MLM - Multi Level Murders

Robert Arnold Kay

Published by Robert Arnold Kay, 2024.

MLM - MULTI LEVEL MURDERS

First edition. January 21, 2024.

ISBN: 979-8224234400

Written by Robert Arnold Kay.

Table of Contents

This book and all my books are dedicated to Swami Muktananda.

Chapter 1: Lyin' Eyes

"Is that a phone in your pants or are you just excited to hunt?" Bart sarcastically stung Maachi. The volley would be served up nasty and hot quicker than you can say headcase. Maachi was so much more than a headcase. He was a full blown, megaton, depraved soulcase. Five levels of compassionate illumination ranging from dark to no one ever sees again.

"Okay funny fuck. Maybe you should suck on my buzzer and let me know if I'm eating too many mangoes," Maachi flipped the retort pancake on the sizzling iron skillet. He squirmed a lefty into his hip jean pocket to paw his phone. He ballet twisted it to check out the dimmed screen. "Shit goddamn fuckety-fuck. That dumbass Indian gash is trying to call me. No matter how many times I bang her in the head to make sure she never calls me when we go hunting. *Ovahandovahandovah.* Too much curry must be screwing with her head. Hey Bartboy, do we know anyone that can do a bit of brain shock therapy?" The Maachi look at Bart clearly indicated he was on another emotional roll into Mr. Toad's Wild Ride. Hang on boyz, it's gonna be a rough ride.

"Jeez man, this really sucks. You know that one of the rules is no cell phones on when we're kitted and rolling. That's how people like us run into big trouble in little Atlanta, or Philly, or where are we now?" Bart was tippin' light krink and his pharma chemical lubrication was slimily oiling the gears in his shell-like head. Let's cut him some bloody slack though. When you travel as much as these two bipedal dirt ball Massengills do, you sometimes need to use your phone to geo where the heck you are.

"Migo, don't fucking lecture me. Do ya' think I'm some kind of hillbilly? Hey, we do live in Georgia, but I'm not some five-tooth grinner. Shit. Why the fuck does she do this?" In mid-phone buzz, He stabbed the red dot to disconnect the call. He was on the verge of an angry pop shot of 'drenalin.

His brow was more intense than Defarge's knit-knit who's in the shit? It was a Three Fates knit all pearl necklace.

Bart jacked a look at Maachi and even in the shadowy darkness he could see that he was totally pissed. Maachi took his phone and tossed it down and crushed its existence to dream of electric sheep. The craaaack that made sure he would not get a call on *that* phone. Alas poor phone, I knew him, it, her, whaa-evah, well. And now it was cast to that great big electronic wasteland of disrupted intelligence. Cast an electron tear for the departed. Go for two and show that you have compassion. You can do it. Give it a squeeze.

"Wow dude. Getting a bit intense. The phone ain't the target here. Pull your shit together."

"How about if you do the universe a favor and go Matrix and melt your mouth. Okay? Do ya really want me to pop the trunk right now?"

Bart didn't push the issue any further. When Maachi totally went animal for whatever reason, anything near him got bitten. Some folks are assholes some of the time. Maachi made it his full-time job to be the biggest whatever it may be, even in regard to being an asshole. Bart made a quick mental note to himself to make absolutely sure that the departed phone wasn't left behind. Dead phones tell no tales. Maybe so or maybe not.

Chapter 2: We Own the Night

❝ *How cool is this*? Knocking down a twelve of thirty-four-degree Tsing Tao with some really pure blow. I don't know 'bout you, but if I were any higher, I'd be hittin' my head on the space station. *Boink*! Hot damn, I love this shit!" Bart excitedly spat out the words like a shark casting off teeth so bigger, sharper ones could grow in their place. A thrill junkie hunter who didn't care what season it was. It was always open season. And doing all this in the purity of darkness with night vision just made it all the more cooler. Dark-camo wrapped cool fools that prayed for prey.

"Fuck man, I can't believe we got this lucky! Hey, toss me another Tsing will ya'? Migo, why do you still do blow? You have a tacphone," Maachi snappily danced his tongue extemporaneously.

"I love the sizzly rush up my nose. You gotta' an issue with that? To each his own poison and pleasure. Here ya' go migo, catch!" Bart tossed the beer over to Maachi. He snatched it out of the air like a pit bull on a blood-soaked tennis ball. "Hey, nice catch! Wanna opener?"

"Dude, they're twist-offs. So, nah, but watch this." Beer bottle in his left paw, he yanked out his switchblade and smacked the blade. The knife got all excited and went stiff. Shiny metal phallus worship. Maachi took the very sharp tippity tip of the knife and like he was some kind of superhero with amazing, blazing speed, tucked it up into each little groove and deftly flipped the twisted metal up. As he flipped the last fluted edge of the cap, he retracted the blade and turned the knife over and solidly tapped the bottom of the bottle. The cap jumped up a short way and Maachi caught it in his teeth. He retracted the blade and dropped the knife like a high diver into a cup of water that was his vest pocket. A metal on cloth sliding sound and then the knife was out of sight. He spit the cap out and caught it between his index finger and his thumb and frisbeed it towards Bart.

Bart was a little more pissed at this than usual. He reflexively tilted his head to the right in response. The metal cap was going so fast it left a mark in Bart's Cantank Rus Pharma logo hat.

"I hate when you do that. I just *hate* it. You could take an eye out doing that!" Bart contemptuously shot out the words like bolts from a crossbow. Ka-zing, now that's the thing!

"Hey, that's a great idea! After I finish this one, toss me another one and let's see if I can have you *less see* by taking out one of your eyes. Which one isn't your favorite?" Maachi childishly quipped as he took a big, thirsty challuga-gulp of the frosty cold beer.

"You're a total asshole. Ya' know that?" Bart was now a gas pump hose pissing his words out. Someone loan this guy a Bic.

"You didn't answer the question. I'll just take my pick," Maachi darkly chortled.

"How about if we cut the shit, you drink your beer, and we do what we paid to do? It's huntin' time and all your bullshit won't bag us anything except having to take a leak more often cuz of the beer." As usual, Bart tried to be the cool one and bring the game back to its point. Shoulda brought an industrial-size tank of liquid nitrogen.

"Okay, okay, okay. I'll stop. But by the way, maybe I'll try for a twofer. I'll buy the cane for you so you can cross the street safely. Or not. I can put the odds up on the board with the company and make a chunk of cheese." A mucusy, guttural laugh frogged out of Maachi's throat. He spat out a huge yellow-tinged, gooey loogie. It landed about half a meter from Bart's kit.

Bart projected a *cut the shit, or I cut your lip, face meets knuckles* look. Maachi got the message. Maachi was such a fuck ball. Skinny as shit. If he turned sideways, he'd be invisible. Two-dimensional in the physical, and personality wise, also two-dimensional. Always stuffing some protein bar thingy down his pie hole to chase after his ever-present gnawing hunger of low blood sugar. The guy had problems. He wasn't just bipolar, he was multipolar. His poles randomly shifted with no advance notice. No warning lights and no klaxons. You never knew if he was serious, sarcastic, crazy, just goofing around, or mix it up and take your pick. But that was all irrelevant. Never fear the smart bad people. Don't fear the stupid bad people. Fear the majorly fucked up, walking crazy bad people. Their motivations are driven by really staticy wiring and chemical dependency imbalances that run the gamut of what's for sale *today*? to *how much of it can I get*? Maachi never met a drug he didn't like. It wasn't always the other way around. He made sure he had a healthy skoosh of naloxone in his tacphone just in case he dribbled in too much of a smashed-up opiate or something stronger this way comes like fentanyl. Drugs and supplements were how he made his puppy chow and it's how he made his inner dog roll over for a tummy rub. He was all-good with his tacphone dealing custom-mixed poisons, especially those that were more intoxicating than white lines on a mirror.

Unfortunately, all that spaghetti mess metabolism of his layered onto bad wiring from when he was old enough to pull his first fly wings, resulted in a sadistic, self-righteous asshole. He was lucky that Bart put up with him. Or did he?

"Did you hear that?" Bart queried Maachi.

"Yeah, I heard something. Let me turn up my ear monitors." He tapped his phone, and the volume teased his ears with crispy-clean louderness. "Yup, gettin' closer noise.' Couple more minutes and we'll have some really clean shots."

"Coolness *is* tech, and tech just makes this *so* much more interesting." Bart irrelevantly commented with a very slimy smile upon his haunted face. They both tapped the tech to jack the mood to morbidly ecstatic.

The sounds kept getting louder. They really lucked out. Another awesome night of getting fucked up higher than a twenty-foot ceiling and juiced like King Kongs on industrial strength Georgia hammerhead-worm-moonshine.

"I'm gonna spike now. What about you?" Maachi asked Bart.

"Great idea." Bart answered as he took his phone out. He tapped the screen to bring up a menu of drug selections. Coolness *is* tech. He had his phone preloaded with stims, opiates, and his favorite crazy item – PCP. All among a small smorgasbord of other tasty best-of-science happy brain and body candies. He tapped the stims selection and another menu appeared. He chose a preselected dose and smiled in anticipation of the next roller coaster brain toaster. A low dose of stims now and maybe later a nanoparticle time-release version. He closed the menu and then tapped just the PCP image and another movable arrow popped up so he could select a low dose.

The phone waited. And then, receiving no further instructions a message appeared on the screen. *Dosing calculations completed.* Bart paused and shoved his left cuff up a bit. He held the phone over the back of his hand and tapped the wording. The phone squirted out an alcohol-based antibiotic and then as a playful honey-pooping bee it jabbed a Teflon coated needle through his skin and injected its recreational compound payload. "Aaahhh, *soooo* nice" Bart oozed a sensual drug laden aura of happiness. Lids closed, all smiley face. Nirvana is as close as a poke with a major sharp 28. No need for soul warming velour opiates yet.

"Shit. You baby ass this stuff. Let me show you how it's done." Maachi picked up his phone. Same menus, kinda sorta. He selected a higher amount of stims, a generous dose of PCP, a smidgeon of ketamine, and a time-release dose of opiates. "This is what I call a Murder Hornet, no pain and lots of gain." Maachi smiled, Bart didn't. When Maachi played *it's better living through chemistry roulette* mixology you never really knew what was going to happen except it sure will result in meaningful degrees of randomness. When the phone had completed its injection of the happy face venom Maachi sighed a melt into the landscape chemical wonderland moan. His exhale was as though he just finished bogarting some sativa and he couldn't hold it any longer. Sans the requisite cough-cough chokey reaction with accompanying strange clouds of smoke.

The sounds kept getting closer and louder. The disharmonious band played on. The percussive steps of the human megapede tapped out a random rhythm.

They nodded to each other and picked up their firearms. As though with choreography, they pulled back on the bolts with a subtle, lubed, slippery metal on metal clack. Racked and ready. Heavy metal love was in the offing. Literally. Maachi sank the butt end into his shoulder and held the Christensen up and pointed it at the stars. He hit a membrane switch near the trigger and the glass got all smiley. He looked through the scope and it was like looking at daylight. *Ain't the tech cool?* he thought.

Maachi's favorite toy was a carbon fiber wrapped Christensen with an extended barrel and a compact suppressor. The carbon kissed the barrel and dissipated the bullet heat in zero time flat. Bart walked a more conventional path. His pet was a SCAR 20S with a scope to kill for. Misstatement, kill *with*.

Both were tuned for Grendel 6.5 just in case they needed to begrudgingly share. Covetous bastards they were. The perfect pairing of ordinance and targets. Ideal metal projectiles to reach out and deliver a terminal touch. On the menu tonight was human flesh on the kicks.

They peeked over the edge of the roof wall and checked out the approaching images in their scopes. The group of raucous, rioting protesters was randomly marching down the city street with reckless, feckless abandon. Dressed up like Mad Max extras with an assortment of homemade and store-bought items. There were football helmets and militia headgear. There were crowbars and sledgehammers. All that was missing was them chanting, *kill the beast!* The beast needed no chanting to come out and play. It wasn't an outside hateful vicious beast. It was the monster that was writhingly alive in their dark hearts and pitch covered souls. The beast they sought was tucked within. The beasts were out tonight in force, of course.

Centipede action with a badass bunch of arms swinging medievalness.

They were smashing, grabbing, and arsoning as they passed stores and vehicles. Behind them was a blistered and battered war zone that was turning to darkest charcoal and smoldering plastic. The police were about half a kilometer away in front of them and approaching with focused order and confidence. Spartan warriors dressed in blue with full riot gear. Shields, batons, and visored helmets walked forward as the thin blue line. Some officers carried reinforced bicycles as an added crowd-sweeping tool for law enforcement. Visions of Soylent Green people scoops.

This was the twenty-fifth night of *peaceful protests* in Portland that had pivoted on *peaceful* to a rapid march towards spasmodic, malicious mayhem. Multiple blocks of mom and pop's boutiques and large, exclusive chain, retail brick and mortar buildings were shattered and broken, burning hot and spewing smoke. The will of those insentient collections of steel and concrete broken and tattered. The goods were liberated and were moved on to the less fortunate. Or the evil intent Robbing Hoods would have you believe.

"You good?" Maachi asked.

"Shit yeah! I already have mine picked out. Swing your scope to the far middle of the mob. See the guy with the yellow starred, dark blue mask?

Trackin' 'im. One melon shot. Boing. Another one bites the dust. You?" Bart demonically grinned and shared with Maachi.

"I'm gonna do a chick first. The fat walrus on the left. She's the one with the *cook the pigs* sign." Maachi's pupils were wide with sadistic drug-induced delight. His eyes were dancing and laughing in their own surrealistic brain mush.

"Five by Five, migo. You or me first?" Bart politely asked so as to not destroy the feral etiquette. The ambience of the carnival of nastiness was so delightful he didn't want to disturb the moment and kill the flow.

"We'll wait until the unis are up close and personal with the circus. And then it's go Latin, go *ad libitum.*" Maachi responded with focused intent. He was calling the shots for now.

"Dude, I'm getting pretty zonked. You do have your can on, right?" Bart could have simply snap-looked at Maachi's rifle, but he was focusing on his own glass.

"Do *I* look like a *freakin'* newbie? Don't answer that. Just keep in mind, I *am* the smartest guy on the roof," Maachi chidingly, self-righteously chuckled. Bart was not second fiddle; he wasn't even in the string section as far as Maachi was concerned. Maachi was like an Agent Smith in The Matrix. He only saw himself as the major actor in all that occurred around him.

The mob of miscreants was now face-to-face, in the grill of the blue. Maachi let it rip. The subtle *pop* was a champagne cork-a-flying sound. He hit the fat lady right in the neck. The bullet passed through her blubbery throat and blood flowed out of both holes. She had no idea what had occurred. She opened her mouth to yell but to no avail as she put both hands around her neck with the blood squishing out between her chubby, sausage fingers. She took one look at her crimson-colored hands and tried to scream *bloody* murder, but her larynx had been trashed. No one noticed the frantic silent utterance of the BBW. There was so much noise and cacophony in the street that her blood-burbling chirps were just another little bubbly, squeaky squawk in the jungle. She ran off to the side of the jostling crowd and fell on the concrete sidewalk near the broken glass of the trashed Nordstrom. Her head bounced on the cold hardness. Nobody noticed her panic attack drop to the ground. The crazed mob was so intent on smash, grab, and poke the pigs that she looked like just another drugged out nasty reveler who couldn't take all the excitement. She quickly bled out on the sidewalk. The blood flowed onto the edge of the curb and down the sewer opening never to be seen again. Irony. The rivulets of her crimson blood mixed with the debris and tear gas volatiles to be carried away to the river in the storm drain. A syrupy, oozy human and chemical smoothie. Flowing away never to come back another day. But it's illegal to dump toxic waste into the storm drain in Portland, right? Laws, shmaws, and *maws*.

The acrid, oily smell of burning plastics and automobile carcasses swirled up the walls of the buildings and rolled over Maachi and Bart. Bart took his shot. A subtle *thuddd* burped out from the suppressor. *One shot, one kill, ammos expensive!* He joked to himself. Perfect melon hit on the masked mayhem bandit. Banged him right in the little star on his mask. At this range there was no exit wound. Just another piece of rattling metal inside his cranium. Brain salad Pachinko. If this were an Olympic sport it would have been a ten-ten. Difficulty and perfect execution were in the mix. The man fell back with a shudder and the thronging, spastic monster mob just shoved him aside as he dropped to the pavement.

Two points up; one each. Even game so far.

Chapter 3: Riot

"Man, it just doesn't get any better than this! We're doin' stripes and solids, right?" Bart asked Maachi.

"Yup. And don't forget our stretch bonus game. Twofers count as double points.

One bullet-two kills. And if only a maim, you lose two points. Agree?" Maachi questioned back.

"Standard ammo or the hot stuff we cooked up?" Question to question-to-question spooling up into a shaky Zoom call, or *something* zoomy.

"Dealer's choice. You can use hot if you want to, but just remember I'm going to call you a gender-twisted pussy that bent to brute force over a desk versus finesse. Muscle versus skill." Maachi laughed a snide giggle and closed the question gap with that snarkled answer.

"Fine by me. Hey, douche-bong-dick, y'know your words can never hurt me. Sticks, stones, brass knucks and balisongs, different story." Bart chuckled over his lame attempt at dark humor and showing he was one smarty pants mother fucker, *yes, he did his best to fuck as many at-home moms as possible*, that could recall nursery rhymes. A pedestrian snappy repartee at best. Blague drole at worst.

"Time to show you, migo, *I'm the boss*. The big boss at the end of a level. Don't forget it. Time to go back to playing. We only have about another twelve minutes before exfil.

"And no, ... I'm going to answer that question I know you're goin' to ask right now! We're not going to chew up time by goin' street level. We could get some extra points, but you tell me you're not crazy on going street cuz of the covid mask thing. That mixing karma with the masses is only okay if we're really zonked. Cuz when big comets drop it's always on a group. Group

11

karma is not to my liking, nor yours regardless of the points. Easier to dodge comets by being solo. Ya' know what I mean jellybean?" Maachi delivered a remarkable set of insights on the human condition where the dogma gets run over by the karma. He had no intent of getting run over, *ever*.

"Roger that! I'm with you. That mixing it up on the street with having to wear a covid mask isn't my game. You know I really don't like going elbows while this pandemic thing is cooking." With those words Bart turned away and checked his chamber. He was on a buzz like an angry African bee and with the jabbering he lost track if he racked or not. He was the body electric and soon to be the body kinetic. "I got stripes! If it's got a stripe on it – it's mine! So don't fuck with me" he chopped out his words like a Paul Bunyan axe man on oak. Clack, clack, time to make a whack.

"No unis, right? They got stripes so no cheatin." Maachi was now orbiting the cognitive planet of Uranus and was caught in an intoxicating gas cloud.

"Double roger roger that that. We start knocking off unis and our cleaners will have a challenge picking up the parcels. We want the unis to keep all our two-legged targets in basic rotate on their ass shit. Better for us." Bart dropped the gate on that issue. No unis.

Bart had his I-spy-eye focused in his scope and in the middle of the reticle was this goofy *it*. It looked like it was a guy. But he had a dress on, jeans underneath, and hiking boots. With long dyed purple hair with some kind of dangling bullshit shiny costume jewelry strung in it. Pancake makeup on thick as putty. It was hard to be sure which side he wore his pants on. In his skirt and under the jeans did he wear panties, jockeys, or boxers? He thought, *if it's that hard to tell, who the fuck cares what it is.* Bart continued the thought thread, *it ain't the gender – you got stripes!* He blinked and refocused. Yup. Striped dress. "You're mine you stupid mother fucker!" He whispered a rhetorical poof.

Before he could hit the second stage on his trigger, he felt a poppy sonic wave go through him from Maachi's Christensen and the follow-up *kachunk* sound of another round ready and in queue. He hadn't noticed that Maachi went heavy on his loads. He had pegged a goofy looking dude who was wearing a bicycle helmet with a flashing red light on it, a camo bandana, and some kind of dirt bike body armor. Maachi's round smacked right into the flashing red LED. The guy keeled off like a listing ship in the harbor. The sound and impact of the round gave away that it was special ordinance. Lights out.

Son of a bitch. He switched. Must've gone to the hot 123 stuff. Shit. I gotta get goin here. Hot damn, he notched a point! Fuck! With the thought of the word *here* in his head, he teased the trigger with a soft caress and his round went true. The punctuation on the deadly nonword sentence was a *Kachunkkk* of another round up the magazine elevator and into the receiver. How fitting. A heart shot for his cute little whatever it was out there. Another *one* for Bart.

Maachi, at about the same time Bart was scoping some arsonists who were about to go flambé barbie on the Nike, was lost in his scope. Oblivious to what was going on around him. He didn't even bother to think about the body count. It was all being recorded in their scope chips and uploaded anyway. Over to the left were about four peaceful protesters rolling a very large, topped out dumpster towards the unis. *Too hard.* He thought. And then he saw it. A cute girl with her legs wrapped around a tall guy's neck. Both dressed all in black and the guy had a rough-cut balaclava on. It was a goofy head covering. It looked more like a tattered pair of Under Armour than a real ballie. The girl was playfully riding on top of his shoulders. *Decisions, decisions, decisions.* He thought. *If I pop the chick first, she could fall forward over the guy's head. I gotta try some kind of twofer on this one. Gotta increase my lead. Can't let Bart win. Cuz I'm the smartest guy here.* His thoughts ran wild on the tactical aspects of killing a chick and her ride. He popped the guy in the head and as his target started to crumble and melt down Maachi quickly chambered a second round and took another quick shot at the girl as her mount was turning to crumpled paper. He popped her melon. He wanted to be consistent. *So glad this is all being vid. That was a thing of beauty.* Yet another macabre thought slid through his mind. *Not a twofer but wicked cool anyway!*

Bart snap-looked just in time at the crowd to see more of Maachi's handiwork. Bart sweat a bead or ten, refocus on new. It was four to two, and he needed a twofer. His next shot went right through the necks of a guy and a girl who were doin' the *hold me close baby* PDA. Carotids pumped out red mists and pulsing red streams. *Ha. Six to four, eat it Maachi. Gotta kick it up a peppa* he thought to himself. He scanned the mass of vitriolic human compost and settled on a couple of guys readying up a Molotov. *Let's see him beat this*! Arose the nasty, drug-induced thought in his head. The targeted men of mayhem were standing about four meters out from a bunch of smashed plate glass windows. One guy, dressed in a black hoodie with jeans, a striped durag that matched his bru's, was holding a bottle of gas with a rag in the neck. The other guy with an *Eat the Rich* t-shirt lit up a hand torch. In the scope Bart saw that it looked like the little torch he used to make the glassy sugar on his signature Baileys – Kahlua crème brûlée. Yum. Time to turn up the heat.

He started to get lost in thought. All the chems were colliding inside of him. He waited until the protesters had just lit the rag in the bottle. He held his SCAR firmly against the mortar notch in the roof wall tile and buttered the trigger. The shot was another one of those award-winning efforts. It blasted the bottle and the fuel fountained all over both of the douchebags. The lit torch took care of the rest of the hit. They lit up like Halloween ornaments. Two more quick shots at the Vitus' dancing candle brothers just to demonstrate his version of finesse. "I should get bonus points for style. 'Check it out, eight to four." He barked at his buddy through his throat mic.

Meanwhile the unis were popping and tossing tear gas canisters deeply into the crowd of angry bee-ings. The clouds rose up in the little eddies made by the movements of the protesters. It added a bit of depth to the delightful visuals. Devilish Whirling Dervishes in the mist. The ballet troupe of night creatures in the shadows of the fires and foggy chemical deterrent were mystically macabre. Maachi and Bart would have to be more selective now. Neither wanted to err on hitting the opposite's stripe or solid. That could be an immediate loss due to not following the basic rules they had agreed upon earlier.

Sharp sands dropping down through the borosilicate tempered glass hourglass. Time was doing its thing and rapidly slipping into the future. Both of them lost track of the number of kills they had. Unfortunately, Bart had actually only injured one of his burning man trophies and death by fire is not a point-add. At least that's what it looked like. He was going to get dinged a few points. Their wrist transponders silently vibrated to let them know, *time to go, fellas.*

Choreographed reverse motions were in order. Both of them slid back away from the wall and being good little kids, they cleaned up their play area and they even picked up all the spent shells. Tidy-tidy time to say good-nighty.

Bart was doing a hunched-over walk-thing seeking to ensure his head didn't pop up over the brick wall. Maachi crouched on his haunches and took his phone out and rolled up his cuff just enough to dose himself with God only knows what. He dropped the phone and put his hands on the rooftop to steady himself. And then, as though a startled cheetah, he picked up his phone, his kit, and his rifle case and beat booted feet like Usain Bolt. Bart was startled to see him whiz past. He almost dropped his rifle case in surprise. Meth in that sting for sure.

They had memorized the path to vacate the premises and exfil. There was only a short window to be at the pickup. As in seconds, not minutes. It was a portion of a tick and not a full tock. They jumped over the side of the roof and began the seven-floor fire escape descent into the alley. A clip-clop trot to the rear of the building where they had disabled the street and business cameras was in order. If it ain't videoed, it never happened. With cameras everywhere it was as much of a clever trick to identify and disable the ones that could expose them to inquiring minds during a replay of events as it was to be on the field and invisibly sport their kits.

The van pulled up next to them. The body of the vehicle was blacker than black. It had some type of high-tech nanotube on aluminum wrap. It was darker than even Vantablack. The mechanical gorilla in this mist was a four-wheeled wind in the forest of concrete and steel buildings. A blur that could sneak among the narrow alleys and one-way streets without being noticed. How quaint though. Part of the graphic wrap stated *Satriale's Pork Store we pick up and deliver!* In a deep, metallic shimmering purple hue. There were no glaring, tuner blue-light headlights. The headlights were invisible. They were custom-order high-tech infrared. The driver and the navigator used uniquely calibrated night vision goggles to see in the darkest in the darkness. All the preparations with the single intent of not being discovered. Maachi and Bart saddled up to the parked vehicle and the door slid widely open to welcome them aboard. They tossed their gear in and quickly followed it.

Whoever runs this game has a very sick, twisted sense of humor and lots of serious bitcoins nested somewhere safe and sound and captured in the dark net.

Bart thought, *I won.*

Maachi thought, *you lost Bart, the human torch thingy blew your game. Besides, I always win cuz I'm the smartest guy in the hoodie.*

Chapter 4: Ghost Out

They drove out to a remote piece of deserted farmland where there was a single, dull black, totally tricked-out AW109 with its rotor spinning. The van came to a halt and the driver asked them to stay inside until he gave the all-clear signal. The guy riding shotgun popped his door and did a duck out on his get out. He silently circled the vehicle and then tapped three times on the rear door. The dude went low and ghost on the ground. Nobody gets full pay if the cargo is damaged in any way during transit. He was heavy with a Sig MCX topped with an Eotech ClipIR.

They couldn't see anyone else around and it appeared that they were the first on the scene. They bounced out of the van and reflexively ducked down as they crouch-ran to the chopper. The door was open, and the walkway was extended. The mouth of the beast with a tongue made of aircraft aluminum awaited their arrival. It swallowed them up and was going to take them far from the social shitstorm that had spawned forth from the city of Portland.

There were already two early arrival players tucked in the front end of the bench seats. Maachi, as his typical *it's all about me* disposition, gave them an up and down laser eval. Not the one he used on chicks. It was a *what the fuck?* look, and he wasn't looking to get fucked and situational awareness is a deal breaker must have. The two dudes being evaluated didn't move a muscle. Stoneheart contractors out for a thrill? Or CFOs dreaming about how to lay off a couple thousand droidlets?

Once inside the belly of the beast they stowed their gear and melted into the comfy rear of the benches. Butt on cushion beats ass on roof top twelve out of eleven times. It would have been Miller time, but they only had a couple of Tsing Tao to quaff. They popped the tops and guzzle-guzzled them. Even warm beer can be mightily refreshing when you're dehydrated.

They smelled of burnt-stuff mélange that left an amaroidal taste on their palates that even the Tsing could not wash off. It was always a challenge to get the stink off the tongue and the gun metal.

No pilots were in the cabin. These guys never want to be sitting ducks. They're out there somewhere being discrete and invisible. Just in case something goes wonky, they won't be wonkied in the middle of it. Nobody gets full pay unless the cargo arrives intact during transit. The whole team gets dinged. Good guys don't let comrades get dinged. Especially since every person on the team is strapped and toting sharp toothpicks. Tempers would flair and the devil may care there would be heavy doojas in the red mist air.

"Here they come." Bart calmly shared with Maachi. Sure enough, the last group of two were about thirty meters away and making their way to the limo chopper. One of the guys was holding his left arm. Not a good sign. When someone returns with a broken wing it means some really random event transpired and most likely a bit of mano y mano went down. Drippy, red sweet stuff was the aperitif to stitches and antibiotics accompanied by the ouch chorus. The guy was majorly wet. Main line time for a pint o' deelishis, plasma expander, and maybe super-size it. Give that bleeder an extra-large Octaplas with a solid jigger of Dextran 70 to sweeten it up.

The newcomers ambled up and took their assigned seats. The stairs automatically retracted, and the door gently closed with a *pfffffvvvtttt* note of finality. The cabin bounced as the pilots entered, jacked their doors shut, and took command of the aircraft. Maachi could see they were double strapped with suppressed Glocks and FN five-sevens, and they weren't shy to show 'em. Good choice on 5.7 fast close-encounter body armor piercing bullets. Probably some kind of banned custom rounds.

They hit the accelerator and the blades whirly gigged at an ever-increasing speed. The whoosh and the roar of the engines drowned out all other sounds. A demonic ghost of a tilt-a-whirl spun up the dust, dirt, and detritus underneath. A warning to the earth that an evil, powerful, demonic windy storm was en route.

Then came the ritual. The dark, shiny helmeted phantoms in the front seats retrieved Glock 18s and held them up so everyone could see them. Clearly a Gun Fu message with synchronous racking of a round just to demonstrate no racking needed *but just to make sure you understand, be nice.*

With the Glocks in one hand, they both turned their helmeted heads and looked back into the cabin and did a mini-mime thing. With their other hand exposed, they wiggled their index fingers. Sign language for *funny stuff will meet extreme prejudice*. No one laughed or even smiled. Redundant messaging just to make certain everyone knew that the guys in the front bubble were the Masters of the Bird. Very clear. The 18s were as illegal as all shit and were full auto capable. Not toy Glocks by any means. Just mean shiny death dealing machines. If they went rinse cycle it would be messy. These guys always played for keeps. The stakes were high and so were all the players. If some wise guy went berserk-o in the cabin, he could get shot and everyone else in the cabin would be the collateral. Ya' don't shoot the pilots of a chopper. This isn't Flight Simulator. Dead chopper pilots make helicopters go crash. So no one ever even made fast hand movements. Everyone went navel meditating. Malevolent balaclaved Buddhist monkey boys in transit.

But not Maachi. Maachi was ever the jacked-up fuckball. You had to be careful wherever you took him. He was the evil, nasty, greasy Italian uncle who wasn't even an uncle yet. He was capable and skilled in random acts of violence and cruelty. He looked over at the guy next to him holding his arm. The sleeve was cut away and a tourniquet was on duty. A large wad of quick clot was wrapped around his bicep with black duct tape. Wonderful, sticky, thousand-uses duct tape. Good stuff that can even be wrapped around a gut wound as long as you did a decent job of stuffing the hosing back inside. Awkward though if the adhesive on the tape was smacked onto some intestine or organ. Pulling that band aid off later would be supersized *Youchiness*.

"Something random this way comes?" Maachi queried his fellow passenger.

"Yah. We were doing great. And then all of a sudden, some big jabronis is up on the roof with us and he's poking me in the arm with a KA-BAR Snody. Fuck it hurt. My partner hit him in the head with the butt of his rifle and knocked him off his feet. He dumped a close-range load into his head. Wow! That was messed up. Close range getting popped in the head with a 308! Like a big pimple exploded. He pulled the knife out and straightaway clotted me. Lucky, lucky me. Could a' bled out in short strokes. Thank God for our tacphones. Dosed myself up. I lost the match to him, but hey, there's always another peaceful demonstration, isn't there?"

Maachi simply nodded and asked "Artery?"

"Hey, guy, you a newbie? If he'd sliced an artery, I think I would've gotten offed and picked up by the Indians. Very lucky. We never heard the mook. When you get in that zone though, ya' only think about the targets and the counts. You catch my drift, biff?"

Maachi steely-eyed the bleeder. No-body calls *him* a newbie, but no need to do the fuckemup backup the dump truck. He already did that with being an unaware douchy-bag.

So he just nodded, but the thought in the back of his head was the rules were simple. Have to have eyes in the back of your head, an army of guardian devils, and situational awareness on the level of a Borg.

If you get mortally wounded, your partner has to off you and you get taken out with the rest of the carcasses by the Indians. The Indians had a very stealthy, simple job, leave nothin' behind. Anything they snatch from the husks is theirs. Credit cards, debit cards, identification documents, phones, firearms, and even other useful items that can morph into very profitable short-term assets. They take it all. Even body parts if there is a need and to their liking. It wasn't their preference by any means but if the billet says kill it and chill it and bring a trophy, then so it goes.

No more talking, speech was a June bug on the windshield of a speeding Kenworth. Talking was gossiper-rumor that had no value. This wasn't about chatting about the game they were in. Maachi and Bart knew this, and they went Silent Bob-Harpo.

The chopper rose up on its air column. No lights or transponder. No markings either. Just a Ninja light-absorbing blender spinning away to move the packages back to some mysterious drops. The dark black was the same nanotube wrap stuff. In the night sky all that would be seen are the stars being momentarily blotted out. A shadow passing over the blinking celestial lights. Even if anyone saw the dark metal beast in the air, they would draw their own lines between the dots to create a constellation of believability.

A big, dark chopper flying low, with no lights and no markings? Must be some military thing. Maybe a Homeland Security thing. There are so many quasi-clandestine government actors in this carnival of country chaos it really didn't matter. When the angry, infected public blisters pop, the citizen protectors come out in force. All different types of groups. Who knows? Maybe even the CIA. How could anyone even remotely imagine the behavioral trajectory of this *specific* chopper? People make their own connections per what they're accustomed to. Creativity is not the piercing of the veil here. The lines between the dots are simply thin. Only the military or some other flush with cash agency would do something like a covert flight in the inky night. So there you go. Nothing to view here, and nothing to hear here except for the sounds of the roaring engines going doppler and the giant insect wings rotating in the air. *Now, where is that double vanilla deep raspberry mocha latte I ordered?* Back to personal reality. *Dingaling*, and who is that calling me *now?* Gotta bolt. Got shit to do, ... see ya all later. The already forgotten passing helicopter in the night was nothing more than. Nothing.

And so the mind goes on to the known and accustomed trappings and predictable cause and effect. Goblins, witches, warlocks, Morlocks, gremlins, and vicious creatures don't really exist anyway. There are no three-eyed, armored, big-bug beings with death sticks. Right? No *real* monsters. No weird things from another planet, Right? No giant reptiles eating humans for brunch. Right?

The flight was smooth. It was a flying fish in the ocean of air, and it sliced its way towards its destinations in slippery fashion. It only took about thirty-five minutes for the first drop. On top of a high rise in Seattle the chopper unceremoniously landed. The speed of the blades slowed enough to not create too much of a cool, urban dust devil.

The copilot, without looking back, held three fingers up. Such simple beasts. Front passengers-time to get a move on. The silent pair unhitched the buckles on their straps and arose from the bench. They cast no gaze at anyone. The *dos amigos* were spit out of the dark conveyance and it was boots on the roof time. The door opened, the stairs tumble-danced forth, and the somber ones climbed down, out, and onto the rooftop. They hustled to the access man door, which automatically opened when they were within about three meters of it. No hall lights. No flashlights and no beacons. All were specters in the inky darkness. They disappeared into the stairwell and the door closed with a ghost's hand. *Kaaalack* in the black.

The whole adventure had very orderly actionable points and places. Randomness remained in the domains of the very well-paying passengers. The company goal was to provide the epitome of a life and death set of experiences to the minority of thrill-seekers who had become jaded with their successes. It was the quintessential provider of unique one-of-a-kind experiences. All the thrills for a very significant financial paid-up bill. No tipping, please.

The steaming heaps of human compost, the other part of WestWorld meets Stepford Wives in the Matrix were so preoccupied and smothered in demigod worship of consumerism in all its forms that they were almost completely oblivious to any thoughts other than where to buy the next accouterment. The ninety-eight percent of pink bags containing DNA were benevolent garbage disposals of all things that really don't matter. The edited news, tidal waves of deliberate misinformation, the fake reality shows, the upgraded coffee maker, or the next ever larger, ever so-much-more real-life plasma display were propagandized as being the required focus of your attention. Reality had become surreality to the ninety-eighters. There was more realism in what they watched than in how they lived their lives. During the day, Starbucks quaffing corporate droids. During the night sedated sentients became hypnotized by flashing little lights in various sized displays. It made no difference if the piece of the unreal were a video game or a lame game show. So many people had become some form of workplace robot that plodded, plopped, and landed in some sort of routine furrow. They were in ruts and rutting on a daily basis. Maybe even hourly if they could stomach 100 mg Viagras as M&Ms. Where are those Tums, honey?

The other two percent were far past the mundane. In that two percent were the adventurers, the entrepreneurs, the builders, and the darker beings. Some of those folks wallowed in inflicting some type of societal or personal pain for gain or amusement. They were cosmopolitan sadistic sociopaths. The two percenters needed their thrills whether pills, injectables, or real live-action drills.

The masses were the Eloi, and the two percent were the Morlocks who ate their fills of kills and hid mostly in the two percent. There are always exceptions though.

Next stop was the parking lot of an abandoned strip mall. All the streetlights had been removed so that the chopper would have a nice level, smooth place to land its feet with no sharp, tall, pointy things to dampen the mood. A delicate kiss to the asphalt and the chopper was pillowed and ready to disgorge pair number two. The stuck-pig, now pale looking guy and his compadre were not so elegant in their exit. It was obvious that the bleeder guy was numbed and bummed. His buddy held him up on the stairs and they did a wobbly-bobbly duo fox trot out front to the main mall doors. As though they had taken a queue from the roof top man door, the glass opened without being touched and closed in the same but reverse manner. The light thudding of the electric doors was a wave good bye to the other travelers. The only light was from the half-moon above.

The next LZ was on top of a leveled hill. The big rotary bird swooped in as though an osprey to catch a fish in the ocean and landed with the softest-caress-me bump. The rotors slowed and the walkway deployed. Maachi and Bart picked up their kits and their rifle cases and dechoppered.

When they were about twenty meters away, the blades spun faster and the dark phantom in the night vanished into the coal blackness of the sky.

They were still-lifes who gazed towards the tree line. "I got this, migo." Maachi grabbed into his side pocket and pulled out an infrared hand scope. He scanned the edge of the forest for their ride. "I see it, a big heat sig is over there at two o'clock. Let's fast scamper and get the fuck out of here. The woods always give me a shiver. The not seeing thingy makes me edgy. Especially when I'm volleying." He nervously shared with Bart.

Bart just nodded. He knew this. Never knew why and never asked about it. A guy thing. A hidden personality gremlin that Bart preferred not to open the door to. Batten down the hatch and don't open it to the inner creature of Maachi.

They struck out towards the red glow signature of the car. As they approached the ride, the back doors, just like with the other two drops, opened without human touch. The plush Hummer limo sucked them in and plopped them down along with their gear. It was a short bumpy ride to the country road. Maachi nodded off and Bart enjoyed the surreal tree-laden scenery.

Chapter 5: Black Cadillac

Without blingy pimp-pomp and circumstance the black hole dark Hummer drove to an abandoned oily smelling automotive parts warehouse and dropped them off. The side man-door popped open and beckoned them in.

"So, how was this one?" The jowly-faced, plaid jacketed man in the center of the warehouse asked with a throaty loud whisper. He cast the presence of a *step right up* carnival sideshow hawker who had a big alligator smile etched into his giddy deceiving face. The smile that equally let you know, happy to see you, ... happy to eat you.

"Predictable. Not boring, just a wee bit predictable. A movie we've seen before but it was still fun watching it again." Maachi responded with his characteristic *ho-hum, is that the best ya' got?* tone. The implication to anyone who cared was the message *do better next time*, regardless of the current endeavor.

The man laughed as he confidently paced his saddle shoe saunter one foot in front of the other. A stride of a man who made you think he was some sideshow jowler. Inside that disarming, rotund exterior was a crimson creature of potential influence that could be unleashed at any moment. Like a cobra strike, when you saw it, it was truly too late. You wouldn't be able to identify the social venom he injected into your world. There is no universal antivenom.

A welcoming outstretched hand, a couple of handshakes and a *glad to see you made it* macho look in the eye. "So, Dr. Panicles does that mean that the thrill junkie inside of you seeks a little more of a significant challenge? A more visceral activity? " The plaid clad man half mockingly commented. The kind of mock that says a lot. It says, *you think you're hot shit? You think you know how to handle yourself all the time? You really think you're the smartest two-legged pink thing on the surface of the planet? Well, all that you see is not necessarily what you think it is.* He thought to himself. The way the custard-words projected was innocuous, innocent. On the verge of platonically, sickeningly sweet.

"Look McCarty, we've done this since the *peaceful gatherings* began months ago. At first, ya' know, it was novel and juicy. Now it's more like going bowling. Don't think me unappreciative for the sojourns into the dark side, but yeah, it's getting predictable and predictable means boring, but still potentially interesting. Some new twisty slidey unexpected stuff would be nice." Maachi smonked with his full elitist attitude.

Every word is always a challenge to him, and he just had to always, without question, view himself as the shiniest apple, the machoist tough guy, *all of the time.* Bart cast some slinky shy sly eye his way. The *Bart look.* It was the same ole same ole and he just tolerated Maachi. His tolerance was based upon the blood, sweat, tears, and pain they took to create the dietary supplement-pharmaceutical behemoth of Cantank Rus Pharma. Yes, they did build it. But they built it upon lies, deceit, and various mischievous corporate activities. So much was illegal, ... but it's only illegal if you get caught. Right? They never got caught. No videos. No incriminating written notes on any type of paper or tablet. Every disgruntled, wrongly terminated employee had the fear of the bad things that could happen to them if they ever cast any type of disparaging commentary into any kind of media, as a long mantra of intimidation. Grrrrrr, the bear growled.

When they sliced and diced the human assets of their business it was nothing personal. It was just a bunch of fruits, vegetables, and nuts that they leveraged to make yet more money and ensure their twisted livelihoods.

When someone, or even small groups of someones pissed them off, Maachi and Bart didn't waste time. HR was nothing more than the machine that ground the grist. Bloodless employment death. They simply severed the cord and cut the employee loose. Lots of *shut your mouth!* Retaliation stuff. But no one was every able to glue the rats to the board. The severance agreements they concocted were legally tight and quite stingy but it's amazing what bravado and a loud voice can do to project bogus, definitive superiority.

When employees get thrown out of the company and get their asses bounced to the curb with no explanation other than *at will*, it focuses the person being bounced upon one thing. How to get a *new* job. The clock is always sliding its numbers into the future. Rent is due, electricity needs to stay on, and family matters are never free. A bit of cash in-hand to buy a piece of the discarded employees' soul and keep them from loose lipping was the lucre that hit their Jones. That was what the severance package was intended to do. Not decent enough to ease the loss of the job but just enough to survive. Survival is a noble thing in the ebb, flow, and riptides of life.

The people who went to the wind discovered that the folks they formerly worked with at the company corporately gaslighted them. Once they become an ex-employee, they ceased to exist 1984 style. Even their work buddies would refuse to connect through social media and such for fear of *their* asses being dribbled on the pavement next. Bounce left cheek. Do it again right cheek.

Maachi and Bart would laugh in private at the silly HR issues. Heck, they fully used the department as their human asset hitmen. They learned long ago that HR had a sole mission to protect the company and not the employee. It was like playing stripes and solids, it was fatties and skinnies, and it was bimbos or pencil neck geeks that they corporately disposed of.

Sometimes just for the fun of it they would pick a manufacturing facility, a warehouse, or a front office worker confine and just stroll through them and give random people notice. It was a joke to them. They banked a million here a million there and exjecting an employee as flotsam and jetsam, or simply lagan was entertainment. Nothing more than that.

They would collectively decide upon an office or work area, walk up to the person, and tell them they were fired. No notice, no reason, just for humor. Maachi was always the lead. Bart invariably went method acting. They appeared to collectively love to see the shocked, pained look on the face of their victim. They would move on to some other area in the building and just send a *711* note to HR with the work area or office number. In minutes the HR hyenas would pad their way to the designated hunting ground for the person, empty the desk into used bankers boxes, and escort the poor soul off the property with a plop, plop, box dissed on the sidewalk. The dazed and confused employee was now one of the departed. All videoed right on down to the ass shot as they exited the doorway.

Maachi and Bart were feared throughout the company's facilities. Fear is a very effective motivator to enhance compliance. But just compliance, not exemplary performance. Acceptable but marginal performance as in stealthy quiet quitting.

When notice came around that they would be visiting there were conspicuous PTO days taken. Out of sight means out of mind and no questions about *what do you really do here?* They had so many employees that if you were clever and didn't let them see you, they would pass over you like an ant hidden in the deep grass under a lawn mower's spinning, sharp blades. Thus, if you weren't on the premises that day, your chances of having an invidious visit were lowered. Although upon occasion, Maachi and Bart would use a Zoom call for some worker who was working off-site and bombed them then. They liked to mix their macabre experiences up. They hated being bored. Being bored was being gored by anesthesia to them and being forced to view another sexual discrimination vid, complete with a knowledge test at the end.

Building a business is in some ways like going to war. Sensitivities and compassion can dim, and the thrill is anything that is different and exciting. Maachi and Bart were entrepreneurial corporate-war adrenalin junkies and had their own special version of CIS, chronic insensitivity syndrome.

They lived by a very simple credo, *love us or hate us, we don't give a shit, just do as you're told.* They only cared about the money and themselves. Bad wiring, abominable intent, and a casserole of just evil fuckedupedness. Maachi led and Bart followed like a loyal sidekick. A dastardly duo. The leash was the huge financial assets Bart would lose if he crossed Maachi. He was a money junkie, and his fix was more than most people earn in a year. Correction, years.

"How about if you fellows follow me to the other side of the warehouse where your rides are? We can chat along the way." The plaid-clad hawker said with an overly pronounced smile.

"Sure. Great idea. Let's go Maach', we've got people to do and places to see." Bart squeezed word farts into the dialogue so he could get Maachi to just shut the fuck up for a while. Silence was not golden when Maachi went heinous extemporaneous, if you could have him close his self-aggrandizing yapper, it was palladium anodized platinum. Bart seized upon the opportunity to move the exit process along more quickly.

Maachi is a tennis ball chaser. You just have to keep throwing the tennis ball a further each time to keep his caffeinated squirrel-mind under your control – you hoped. If not under control at least majorly distracted.

Maachi viewed Bret as a *look!–shiny metal thing–look, look*! Maachi knew that Bart was like a chicken on a juicy worm whenever the thought of *mo money mo money!* hit the dialogue. Bart would throw tennis balls and Maachi would up one him with shiny thoughts paved with greed. Not so much a battle of wits. It was more a battle of covetous ditz.

There wasn't a lot of chatting and verbal cavorting during their walk. Maachi was still boingled with the recreational pharmaceutical compounds he took, and Bart was dick-thinking about what was in it for him. His mind lock was his own special design. All he could think about was what he wanted and everything else, even Maachi was on the bottom of the sweaty, three-day used, waxy-sebum coated jock strap.

They stood next to the stretch black Cadillac XTS limo that waited patiently beside them. The engines were off as well as the attention of the very well compensated driver. Cars, chopper, cars, plane, and cars again. Private contracted carriers both van wise and plane wise always shipped the kits. The help would wipe all prints and barrels would be swapped out and destroyed. If needed even the firing pins where replaced. Just for safekeeping. Out of sight, out of mind, and hidden from the attention of inquiring souls, should those bodies with the minds with names like FATE, BIF, or even Georgia Bureau of Investigation just happen to appear.

The driver listened to tunes while she readied up to take the two VIPs to the small private airport where their jet was patiently sleeping. She'd pet the kitty engine of the Caddy and have it purring horsepower and pawing the pavement in less than no time flat. *Cattus fugit memento mori* – the cat was well-armed and more than a match for any type of needed dispatch.

Bart wanted to leave *now* and Maachi went monotrack and reopened that *last word* monologue with the barker. "So, yeah, ah like, can we kick this up a peppa'? I mean like not right away, not pushing you, ya know?"

McCarty gave Maachi a McCarty – *who the fuck do you think you are?* eyeball blast. The yellow, toothy smile melted a bit at the edges like a sanguine candle burning at both ends.

"Oh, Dr. Panicles, I am certain we can accommodate your wishes. It really is just a matter of agreeing upon the compensation for our services. But you knew that already." The words dropped from his mouth like frisky maggots seeking something dead to eat. As far as he was concerned all his clients were already dead when they decided to engage his services. They were lifeless debit cards with an embossed name on them. McCarty was just a thrill-junkie broker with all sorts of business intents. He got paid on both ends. "Any limits on the expense?" He further inquired.

Bart turned his head and looked into Maachi's eyes. Dark coal meets volcano passion logic. But that's an oxymoron, *passion, and logic*. When Maachi and Bart slipped and oozed their way to their most cruel and callous side, all bets were off. It was thrills, pills, chills, and overbearing wills that became the chutes and ladders of their lives.

"Nah." Maachi puked up his monosyllabic response. It bounced around the three of them like a putrescine smelling, decaying tissue pig-scrotum racket ball. Who was going to kick *that* peppa' up a notch? Hacky sickie straight out of Portland.

"Superb! Gentlemen I shall act in the interests of your desires. It may not happen on your next *dance macabre*, but I will endeavor to deliver simple delight to you and tickle those dark fancies of yours! Sound good?" More wriggling maggot words slithered out of his jowly mouth. As they fell to the floor they wiggled in Bart's direction. Where's a shop vac when you need one?

"Yeah, all good. Whatever he says. Just let us know a in advance how to kit up. If we do have to go to a gunfight with a knife, we want to have a couple of Spetsnaz ballistics. Okay with that? Just a note to us, you can be cryptic or not to let us know how to show up first cabin." Bart soliloquized his elegant and refined comments.

"Oh yes, I do understand Mr. Henderson. I most certainly do understand. By the by, Mr. Henderson, our preliminary scoring indicates that your business partner did far better than you by a few points. You did not fare so well because you did move astray of our guidelines and did leave a damaged and not mortally wounded participant in the fray. There were other policy violations that hopefully you will not make a habit of demonstrating.

Our Indian friends had to use a yellow sash to complete the job. And please do note, there is an extra charge for the sash cleaner services rendered for that *a la carte* addition. Shall I use the same bitcoin accounts as we have in the past?"

"Yup. Same, same, same. Let us know about the next soiree." Maachi snapped back. He further turned his torso full on to Bart and pointed his stabbing, index fingers at him. "*Told you I'm the Boss*! And you know what that means!" a domineering set of muffled words that did a double tap on the thought that he crushed Bart with his score.

"Yeah, I owe you a real dead president dollar bill. Thanks for rubbing it in." Bart stated with a smidgeon of sarcastic resentment in his voice.

"Dr. Panicles, if I may interrupt, I shall do my absolute best as always. These opportunities do have randomness though. We do endeavor to anticipate and encourage, but you of course realize the path of a raging beast is somewhat unpredictable. I do expect that there may be events a little closer to home for you fine chaps in the near term. But we can never tell when the next incident will accelerate to a full-blown playing field.

Atlanta has been on a medium high boil and our algorithms suggest an upcoming set of events may be in the offing. At least you won't have to travel across the country again, for now." The larval words morphed into miniature Dubois' sea snakes that slid upon the excited mucusy spittle from his mouth.

Fini and time to be engorged by the Caddie. The purr became a roar, and it was tally ho to the plane they went. In a few hours it would be Maachi in his silver Audi A6 and Bart in his black F350 tooling it out to their respective humble abodes; a nine thousand two hundred square foot fortress complete with an underground sixty-meter firing range, and the seven thousand four hundred square foot cabin, respectively. It's amazing what you can afford when you buy the cheapest APIs and supplement ingredients, relabel them as some other material and junk the data up in the ERP. *What* trail? There's no trail here, look for yourself. The ERP system that Maachi monkeyed with as the world's smartest programmer truly was a masterpiece. The only person who understood the stinky, bloated, programmer's underbelly in the whole entire complete organization was? The eviler Maachi the Magnificent. A legend in his own mind and a behind in everyone else's.

So many ways to make money in this business they were in. Just hide everything and hacked bits in a computer rack. And if someone did discover something? No big deal. Delete, demag, frag, and poof, the data is for some unforeseen reason, gone. Minor infraction instead of the critical issues that were tossed into a data meat grinder and extruded out into a tasty buffalo post-digestion corn chip of information that bore no genuineness to the original product issue.

Chapter 6: Coming Home

The first thing Maachi did when he got home was to pull the chip data from his scope and view the replays while sucking down an almost frozen Stella. He couldn't wait to see MOI – *moment of impact* and how it ferried the living across the Styx in a competitive 4t GTO Huntress at full throttle. It wasn't a slide of consciousness into the unknown. It was a direct heart injection of adrenaline while being subjected to an electroshock therapy jolt. The unfortunate soul perished with no ectoplasmic impressions of anything. The to-be-capped asset target look of *Whatthefucketyfuckfuckfuck just happened ZOOIINNK!* That's the part that Maachi loved. It gave him a camelthorn woodie. Playing those scenes in loops was like one long masturbation session. Such odd reinforcement wiring. Pain and suffering made him pop his nut.

Bart settled himself in after he put away his toys. But just for the fun of it he went to his armory room. He liked to stand in the middle of it and breathe the scents of ammo, gun oil, and metal. It was militaristic aromatherapy. In his mind he thought of all the cool ways bad guys called the game. From, say *hallo to my leedle friends* – to *they feared me because I feared nothing.* The inner image of himself was far larger in the rear-view mirror. In actuality he was nothing more than a very financially well-off white-collar nipple-headed crook. And those actions he and Maachi had taken to be crooked were simply the behavioral rebar in the foundation for the rest of their outrageous inhuman practices coliseum. They were not super predators. They were the epitome of soulless *apex* super predators. They ate predators for breakfast and even with no laxative, shit them out by noon just to make room for more.

In theoretical genetics, Maachi would be a transgen of a tiger seal and a salt-water crocodile and Bart would be a goliath heron and a tigerfish. Suggesting that there was anything in their charred souls other than cynical, sadistic cruelty would be in error. Maybe that's why they got along so well, in a rounded-up way. Maachi was the darker of the two and Bart was a very subdued recalcitrant *time to fuck over* accomplice.

The sun would arise tomorrow, and the world would hope for better. Expecting little and getting less. Even the soulful sun is obscured during a moral eclipse.

Chapter 7: Faking the Folk

"What is it you don't get about me telling you for the third time that I don't know where Archie or P'sue are. I saw P'sue on Archie's shoulders and right about then those guys blew up with the Molotov and I lost sight of both of them!" Paul unapologetically stated at mega disco dB.

"But that's the only thing I asked of you! We agreed that when those guys showed up at our meeting that we would use the buddy-buddy-buddy system. Things go so rad-random at those gaggle of people events and ya' never know what's gonna go today's selection of vomit. We really need to find them. They can't just've vanished. Maybe we should go back to the mash up and see if we can find 'em." Andell chipmunkedly offered up.

"Now that's the smartest dumbass thing you've said in a long time. Like since, yesterday. Yeah, super. Let's just stroll back over and play NCSI, *no* crime scene investigation. We go back there with no crowd around us and ya know the pigs will snatch us up for nuthin' truth or dare?" Paul piled on the *let's not do something really stupid here*. "Look, they'll show up. I know they will. This isn't our first burning horse rodeo. It was one of our best, though, wasn't it?" Paul rambled on.

"Agree, agree, okay, I'm down with it. Yeah, how grody chill it was. The extra money sure did help us out to put this together. I still can't figure out who those guys were who dumped the cash readies on us." Andell had a childish grin across his face. His memories were dollar bill relished with honey mustard on a Kosher dog.

It was the *other* kind of Men in Black who made the mustard *and* the dog.

Chapter 8: El Urgencia

"Interesting text from our best-event organizer friend." Maachi shared with Bart.

"Yeah? What's it say?" Bart queried with wrinkled brow.

"Hey, go get your phone, okay? I think you have the same message. It says, *let's chat, secure line, one hour.* So go get your phone. Hey before you go, look, you really need to have your phone with you *all* the time. If you or I miss anything on this China bullet train it could be more than a little micro aggression issue. Get it? So no more *Dude, where's my phone?* Do you really get it? Sign of life, puuhlease!" Maachi caustically chided Bart. Maachi just had to control *everything.* For him, controlling every little drip and drop of life around him meant he would always be the smartest guy in the room, a gringo *El Hefe.* A small dick way of protecting himself from his own insecurities and deficiencies. Project unto others that which you are.

You earned brown-dabbled nose brownie points by stating his imaginary title when you met or spoke with him. Even bright burning candles, like him, love to be bathed in glowing adulation. They're just blind as to if it's genuinely stated in an endearing manner or not. The *or not* never enters their mind because they could not possibly imagine anyone being so irreverent in a statement of truth! A blind spot for an inquiring mind to squirrel away in and easily leverage.

Bart tried his best to hide his latent, slow boil disgust. His phone was connected to the emotion ring on his finger and let him know when it sensed his below-the-skin tolerance of Maachi's nonsense by going from acute temperature spike to consistent contempt. It would vibrate when he was getting ready to blow and the biofeedback slid him back into a blander vanilla, casual demeanor. He was very clear on how Maachi would react if he let him know his true feelings.

He was quite aware of how his sporting buddy was on a continual blend of drugs, screwed up metabolism, and innate cruelty, in short, nuttier than a Mr. Peanut rack in the grocery aisle. And he avoided tapping the keg o' self-centered viciousness. He just smiled and stated with a laugh, "you got it El Hefe!" Maachi smiled back with a look of *now that's what I want to hear.*

Bart went full character, shiny toothy smile that bounced the image of Maachi's face in reflection, and snapped a two finger *V* at Maachi as he left the office to retrieve his phone. Rather than have to interact with Maachi anymore over the phone issue, he simply texted back, *Mine is in two hours.* Badda-bing-badda boom.

Maachi though, always has to have the last word. He texted back *Tell me what happens on your call. I'll have my phone W/me for your text.*

Bart glared at his phone. He thought, always a dig, always textscreed, always just poking himself into everyone else's world – you'd think we're all his little robots and all he has to do is key up a few buttons and we obsequiously pay homage. Total fuckhead but he sure does know how to make money! *Hey, Big M, LYK after the call.* And then he cathunked his phone into the desk drawer, hit the reactive graphene glass shades control, and took a nap in his designer, ergogenic, weightless chair. He let his brain shrink and clean out the thought wrinkles of Maachi's arrogance. Should hit the turbo spin rinse cycle. Fuck! Where is that selection on the screen?

Chapter 9: Shout at the Devil

"We both had a mick-chat." Stating the most incredibly obvious. They were private dialogues that occurred within an hour of each other. "You spill first." Maachi matter-of-factly stated.

"Why do I have to cough up the sprinkles first?" Bart chirped back.

"Well let's try this. Who am I? *El Hefe.* Got that. And I *did* ask you first." Maachi took the highest alpha ground he could. It was weak, but when things are said loud and often enough, they can become very real for some people. All that would add to the ambience of mind control would be Super Trooper lights directed right at Bart.

"You suck. You really, really suck. You always pull this one-upmanship crapola." Bart hung on to the insulting behavior with his canines.

"I know you're trying to make a point. Let me offer up a different perspective. We've known each other since our puppies were bigger than us. We committed to each other there's always a leader and a follower. If you burn fast and make lots of decisions in snap time that would indicate, you're the leader. Otherwise, you have to put up with this and we keep rolling with this codependent-odd couple relationship in real time. And look at us now. Ain't America awesome? We built our company out of nothing to become a major something. We can do what we want and when we want *in perpetuity.*

Anytime you think you can move the pieces first in whatever we're doing, take your best shot. Some of your endeavors didn't turn out so well though. Remember? Mine? *Baaatttinggg* a thousand. So right now, I'm processing all the shit we're doing, and I need your pieces. I already know my thoughts."

El Hefe morphed into a guy on a shiny, marble balcony espousing and pontificating his thoughts on universal order as a current day techno *Il Duce.* Still, both are romance language names, and the comparative insinuation has some consistency. "Like I said, you first. One to one to two and you, and *you!*" Maachi took a half-meter higher perspective on the little faux marble balcony he had built.

"It was an offer." Bart reluctantly shared.

"And that's it? That's your first piece on the board? Shit, no way – you need to go wide and deep. Don't stop until I tell you to. I told you I know what I know, and I need your notes. Trust and verify, migo. Blade's out at you Mr. Pikachu." Maachi was ever the confrontational dickhead.

"He said that we had mightily impressed some of the foundational company board members. We always sluiced the crypto to them ahead of time all the time. They liked our numbers. It appears that the Board members also have some kind of bent wagering system on who's going to score how many points and how they get them. Like betting on horses. You don't just bet on one and you don't just bet for first place. We're amusement to them, in a rather bizarre world way. It's kind of like the hair club *whatever* for men. They like to have customers but having people recruit others by letting them know, not just as customers, but as some kind of ownership skin in the game guys, that this investment of time and energy is a great ride for all. Not quite sure what all that meant. A bit of McCarty fast barcode mode blabber. The punch line on all of that is they would like to know if we want to have equity in this rumble in the urban jungle business." Bart slowly slid the door down to close off the commentary.

"Yeah, I got the same story line. It sounds attractive. How much do we spend now? Annualized on our big boys go bb gun hunting adventures? Between the two of us that's about hitting the ceiling of five mil. You got the rest of the blabber from the carnival hawker, right? The part about we get a hefty percent cost reduction on all normal parties and for the challenging ones we get a straight thirty percent reduction. That's a win for us. He's waiting for my text to go green on this. You green on this or do you have some other ideas?" Maachi questioned Bart.

"No amber and no red. Seems like our lifestyle just may get more lively and less boring, and at a discount. Separate calls, same desired business outcome. I say we do it. I'll key him up and let him know we are a go to have a face-to-face in three D meeting." Bart concluded.

"All go for me. And let's remember that you called this one. Let's go roller and have that meeting." Maachi dryly responded.

Chapter 10: Pimpin

Hey, Lati, my office, now. Maachi Slacked a terse note to Latika.

Sure. Be right there. She flashed a disdainful look at her computer monitor. She never could recall a good meeting with Maachi. Her level of expectation was dread or lower.

"Hey Latika, c'mon in." Bart congenially commented with a warm, inviting smile.

"Thank you, Bart. How can I help? What do you need?" She politely asked as she cast her eyes downward. Not so much in appreciation of being politically correct. It was a glimmer of embarrassment that was well founded from her experiences with Maachi.

Latika was that special sort who wiped the ass of El Hefe sans toilet paper. Smart, good looking as front desk eye candy and most importantly, she did what she was told. Always. Latika was *culled from the herd* as Maachi had shared with Bart. Maachi had gotten word a while ago that some gray labor was going to be available. There was some importable Indian talent to be had. A *human resource broker* had called him and let him know he had a good one on the line and there could be some nice leverage. Maachi was a predator in every sense of the word and there was one word he loved, leverage. Leverage meant control. Control meant he could add another squishy robot to his warehouse of talent to do his bidding. Latika was a special asset though in more ways than one. An Executive Assistant with benefits. Unwilling benefits but benefits, nevertheless.

She had anchors, her husband, and children. What Maachi loved about making her one of his windup toys was that those anchors would make her far more passive. He could box her in and since she wouldn't have any local family social support, she was an easy one to be controlled and manipulated. Maachi had his very own human asset acquisition punch list. On that list of attributes importation, anchors, and a lack of local family support were high on it. Good looking was a major plus. Latika was not some lower administrative bimbo. She was highly educated with a master's and of note, from the Brahmin caste. And she had an awesome honey-peach ass that just wouldn't quit.

"Where is it?" Maachi asked.

"Dr. Panicles, where is what?" Latika questioned as her brow went lightly wrinkly-skrinkly.

"Your fucking Surface? How many times have I had to tell you to *always* have your pad when you come in here? And I don't mean a maxi pad. Do you think we're just going to bejabber some Bengali nonsense?" Maachi chunked out his so very typical, ethnically insulting, misogynistic nastiness. Latika just stood there frozen in time. She thought she had become accustomed to his insults and bullying. But no, it was always a shock the monkey moment.

"There isn't a bus stop here. There's no what-the-fuck Tuk-Tuk either. Go get your pad." Maachi was a master of insults. He didn't hide them either. His ethnic slurs and insolent behavior just rolled from one day to the next. He truly believed he was invulnerable to the outrageous slings and arrows of modern society. Thuk, thuk, thuk, arrows missed but the hurt was not remiss.

For him it was a matter of *next victim, please.* Right now, Latika was the *victime de l'heure.* With all the jibber-jabber Bart just kept a major poker face on. His ring started to do its thing. He had been to this sadistic poking session before. Far more than once. To come to the aid of the victim was like trying to pry a struggling, panicked baby seal out of the maw of a great white shark. Not gonna' happen unless you have a desire to perish during Shark Week.

Latika looked down, turned around, and walked out of the office. "Is that the fastest you can move? We've got our taximeters running here. Time is money. Speed up your butt, and the rest of you. *Pronto Ms. Tonto!*" The insults hurt *in perpetuity* as a soulful burn that's more destructive after the initial scorch. The noxious words resounding on the stony hard grey matter with harsh echoes. The unwanted gift that just kept on giving.

Latika quickened her step and repeatedly recited a short Goddess Kali mantra.

"She's always soooo stupid. You'd think by now she would've gotten the memo. *Do not come to a meeting without your pad.* But no, she just doesn't get it. But ya gotta admit, nice eye candy. I really like it when she leaves my office." Maachi's eyes widened as he thought his salacious, disturbing mental meanderings. He makes everyone a thing. Bart just managed a slit-smile and nodded a shallow-head tilt.

"All set. How can I help?" Latika had returned and was doing her best to mask enmity with helpfulness.

"You could sit on my lap and take notes." Maachi never let a sex-laden moment go to waste. Latika feinted a smile from a grimace.

"Here, now?" She politely asked as she embarrassingly looked over at Bart.

"Only kidding. Later maybe. Kidding, ... sort of." Maachi's eyes lit up and his words redirected his blood flow. "Here's the deal. We've gotta' VIP of sorts visiting. Make sure everything is cleaned up. The coffee bar area, your desk, my desk, Bart's desk, and even the men's room. Make sure you do a great job on the last item and polish everything. Let me know when you clean it up. I want to do a personal inspection." Greasy fried chicken-crispy coated words spewed from his mouth and onto his desk. Crunchy, saucy style. When slime gets on Maachi, the slime feels it needs to be squeegeed clean. Sqqkwaaaeeeek. The smirk on his face held in place after his last lascivious comment.

"Latika, my office is fine. No worries. Got it covered." Bart tried to provide some form of shielding manliness. Lame as it was.

"C'mon Bart! Doesn't some of your furniture need to be polished? Maybe some door or a cabinet *knob?*" Maachi just never gave up. Insults and demeaning behavior were his forte. He grinned a bit wider. Latika just remained motionless and recited mantra to move her awareness from this awful place. A thought popped into her head though. *What samskara did this nightmare sprout from? Was she a demon in a past life who ate babies and slow boiled small animals?*

"All good, honest El Hefe. I'm in good shape." Bart was now getting edgy and trying to chainsaw a hole in this situation to allow both Latika and him an escape route.

"I'll make absolutely certain all is in order. Do you wish to have any specific refreshments for your visitor?" Latika moved the dialogue to the present needs versus the future potential for misdeeds.

"Nah. He's a yokel. Dresses like he was mugged by old obese comedians. Water, coffee, tea, and some of those Krispy Kreme doughnuts. The cheap day-old ones. He's a pudgemaster and probably has a wide gauge needle to inject them." Maachi was a Gatling gun of derision.

"Okay. Anything else?" She very politely asked

"Nope. Except tell me when you're cleaning up the restroom. You can go now and get to work. I expect every box to be checked off. At the end of the day I can run through your list." Hidden meanings, false words, and self-serving intent permeated his last comments.

Latika turned to walk out the of the office and Maachi raised his finger and pointed to her behind while he wet his lips with his tongue. He nodded to Bart and mouthed the word *tasty peach!*

Later, in the early afternoon Latika Slacked Maachi to let him know she was finishing up cleaning the restroom just as he had requested. She had her pad with her just in case she had to take notes. Her pores opened and tiny beads of perspiration coated her skin. She had a frosty glisten. She was very anxious about meeting him in here. He demanded so much from her on every level. Mostly levels beyond acceptable proper supervisor-subordinate depths. He often had her service him. Hopefully this was not one of those moments.

"So, let's see how you did here. I think you missed a few spots on the floor over there. How about you take care of 'em right now?"

This was not going well. She did as she was told and bent over to clean the imaginary spots. "I think you need to get closer to really see how dirty it is." He tapped her on her shoulder and then took a step away. He tapped again. "I think you need to get *very* up close and personal. Try on your knees." Maachi was moving his piece forward. His pants were bulging. She put paper towels on the floor and knelt upon them. She knew what was going to happen. Like so many other times. Her painful discretion kept her and her family in the States.

Maachi began to unzip his fly when the door opened, and Bart started to walk in. He quickly pulled up on the metal tab *zzzzzuuuuppp.*

"Hey, sorry. Everything looks shiny and clean? You did a great job on spiffing up the digs. Hey, okay with you guys if I use the lav? I really gotta go." Bart knowingly or unknowingly had come to Latika's rescue. She took her cue and stood up and cautiously crab-walked to the door while Maachi slowly turned to follow her with severe disappointment. *Oh well, we can make up for this later.* Maachi one-eyed pythoned his thoughts. He would have to wait for another opportunity to be lecherous. He was as good at that as he was with his vulgar snappy repartee.

Latika looked at her watch and was delighted that time was moving on towards five o' clock. Latika was more than eager to hastily leave the office as soon as she could.

Chapter 11: Save Me

Lati, need you to work late today. Until around 8. Mt/m @ my office at 6. Maachi keyed off a Slack note to his favorite and only executive ass-istant. She was now one of his most treasured indentured servants. He had massaged a group of documents to get her and her family into the country from India. Unfortunately, he viewed her as his personal hand puppet robot. He knew, and leveraged the fact, that he had scared the *mal* out of her. He made her very aware that the documents she signed were not all that accurate. And she *did* sign them. The errors and omissions, if made public, would place her whole family at deportation risk. At least that's what he made her think.

Overall, her job responsibilities were quite reasonable. Operative word her is *overall*. She kept his travel schedule, meeting appointments, and some personal items under control. Maachi would terminate her if she let him look foolish by missing a meeting or not having the correct notes. She knew this and kowtowed to any need he required to have addressed. *Any* is the appropriate word in this reference.

She responded with her typical truncated response. *Okay.* She had learned early on that Maachi had this crappy habit of deriding her English skills or somehow making wild speculations out of her simple, straightforward words. Sometimes it became ridiculously onerous. He would even claim that she said something she didn't state and impune, *but you meant this!* It didn't help that it was rumored that he referred to her as his *robot bitch.* She had become numb. She needed to financially support her family and make sure she did nothing to poke the lizard king. She texted her husband with a short note, *need to work late, be home/8.* It was now three-thirty in the afternoon, and she hadn't had lunch yet, ... her energy was low. Time to warm up some chicken Madras in the microwave. It was going to be a long day's journey into the late afternoon and early evening. Her mood switched from *excited to leave* to a major downer.

Clocks don't tick and tock. They just play temporal blackjack and there's no point in betting against the house. You never win back the time you spent doing things that were of no value or at worse, soul crushing. Little lit up numbers on a panel, phone, or pad let you know *tempus fugit*.

Five o'clock dripped into just a few minutes shy of six o'clock. Dread by a thousand seconds. Latika opened the glass door to the anteroom adjacent to Maachi's office. She paused for a moment and took a deep breath; and with a very slow exhale she silently chanted *Om Krim Kali*. She walked over to the mahogany door, timidly knocked once, opened it, and then entered the den of the scoundrel. All fake-smiley she held her pad in front of her with both hands. Her body language signaling a need to be protected. It was 5:55 PM and she always believed being a bit early showed respect.

Maachi was staring deeply into his monitors and didn't even look up. Latika just stood there. An attractive helpful goddess who was at this moment not even worth a look of recognition. Her smile froze. She knew how to bury her feelings and cloud the microexpressions. *Om Krim Kali.*

After a minute or so, Maachi looked up. "What the fuck are you doing here? I said six, not five-fifty-three, or five-fifty-four, most assuredly not five-fifty-five. How about you go back out and when you count off the numbers from five-fifty-nine, you come in exactly ten seconds before six." With the last word he just face-darted back to the monitors. Latika exited and started counting seconds. *Om Krim Kali, Om Krim Kali.*

At exactly 5:59:50 PM, she walked back into Maachi's office. "Sit over there, I'll be with you in a couple of minutes." Maachi snap-barked at her. She didn't look up. She intentionally gravitated to studying the intricate designs in the Pasargad antique rug on the floor in front of her. *Om Krim Kali, Om Krim Kali.* After five minutes had passed, she hoped that he would dismiss her. Not so lucky though.

"I want you to take off your skirt. You know how to do that, right? Or do you need help?" Maachi pasted a slimy smile across his face. His pupils were dilated and wet with touchy-feely anticipation. With those salacious words he calmly took out his tacphone. He dialed up a cocktail of a rather random design. She looked at him, stood up and did as he had asked. This wasn't the first time, and it wouldn't be the last. Her paisley skirt fell to the floor, and she stood in the middle of the crumpled garment like an animal waiting to be directed on what to do next. She already knew what that was. *Om Krim Kali, Om Krim Kali.*

Maachi unfastened his Tateossian skeleton gear cufflink and pulled back the monogrammed French cuff. Over the naked skin he zeroed in the phone and keyed up some additional numbers and let a modified Murder Wasp with benefits sting him. It was a powerful pharmaceutical venom sting. It burned and he winced. *That was different!* he thought to himself. He spasmed muscle-rigid and pushed back on his black leather chair. Eye-roll whiplash snapping up into his head and a short husky gasp spit forth from his mucusy throat.

Maybe this one will kill him. Latika's thoughts were unusual in that she was not prone to wishing anyone harm. But this man was not human. He wore a human skin. He spoke words like a human. He walked like a human. But he wasn't human. Maachi was the living embodiment of Tarakasura. He was a vicious, demonic animal that lived for the next excitable moment. He fully intended that this was going to be one of them.

After chilly, foreboding whole body shudders, he stood up and walked a bit tipsy to the other side of the desk where Latika was standing half naked. A chill went up and down her spine like a vajra from hell frozen over. She shivered. Her chant changed and she sought protection and detachment. *Om karala-badanam ghoram mukta-keshim chatur-bhuryam kalikam dakshinam dibyam munda-mala bibhushitam sadya-chinna shira kharga bama-dordha karambujam abhayam baradan-chaiba dakshina-dardha panikam.* The words in her heart and soul were loud and drowned out the foreboding feelings she had.

"Are you cold? I can take care of that." Maachi's pupils were as big as saucers with droopy eyelid shades obscuring half of his inner darkness. He was standing behind Latika and placed one arm around her waist and the other encircling her throat. "Remember, no screaming and moaning unless you really mean it. I hate fake people. Warmer now?" He pulled his body closer to her. "Do it. Remember, *no teeth.*"

She reached behind and unzipped his trousers. Each metallic squishy-squeak on the teeth of the metal gate made her flinch evermore.

Time ceased to exist and the sounds from the zipper were shrieks and screams of what was yet to come.

She reached into the opened clothed veil, hesitating for just a moment. Maachi barfed out the words, "I said, *do it*." She slid her hand inside his trousers. Maachi never wore underwear. He said it was too civilized. "What the fuck is wrong with you? You know what you have to do. Let's not forget about your lovey-dovey family all safe and warm in that little apartment of yours and what it was like living in the urban paradise of Kolkata." She shuddered. "Is that an *excited to feel me* shudder?"

Latika knew what was at risk. He wouldn't hesitate to throw her to the street and use all his connections to have her and her family shipped back to India like dogs in a too-small crate. Not because he really cared. It was just because he could, and he would, if she let him. She grabbed his penis and gently squeezed it. Maachi smiled. A syrupy smile of knowing he owned her and everything around him. He was El Hefe. And right now he was going to have his kind of fun. Unfortunately, whatever was in the pharmaceutical cornucopia he injected wasn't helping to stiffen his resolve.

"Mmmmmmm, jeez Lati, that's nice but it isn't getting me there. I have a feeling that this won't be over quickly, and you won't enjoy it, but I will. Gotta hit this up a notch or three." His voice a toxic, syrupy evil male siren's song. He was a nauseating triton. He dropped his hand from her waist and slid it into her panties and onto her crotch. He slowly stroked her soft fur. He loved it; she was ready to vomit. He ran his fingers up and down her lips. She went mindless and pretended this was all just a disgusting nightmarish dream. A very bad dream. A dark, snarling cloud of a dream that would pass and disappear. She sought dispassion and refuge in her mental chanting. *Om karala-badanam ghoram mukta-keshim chatur-bhuryam.*

He twitched-slid his maleficent fingers more deeply between her legs. His pinky penetrated her. "Babeee—you gotta get wet. C'mon bitch, get wet. Loosen up. Maybe you'll like it. Just pretend I'm your little hubby. How big is his cock, anyway?" He chortled a Cane Toad laugh.

She didn't even hear him. The sound of his voice passed through her like a bad wind. She just let him do what he wished with her. Her mantra chanting provided refuge from the reality of being sexually abused.

He was getting tipsy from the recreational cocktail and he tilted to the side. He took that serendipitous tilting and morphed it into a slide around to the front of Latika. Face to face. He was a drooling, nostrils-flared demon and she was a rigid statue. He put his hands on either side of her head and kissed her. He shoved his tongue deeply into her mouth and she repulsively gagged. He pulled her head so tightly her lips almost bruised. She could barely breathe as he held her nose pinched closed, and his mouth totally cleaved to her lips. She gasped and writhed with the evilness of his actions. He shivered with the rush of being in total control and he started to drip. He firmly placed his hands on her shoulders and forcefully pushed her down to the floor.

"Move over. No dripping on the rug, it's expensive. Over here." He pointed to the hard plastic floor protector. It hurt her knees.

"Time for some light refreshment, catch every sugary drop."

Latika had a macabre feeling of relief. This is the part where he blessed her with his all-powerful sacrament and made her swallow while he continued to thrust. It was the crescendo. If she could get him to quickly climax, he would drowse out. He'd either collapse on the carpet or blind man his way to a chair and fall asleep in it. *Almost over.* She consoled herself. No tears. No strong, stiff memory wrinkles. *Om karala-badanam ghoram mukta-keshim chatur-bhuryam kalikam dakshinam dibyam munda-mala.*

He mashed his cock into her mouth and slid it around her face. She kissed him and licked him. He forced her lips against his balls and gyrated his groin into her face.

To her surprise the focus of her intent was rather unresponsive to her choreographed wiles. She thought to herself, *this is not good, this is a first, drugs, it's his design by randomness.*

"What the fuck is so messed up with you? *Get me hard bitch!* I really need to feed you a creampie! C'mon! Wetter, wetter. Spit on me and slide me, tug me! Way down that tight throat of yours." Maachi had tipped over to being feral and that was going to increase the bizarreness of the noxious encounter.

He grabbed her hair and yanked her head off his cock and tilted it up. "Look at me! We need to jump further into that tasty rabbit hole. Right *rabbit*? Rabbits love to fuck so let's get to it. You can do better, can't you?" She was in shock. He wasn't going to penetrate her, or was he? He had never done that before. He was always satisfied with her warm lips wrapped around his cock coaxing his vile, bitter syrup into her mouth and down her throat.

He grabbed her off her knees and pulled their faces together. She went limp with the resignation that this was going to be so much more than just a bobbing head. "Take off everything and go over to my desk. Stick that luscious brown ass out I'm gonna' round the world you. Nice wet, sticky sweet. I really want to taste all of your drippy meat. Your lips, your clit and everything in-between!" His voice was a low intimidating, insensitive growl.

She took off her print blouse and brassiere and let them drop to the floor. She started to bend over to remove her panties and she was surprised that Maachi's hand was the hare, and she was the tortoise. He forcefully pulled the fabric up into her lips. She winced in pain. He then pulled her panties down to her thighs where they obeyed gravity and fell to the floor. He followed the paths of the gravity-captured clothing with his tongue. To her soft neck, to her squishy nipples he wet her with his mouth and tongue. He dropped to his knees and stuck his hand through her breezy-gap to pull her pussy to his mouth. Reaching between her soft thighs he yanked them more apart.

He drunken-dog lapped her and forcefully sucked on her clit. *He was right. This wasn't going to be fast.* She thought to herself in abject, mortified disappointment. This was new skin oceanography that the bad ship Maachi was navigating. He was going submarine watching and she was drowning in an ocean of self-contempt. *Om karala-badanam ghoram mukta-keshim chatur-bhuryam kalikam dakshinam dibyam munda-mala bibhushitam.*

He pushed her upper thighs further to the side so that he could explore all her caverns with invidious intent. He licked, poked, and stroked. He bit her labia and drew blood. His tongue sucked in the little red drops, and he smiled. Salty, metallic, and sweet, the essence of her meat. *Yum, blood play!* he thought.

She contracted. Not just from the abhorrent act. *It hurt.* He abruptly stopped. He was a speedboat that slammed into reverse and totally froze. His hands squeezed her thighs so tightly it immobilized her. His grip loosened and he arose from his knees like a cadaver from an open casket. *This is going from bad to worse. He is going places he never went before.* Latika's words banshee-screamed in her head. Disgust, revulsion, and fear had taken over her spirit. A sickening, choking pall swept her being. *Om karala-badanam ghoram mukta-keshim chatur-bhuryam kalikam dakshinam dibyam munda-mala bibhushitam sadya-chinna shira kharga bama-dordha karambujam abhayam baradan-chaiba dakshina-dardha panikam.* She panicked to a level she had never been to before. She had become detached from the less invasive sexual assaults with the knowledge that the episodes were predictable and not very long but had become more frequent. This was taking a physical attack to a full-blown rape. She was feeling faint, and her hands were clammy.

"There really is something wrong with you! You just aren't doing it. You need to do way better. And I don't mean just longer or wetter. I know just the thing." Maachi rattled on his vulgar, throaty screed. He pushed her away and her eyes again cast downward in shame and embarrassment.

Maachi grabbed his tacphone and placed it on a small, shiny metallic stand at the edge of the table next to a snake plant. He pointed the camera towards the front of the desk. He tapped the screen a few times. "C'mere you! Let's get this *parteee* started!"

"Maachi, please, please. Please, no videos, no photos. We agreed, no photos, no phone photos," she pleaded with him.

"You cunt! I do what I want to do! Get it? What the fuck do you care? I keep these to myself dontcha' know!" He stumbled over to her and grabbed her around the waist. As to an animal on a tether, he turned her around and pushed her face first over the wooden desk and spread her cheeks. "That should do it. Pull back on your ass cheeks! Stick that pussy out! I'm goin in!" Without any hesitation, he jammed himself into her like a malicious, steel spike. She was dry and his cock was locked in an awkward position. His harsh action tore at her tender inner lips. "Wutz it take to get you fucking wet, *bitch*?" With that, he pulled his cock out of her, looked down and spit a gooey mass of yellow-green mucus onto his dick. He rubbed it around and then went right back into evil action. He slid in like the greasy thing he was. She arched her back. It was screechingly painful! It was sharp and nasty. It made her bleed even more from where he had bit her. He now had blood on his cock. "Wow! Looookeeee here! I got me a virgin! Waaaaaahooooo! I'm gonna ride you fresh bitch like a rodeo!" And with that he plunged in and out, deeper with each assaulting hip thrust. He took one hand and placed it around her neck. He was totally limbic feral. There was not one shard or shred of human soul left in him. Not one little ectoplasmic drop. Just pure, primal fuck energy. He was truly full of sadistic intent. He became a thrusting nasty Tarakasura.

Latika grabbed onto the desk to stabilize herself against his thrusting. She focused her meditation. She went deeply within her being. *Kreem* and an inhale. *Kreem* and an exhale. With each of Maachi's pumps and thrusts she coordinated her breathing with his vile actions. She focused upon the space between each of her breaths as she chanted *Kreem*. It was not a loud chant. A chant from the mouth is of marginal power. A chant from the gut has greater power. A silent vibrating chant is a tuning fork that springs from the heart and soul and is the power of the universe in light-body words, the mantra. Practiced for generations by devotees the mantra takes on a power of its own. Like a brilliant blue, sparkling dot, it unleashes the best of the best in us. It's a matter of tuning which mantra, when to chant, and to what intimate power level. She was oblivious to his rocking motions and thought of herself as being in a small boat upon the waters of Aksa Bay that was gently pulsing with the waves. The sound of the slapping waves were that of her own being, the recitation of the mantra coinciding with her breaths and pausing for a brief moment as an exhale became an inhale. She further focused on the space of no-breath.

Maachi was grunting as the animal he was. He then stuck his thumb in her mouth and told her to suck on it and get it wet. His hand slid down her back and he penetrated her behind with his wet thumb and he fishooked her while his cock was pleasure pistoning. It hurt her beyond her imagination. This nasty creature pinched her from the inside out and the pain was nauseating, and his actions were reprehensible.

"Hey, cutie, with chocolatey-skin so soft and delicious I got just the thing for you!" Maachi barked out the crescendo to his sadistic faux mating ritual. Latika was harshly brought back to reality. With his words she anticipated that this rape would end soon with him climaxing inside of her. The thought of his slimy birya moved her mind back onto the boat in the ocean and the song of mantra. Her perspiration dripped to her mouth and in her mind, she was in a salty ocean spray.

Maachi slowed his hip-kiss dance. He turned and grabbed his tacphone again. He held it up over the back of Latika's head and started keying in a song of pharmacopeial discordance. It was always a toss of the dice, but Maachi was drug master flash, and he created a potpourri of opiates, Addyii, fentanyl, and for some reason pilocarpine hydrochloride.

Latika felt a sharp pain in her left butt cheek. She thought he pinched her. The pain turned her focused meditation into a right here right now awareness. She quickly glanced over her shoulder just in time to see Maachi toss his phone to the seat of his chair. It bounced on the leather like a quarter on a military bed sheet. As bad luck would have it, cameras up viding her distorted face.

She froze and feared about what he had injected her with. At that catatonic moment Maachi smacked her on the ass and then on the back of her head. "I didn't tell you to stop! Did I! Diiidddd IIIIiii? Rock me and ride me baby like a wild fucking mare!"

Latika felt drowsy and off-balance. Maachi found her squirming to be delightful. It was like the bitches he roofied but so much better. They just passed out and she was quivering and shaking like a donkey with Parkinson's.

He was living his dream. A hot bitch in heat bumping and grinding and moving that soft ass that he was riding.

A warm rush came over her. She was soft and fluid and totally submissive. Latika went limp and slumped on the desk.

'Great, no talking or nasty looks. Couldn't be better!' He thought to himself as he piston-pumped away at her wonderfully tender bottom.

At that moment Maachi throbbingly climaxed and filled her up. "MMMaʋʋaaarrrooww," he groaned the most beastly, unstoppable howl from the explosive climax. And he just kept rolling out the carnivorous notes to the unconscious Latika. She was somewhere else beyond the ocean and had no thoughts about what had just happened. The world was a blur, and she was losing consciousness. In her mind she had fallen overboard from the boat and was drowning in the salty ocean. One twenty, one ten, ninety, seventy, sixty, fifty beats per minute. Her heart was slowing down. The opiates were a bit more than her body could handle. She was drugged and violently raped. She was going to die.

Maachi came back from the pitch-black side and saw that she was going down for the count. He knew the signs. *Shit*. He visited that place like a revolving door but lucky for him when it happened his tacphone anticipated what was occurring and pulled his silver thread in from the edge of the veil to prevent his passing.

He yanked his limp, honey-dripping cock out of Latika and ran around to the other side of the desk and scarfed up his phone. His Pharm D background always came in handy. He keyed up a tune and focused on naltrexone and adrenalin. Turning her over as quickly as he could, he pushed her voluptuous breasts apart and stung her in the chest above her heart to revive her. She was on her back with her legs wide and Maachi between them. "You'll be all right. Just shake it off." He picked her up and held her in a dispassionate bear hug and shook her.

She abruptly opened her eyes and was not clear about what had happened. All she knew was that something extremely perverted and dark had occurred. She was naked and bleeding. She dry heaved. Her stomach pitched with a sickening opiate surge. She vomited on Maachi.

Her eyes were pitch black and furious at being so compromised. She had no recourse though.

"Now was that nice? Didja have to blow lunch on me?

"You can shower up in my office lav and leave. We're done here. We'll have to do it again. It was an *awesome* rush." He grabbed her nipple and squeezed it so hard it went dark purple. She pulled away. "Don't you ever fucking pull away from me! You bitch! Pick up your shit after you shower and just get the crap outta here."

A warm dribble of semen and blood cascaded down her thigh and onto her knee. She slowly collected her clothes and sluggishly walked to the private lav. The shower water rained down upon her. Her head pounded of thunder and the pain she felt was lightning bolt sharp. She prayed to the Goddess Kali to wash away her sinful actions. Her tears and blood merged with the waters of the earth and swirled away to the drain. She heaved again and vomited. With a heavy sigh she leaned against the glass shower wall. A harsh resentful sigh of resignation and shame. She needed to get home. Her family and her husband awaited her.

Maachi had left before she was done cleaning up. He switched on his office security cams and tossed his tacphone into his pocket. A rush of remembrance of his excitement at brutalizing his assistant splashed across his being and coalesced into a single thought, *Gotta do that again. That was so mind-fucking awesome. At least I've got some super wide screen replays!*

Chapter 12: Take Me Home

She nervously finger-tangoed-jingle-jangled the keys to her apartment and dueled with the lock to see who would win. It was no contest. The bits of shiny metal would not impede her passion to be in her sanctuary. She wanted to be hugged, to be consoled, comforted. There was no way she could let her husband know what had happened. It would be disastrous for her family. She was the sole earner, and every penny was precious. If she lost her job, they would have zero income. It would destroy her husband and her relationship with him.

Any big disruption at work would result in four one-way tickets paid for by her and mandated by Immigration at the whispered behest of Maachi. Whispers in the night would create problems and forced flight.

Her husband was eagerly awaiting her return from work. As the house husband, he took care of pretty much everything. Since he had been laid off from his code writing job, he happily shouldered the child-care and mundane householder activities as his full-time job.

His employer had a sharp decrease in revenue during the ongoing pandemic and the fastest way to get back into a more favorable financial balance was to chop heads. His head was chopped along with twenty-six other fellow employees. That equated to over a twenty-five percent reduction in an already stressed workforce. Viral infection labor collateral.

Now he was the home-dad *par excellence.* He took care of the kids. He made breakfasts of chapattis and an assortment of traditional Indian foods to nourish Baku and Saadhaka. The lunches he packed for them were filled with unconditional love. It makes the food taste divine when someone places their positive energy into it.

When Latika was late from work, he prepared dinner in anticipation of sharing life with his entire family. And if she was really late, he meditated on the Goddess Kali with his children before bedtime and sealed the day with a kiss between their eyes. His love for his family was overflowing with the best of intentions and prayers for a better tomorrow. He would do anything and everything for them. The energy flow of karma had placed the four souls together and he viewed himself as their Shiva. Their lives given by God were a gift to further evolve enlightenment and self-realization. In human form, he was their protector, and their apartment was their sacred holy place, their personal ashram.

She slowly opened the door and her kids joyously charged at her. She held her tired arms out as they bunny hugged her while she looked down the hallway. Her husband, with a big smile, awaited her. She still had her mask on after leaving work. The big man enveloped her with a loving embrace. He gently took her mask off and passionately kissed her.

It was a late dinner for all of them. But late was absolutely fine. They were together and her being eased its way into their secure loving sanctuary. Hard memories of the day melted into nothingness as she bathed in the warmth of their generous love.

Chapter 13: Dark Places

Dinner was heavenly and delicious. Bubai had made vegetable momos, a kati roll, and Kolkata biryani. The wonderful scents of spices merged with the love of Bubai for his family and swirled around the room as a playful, heavenly mistral.

Food made without love is not food at all. They never ate food made by another person's hand unless it was a family event. That was different. Family-made food was soul-nourishing amrit. Food was a gift from the Goddess Kali to her committed, beloved devotees.

When they first arrived in America and before they settled into their apartment, they went to dinner once with their extended Kolkata family. It was an Indian buffet, and the food was exquisite. Except while dining and enjoying naan and different regional Indian cuisine, Saadhaka went to Latika's side and said that she tasted anger in the food. They looked at each other and in that communal connective moment they realized that the cook must be in a foul mood and had changed the energy of what they were dining upon. It was food filled with anger and prepared for money and that was prostitution to their bodies and souls. That resulted in a short dining experience as Latika and Bubai politely excused themselves and placed the reason for their early departure upon time zone lag. After that night they agreed that their Goddess and their sensitivities determined that they make their own meals from scratch. They never felt ill again from dining. They never again sensed their bright inner light dim after dining. They followed their inner guidance and then walked into the reality of the real world. Free will to them was only half of the whole of who they were. The Goddess always set the path and they just needed to be sensitive to the cues and hints that the universe danced out to them.

Prior to eating they always closed their eyes and bowed their heads to a small ten-armed Kali statue in the middle of the dinner table and chanted a short chant. *Om Klim Kalika-Yei Namaha, Om Klim Kalika-Yei Namaha, Om Klim Kalika-Yei Namaha.* They paused and took a deep inward breath and then almost as though choreographed silent bansuris they slowly exhaled through their mouth. All were with eyes open and shiny with calm and happiness. Except for Latika. The luster of her luminous eyes was now very dull and her gaze distant.

Latika was poking at her food and moving it from one place on the plate to another. Her fork was the palanquin for the traveling morsels. She took small bites and swallowed as though in a rote trance.

The kids were enjoying every bite and starch molecule of the rice. Food was Kali's way of letting all of them know that she cared deeply for them. They reciprocated with meditation and chanting upon their much-loved deity.

Their chants were not always the same. They used their own chant books and aligned the harmonic vocalizations and thoughts per what the day was to become, what it had become, and then evening closure with utterances just before sleep. They happily paid homage to the Goddess who protected them and gave them a wellspring of appreciation for life in the body. She gave them a tremendous opportunity to simply, ... be.

Bubai dined with a smile but behind the smile there were inquisitive gritty bits of concern in his eyes. His face was a benevolent façade. Something was wrong with Latika, his Goddess consort. They never held back anything regarding their relationship, and something was amiss. They were partners in this world of the mundane. She was the irresistible and he was the immovable, and all of their lives together were a constant play of consciousness between the essences of the fabric of the universe.

"My love, is everything okay? You look tired and depleted. May I help shoulder your burden? Is there anything I can do to help? It is yours for the asking." He calmly said with a soothing tone in his voice.

"Everything is fine. A long day at work and you know how that can be sometimes." She demurely responded with small crinkly tones of defeat in her voice

"Ah yes. That *thing* that you work for. He treats you like you are dalit. Why does he do that? He is insufferable. You come home to our sanctuary and your shoulders are heavy with the burdens of the day. Offer those burdens to Kali. Let Kali take them. She devours the unsavory to create the new." Bubai counseled her with encouraging words.

"My loving husband, sometimes the day is a heavy blanket. Today was heavier than usual but tomorrow we will awaken, we shall take the blanket off and it will be gone. The sun will shine. We will be rejuvenated. We'll say good day to Kali, and request that Ganesh fill us with elephant power." Latika worked her sharing in once-removed metaphors.

Bubai decided not to pursue the topic. They finished their meal and cleaned up the dishes. It was then off to bed for Baku and Saadhaka. They shared the small second bedroom that was decorated with elephant and Goddess statues. Their parents knelt at their bedsides and tucked them in while chanting. Lights out and all was quiet.

Latika and Bubai went to their bedroom that was attached to the single bathroom. Bubai let Latika know he wished to share himself with her. He desired to hold and console her to lift her spirits and cast off the clouds of the workday. Tantric love was in the offing to rejuvenate the love of his life.

She showered while he warmed the bed. Lights out and the two became one. Caress-filled loving embraces that melted away the horrors of the day for Latika. They mingled and gently played beneath the covers and shared their energies and their bodies. As Bubai penetrated her and stroked her most sensitive parts she hid the pain of the torn delicate tissues. She buried the pain within the passion of the moment and the total love of her husband.

During their happiest of moments Latika's phone rang. She knew by the tone it was Maachi. Her core being responded to it with subtle revulsion. She did not answer it and a message was left.

Latika and Bubai merged their energies, and she stirred their warm body fluids within. She held tightly to her wonderful husband. The passionate embraces made the moment more real and intense. The spiritual fire they generated melted her thoughts of the events that had occurred earlier in the day and evening. The crucible of hot, endearing passion evaporated the negativity.

Four more times during the night Maachi called her. Each time he left a voice or text message. Of the four messages, two had awakened Bubai from his peaceful slumber. The second time he was awakened he silently slid out from the covers and went over to Latika's bed stand to check on the phone. The two text messages from *Boss* were almost identical. *RU All R?* and *Are you, okay?* Bubai wrinkled his brow and went back to sleep. Something was not right. The universe was alerting him to this fact. *If she wants me to know something, she will tell me. This jerk of a boss is probably concerned about some ridiculous business thing at work.* Bubai thought to himself. He connected the thoughts with the most likely rationale.

Later at night, Bubai ventured into the lavatory to relieve himself. The amber night-light guided him to the toilet. He looked at himself and was startled. *Oh my! I have blood on me! I must have hurt my goddess!* He was very concerned and mortified. In the morning they would talk. He did not sleep well that night. He tossed and turned as though being stir-fried in his own questioning thoughts.

Latika was always an early riser. She awoke, but before she could leave the bed, Bubai grabbed her arm. "I hurt you last night when we made love. There was blood." He stated with embarrassment and temerity.

Latika was caught off balance. "Oh my sweet loving husband. You did not harm me. I started my period. All is fine. Do not worry yourself." She went blank with those words so as to not generate any microexpressions that communicated that she was lying. Her interactions with Maachi had made her a master at hiding what lived beneath the waves of her being.

Chapter 14: Another Level

"The McCarty unit is supposed to be here in an hour. How about we use my office and just in case, we vid and audio it?" Maachi casually asked Bart. Inside of Maachi there were always eggs with unknown gargoyles and golems awaiting to hatch.

Bart quickly replied, "Okay by me. See you on the time mark. Start, mark, later." Bart knew the drill. He thought it was amusing that Maachi actually believed his comments were sincere as if he was a real bru'. The only real bru' between them was made with plasmolyzed ethanolic yeast, some hops, barley, and had a label *Craft Brew*. It was Bart's way of programming Maachi into just being a predictable prick and have him not even realize it was his character flaw. Slave becomes master as though a virus contracted in the night air by simply breathing. Whiff, whiff, breathe deep the gathering gloom.

At ten seconds before the hour, Bart was in Maachi's office doorway. Maachi didn't look up from the monitors. He had his own private videodrome going on. Could be snuff stuff, bondage, or anything dark web that gave him the sadistic feedback he loved and needed. Even coal fires need to be stoked and fueled. Bart just stood there. No rapid hand movements and no loud noises. The beast was ensconced with whatever was on his three screens. Bart was a rigid in-place green plastic soldier boy. The only movements he made were an occasional clink-clink eye blink. And when he did that, he even wished he had his lids tac'ed with suppressors.

It was as though they were walking down the middle of a carnival extravaganza drunk on more bottles of beer than fingers on hands. And then the barker congenially yells from a distance and as the distance gets shorter, the barker gets louder.

A *step right this way* congenial, gently commanding voice descended upon the room from a mellow Indian lady that was apologizing for the rude intrusion. A trio of ridiculousness.

Not *tres leches* being all sweet, creamy, and unique. To Maachi it was *tres bitches.*

Latika stood behind McCarty and McCarty stood behind Bart. A reluctant voluntary human centipede of sorts. Maachi looked up over the monitors, waved two fingers and just pointed at Bart and McCarty to come in. Latika knew when to retreat. She did just that. She was trained by the man at the center of this small dark piece of the universe. Latika made a wise choice when she backed out.

"Just how are you two fine gentlemen today? Spectacular I hope!" McCarty tossed the first cards down on the grand playing table. Maachi stared at him to let him know to cut the crap and let's get down to business. Bart didn't say anything. McCarty's words were like a bad, sulfury fart that just hung in midair. "How about if we sit down at that lovely conference table there and I can go over some agreements that you both were so kind to agree to *hear more about* and parley with me?" He grinned in anticipation of swallowing another business agreement whole without chewing. This was a twofer for him. His downline would profitably grow accordingly if he was successful. McCarty was a true missionary and spoke of the fact that you could never have an excess of success. Make success your breeder reactor and flame on.

They sat down and McCarty dealt out four manila folders with their names on them. One for each of them and two for him. "Why don't I give you fellas a couple of minutes to review the document?" Maachi and Bart nodded and then opened the folders. All that was in each of them was a single sheet of custom, holographically watermarked rag bond paper with twelve-point sans serif font Arial type. Nothing else. It was as clear as pitch black dried blood on white angels' gowns.

"This is it?" Maachi annoyingly pecked out his words like an irritated rooster.

"Oh my dear Dr. Panicles! Your sarcasm and wit are simply superb. Bart, he's the funny one, isn't he? Admit it Bart, he really is a hoot and a half!" McCarty was in a cocoon space. He was some mischievous thing inside a drippy, cadaverine perfume-soaked wrapper. He was the carnival barrow walker and was waiting to transform into something more charming. What he changed into was totally directed by what would occur. He is a winner in the evolution of interpersonal morphing. Mirror, mirror, *you* I do, just so I can get inside of you. It's his design.

He looked over at Bart. *Oh, yeah, he's the funny one alright.* Bart let his thought cloud linger for a moment as he bathed in the ironic sarcasm that floated in his head. That foggy thought mass above them all was only missing an intermittent, flashing, arcing fluorescent tube to provide soul-staining bright white ambience. All Bart could think of were the times where he and Maachi were kids playing. Yup, *playing.* Maachi pulled the strings, laughed, and then cut them. Funny? Sure. As long as it was deeply dark and at someone else's expense. *Haha look at you, you big ole dumb persona stuluis!*

Maachi's playing could turn on a nanometer disk in a pico click from fun to run. Run very fast in an away mode. Bart remembered the time they were playing together near the neighbor's fence tossing a ball back and forth. Gloved hand and toss, toss, and catch. Throwing became a bit of an issue. It became boring to Maachi. So, Maachi kept throwing faster and faster *at* Bart, not so much *to* Bart. The funky thing is that Bart really is the classier act of the two. One thing led to another and Maachi cannoned out a fastball that was a scorcher. It was a barbeque shot and come smell the pew. Bart effortlessly caught the leather-covered comet. He was belly full of this stupidity but rather than just quit, you see Bart is not a quitter, he turned to the left. He then said to Maachi, "Hey, dude *watch out!* The neighbor's dog is creeping up on you." Maachi glanced for just a moment to his right. As he did that in a microtome slice of time, Bart missiled the dirty white projectile right at his head. It was not just a beaner. It was a *crowner.* He hit Maachi so hard it almost knocked him off of his feet. Maachi took off his glove and firmly grasped it. He took his other hand and placed it on the now growing burning welt. A furious, scowling, true conehead in development. Maachi ran full-bore at Bart as a nostrils-flared, snorting, dust kicking bull going *sentido.* Bart was the matador, and he was facing down a snorting mad *el toro.* It takes two seconds to cover about seven meters. They were only about four meters apart. Maachi was wildly waving his glove at him. As they came within arm's length Bart held up his still gloved hand to ward off the fist and glove of Maachi. Maachi yanked on Bart's gloved hand and went full *desarme*. He pulled the leather mitt off and threw it over the fence into the neighbor's yard. The mitt was now a muleta in absence and that was not a good thing.

The heavily fenced yard was a mixture of enclosure motifs. There were anchor chain sections all around and in some places the metal chain was reinforced with two-meter-high solid redwood plank fence. A while ago Maachi had cut a small hole in the wooden fence just large enough to stick his hand through. The hole was within reach of the chain anchor that was intended to restrain the canine in case of an acute case of Cujoitis.

Maachi, on occasion, was the server of meaty delights. The menu was usually a single item like a table scrap or some squirrel he caught and bashed into unconsciousness. Offerings for the porch pooch beast to feast upon who lived there.

The resident neighbor's dog person was an odd sort. An immaculate well-tended big fluff ball with genuinely impressive canines of the pointy variety. Of course it was one of the breeds that momma said dontcha' play with. It was a Songshi Quan, Chow Chow, if you will.

The neighbor was of diminutive stature Chinese and of such slight size that he probably could have put a saddle on the dog and ridden him. *Yippee Yi Yo Chow Chow*! He lived alone and used the dog as his companion and loyal guardian. The dog was smotheringly protective. Longya was his name, and it was fitting. Dragon Tooth lived up to his tag. He was like a crafty mad dog without the bloody drool and rabies. Longya had become accustomed to the occasional something tasty being sacrificially offered up from within the hole in the fence. Mostly, he would chomp-chomp down on the morsel, yank on it, and run away.

Maachi furiously slapped Bart in the head with his glove. They did the adolescent pugilistic two-step and twisted around like vampiric Flamenco dancers. He maneuvered Bart to the fence next to where the hole was. Maachi, being the guttersnipe of the neighborhood, suddenly dropped his glove and in that moment of change, grabbed Bart's right hand and shoved it through the fence. He then kicked the fence and yelled, *Longya! Longya!*

Bart was a petrified Groot. The change of the scenario from bean-ball thrower to fierce dog lunch meat was in the offing. Maachi projectile spittle yelled at Bart, "Fucking wiseass! Let's see how you play ball now! You'll simply be lefty! Go get your glove you fucking stupid shithead! Don't ever do anything like that to me again as in nevah-evah!"

Bart could hear the thudding paw sounds of the four-legged meat grinder getting closer. It was not a walk, or run, it was a bolt of fur and teeth coming to do a carnivorous, canine clamp down on his hand and pull on it through the fence until it came off. Bart pleaded with Maachi to let him go. His begging in cadence with the dog's padding feet. Maachi wasn't going to let go of him. He wasn't just fucking around. "This'll teach you a lesson! *Nobody* does shit like that to me! Promise you'll never do anything like that again!"

"Promise-promise-*promise* — may my dick fall off if I'm lying, ... promise *promise*! *Never Again*!" Bart tearfully spat out the words to coax mercy from malevolent Maachi. Bart could hear no more dog steps, which meant that Longya was airborne with mouth wide open to snatch up the squiggly, spasmodic pink, hotdog looking thingies. At that very moment, Maachi looked into Bart's eyes and said, "I'm the *big* boss in this video game and *never* forget it!" And with that he did a *JIT* and pulled Bart's hand from the fence hole.

Longya, while quite voraciously fierce was also quite one-pointed. He clamped his jaws down on the phantom hand with a teeth a' clacking and smashed into the fence so hard it tipped the anchor *and* the wood fence towards the two confrontational boys. They looked at each other and became terrestrial banshees gliding over dirt, sticks, and stones to the backdoor of Maachi's house. Maachi, who was always filled with such benevolent compassion, wasn't done with Bart yet though. Bart thought his bowing down to the great Maachi would have been enough. That isn't how Maachi interacts with the world. Give him a centimeter and he eats your galaxy and any small furry animals that get in his way.

Maachi whipped open the outer glass door *shazooonk* and then the inner door. He jumped inside the safety of the house of brick and closed the door behind him and locked it with a resounding *Kalunnk*. He stared out through the windowpane with devilish glee as Bart started bangedy-banging on the door. Bart's face was all twisted up like a coat hanger stuck in a car wheel. He was begging to be let in. No such luck.

Longya was now enraged and hungry. He was the epitome of an angry Pavlov's dog. He had been tempted with a rare morsel and it was gone. But, being classically and operantly conditioned, his stomach juices went fire-hosey and his mindset was *who moved my meat*? *Time to eat!*

He was so focused he kept barging at the fence. A canine battering ram with hungry fixated intent. The anchor fence and the wood wall tipped far enough at an angle to allow him to ski jump over the bent barriers. His teeth were the downhill edge. A forty-kilo gigantic, maw-open fur ball flying through the air and zeroing in on new prey, *Bart*. Bart gave up on obtaining the mercy of the great and almighty Maachi. He ran to the side of the house and put his kicks to good use. He ran so fast the soles should have melted. He bounded over the asphalt road with his pursuer not far behind. As he stepped on to the other side of the road, he heard a loud brake squeeeeaal and then a major *thudddyyythudd*. A speeding red pickup had collided with Longya with such force it almost made him a fluffy hood ornament with a now departing spirit. Dead On Impact – DOI. The karma ran over the dogma F350 style.

Bart was in the clear, or so he thought. Only to find out that Mr. Chen, the neighbor, was furious that his beloved companion was dead. He *stamping-feet-stormed* over to Maachi's house and demanded to know what had happened. Maachi told him that his friend Bart had visited and taunted the dog and it became enraged. It was all Bart's fault.

Bart was wrongfully judged by the neighbor and his parents. He was grounded for a month without a phone and computer use was limited strictly for schoolwork. That's Maachi at his villainous best. Maachi can poop on any carpet, crash any parade, smash the spirit of anybody and then blame someone else. Even at an early age he was a masterful soul crusher. Yup, he was the funny one and the only one who appreciated the perverse humor in inflicting pain and fear. He always had the last laugh.

The silence in the room was negative 128 dB deafening. McCarty was being clever and Maachi was on some metabolic emotional curve or trough. This may not end well. Maachi went all Siberian frozen-look-stare zap right into McCarty's eyes.

McCarty being the chameleon showman he is, didn't blink. Volcano meets a tornado moment. Brimstone spin, always an issue with who would win. But McCarty was a true solid and never met a mark he couldn't win the bet with. He still had a warehouse full of behavior influencing tricks up his plaid sleeve.

"McCarty cut the shit. We're busy here and your whole gig is just an avenue of entertainment for us. I asked you a question and I don't ask twice." Maachi marched out the words like little well-armed soldiers of fortune. Ready, fire, aim!

The man with the ever-worn variety of leather-elbowed plaid jackets laughed at Maachi. This was now one of those twisty, curvy, *who the heck knows where this will go*, moments. Maachi didn't move a single fast or slow twitch muscle fiber. Not a cheek twitch or a slight ear wiggle. He was waiting for more articulation to come bounding over the table. He wasn't disappointed. Bart was totally surprised by what happened next.

"It appears that my jocularity has missed the spot. Yes, Dr. Panicles it pretty much is *the* agreement. There will be an additional document or two for both of you to sign with a notary and some minor details we can attend to, but that's it. A simple signature brings you, and Bart if he so chooses, into the folds of the well-heeled and courageous athletes in a very profitable business model." McCarty was unflappable in his response.

"There's no fine print? Did you water mark it into the paper with the company logo?" Maachi sneeringly questioned McCarty. McCarty transformed from the slimy thing in a cocoon to a full-bore curare-covered stinger of a killer bee, complete with a *What big teeth you got – all the better to eat you up with*! vibe. The larger toothy smile was the nonverbal hovering spirit of the moment. A smirk that could eat continents spread across his face like a never-ending cavern.

"Well, yes Dr. Panicles that is the entirety of the agreement. It is very straightforward." McCarty calmly stated.

Bart ran up to the nosebleed seats and readied himself for the upcoming entertainment.

Opera glasses in hand so as to not miss one single tell or projected spittle drop. Verbal cage fighting at its finest. All that was missing was a collection of sharp bladed items hanging from the ceiling on bungee cords.

"Lemme scan this," Maachi shared with McCarty.

"Certainly. I'll be right here." McCarty said with an acidic stinging pinch of sarcasm. "Doctor, you are a very wise man to question simplicity. To pose antithesis to Occam's Razor is quite noble and appropriate. The entire agreement is on the paper. Consider this. This adventure we are both immersed in is a unique business model. An MLM of *sorts*. May I continue?" McCarty was on a roll. Toss a bit of greed and screed on the table and it might just be so tasty.

Maachi went Medusa victim. Coldest stone in the middle of a North Pole winter.

"I'll take that as a *yes!* If I may wax on, my client has a unique modified, direct-to-consumer business model. You both were introduced to this sport by a Mr. Ben Sussen. Correct?" McCarty was filling up with social venom and getting ready to poke Maachi in just the right place.

"Yeah, we remember. We knew Sussen from our work on the west coast with his supplement company. He was a wild guy. Had family money from his radio personality dad that he parlayed into a vitamin biz. His side gig was far more lucrative – counterfeit drugs. Lived outside of LA, Santa Monica. He had quite the armory for a chap living in California. It looked like he kiked Charlton Heston's stash.

"He had a buddy out of Solano Beach. Didn't he? The guy with the weird nervous, gagging disorder. I think his first name was Scott; last name maybe was Lending, or Longdow or something like that. Have to think on this one. The Scott guy was a real asshole. He thought of himself as some kind of civilian secret agent. His paranoia must have fed his delusionary state. I think he even squirmed his way into some type of sport supplement company. One of those *camel toe nose in the tent* things.

We used to buy some Chinese raw materials through Sussen. He was connected with a couple of scrimy pharma material manufacturers in China. Cheap stuff and if no questions asked, highly profitable for us. How is Sussen anyway?" Bart questioned after his monologue about relationships was capped. Clearly, he was not a social butterfly. He had bigger wings and drank blood on Friday nights. And every night is Friday night.

"Funny you should ask. He's in China. Western part where there is some significant social unrest occurring with a religious group. Ole Benny is supposed to return in about a week." McCarty hid his oozy smile. His anaconda lips writhed in anticipation of revelations. Those lips were eager to wrap themselves around his audience's mental state of being and *squeeze*. "He sponsored you. And *just like that*, you guys were on board. Happily I assume. And look at him now. A rich and international traveler living the dream. He hunts big game now.

"But please, let me continue. We love having our customers achieve ever-greater potential in our sport. Our goal is to have folks like you be both customers *and* owners, or at least shareholders so to speak in the game we all so enjoy. A *skin in the game* relationship. The proposed arrangement is quite simple. You agree to become Associates versus just end-user *prospects*. You'll receive discounts on all services rendered. Payment is not required upfront for booked services and entertainment. You pick the turfs to play on. Wouldn't it be nice to have first choice of some of the finer arenas?

"By having the status of Associate, you can advance to a more elevated participation level with even greater benefits and financial rewards. Try reaching out to your KlikedIn contacts and entice them to play in this modern-day art form. In addition, by bringing in additional engaging fellows such as yourselves, you receive even greater benefits. Its loads of perks for a lot less work." A confident puffy smile adorned his face that accompanied his pulsating, glowing eyes. The ever-morphing McCarty. That puffy smile from a pufferfish salesmen that exuded volatile tetrodotoxin.

"That's it? We would be, what did you say, Associates?" Maachi came out of his catatonic state.

"Yes. All of our most engaging players and athletes are Associates and more. And that really is just about it in regard to the agreement. Well, almost." McCarty replied with a slightly charming thin-lip grin. Sharp little pointy vowels mixed in with chewy consonants of question. Snap-snap went his hypnotizing rap.

"I knew it. Always some kind of bullshit bait and switch. *Almost* is a highly operative word. So, *almost* what?" Maachi's icy visage was melting under his fuse lit heat, but the coldness of his being was still present. His chair needed a sweater and would do well with an antifreeze wipe down.

"My client will be investing heavily into developing both of you into achieving your potential. You are such resilient and inventive fellows and since we have no written contracts, except this one with which we endeavor to be very clear and without unintelligible legalese. Please take another review of section *Nine: Acts of God or Men* and the section on financial incentives by having like-minded folks sign up with you as their sponsor. There are no hidden fees or other requirements. Just engage the process and bathe in the glow of immersive entertainment."

"Bart, did you read this stuff? What is it? This is starting to sound Ponzi-ish." Maachi turned and intimidatingly questioned Bart. The twist of the nipple here, as always, he made undesirable world events the fault of someone nearby. He made a point of hosing Bart with some imagined guilt with one intent, to stay being El Hefe by keeping others way off-balance.

"It makes his client part minor shareholder in our business with survivor rights. And the more people we bring into the game, the better we're rewarded." Bart dryly stated the obvious. Reading really is part of Maachi's job description but he prefers to just ogle the pictures.

Centerfolds are his absolute favorite. Especially if it's the folds between Latika's thighs at crotch height.

It appears that Maachi didn't even really read what was on the paper. He skimmed the text just like he skimmed company profits. His scattered and distracted attention was his *modus operandi*. His fleeting focus was more hocus-pocus-watta-jokus than anything of real intrinsic or emotional value. The delegation of action to Bart was a covert future weapon.

"What does that mean, McCarty?" Maachi turned his head back to the carnival barker as he was spooling up for a tirade. He hated it when someone tried to get over on him. Maachi always had to be the big dick with someone bent over the desk *sans* jockeys or silk undies. No lube unless he wanted to dose himself with it.

"My client invests in you and as you continue to be more successful both with your company and your network in their company, you become a very valuable human asset. If Lloyd's of London would underwrite you as an asset, it would be so. But unfortunately no insurer protects assets such as you and us in this sport of excellence and life-challenging danger." McCarty placed a verbal sentence at the end of his comment as punctuation on the concept versus a simple period. A seed that was ready to grow into a very mobile Triffid. Chompity- chomp-chomp let's field romp.

"So lemme get this straight. You had us come on into this business arrangement as customers or some kind of *prospects*. Now you want us to flip up the game and be some kind of *Associate* and we pull a greater revenue stream in for you. We aqueduct deep pocket adventurers into the game. What's the word you used? It was Associate, right?"

Maachi had a habit of taking a concept or thought he didn't fully understand and sometimes spin it around. Round and round it goes and only Maachi knows where he wants it to go. Or maybe not so much. The verbal redundancy helped him to remember relatively new concepts. His wiring made quick encoding of new thoughts a challenge.

"So, someone up the ladder makes more money, and we get rewarded for that. But your client gets a piece of our game and if something happens to us, I think I get this; they have a much larger piece of us to offset any investment in or risk from us. *Correctomundo*?" Maachi channeled his steamy words to ensure clarity. He was an annoying dogwhistle teapot getting his latent heat on and it was shouting out a Night on Bald Mountain.

"All true. It is a demonstration of mutual trust and camaraderie that also, serendipitously is quite rewarding." McCarty casually answered.

"But why a piece of our business? They already make a lot of cash-readies. We pay out millions to them. Why a piece of us?" Bart inserted his typical logic.

"We are all in a unique life pursuit. By each of the threads of this relationship being woven into each other it guarantees the utmost in confidentiality. A delicate *quid pro quo* with the added benefit that we all understand that loose wires cause fires and loose lips get into significant trouble. As we individually succeed, we all float higher on the sea of revenue. A camaraderie cork in a bathtub of bits gorged with feral juices." McCarty morphed his comments to provide greater context that fed upon a form of mutually assured confidentiality as the meal. Gulp. Some digestive enzymes might help here. Or a very hungry tapeworm.

"Your mutual guarantee is really mutually assured destruction. Ya' know, like the Russians and the US." Maachi quipped in and clearly indicated he felt as though they were being pushed.

"Goodness gracious, oh my no! It is a business proposition that allows you to continue to explore the real you. So many people, almost all, bury their powerful, true nature and are so totally politically correct that all they have left of themselves is how to please society. Civility exists as a humdrum existence in the first world countries and the animals are loose everywhere else. Does this help to clarify? This is a mutual investment – with *in perpetuity* success and meaningful compensation." McCarty delivered his thoughts with what appeared to be true sincerity. "Dr. Panicles, what do you really think of other people? Your employees? The populace in general? Would you dine with them? Would you invite them on your next seaside vacation? Would you even speak with them if it was not a required form of communication?" He continued.

"Total Massengill. Pink robots that are utterly clueless about everything other than the price of a Quarter Pounder and what toy comes with a happy meal. If they had a gram of sense, they wouldn't be addicted to looking at little bright lights on a computer monitor and playing video games, eating tide pods, or featuring very personal details about which celebrity is pregnant with hopefully a gender solid baby. I never could understand how multicolored dots would actually make people think they're doing something productive. It's an opiate of the masses. Good thing there are some very graphic videos that educate you to do ever-more interesting things while communally splooting.

We found one guy who was playing a first-person shooter on a company computer on *company time*. Stupid shit. We have bots in our system that are above and beyond just finding the latest virus *du jour*. Anytime someone goes off the ranch we know about it in real time. We let him carry on for about a month. Then we made a big deal out of firing him. We even had our attorneys go after him for the pay he received while he stole the work time. We broadcasted that this guy wasn't even working thirty minutes a week! We knew we couldn't make it stick but he folded anyway. We made him think we were the all-powerful Oz and that we could actually do that. Right Bart?" Maachi turned and looked for confirmation from his colleague in craziness. Bart robotically nodded while Maachi devilishly grinned.

"Oh, I see. I do understand. You quite logically believe that the vast majority of humanity is just simply, an aggregation of much lesser beings. If I may be so bold, you appear to view them as a different species that are very so much not like you, so to speak. Most of the clients and Associates of the company I represent have the same view. They view themselves as the *Homo sapiens superior* and the lesser beings are a subspecies *Homo sapiens inferior.*" McCarty provided air cover for Maachi's comments while noticing that Bart was distant, yet he played the part of a loyal compadre very well. Bart was swimming silently below the waves. He didn't need a snorkel because he knew how to hold his breath.

"That's hilarious! Yup, that sums it up in a to-go body bag without a tag. Do ya' know the movie *The Time Machine*? Where humanity becomes two very different species? There are the Morlocks who coddle and nourish the Eloi. They only do it so they can hunt them and chase them down. They harvest them as two-legged take home food. Bart, and me we're the Morlocks and we do as we wish. Simple evolution. The more intelligent, manipulative specie always wins out. Especially since the Eloi are playing video games and collecting digital coupons for food shopping. *I love that movie*! Yeah, two different species." Maachi demonstrated quite clearly his disdain for the multitudes of the *lesser* specie. He viewed himself as someone distinctly different from the hordes of human turds. He was more than a piece of corn in the peanut poop of *humanity*. Bart just projected an unemotional kabuki smile. Clearly, he was mentally disconnected and just tagging along with the dialogue to assuage Maachi. He would rather be playing a videogame like Halo or Call of Duty. He never let on to Maachi about his true feelings on so many topics. His desire was to not be viewed as an Eloi. Bravado with a capital *B*, as in Bart.

"Dr. Panicles I do so much appreciate the reference to *The Time Machine*. I recall reading H.G. Wells' epic portrayal of how people react and evolve in response to a massive global catastrophe when I was about seven years old. Stating the most obvious, I remember the utmost horrifying details about that seductive dystopian novel. The images of piles of bleached white, gnawed-upon human bones in the midden." McCarty was now moving his verbal pieces across the room. He was maneuvering Maachi to where he wished him to be. His skills at digging in and mirroring behavior were on the march. More than a simple bumpkin broker, McCarty was an Alpha Morlock in his own right. A fine middle-aged sophisticated cannibal who also had his unique views on society.

"Yeah, the book. I like the movies better. Reading is not so fun-*da-mental*. Takes too long to get to the point of whatever's going on. I usually just read the first and last page. Same story just a different way of presenting it." Maachi always had to validate his rationale. He was not so much a Damascus steel kind of guy as he was a plastic knife that delivered up on situational ethics. He did what he wanted and then blabbered his way into *splainin* why he was right. Having an intelligent dialogue with differing opinions with him was like swallowing razor blades to shave your beard from the inside out. It never turned out well. How can anyone be right in a world created by Maachi? Simple answer, you can't and it's not worth trying unless you wish to become one of the corporately departed. A pile of bones in the midst of the corporate midden.

Bart liked his cushy executive position and he tagged along with Maachi to insure that he kept him close but not invasively so. Bart adored the finer things in life that consisted of awesome whips, expensive trips, and an assorted bevy of curvy female companions with lovely hips who claimed they adored him. Twerking and WAP was not part of the job description but if it was offered up, he was all in. He was okay with a few stretchy truths. Adore him or not, as long as they were accommodating and comfy-cozy it was fine with him. The ends justified the means.

McCarty smiled and nodded thinking to himself that Bart's face was all corkscrewed up like pulled salt-water taffy in a mixer. And that the written word is far mightier than the titillating widescreen edited version. *To each his own.* He thought. And then he continued. "Please indulge me. The commitment to achieve mutual trust as demonstrated by the very clear and simple document is a formality. Nothing more and assuredly, nothing less. You could always contact Mr. Sussen, he is your sponsor, and ask about his thoughts. He too is also on his way to achieving a quite admirable level of success. He has sponsored many athletes in the game. You can line your pockets and enjoy your animal instincts at will if you deem it appropriate. One of the reasons he put his arm around you both as your sponsor was to attain a higher status level. He is a compassionate man and also has a keen nose to smell profit in the wind.

As I had touched upon, he is in China right now. That trip was partially made possible by how he has successfully endeavored to bring more sport clients into our realm." McCarty slowly and confidently moved his pieces across the mahogany coffee table. This was not a *change somebody's mind* activity. This was a sorting activity. Either you're in or you're out. McCarty made his Eloi ribs and steak chow regardless of the choice that's made. Having Maachi and Bart in the prospect category was rewarding but they would be far more valuable in several ways as business-building associates. McCarty had coughed up a big cat, razor wire hairball of a deal that was irresistible. But any deal you can't walk away from is not a good deal. McCarty was disarmingly deceiving. There was far more to this fellow than met the eyes. If he walked away that would be a very demonstrable message to both Maachi and Bart that he could care less if they signed on. That walk away low-level threat made the deal ever so much more desirable and covetous. Maachi had redundant sets of envy genes.

"Bart, what do you think? You're the detail guy here. If you think this makes sense, I'm in. Like I said, the video is more to my liking than the book. Even if the book is only one page. *You're* driving the decision, Bart." Maachi dismissively shared a multiedged melee Morningstar comment. Sure, Bart would be making the decision and he would also be held very much accountable if the results did not satisfy Maachi's belief structure. So typical. Maachi would off decisions on topics like this just so he could state, *not my decision, not me, not at all it was* – pick the victim time. He never accepted the burdens from his choices for anything ever. And yet again Pontius Pilate would wash his hands of responsibility and the repercussions in the waters of invidious intent. He was so very adept at creating a domino path of fall guys and gals. Maachi was the Teflon Pharm D. Nothing ever stuck to him.

"Aha, Dr. Panicles does this suggest that you would rather not sign at this time? That is quite satisfactory. Please do consider though that there are limited spaces at the associate level for this highly rewarding business opportunity. There are many prospect openings and if you wish you can remain at that level of status. That would be unfortunate and more costly, but it is totally your prerogative.

"I do need to share though; time is of the essence. How long do you think you would require to make your decision? Shall I speak with Bart regarding questions about the document?" Check, *not* check mate, yet. McCarty was letting the one-hundred-pound test line spool out to make Maachi *think* he was in control of the situation.

"Bart, whaddya think man? Spit it out. How about if you go to your office and take a slice of time and ginsu the document? I have some things I need to attend to. I'm looking for a 45 cal Vector with a short barrel. Can't find it anywhere. The whole election and pandemic thing has eaten up the inventory of all the best toys. I really want one to play with. So over to you migo. Call the shot. Wow, that was almost funny." Maachi pulled his pieces off the interactive business chessboard. He didn't fold. Like any reasonably good manager of events he delegated the decision to a subordinate, Bart. A fall guy in waiting of a reason to fall. At the same time he polished his Teflon coating with a scratchless white scrubby.

"Okie dokie El Hefe. On it. I can close the loop with McCarty in my office." He glanced over to McCarty and suggested a course of action. "How about we exit and go talk about the lines between the dots? Would you like some coffee when we relocate?" Bart congenially asked.

"How delightful! Yes, let's go secret ourselves away. In regard to the offer of a libation, I shall decline coffee but would relish a cup of any type of tea. White, green Matcha, or any other variety you might have handy. Nothing like a cup of tea to sharpen the mind and titillate the taste buds. Rich in antioxidants too!" McCarty was going to exit the meeting, but he left his pieces on the table. He was optimistically curious to see where the dialogue would meander to with Bart.

"Someone once said never trust a man who doesn't drink coffee, or was that booze? Same difference. Hey, McCarty maybe later we could hit the Pumpus Ass titty bar for a drink to celebrate. That is if Bart says we move forward." Same snooty one-upmanship different hour and day.

"What a generous offer! I shall need to decline the venue though, and the alcohol. I am not partial to coffee or alcohol. Hopefully that will not diminish your trust in me." Not quite a checkmate but darn close to it.

"No coffee OR alcohol? Boring. And no titty bar? Jeez McCarty, what do you do for fun? What twists your nipples? Electric clips? No problem on the trust thing. That's why we have the paper, right?" An obvious parry and thrust by Maachi.

"Yes, the paper. The succinct agreement that foregoes any misunderstandings. Mr. Henderson, shall we retire to your office abode? By the by, may I wash up before we conclude here and whisk ourselves off to confirm the horses we trade are of healthy acceptable value?" McCarty was an artful dodger. Maachi never did get an answer. Good thing that Maachi was preoccupied in his search for *who wants to own a deadly weapon?* Bart viewed El Hefe's deadly firearm quest as an avant-garde compensation for other areas of subsize endowment. And he never *ever* broached that subject with him. Some things are much smaller than they appear in the mirror or scope.

"Let's move the dialogue to my office. I'll have Latika brew up some tea. She's Indian and she knows tea and maybe if we're lucky, she might offer up to read the residual tea leaves in the cup." Bart wanted to close one door and open another. Even he became fatigued at the never-ending verbal detritus games Maachi played.

"A tea bag would be just fine. No need to be more cosmopolitan." McCarty humbled himself. He wasn't looking for any type of tea drinking elitism.

"No tea bagging here! Just the leaves. We have a decent selection." Bart said and Maachi burst out laughing.

"Yeah, no tea bagging with us, that's a big *for sure*!" Maachi continued to laugh like a school boy who got caught looking at racy porn. Bart smiled and chuckled. Every once in a while, he tossed a bone with a little meat on it over to Maachi simply to draw his attention off of the Six Flags wild ride he was on. *Here boy! Go fetch.*

McCarty stood up and offered his hand to Maachi. Maachi stared at his hand as though it were the drippy bacteria laden tongue in the open mouth of a Komodo dragon. "Hey McCarty, are you in the same world as us? A handshake? Ya' do realize we're in a pandemic, right? Hand shaking is not my skin-slapping-microbe-swapping idea of being socially hospitable or compliant. If I swap bodily fluids, this isn't my way." Maachi, the eminent Pharm D bluntly stated. No handshaking to prevent viral transmission but no one wore masks during his meetings. Not a conundrum. It was complicit braggadocio with a lack of true concern for anyone's well-being except for his own. It would be a Festinger cognitive dissonance moment if Maachi allowed it. But it wasn't the case. Maachi made it up as he went along. His world, his words, his control of all things motile or partially conscious.

"Well, I do understand." McCarty half bowed to Maachi as he looked at his hand with a new sense of pandemicmonium.

"Hey, I like that. Bowing to me? Cool. Bart, take a note *employees must bow when greeting Maachi and leaving Maachi.* I really like that." Maachi didn't stand up to bow back. He just made a mental note that his kingdom now had a new social behavior to adopt to stroke his ego that was to his liking.

McCarty was in a stalled half-bowed position. He was anticipating a reciprocal social action by Maachi to acknowledge his offer and respect. Waiting for that to happen would be like waiting for Godot except Godot was in another narcissistic dimension. Maachi created his own universe and on the eighth day he created mayhem to keep the fattened, hypnotized Eloi off-balance.

"Let's go Mr. McCarty." Bart injected his comment to move McCarty from customary political correctness to an advance to the rear. Bart was redeeming the situation and allowing a respectable stage left exit.

McCarty reversed his bow and straightened up. "Ah, Mr. Henderson, yes, shall we go?"

"That's the ticket. You boys go along and play and no sand kicking and biting. And if you go salacious, Bart, make sure the cam is off."

"You know where to find me." Maachi stood up and walked back to his triple monitor rule-the-world master blaster command station. Time to see who might have one of those tricked-out Vectors. Either on the Internet proper that he could have modded or on the dark net already plumbed out close enough to give him a dripless woody.

Chapter 15: Time Bomb

*I*n *WIP? No caller ID* texted in the burner phone.

All copasetic. We are 2/2. Batting 1.000. McCarty responded.

Nxt mvs? As usual or need random? the mystery caller inquired.

Organize gemming first and then may need help. Riots and demonstrations are going as planned. W/need help in stimulating a few more. Consider recreational compound donations. A few words and volumes upon volumes are spoken. Electron smoke signals in the air dancing between the coryphée and his partner. Comforting and predictable words from McCarty.

Use whatever U need. This is not a cakewalk. It is a moonwalk. TNX/ tonnes. The secretive caller stated.

5X5, W/work details with downlines and promotion. McCarty concluded the conversation. All Utah communications had to be very staccato to prevent the remote possibility that the burners were being tracked. One never knows who is listening to whom. So many little wires and photons just waiting to be captured like pulsing fireflies in a jar. They light the way even in pitch-black darkness with trails from here to there.

McCarty pasted a greasy, jowly smile upon his visage. He loved when a plan went well. This one had tremendous potential. Utah would be thrilled. Building mountains upon mountains that reached the stars and creating financially rewarding tributaries that flowed to the downline earners was a plan made in heaven. Lovely.

Chapter 16: Worth It

"Thank you so very much for organizing this call, Bart. Travel these days with the pandemic is a challenge even with private jets. Are we in a rather secure sound and signal blocking environment?" McCarty cautiously inquired.

"Hey, M, get a clue Mr. Magoo. Do you really think we're hayseeds who fell off the back of a used *pickemup* truck on the way to the Farmers' Market to sell mostly potatoes with a few heavy rocks built in? Yeah, *my* office. IR couldn't pick up anything. We're like in a Faraday Cage exemplar. So what's so freakin' important for this call? We took care of the documents—and BTW, do we get hoodies or something that state, *Associate in Training*? You slid us from a couple of customers to prospects and then on to Associates with sleight of hand and we're okay with that. For now. So what's the dealio?" Maachi spewed out his sharp-tongued, diatribic monologue. As usual, Bart just sat and vacantly stared past Maachi as they listened on the conference phone. He probably was thinking about the next level on Call of Duty War Zone. Every day with Maachi was like being in a verbal combat area.

"My, my, my that is quite an excellent idea! I am surprised that someone in corporate marketing hadn't already thought of that. If it is acceptable to you, I am going to make a suggestion to the sales and Associate development groups to put that in the ratchet and see what they can come up with!" Naivete in some things is truly a blessing. It helps make insults and rude sarcasm drip off the roof. McCarty really did think Maachi was serious.

"Yeah, wow, *whaa-evah*." Maachi sniped back and his imaginary swagger stick tapped his thigh. Il Duce-*Hefe* was on the loose, again.

"Thank you for that. I shall give you full credit for the insight! But the purpose of this call was regarding some exciting news other than MLM bling. It's the end of October and we have been so blessed to have a unique opportunity. In a few more days it will be a full moon, a Blue Moon. The moon could be very much a blue moon with the smoke and ash that arises from the demonstrations." McCarty was becoming extemporaneously animated. Strange clouds in the offering.

"Oh goody-goody-goody. So what? Who cares? Do we go sacrifice chickens in the parking lot in the middle of the night for good luck? Or maybe even a goat? And save its eyes? By the way, the moon isn't blue it's grey. Always is. Probably always will be. Your point? Hope you have a good one." Maachi chirped out grade F sarcastic snipe.

"It is unique in that it nicely illumines the panorama. Full moons are our best-selling season. It allows our fellow athletes to use less illumination and they can have some very engaging up close and personal encounters. There are two full moons this month. And that equates to greater revenue and challenge. Now that you are on the next level you also benefit from this double revenue opportunity. The space is very limited, and we only have a few more vacancies. We have had so many reservations in light of the pandemic and the pandemonium it has handsomely created. Please entrust me, this is an experience that should not be missed or dismissed. But, as always, the decision resides solely with you. The venture at hand only requires a *yes* or *no* and I shall take care of all the otherwise dithery details for you both. Also, if there are some specific swat bag items you require, I am at your service.

"Either way is perfectly fine. I did not wish for you to later on be dissatisfied with my customer service and feel any umbrage towards me because of a lack of letting you know about the more engaging events. I did commit to you that as you advanced you would be notified of any exclusive events and their advent. I am here to support your business and recreational activities.

I believe you had shared with me that the events were becoming *predictable*. In the colloquial, meaning *boring*. The full moon activity is nothing if not considerably more random and potentially quite unpredictable. It's an edgy endeavor." McCarty's voice smoothed out to ice-on-ice slidey-coated opiate.

"Interesting." Bart indicated with one word that they had an interest and simultaneously projected a tell-me-more intonation. McCarty was a

Rottweiler who just trap-snapped shut on Bart's curiosity. One word hit the trick switch and McCarty's instincts let him know, *got em.*

"You could infil and go to the rooftops but to be true to myself and letting you know the most delicious options; I would not recommend a rooftop deployment." McCarty morphed yet again. He became an urban engagement tactician coach. He wanted his newbies to succeed on all levels. There is no profit if your downline associates end up as prime cuts at Satriale's. He was going Yoyodyne Skynet in miniature.

"How so?" Bart inquired.

"Thank you most kindly for asking."

Maachi gave a silent shrug to Bart.

"The risk is greater, and we have had more than one situation where the well-lit sky enabled the detection of our associates' shadowy shapes by the denizens below the precipitous roof top ledges. It does not end well at all." McCarty detailed his rationale.

"Was that English? M, was that English? Is that a subdialect of Utahan? Could you just spit it out? Why is it all the times we have these little get togethers you go mumbly bumbly? English *please.* It's your first language, yes?" Maachi classically chastised McCarty's obscure choice of words. In the land of Maachi it is imperative that all speak the lingo of the land, Maachish.

"My sincere apology Dr. Panicles. Stated more succinctly, our athletes can be seen more easily against the lit background of the moon. Silhouettes in the night sky. They become targets versus targeters. Thusly, and so forth, for your consideration, going close to or on ground level is the most exhilarating. What is it they refer to it as? *Boots on the ground* is where you want to be around? Of course longer distance, larger firearms offer no advantage. Short barrels or pistols with suppressors are of the greatest benefit. Oh, let me add, short-barreled shotguns are not allowed. Other reduced barrel firearms that utilize .556 or .223 are acceptable. Surgical precision obfuscation is what works most optimally. Higher counts and less potential for detection. And no .410 rounds either. Mmmmm, am I rambling on? Are we okay here?" McCarty was verbally chumming. He knew he was fine. He was the Gatling gun of charming articulations. But even a plaid jacketed jackal has to strut its stuff. Knowledge of firearms is not the sole property of Maachi.

"I get it now. Yeah, we're in." Maachi put the cork back in the conversation. *Thumpt.* He looked into Bart's eyes with the visual messaging of *that's a done deal babee.* Bart just blinked a few times, thinly smiled, and remained still and dispassionate. Eyes wide shuttered.

"Splendid choice! I shall transmit to you the details. I hope you have satisfactory tools to use. I also would be remiss if I did not let you know that standard nine-millimeter ordnance while of common more banal use, is not advantageous at this time of year. It's cloudy in Philly and in the fifties. Some of the marks could be attired with more cumbersome clothing. Nine millimeters at the ranges you will experience rarely are successful with a single shot. Firearms experts have commented that almost all smaller less potent calibers would require a, what is it called? A *double tap.* Those lighter weight projectiles may produce unsatisfactory results. Ammunition is expensive so we all strive to only use one round per item. Weighting of the points is also more favorable for going less versus more.

You may wish to consider more exotic tools, ordinance, and augments. If you do select to utilize the smaller calibers, please be advised that you may desire to modify the ordinance for better penetration. But you're very intelligent fellows and I am quite confident that your choices will result in stellar success. This is a double point game on ground level." McCarty just sold the washing machine, the refrigerator, and almost a significant makeover of the entire kitchen.

"Smoking! Yowzah! Now we're talking. So when's the exject?" Maachi spoke and Bart didn't. It was clear that McCarty had been quite effective with his sell. Too bad there were not upsell options for him because he would have chunked those out in a Philly Cheesesteak heart stop.

"Tomorrow. Same pickup time. I shall forward to you the place for the assemblage thirty minutes before you lock into company transportation. At the risk of incredible redundancy I will inform you an hour in advance of the general vicinity to park your vehicles. I will not place you so far from your connecting spot that you have to hustle and breathe hard like quarter horses. In closing Dr. Panicles, I am absolutely confident that you will yet again be the number one athlete for this event. As I had shared, my superiors are very much impressed with your skill level, if I may comment. My client did conduct a comprehensive background check on both of you and they were titillated by the fact that you, Dr. Panicles, had some experience in training others in regard to weaponry. A true plus, indeed. Could be a magnification of a real set of facts, special weapons if I am correct, no need to reply. Regardless, legends live on regardless of truth. Your superior skills will be put to the test on ground level interactions. Overall, those talents are a true plus."

McCarty had yet again chummed, baited the hook, and sunk it soul deep. Stroke the big dog ego and get a hypnotic low tone growl in response. If he keeps this up, he might get a weighty bonus for a job very well done. A smile stretched across his greedy face. Each tooth had an imaginary bitcoin design debossing.

Maachi cast his gaze to the table's surface and didn't wish to catch the Bart's eyes. When Maachi goes emotionally closed door it is wise not to ask why. Always leave that door hermetically sealed. Bolted. Welded, and buried in a deep cavern.

"Are we good here? How about we lid this so we can ready up our kits. Send the text on the burners. Okay?" Bart is the skilled distractor and the accomplished closer of events. He didn't suffer excess blabber well. Much like Maachi it was cut to the chase and erase all hope of spoinking catchy verbiage. Time was ticking and that meant it was time to schlepp on out and beef up the bags they were going to tote. Come in heavy, land hot, don't get caught.

Chapter 17: Immigrant Song

Need to C U Now! Lookin for an important parcel. Know anything bout it? Maachi Slacked Latika. An exclamation point bolt of lightning to emphasize a sense of urgency was unnecessary. But he stuck it in the note just to be a dick. *Everything* was maximum-urgent-right now-super-duper overthruster overdrive for Maachi. When he wanted something, he wanted it a year ago. Even if you were engaged in another project for him, it made little difference. Stop, go, start up again, pause, faster, hurry up and make it so. No matter what the IM stated it was always a tense moment for Latika. Her stomach was already so queasy that her knots had knots. The Gordian ain't got nothing on her. After the most recent evening encounter she felt sick to her stomach. The queasiness was pretty much an everyday thing for her now. She wished she had some ginger tea to soothe her insides. The stress of working for Maachi was over the top with the needle smacking the far-red side of the meter. Smackety-smack-clack-clack. *What now?* she thought. Delaying a response or being untimely would result in yet more misogynistic, racist behavior. He never put the viler stuff in a text or email. Always by *WOM*. No recordings, no vids, no nothing. Words are cheap and the currency of the ignorant and the wily. Maachi was a clever soul and he knew that proof was in a video not in words or hearsay. Except for the video he took of him violently raping her, and others. That was on demand drippy eye candy.

To Maachi, if it isn't written down or videoed, it didn't happen. She arose from her chair and did a mild quick step to Maachi's office. Lucky for her there was no time stamp to satisfy. Well, not really. When Maachi indicated *Now* it meant right this very minute and not as soon as possible. Early on in her indentured servitude, slip of the verbiage, her *employment*, Maachi had made his verbal expectations as clear as a freshly washed window on the Sovereign. ASAP – meaning *as soon as possible* was a stupid thing to say. Maachi wanted no ambiguity. ASAP could mean today, tomorrow, or next decade. Things were done for Maachi in real time. He rarely stated that a person needed to hurry up. It was understood that everything he requested was in the now and that all else should cease being worked upon. A simple expectation. Be here now or not be here tomorrow. The hands of time shake in fear of Maachi-time.

She thought, rightfully so, that he truly treated her like a dalit. And, unfortunately, he literally owned her existence in the United States, which was a powerful piece of leverage. He had her papers and her passport. Not just her passport but also her whole family's passports.

Macchiato Poco Panicles hated his given name. He felt it made him look like some kind of a special holiday coffee drink served in a small cup at Starbucks that celebrated the birth of Sicily. He never signed his full name. He simply signed his documents as Maachi Panicles or Maachi Panicles PharmD, all internally sensitive items were simply signed, *M*. No one ever questioned him about it. No one would even know to ask. He was as Sicilian as arugula, you know, a vegetable. His Italian lineage was not something he was particularly proud of. Poverty was the soil upon which he came into being and his current successes created an early life story tabular rasa. He liked it that way. The past only happened in his head and bent him accordingly. No videos of kid Maachi tying up small animals or tormenting the neighbor's cat. Nothing written down or memorialized except the vids in his head. And tacphone.

In actuality he was the runt of the family. He was his parents' fourth child and the other three boys, even the younger brother, made sure he knew it. He also had a sister. His clothes and shoes were all hand-me-downs or hand-me-sideways. He was bullied and ribbed at school all the time. Older kids who knew his brothers would see him with his older brothers' clothes on and mock him, *Gee looks like you stayed back a year*! Yeah. Right. The insult was both to him and his brothers., but his brothers didn't need to shrug it off. They would just go *au grille* to the verbal offender and insured that a very memorable and painful event occurred. Sometimes reparative dental repair was required. Negative reinforcement with a very healthy dose of aversion behavior was dolloped out for the transgressor. Those brothers were a force to contend with. Meaner than deranged junkyard dogs who hadn't eaten in a week. Step on them and they'd break your leg, in two places and then search out your brothers or sisters to teach them to keep their sibling in-line. Maleficent mini-milieu therapy delivered *in situ*. A parking lot primitive double tap of sorts.

But then there was the most embarrassing year. Between him and his two older brothers was his sister. A gangly girl at that age with teeth too big for her mouth and ears that looked like a squirrel's. When she laughed you could not be certain if she were asking for nuts, or someone was tickling her. And that was a problem. Maachi's older brother had gone through a significant growth spurt and the clothes that he was wearing were quite large on him. His mother, ever so thrifty and creative having learned life's talents from having very little, took some of his sister's blouses and tailored them the best she could on a limited budget, to be a new set of slightly used but not abused *shirts* for him. They were actually *blourts*, not shirts. A seminal year of heavy gravity mortification occurred. Ten G social gravity. Everything was heavy doojas. It all amped up with the girly shirts and even worse, girls' jeans. Girls' blouses button on the opposite side of a boy's shirt. They also don't have a pocket. Shirts for boys all had the omnipresent chest pocket and even for the most part a little tab at the top of the back of the shirt.

Maachi's mom was so proud of herself. Maachi, not so much. He didn't have a lot of options. Big bro's shirts and pants were too large for him. His younger brother's wardrobe was too small. So for a year Maachi wore pants that were thread-worn and a bit tight or upon occasion, his sister's jeans, which made his manliness, show up at the most awkward times. Those gawky times coincided with the ogling by some sweet young thing who would giggle and whisper to her friends. Hand to face and finger pointing, Maachi was being noticed for not so wonderful reasons. And before you knew it, it was a field of laughing daffodils and roses with thorns.

The shirts she tailored were very delightful flower prints, animal images, and an occasional my little pony design. Nothing like dancing ponies to bring out the animal in you. There was also the occasional red or purple polka dot item. It didn't take long for him to become a branded outcast. The bizarre, subdued cross-dressing was the signal that a new animal was in the prepubescent zoo. He was an Eloi on the playground and in the locker room. The jock Morlocks made sure that he was aware of the situation on a very punctual regular basis. If he had lead underwear, he might have been able to avoid the atomic wedgies. Nah, kidding.

Then one day he returned home covered in bruises without his shirt. He was angry with his mom and swore never to wear girls' clothes again. From that day on after school he scoured the Goodwill clothes boxes for something more suitable. He didn't care about fashion. He cared about being clothed as a boy. Unfortunately the school miscreants continued to mock him for wearing tossed out donation clothing. Once effectively pecked, pecking becomes the new normal. Get with it or do something real fucked up like just offing yourself because of the tormenting bullying. The bullying was online as well. It was incessant. It was a real-life Lord of the Flies on an island in the middle of public education.

He was different and once cast out he become a target all day and all night. He had more than his share of beatdowns and head in the not-yet flushed toilet episodes. They called him a fag, a cross dresser, digit between zero and one. He fought back but his stature even then was an ectomorph. A skinny thing in their eyes who was worthy of derision and denigration.

It didn't help that he was a raging hypoglycemic. The low blood sugar made him Jekyll and better hide. He often became limbic in mid-morning and would almost pass out. First early recess break meant the raging monster inside of him would go hidden berserker mode. To further exacerbate the whole situation he often had his snacks and lunch stolen or absconded with by some bully who made sure he knew who the thief was. Inevitably the larger beast would inquire, *so whatcha gonna do bout it fagot?* End of dialogue. Turtle head back in shell.

A fight or nasty kerfuffle was very often on the school day agenda to be followed up with a *mano y mano* event after school. He learned to hate school and everyone in it. His hatred extended even to his siblings who never came to his aid. He was an embarrassment to them. Only his mom comforted his wounded bruised body and soul. He resented her because he felt that she was turning him into a momma's boy. Sometimes he wondered if she wished she had two daughters.

And even more egregious was the very existence of his sister. She was the bane of his clothes selection. When he wore her modified blouses even for a short period of time, he felt like a seal on an iceberg awaiting the teeth of an orca or walrus. Chomp gulp. If only she had been a boy, then this would never have rolled out the way it did. He despised his sister and his mom for the torture they so casually allowed him to be subject to. The deep resentment with the negative passionate events short circuited his brain and made him regard women as less than animals. They became nothing more than fur covered kitties or eager toothless beavers. They were simply things to be dealt with or manipulated to do his bidding. They were nothing more than sperm ashtrays.

As for the school kids, that year was the trigger event time period that made him become a recluse. Moody with a bad disposition and soon a rep that was worse. Whenever he would read in class there were snickers and whispers. *Boy-girl* was caught in a gender no-man's land. The tree was bent and never recovered. Each year afterward the punches and kicks just became more intense with different size shoes.

Maachi though became not just immune to all the confrontational and demeaning bullshit, he used it to get stoked. His credo rapidly became *nemo me impune lacessit.* He used the psychological and physical scars as bowstrings to catapult him to not just being superior. He wanted to make whatever he wished, happen. Target, load, release, hit the objective. That came to people, events, business, and the world in general. His twisted logic was that he was not in the world. The world was in his cage, and he was adamant to dominate every situation no matter how minor. Control was his mode of interaction with everything. If he could control it, it couldn't hurt him.

Let me check. Latika Slacked back.

Check!?! WTF. Don't you N? Your job is TO N! Maachi immediately volleyed.

I'll be right back. She had learned to not take the bait. The electronic dialogue door softly shut. She took a mailroom walkabout to see if the parcel was in some twilight place graveyard where all mislabeled parcels die a slow death. She went to the back of the room and sure enough. Under the counter in the *?* labeled cubby area was a relatively large box. She crouched down and tugged the box out into the light. It was mislabeled. It only stated the company name with no actual recipient indicated. *This must be what he is looking for*, thought Latika. A car without a VIN can end up in the strangest places. She left the parcel on the floor and retrieved a small mail cart to place it upon.

She wheeled it into Maachi's office. He growled and gutturally uttered one word. "Bouttime."

"Dr. Panicles, it had no addressee name. It was in the mail hold question mark box." She politely stated.

"I think you're trying to make a point. I hired you to take care of shit like this. I told you the order was coming, and you should've known to check everywhere in the mailroom at least twice a day. Same old shit. You just don't get it. Do I have to tell you like some droid to keep on top of things? I probably would have gotten this earlier if you had decided to stop eating biryani and take care of business. Do me a favor. Leave the cart, do the same, leave, and close the door behind you. *Get it?*" Maachi spit out his insulting acidic words. Extraterrestrial villainous acid drooling monsters have nothing over Maachi.

Latika took her hands off the cold cart handle, looked down, turned around and did as she was told. At least it was a verbal bamboo cane and not a pine two by four this time. Or worse, something like the other day. She concentrated on her breathing and silently chanted to the Goddess Kali.

Fuck yeah, dumb bitch. So stupid. I intentionally didn't want this with my name on it. About as illegal as it gets. It was Frankensteined from parts and now, It Lives!' That would just be super d-duper to have my name on this and have some snoop dog ATF dudes rappel ninja style through the skylights to catch me with it. Maachi thought to himself in an almost giddy, woody high. Someday though internal thoughts will be recorded. Oh wait. The universe already does that. Thoughts are actions in the universe. Nothing happens in a vacuum. Cause and effect are always in play.

He danced his balisong and snapped it to attention. A gentle surgical slice here and there and the security tape split and opened up the box like a gutted barbecue pig during a butchery. The box volcanoed out pink fluffy noodles. Maachi just stared at the contents. He became entranced. Circling through his head was his own mechanistic mantra, *Ain't tech cool!*

The Cracker Jack box of pink packing fluffies revealed the toy. A macho-macho tricked out short barrel, fully automatic Vector SMG .45 caliber. He took the pet out of its bed and placed it on his desk. He paused for a moment and caught himself in dreamy thought. He glanced around the room and went through his mental list of security items in the office. All off. Perfect.

Glock mags rapidly accompanied the Vector resting on his desk. MagEx2s with thirty round capacities. Maachi started to feel a bit moist in his jockeys. It was a real challenge to keep his juices on hold.

The chocolate fudge on this sundae was the suppressor. He liked to keep his tools very factory complete as much as possible. No off brand stuff. In the box was a 4GSK can. But wait. *There's more.* His smithy had taken the trigger out and tuned it to be one and three quarters pounds. Lighter than shit. The combination of the tricks made this a spitting lead, badass, mad honey badger. It would have taken months to get this vicious animal out of the ATF zoo if he was a dope and followed the rules. Rules are for mules, robots, and executive assistants. Going through ATF was like putting rib eye steaks on a trail right to his very doorway. Not today. Not ever.

Not to be outdone it was glassed with the tightness of a tricked out Eotech thermal. The almost infinite range made this the ideal tool to somewhere where someone doesn't want you to be.

Maachi lost his load. It was almost too good to be true. But it *was* true! This little single headed Cerberus would have required so many stamps to get legally it would be eligible for frequent taxing miles. And it was all his and no one knew he had it. He loved his smithy.

Chapter 18: Second Chances

In the confines of the temple they chanted in unison. It was a concert of human voices reaching out to the universe and specifically to the Goddess Kali Ma. "Brother, you can never speak of what you do when you are with us. We are well compensated, and our obligation is to never divulge, never speak to anyone but to each other regarding the acts we commit. These acts are in honor of the Goddess and our lineage goes back to Mother India and the Thuggee. We are today's incarnation of our forbearers who made sacrifices to the Goddess protector. If we reveal any of what we do to others she will look unfavorably upon us. We need her protection. Long ago the bond was broken when our lineage tried to view what she did with the bodies of our worship. Now we are responsible for the disappearance of the bodies of the departed souls. We are committed to never broaching the sanctity of our connection to our heavenly benefactor. I thank you for traveling with us to Tampa to meet in the sanctuary of the temple. We are shaptam. There are only seven of us together at any one time. You now are the seventh in this group. We are mostly from Bengal and Kerala. You are welcome to our enlightenment. Take pride in knowing you are now Thuggee. You are one of many who worship the goddess. We work together when the need requires it.

"Near where you live is an Indian restaurant. I shall not provide the name. You will need

to discover with your own cleverness which one it is. A large part of being Thuggee is being profoundly able to distinguish truth from falsehoods and how to deceive all who you wish. You will need to refine your understanding of viveka and vimarsha. Critical truths lie within all that we experience and our ability to separate the invisible from the visible is what enables our successes.

"The restaurant is your local refuge. Within that dining establishment, all are our friends who work and habituate there." Ramakrishna quietly stated with a powerful hush of words. He spoke in perfect English.

"I am honored to be one with you. My lineage does not extend to the Thuggee, but my heart and soul are committed to do whatever is necessary to take care of my responsibilities. I have been unable to maintain gainful work since arriving in America. I commit to you that I will honor the sacred traditions of the Thuggee and bow to the will of the Goddess in all things." Bubai shared his heartfelt feelings.

"We do not always have meaningful advanced notice of where we need to be. Here is a phone that must only be used in our service. It should not be used for extensive texts or messages. You will need to attune yourself with that which we engage, and all messages will be clear to a true devotee. Our sponsors expect perfect action by us. We cannot leave any trace or hint of our presence and absolutely no evidence of mortality. We are the wind in the trees that shakes the leaves and cannot be seen. You may be asked to commit acts that are unusual but necessary. I have a haluda syāśa for you. Do not show it to anyone other than your brothers. You must bring this with you on all of our travels. Do you understand?" Ramakrishna asked with a penetrating, dark stare in his eyes.

"I understand. Is Ramakrishna your real name?" Bubai inquired.

"It is my name when in service. We shall call you *Ramprasad*. Do not use this name except when we are together. We have secrets within secrets, tucked within rumors, held closely under our yellow sashes. That is the way it has always been and the way it shall always be." Ramakrishna shared with soulful intent.

"I understand. You have my word that my loyalties shall be to you, our brothers, and the Goddess." Bubai sincerely shared.

"When you return to Georgia, please keep the phone with you at all times. Our benefactor does not accept excuses for a lack of timely communication." Ramakrishna instructed him.

Chapter 19: Idol

"The Goddess is smiling upon us. I have some very good news to share with you tonight. Let us sit down and eat. I'm starving." Bubai was all grins and was eager to share the recent auspicious events with his lovely wife and children. "You've looked a bit tired, so I made you something special." He continued with culinary pride. The wonderful curries, cardamom, and delicious aromas filled the apartment with a welcome of warmth and goodness.

He had made Latika's favorites. Kosha mangsho, macher joi, and alur torkari were all on the menu and the desert offering was scrumptious mishti joi. The kids were so excited. It wasn't often that they had mutton and they thoroughly enjoyed it when they were so fortunate. They lived on a tight budget. Lamb was expensive. Latika was the naan winner, and the rent and other expenses chewed away at her income like an angry sloth bear. The first of the month was always met with cautious anticipation. She knew she was worth more than Maachi paid her, but she was tied to him as though a young elephant to a tree. Her choices were nonexistent. She just hoped and prayed that the Goddess Kali would smile good fortune upon her and her loving family. She chanted *Om Maha Kalyai, Ca Vidmahe Smasana Vasinyai Ca Dhimahi Tanno Kali Prachodayat* throughout the day and before she fell to sleep.

Bubai and the kids sat at the table awaiting Latika. She had excused herself for a moment. A moment became moments and dinner was becoming cold. Bubal's face became a bit rigid as he waited for his lovely wife to join them.

"Baba, I am getting very hungry. The food smells so good it's making my tummy angry." Baku said to his father. "Me too, baba." His sister tagged on to her brother's comment. Growling tummies need something yummy to be tamed. The animal within has little patience when blood sugar levels plummet.

"I will be right back." Bubai slowly and gently pushed his chair from the dining table and left to see what was going on. Just as he arrived in front of the bathroom door it opened. "Are you alright? You look pale. Can I help you wife?" Bubai inquired.

"I am feeling a bit nauseous. Work stress. It is of no use for me to share all that happens. I then have to relive the moments that were distasteful. Shall we go dine with our children? My sweet, loving husband, thank you so much for being you. Your kindness melts the icy cold darkness of the day. Shall we?" She asked and walked out to the dining room not waiting for his response. Upon his brow a furrow did plow. The wrinkles of concern were punctuated with a focused curiosity.

At the dinner table the children were squirming in anticipation of their taste buds dancing Tusu. They bowed their heads and chanted thanks to the Goddess Kali for the bounty before them. It was a gift from God to her faithful devotees. Latika was still a bit peaked. She took small bites and pensively chewed the tasty morsels with little joy.

Something was very wrong. She pushed the biryani back and forth as though searching for a mischievous hidden cashew. Bubai looked at her through the top of his eyes as he dined on the delicacies he had created.

"My family, may I share some wonderful news with you?" Bubai asked. As he spoke, all six eyes focused upon him with interested anticipation.

"Baba, what is it? Please do share with us the bounty." Baku happily inquired.

"I have a job. It is at night so mum can be here with you when I am away. The pay is quite exceptional, and it is good strong work. I may have to travel on some days but your khālā

will be here to take care of you and see you off to school and pick you up later." Bubai shared this great news with his loving family.

"Oh, that is very fortunate for us. My dearest sbāmī, how did you find this job? You don't have the documents to obtain work yet. You were lucky your previous employer had a blind eye to a nodding horse." Latika politely inquired.

"I networked at the temple. We spoke and they offered to see if they could get me a job. I have been working on this for a few weeks. They created a relationship with some devotees at a temple in Florida and I traveled there last weekend. Today they called me and told me the rest of the details. It is wondrous news!" Bubai replied. "Even more auspicious, I will be paid in cash." He concluded the lovely sharing.

Chapter 20: Day of the Dead

They arrived on Monday evening, the 27th of October. Philly was a raging mass of angry people. A thronging beast of so many plebes that had gone berserk. Rightly or wrongly it made no difference to McCarty, Maachi, or Bart. A playing field is a playing field regardless of the type of social upheaval.

The triggering event appears to be that a man with a significant criminal history had a weapon in his hand in the 6100 block of Locust Street in the latter part of the afternoon. The cops moved back from him in an effort to defuse the situation, but he just ran at them. Whether it was death by cop or drugs-on-thug made absolutely no difference. The police killed the knife-wielding fellow and that unleashed the beast of a thousand twisted-in-rage faces and clenched fists.

The thug had kids and a rap sheet that went back to at least 2006. When he was thirteen, he was arrested for assaulting a teacher. There were so many mugshots of him with different do's it looked like a barbershop poster that let you know what type of buzz you could get. It wasn't pick-pockety stuff either. It was assault, firearms, and the general kind of behavior that is more than potentially just a community irritant.

Maachi and Bart stylishly dressed close in style to the gobs of enraged people they mingled with. Traveling gray here meant gangsta-nouveau millennial with a tude.

The thronging insanity had bricks and light bulbs as their mini-melee weapons of choice. The unis? Equipped as expected in full riot gear. Current day benevolent storm troopers dressed in blue and black with shiny face shields attached to sturdy helmets. In front they held polymer shields to deflect tossed feces or bricks.

Aramingo Avenue in Port Richmond was bot fly-decaying as they arrived at the edge of the intoxicating madness. It was on its way to becoming a total loss. It was a well-planned rather humorous insert. A U-Haul truck picked them up on Weikel Street and then drove over to the U-Haul biz location on East Tioga. The funny part is that their asset driver knew that if dumped his truck at the facility and left the keys in it someone would scarf it down like a coyote on a tasty, naïve rabbit. Chew, gulp, gulp, and then gone in sixty seconds. Prints, hair, videos would just show another gangsta wannabe or frantic nut job driving it around. The connection to the Company? Zero. The truth was hidden in the deliberate clues.

He let his parcels out as he slow-braked the truck. They boinked out of the back and trod into the night like a couple of horizontal paratroopers. Infil done, the driver exited the truck tastefully dressed with a BLM emblazoned hoodie disguising his true trajectory and intent.. To be unnoticed you need to be noticed in just the proper manner to make others think what you wished they would. Easy manipulation of the perception. And the boys jumping out and gravitating to Aramingo made them look like just another couple of bits of wits entering the flat anthill. Two more outraged rioters who were looking to bango-tango.

They had kitted out with *insurrection light*. No long rifles and heavy gear. PACA Thrustguard vests just for good measure under the hoodies.

They fit right into the swaying madness before them. Just another set of bobbing heads and roving bodies. They were not interested in filling their backpacks with goods and drugs. Their packs were already filled with their chosen tools of the sport. Their tacphones had more drug choices than a CVS.

The choking, acrid smell of burning police cars and buildings created the perfect ambience. Maachi was already jacked-up with a phone inject. He was giddy at the thought of going skin close to his chosen trophies. Bart was a bit more sedate. He really hated being in the middle of crowds. When the pandemic hit, he decided to not even go to the movies or even restaurants. Bars were totally out of consideration. With the covid thing fogging the entire country it just pushed Bart further into being an asocial hermit crab. Covid had added an ingredient to civil disobedience that was unrivaled in history. Both of them wore masks to help limit the potential of contracting a random set of covid virus particles and to disguise their faces from any facial recognition software. Maachi had a wide skeleton grin gaiter. Bart chose a balaclava with a devil face on it.

As budding business builder associates, they were also privy to the overseas opportunities that McCarty offered up. They just didn't yet qualify for that level of play. They were domestics only. They needed more experience before they played in the international venues. They had to rack up the points and use those numbers to qualify for bigger and better tricks and treats.

In the United States the swell of violence was a pressure point profile. A man or woman gets offed by a uni and that pressure point explodes into a societal reason to be violent. A boil that popped and spewed hatred and violence like a skin borne disease. The splatters of boil goo infected and inspired others to ever-increasing levels of violence. It was a feeding frenzy of all types of sharks, piranhas, and lampreys.

In the EU it was a bit different. The violent social events were centric on a *control* or *controller* hot button. It was all about masks and quarantining, mandatory vaccinations or not. To Islam or to slam Islam. And the disappearance of self-determination in regard to personal issues like abortion. There is a limit to what people will tolerate when you order them around. Push them up against their internal walls of go no further and then expect the unexpected.

The tsunami of worldwide unrest and anger had root causes that were like ghosts. The problems under the pimples and boils were not perceptible to the masses. The rabble had their attention on immediate up-close and personal events and were not capable of big-cause and effect thinking. They were enraged Eloi with designer kicks.

Eyes blinking before you know why you blinked is just what was occurring. The guts of society were heaving but for disparate reasons. In Thailand the order and control tug of war was about a monarch. In European countries it was government sticking its big, intrusive nose into the personal health decisions of the populace. In Africa, it was violent unrest in several countries. The US had its own mishmash of inflammatory issues. It was right wing versus left wing. Antifa against the Proud Boys. It was BLM squaring off against conservative values. From a light year view above it was simply the rhythm of societal disruption and change. A twisted form of societal evolution. It was an enormous bran muffin filled with senna causing purgative regularity with a big emotional, flatulent poop. Everyone had a royal reason to be totally pissed off and the spooling illusions hid the core issues. All of the tumult made Maslow's Hierarchy a slippery slide down the polished pyramid into the bottom-most level, survival.

While the world vomited and contorted in its own geocentric ways, it provided reality TV entertainment for late night newscasters. Not to be outdone, Maachi had his own warped sense of entertainment. Tonight he was taking his virgin Vector onto the playing field. Time to pop its cherry and let the virgin taste the blood of others.

The worldwide unrest provided innumerable opportunities for the folks in Utah to place wagers, charge fees, build a pay-to-play multi-level business, and video days and nights of up-close tumult for replay on demand on the dark web or in private showings. It was a massive passion play snuff movie that the actors didn't even realize they were in. It wasn't just the *Tempest*; it was *Rambunctious Rambos On the Loose*.

Utah was swimming in crypto and laundered money in a Mount Everest pile as they harvested the anguish, pain, and suffering of humanity all for a bet or an entertaining diversion. Their money as the root of all-evil became a Hyperion Redwood painted green and adorned with shiny dark net bitcoins hanging like Christmas ornaments on the limbs.

The police scanners loudly rattled on about unis breaking a car window and pulling a man from its innards; a first responder to a fire being shot in the back with a pellet gun; and the litany reads on like a Star Wars scrolling opening text. It was Skull Island, and everything was being eaten up by something else. Benevolence became bent violence at street corners and in trashed buildings.

Maachi was digging the scene. His eyes wide behind his tacshades. He looked like a two-legged Mimic. Bart appeared to be more like a large spooky devil dog that was looking this way and that out of the peaks and valleys of its internal anxious anticipation. He was double strapped and more. He was rolling with .40 cal fragmentation hot loads. Maachi had his Vector on its bloody first cruise outing. .45 cal at close range and rinse cycling was nothing to fool with.

They slithered through the crowd as clear glass mambas. Two very rich tech guys seeking some points. And it was a double points event because it was ground level and bumpin' titties was in the offing. Each hit was worth two to help them qualify for the month. Maachi was counting on his auto to make big points over Bart.

They meandered in a random fashion on into the 18th district. The hard and slippery street underneath their feet added a nice texture to the whole affair. It was like walking on an open artery. A bit of blood here; some motor oil there. All mixed in with smashed beer bottles and cigarette butts. Sticky sweet and oh so replete with potential points upon points.

"Watch this." Bart whispered into his comm to Maachi. Bart with his head down from behind was moving up on a twenty something protester. Bart's hoodie had two enlarged side pockets. He poked out two suppressed CZ75s. One pointed up to the back of the man's head and the other a short distance from the man's spine. *Pffftt, pffffttt.* The man helplessly fell to the asphalt street. Bloody ragdoll time. Two points for Bart. He might get dinged for using two bullets, but he would plead that the spine shot was just for practice. The melon shot was the plan, and the slinky bones were an exercise to insure that his two-fisted pistol skills did not perish. The hole in the back of the man's head at first spurted out fluid and blood like a wine bottle tipped over. Some clumpy brain matter squished through the hole and blocked further pink mist. Bart decided to look down and use his shade cams to video the live snuff details. *Hollywood Undead got nuthin on this boy*, he laughingly whispered in his head as he recalled some very racy lyrics from that awesome masked band.

Not to be outdone, El Hefe crabbed his way up behind a nearby disrupter. He slinged his Vector up under his oversized hoodie and poked its nose out through a strategically placed hole. He made sure that the tricked out Holo and minicam was outside the fabric so that he could document his points. If not videoed, then it didn't happen. One *click* and full auto was on. He sensually teased the trigger, and a short band of deadly bees left the hive and perforated the man's back. Tissue, muscle, sinew, and bone splattered out and reddened the gaping hole in his back. Two to two, score was even. The man tipped over like a drunken bowling pin. Strike one for Maachi.

Even-Steven scoring between the two athletes. Maachi had programmed his tac to deliver a steady stream of meth. Jackin' him up like a lift at the truck garage.

Twofers were a challenge. Maachi was packing .45 230 frangibles. They poof out if they hit something solid. Both Bart and Maachi had ordinance that was not able to inadvertently overkill. That would be pee in the pool if they had splattered the area with random collateral hits. In such close quarters a bullet that passes through someone chest buster style and the exit wound ports the round off to a nonpredicted target would be a point loser. You couldn't just tote a full auto and waste a bunch of Eloi. All the point action was in the finessing of death. A *call your shot* and *make it so* process was the rule of the moment.

Just like billiards you had to call your shot pretty much by your actions. The frangibles were great at lead dosing a single asset but not multis. No handicaps were allowed. You were either all in or all out. Actually, you had to be all in prior to getting plotzed-up in this deadly blender.

National Guard is on the move. The calm words flowed into their monitors and on into their brains. Both Maachi and Bart were five by five with that. If the Guard came on the scene that meant they would have to make a very hasty advance to the side or rear. It would be time to part the waters of steaming heaps of humans and make a subtle yet potentially deadly exodus. Waiting for the Guard to show up was dancing with the devil in the moonlight and exposed them to orderly randomness. The Guard were nothing to fool with.

On the move. Enforcing curfew. Exfil now. The most sedate words were the most jeopardous words.

"Shit with a fuck head on it! Just when this was getting interesting. The random turned to run-dumb." Maachi spat contemptible words into his comm. Bart just nodded and shook his head forward. He was leading the nav now. He was running point and Maachi was in tow. This was *off the plan* action time.

The mercurial flow of the people flux had a high tide and now a riptide. The crowd would soon be aware that the Guard was hoofing it towards them. When they realized what was occurring, they could stampede. Crazed two legged hominids on the run. The Eloi would panic at the thought of real muscle on the field. The Guard meant federal charges and not the kissy ass *catch, and release* bullshit imposed by the disjoint community leadership. The frantic Eloi would mash up with the karma of Maachi and Bart and that wasn't going to happen. Mixing karma is not compatible with what they believed was their dharma. Anyone who got a good look at them would simply have to do one thing, ... die, fast.

Bart saddled up next to Maachi and tapped his wrist. They looked each other in the eyes and in synchronicity they nodded. As mirror images they double tapped their tacphone screens. Perverse humor. Ironic that the universal pickup communication for a speedy exfil was a double tap.

The police in the 18th district in west Philly had just been made aware of a double homicide. It was a twenty-six-year-old male who had gunshot wounds to the back and head. He was DOA as he was slabbed into Penn Presbyterian hospital. The second victim had multiple tight spread gunshot wounds and was sent to the hospital and died a bit later. The art of the death dealing, and their handiwork, was unfortunately discovered. The company yellow sashed cleaners had no chance at picking up the cadavers and squeezing a bounty out of them. The dead were just meat with John Doe toe tags in the cold lockers of the hospital morgue. Collateral damage would be the cause of death. Shitola, in an undulating mass of angry humans, how do you find the real perp? Ya don't. Just blame the pigs. They did it!

As they neared the Philadelphia police department 18th district, Maachi and Bart encountered the fringe of a group that ran into a pod of police. Bricks, bagged feces, and other sharp pointy objects were being hurled at the thin blue line. Maachi and Bart went stealth and slithered their way out of the pig squirm. Over the course of just a couple of days tens of unis were hurt and the confrontations dialed up a bunch of degrees. It was getting lots less nicey-nice.

No one had any interest in playing nice. Sand in the eyes, bite on the arm, stone to the head then all dead or close to it.

It was a large playing field, the 12th, 15th, 16th, 18th, 19th, 24th, and the 26th districts were hit hard and vulturous news helicopters darted back and forth through the night sky. Target, Foot Locker, Burlington, and a Dollar

General fell victim and fed the riotous hungry maw of the violent crowd. Everything was on sale. A BOGO, ... boost one, get one. For the sum of no dollars you could have whatever you could carry. A KYW helicopter flew over and videoed a large fire in the road at 10:30 PM.

The National Guard was mobilized and Maachi and Bart needed to prematurely scamper off from this current episode before the guardsmen came onto the field. There are many opinions about what clicked the switch to open the current floodgate of mayhem. It was hydra insults and responses. But the cause was not as important right now as were the rising flames of violent engagements. It was a roiling, broiling moment in the City of Brotherly Love. Hot love gone bad.

Maachi and Bart knew that if the Guard came in then they could easily be compromised. Unis with orders to just hold the line and make no arrests for looting were one thing. Guardsmen kitted up was a whole *nother shake, rattle, and bleed* potential experience. Guardsmen are military. Period. Unis are civil servants. Exclamation point. Both Maachi and Bart had no desire to mix it up with the milis. Both of them had body armor but nothing that would stop larger, higher velocity calibers if click came to big bangs. Discretion and retreat are noble acts when faced with overwhelming firepower. Offing unis or milis was highly discouraged. No points at all could be earned by raising the body count with bags filled with blues. It wasn't so much some kind of bible-thumping righteousness that tempered mortality. None of the players were so noble. It was far simpler. A wounded or killed uniformed entity on the field would be very hard to recover by the Indians. The motto of the congealed law enforcement folks would not let one of their own be torn to bits by the devil dogs of destruction. They would recover the injured or mortally wounded colleague and then all kinds of questions could be asked. Especially in light of the types of ordinance that the athletes were partial to. Street criminals preferred more commonly used bullet calibers. Cheap rounds used for intimidation and the occasional capping of a banger. The stuff that Maachi and Bart used was to say the least, a rare find at a roasty event like a riot. It was also quite clear that the capping from the athletes would be viewed as assassinations and not just bullets gone wild. So it was no-go on unis or other law enforcement folks. After all, the LEOs kept the herds of screaming meemie Eloi in place and channeled them to areas that were very accessible to the players.

The commissioner had ordered the police to *not* make arrests. They were told to chase looters out of stores like frolicking, highly caffeinated chipmunks. Shoo-shoo and not a big bad blue boohoo. Their pouches filled with all sorts of stolen goods. It was a large group of ants that washed over the body of the city to eat pieces of it one bite at a time that made the unrest an overwhelming experience for the city.

"Perfect." Maachi said to Bart.

"How so?" Bart responded.

"Unis will just let the human swill go back and forth like corks in a full bathtub. The thin blue line will just keep our quarry in-place. That's *how so?* It's perfect. We can just drill in and move forward. Okay?" Maachi directed.

"El Hefe, your call. You move and I'll shadow you till we get to a secure lockdown place. I'm on your six." Bart calmly responded. His calm was not from working on his inner peace. It was his ring and tacphone that detected his vitals changing and acted appropriately. The calm of his demeanor was deliberately chemically induced. The watch signaled his phone, and he always accepted the pharmacological call of the wild. It made him feel yummy and very alert. A James Bond thought romped through his chemicalized being. The mix was so good he thought he should patent it.

They soaked in the cautionary comments that hit their monitors. This was the time to get the hell out of Philly. The degrees of random behavior were increasing in magnitude. The algorithm of the angry, capricious crowds mixed into the parenthetical pieces of a reluctant group of local LE talent with a highly motivated Guard weighing in was far more than either of them wished to dance with. Time to keep the points they had and move on to play another day in another berg. No shame in retreating with honor. Especially when a large part of the motivation was coming from the directions of the company coaches who guided their way to safety. The company had disdain for taking unreasonable, uncontrollable risks that posed the jeopardy of discovery of their multi-level adventures. Regardless of how many points and bitcoins were in the mix.

Chapter 21: Dove and a Grenade

They were provided with only a few options for leaving the area. They decided to head towards the river and let the coaches know they were on their way in hustle time. The *x* marks the spot was East Alleghany and North Delaware. It wasn't far and they could easily trek the distance in a very short period of time. Happy feet moved in meth time.

As they traveled down to East Alleghany, they saw a small group of protesters in a loose knit circle in an open area. The deviants had a cop down and were playing their version of east coast hacky sack. Their actions were not rabid. It was a game to them, *kick the cop, tenderize the pig.* It was very evident that the cop was not going to be one of the survivors.

Maachi and Bart cat-stealthed along the building's edge and crept on up to them. And as the two of them realized what was occurring, they looked at each other and with excited lips soundlessly saying, *points!* The last lip movements sent a signal to their hands and trigger fingers. Time to wake up their sleeping little friends. Palmed, racked, and time to get some more points on the board. Before they entered this part of the playing field, they dumped their magazines into their packs and went full load heavy.

They were only two to two since the environment had changed with the Guard coming into the area. They weren't going to leave the field with an even score. Nope. This wasn't going to be a Mexican standoff. Bart had a CZ in each hand. He wasn't concerned about placement at this range. He just needed to even out the auto of Maachi's Vector. They were about ten meters away from the bangers and Bart started running at a decent clip. They set the vids to record at close range. Closer was better. Two pistol Bart was barreling forward to close the gap. Maachi saw what he was doing and picked up his pace. Their hasty run was not detected by the beasts who were very focused upon kicking the officer to death. They were so intent upon using kicks for kicks they didn't even look up.

Before Maachi could massage his trigger, Bart was almost on top of the sadists. The CZs were true to their fame. Bart had a melon shot, one miss, and two heart bobbers. Both of his assets dropped like a box of blood-spurting rocks. Who says you can't get blood from a rock? Balderdash and poppycock! If the grouping is right, you can even get grey goo and bile from a rock. Lest we forget the dump in the pants and the pee in the man panties from the dead and dying last moments. You sure can get *lots* from a rock, even more points!

The other two ding-dongs looked up but before they could do anything, Bart fired a couple of rounds. His bouncing while running resulted in three near misses. Maachi took advantage of the situation and went rinse cycle on those unlucky souls. They whole bodies twitched with the impact of each bullet until the last round had smacked them. 45s are a punch too much. They too fell to the ground. "Hey, number one, you almost hit me!" Bart annoyingly shouted.

"Almost doesn't count. Should I reload and try again? Would I get a couple of points?" Maachi sarcastically countered. A snarkolitic smile spread across his hammerhead worm lips. They stood over the four carcasses and Maachi just shook his head. "This makes us six to six. There's one more and we can pop the tie. Let's go rock, paper, scissors." With a ghoulish grin upon his chin, Maachi nodded his head to the unconscious cop on the ground. Maachi figured that the body bag packers, the Indians could cart the cop off and reap a bounty of LE gear. The only thing left would be his last death rattle gasp burping out.

"Migo, no points for anything almost dead. Especially a cop. That would be a real cheap shot and it will all be on vid. You might lose a couple of points for that. Do I hear you want to lose this affair?" Bart smiled under his mask. That option he served up and fed into Maachi's desire to not ignominiously crash and burn. A tie for Maachi would be better than losing out to Bart. Maachi loved winning and had deep, dark, smushy vomitus disdain for the other side of that coin.

"Yeah, well rules are meant to broken. But a big for sure, I'm not goin' to let you get a win due to my offing this uni. So, good thought. Let's go!

We need to exfil now!" Maachi injected his thoughts and directive. Bart had tossed the yellow tennis ball and sure as shit, Maachi was all over it. Woof!

"One second." Bart bent over and grabbed the cop's comm and clicked the button. "officer down near East Alleghany and North Delaware. Need paramedics stat." Bart barked at the radio.

"Who is this? This is Marshal Tannin here. Who's calling this in? This is a secure line." Marshal Tannin was concerned that this was some type of setup for first responders to rush in and get compromised.

"Calling this in for *Bart glanced at the fallen one's tag-oddly the officer had left his name tag on*, Officer, ah, Aidan. No last name. He's out cold. Clear here. Come now if you want him to stay alive. Trust or no, it's on you now." Bart responded and tossed the mic down with a dirt-kicking kathunk kiss drop as he stood up.

"Whoever you are, if this is some kind of setup, be warned, we're coming in armed and will not hesitate to do whatever it takes. You've been notified." Tannin responded. Aidan and Tannin were on quiet loan from the US Marshals office in Philly. This was their home turf for now and they were the most competent blue in the tumult. They volunteered to jump *boots on the ground first* into the bedlam to help out with logistics between the unis and the Guardsman. They were *siamesed* during this craziness. It was Tannin's responsibility to cover Aidan's six all the time and vice versa. But in the bustle and hustle, the tussle of muscle, he had become separated from this partner. His going in to retrieve Aidan was not just as a fellow Marshal. Tannin and Aidan were the best of buds and swore to be the shield for each other. They had worked for years together as SOG Marshals. Mostly out of Philly right now but their home station was further south. This was a personal issue now. Tannin tapped Armistead and Gilles, two of his fellow local talent officers and mumbled to them. The three bolted off in their riot gear. Tannin was coming in very heavy with armor, a short barreled 870 as a *just in case* crowd clearing addition, and his STI. Safeties were off and they were in the running to leave no man on the field. No one left behind. Ever.

Maachi looked at his tacphone and then pointed in the direction of the river. As they were getting ready to hoof it, they noticed the clamoring three unis approaching the horizontal blue. Maachi, ever the chameleon, stopped chugging along long enough to turn and face the officers and send them four fingers. Bart had already passed Maachi. He really wasn't interested in cop gang signs. He wanted out.

Maachi waited for a moment and one of the officers hesitatingly splashed back four fingers. A chuckle was in Maachi's head. *Yup, looks like he saw our design. Just hope he passes over it. Sure didn't want him to think we were the perps here.*

Maachi's tacboots kicked up a bunch of dust and dirt as he sped up his pace to take the lead dog position. Bart anxiously followed in his footsteps. Neither looked back again. You should never look back. That chunk of milliseconds could allow whatever is chasing you to catch up. But the macho in Maachi made him stop for those milliseconds to signal the unis. Upon occasion though your ego pumped up macho-ness can be an undoing. For now, though, it appeared to be a smart, safe move.

As they approached the river's edge, Maachi looked through his scope. He saw a bright red light bobbing up and down in the water. He flashed his bright white weapon's light three times, and the red dot rapidly came closer to the water's edge. Bart and Maachi walked into the chest deep water and two guys in the XSR Interceptor reached down to lift them onboard. The sixteen hundred horsepower engines thundered to life and the Interceptor rapidly went on its way. Behind it a wake of water that washed away their trail into the night. Water leaves no footprints.

"Tunas on the cracker" the balaclava-faced tour guide clearly stated into the radio.

"Five by Five" a deep, monotone, noncorporeal voice responded.

Chpt 22: Empire

"Shiz. Unfortunately, the sojourn was interrupted for the tunas. Tender mercies were on our side this day. The Philadelphia adventure was a complete success otherwise. The other four athletes were a bit farther out and their scores were quite admirable. You can pull up their stats at your convenience. They found the fact that the looters were actually shooting each other a plus and a minus. Our cleaners will be happy because they still get paid regardless of the official counts. I think the second team may be worthy of being considered for advancement. Not right now but in the very near future. They are a huge part of our plan. The tuna aren't asking for a refund. They know the guidelines. Yes, it was a draw. Did anyone have odds on this one? No. Okay. Good. Should I offer up some options to them? Understood, I can do that. Truly a capital idea! It's a great idea to reward them at this point, so the even scoring does not dishearten them.

I do agree that it is time to engage them more fully. The ingenuity they demonstrated during the Philly excursion was more than admirable. They played by the rules and should be handsomely taken care of. My thoughts are that we have them gem chipped and as a reward for the chipping, a positive reinforcement, we raise them to an Emerald One Star Diamond level and award them with the fine tokens of our appreciation. From what we have discussed I believe that would be agreeable to all of the Boards, ... good. I shall make it so. It will be my pleasure.

We have a nicely active set of affairs happening in France, curfews, and such. Or maybe we should revisit Seattle or Portland. Thailand is a no for now. It isn't hot enough.

Paris really is out. They have a tough curfew after 9:00PM. The curfew is making the commutes look like a senile millipede after drinking too much cheap French Elderberry wine. Streets would be empty. Our best opportunities are where mayhem rules over the scattered frantic wits.

Eastern Europe has some real potential. The most significant issue there is that it is a war zone and while our athletes are quite skilled, the potential for being discovered due to military asset elimination is quite large. My suggestion is that we wait and see what happens there. We have more than enough other playing fields to activate. But if some of our athletes are adamant about traveling to that area, we can accommodate for a substantial surcharge fee.

We could use an accelerant asset in one of the other areas to create a playing field if we wish to. Our friends in law enforcement could execute extreme prejudice under the guise of an appropriate force response. It has always worked well for us in the past. The Kenosha thing went off the rails with that fellow who shot a few rioters. Very unfortunate. We might wish to entertain bringing him into our fold. He does show great promise. If you agree with connecting with him, I can have legal reach out. Just let me know and I shall make it so. I will exercise a maximum of discretion. He is the poke in the public eye and may be problematic by being so thoroughly monitored.

Let me evaluate the options and will revert to you later. May the good in us spread to others. Good day." McCarty made the call short, to the point, and conclusive. It was a staccato-bar code dialogue that had so much to say among the words that were not spoken.

Chapter 23: Live Forever

"Hey, Aidan, it's me." Tannin compassionately said to his partner who was sedated and very much welded to the hospital bed. Aidan was all Borged up. Tubes and wires, pumps and meters, vitals monitor blipping away, and a small flat screen beaming out in muted sounds the latest news from Philly. It was tires, and fires, and drippy blood, oh my!

"You're going to be okay. Man that was so lame. I sounded like some kind of dumb ass actor in the latest edition of Gray's Anatomy. Bud, you got smashed in places that smashing is not supposed to happen. If we didn't get to you when we did, you'd be in the *in perpetuity* horizontal dirt dance and feeding worms. You were so lucky that your SitRep was called in. Minutes lost would have resulted in you facing eternity." Tannin knew Aidan was in tough shape but he's a tough guy's tough guy.

"What the crap happened. All I can remember is getting cut out of our line and getting lost. Next thing a bunch of toughs start jacking me around. I gave, but they gave better. Four on one usually means *they're* outnumbered. Not this time. The mutherfuckers were high as shit. PCP or something even more jacked. It was like I was in a my little pony dream. Everything I did was soft and tidy. Everything they did hurt like a son of a bitch. The look in their eyes, Tannin, it was more than PCP. Did you shake their bones and get some clues? Especially drug stuff." Aidan's voice trailed off. He wasn't kidding when he shared that when it's four to one, Aidan is the only one left. And that's a fact, Jack.

"I don't get what you mean. Go deep." Tannin quizzically responded.

"You and I have been working together for more than a pensioner's employ. We're what they call married *at* the job. We hate bullies and when the innocent are being fodder, we do what we do best. Stop them. But with these guys it was like seeing a videogame and the baddies just keep grinning, punching, and kicking. And that's all I remember. It was lights out in Philly after that until now." Aidan nonchalantly chanted out his song of woe. He had more than his tastes of the different powders and such to know the effects. Whatever those guys were on was super villain doojee. It was different.

"Aidan, something is wacked here. I can't tease out what yet. But something is making my Deadpool commonsense tingle. And no, not that leg. Up here." Tannin pointed to his head and sliced a clever man's smile across his face complete with puffed out cheeks.

"There you go again. Twitchmaster Tannin. Maybe you just need to stop going all cray on me. You're a bright guy, nah, brilliant, but sometimes you have to be comfortable with not being able to fix every twisted fuckhead out there." Aidan stated with a velour scoff. Tannin just stood silently for a moment. He didn't even blink. His eyes rolled up and to the left. He was searching mushy, wrinkly brain datum. Hard numbers and algorithm data. Not the creative side. He was taking a walk on the calculating side.

"I think we have looters shooting looters. No, let me share what I saw. First, we get a call of an officer down. No ID from the caller. He used your comm. We bust chops and get there pronto. Me, Gille, and Armistead are on the scene. We hover over you, and this is weird, there are two hoodied guys leaving the area rather quickly. Weird? Or what – it got more bizarre. One of the guys turns around, pauses his jaunt and flashes four fingers. Yeah, four fingers. That was kind of crazy. Letting me know he doesn't need help? I was stalled and flashed four as I was looking down at you and four dead guys. Undercover guys from where? They're not marshals because we would have known about it. We were the top of the command for this adventure." Tannin went on with his speculated spook tale. Aidan listened and just nodded.

"Tannin, back to my question, pocket contents please." Aidan wanted to know just fuck the what he got run over with. To him, it was a bunch of overly jacked overlords getting whacked by some rivals who just knew how to dress up for an early Halloween in Philly.

"Oh, yeah, let me get my pad. I'll letcha know in a few minutes. Be back in a flash of the Flash." Tannin retrieved his pad and blinked it on.

"Well? Spill the meth tea, migo." Aidan was getting trigger antsy pantsy.

"I'll read it to ya." Tannin began the litany of gangsta stash.

Chapter 24: House of Mirrors

"We have a quorum of the Forty-two Boards, am I correct?" The grey bearded, balding man in the blurred monitor questioned. And why blurred? A very good question.

"I can see by the nodding faces of those that are physically present and the green toggle lights beneath the facial images in the monitors that we have satisfied our governance needs to be in concordance with having the proper number of voting participants. A note though to you all, none of us suffers foolishness or failure lightly. We are the colliding edge between the two sides. Our existence is the greyness where daylight is surrendering, and twilight vigorously marches forth. As shadows we live in the grey.

We are the missionaries, apostles, sixty-nines, acolytes, or prospects. And Jeremiah, I can still see it is you in that fuzzy image. This is not the time to yet again bring up that we should change the number from sixty-nine. Topic closed. In my position as Premier, I shall now share with you the unfolding vision.

We are between Scylla and Charybdis. We are the space between order and chaos. The friction of creation is the energetic exchange between the two absolutes in the universe. It is acid and base as they combine. It is an electric surge through wires and optics that plays between the positive and negative forces. We are the creation of the interactions between the immovable and the irresistible. Some might think we are the devil, and our only function is to negatively impact all of society. Duality is a human perspective, and its accuracy is lacking in multiple ways.

Yes, I see the amber light from Mr. McCarty. I shall provide the dialogue to you Mr. McCarty. You are on, sir. Go ahead." The man with the beard relinquished his bully pulpit for now as he cautiously scanned the room and the monitors for tells and tell-nots.

"I so apologize for this rude and unexpected interruption of your sermon for today and tomorrow, Mr. Premier Provo. I am thrilled to be able to share today some recent events of which there may be some of our esteemed Executive Board, Operational Board, Recruitment and Retention Board, the other Boards that I may fail to mention, the Premiers, Ambassadors, and qualified Associates who wish to partake in the various games and playing fields we are currently engaged in. So many terrific choices. Some are very unique and spiritually enamoring. Again, please excuse my brash interruption. This is an early and special note to review the sport venues in real time for the most enlightening opportunities to explore all that we are. The spaces are being quite quickly filled. So if you have an interest please do stay in presence. It will be worth your time shared.

The course of inhuman events is unpredictable and one day's pleasant Ozzie and Harriet neighborhood moment rapidly changes to a suburban war zone in the middle of a catastrophic purge. Since our ability to predict those potential venues is limited, short notice of events is the master of the day, and night." McCarty completed the thought-provoking commentary.

"Thank you for that information. We are very fortunate to be the first to decide our paths. When Mr. McCarty returns to command the space, do note his suggestions. I shall now continue.

"We have reports on the agenda due from several of our Board speakers and then we shall move on to more general discussions and the smaller groups for voting on pressing issues. Steward, please be so kind and activate the essentials for the members present in the Temple Oval Boardroom." Mr. Provo dryly and in a very perfunctorious manner requested assistance.

No one spoke and the sounds of hissing, soul-inspiring scents of the most exotic natural oils from plants and other living creatures spooled and winded through the Boardroom. In the monitor speakers there were those that did not mute their mics and the sound of portable vaporizers could be heard accompanied by the most delicate concert of inhalations and snortings. Personal concertinas. A very elitist feral ritual that served its purposes physically and mentally to tap the innermost emotions and motivations. The fragrant touches reached in through the nose and held each participant by the olfactory bulb short hairs.

"Let us now in our quietest of voices, have each of you recite your prayer in the moment." Mr. Provo commented after the *inspiration* ritual. Wondrous odors as determined by the Board Oracle were compounded just prior to the meeting. The offsite believers would have to be spontaneous and creative and connect the best that they could to mimic the cornucopia of intoxicating scents. All appreciated the spontaneous spicing of the controlled set of events that occur between this very present contraction and expansion of the universe. The delicious scents stimulated specific areas of the brain and soul.

"Lucidity is now the presence in this meeting. Are you all lucid?" Provo rhetorically queried the attendees.

"Steward, please monitor the meeting and insert appropriate commentary. Thank you.

"Let us proceed with the litany of activity areas first. Financials, then Marketing and Sales, followed by Customer Service, and to close out the initial agenda, Theocratic Research and Digital Presences. You will all have your moments.

"Firstly, let me share with you my specific areas of interest and those of you that are responsible for those items, go three and no more than three." The words were so dry they could squeeze water out of the desert sands in Utah.

"And now a Sino interruption and recitation of activities; Mr. Chen you are active, please share your three with our esteemed group." Provo continued on and handed the dead fish to Chen who was now the blurred image and voice that dominated the moment. Thank goodness that Chen's language skills were superb and he didn't need the Babblepisce software.

"Our seed program is already underway. Multiple seed packets had been shipped to the US. The seeds are our most recent innovation. They have between five and seven phenotypes and use only three commingled genotypes. In the very near future we will see how this remarkable program develops. It holds great promise in disrupting the status quo.

"We tagged the genomes in all of the plant matter. We will be able to track results in real time.

"Secondly, we have been extremely successful in negotiating with the grey organ market in China. Please be mindful that we in the upper tiers have first right of refusal for any of the commerced tissues. Our protocols insist that we run detailed gene matching between donors and recipients. By doing so we limit the need for multiple sequential organ transplants due to rejections.

We are seeing a large demand in the Middle East for our products from the western part of China where there is a larger reservoir of Middle Eastern genotype derived tissues and organs. The similarity in the gene profiles within the geographic area allows us to provide a minimum three-year warranty against any type of rejection. That is three times longer than our nearest competition.

There is a brisk market spike for corneas, especially in Turkey and Morocco. Again, gene matching works well with the western Chinese products. If any of you have special interests or requests, inform me of them as quickly as you can. These products are highly perishable and some of the gene profiles are in very limited supply. If you monitor your Genedat software dashboard you can track the available materials and determine if anything is of value to you.

Thirdly, the Covid Initiative Phase Three is underway. The initial Chinese subterfuge vaccinations over two years ago have created a magnificent foundational piece for creating global hegemony manipulation. It was a matter of pure genius to have created the faux vaccination program for brucellosis two years in advance. Within that vaccine, while it did allow immunity to the now occurring brucellosis outbreak, it had within it the titers for the coronavirus we were working on in Wuhan. It was a bivalent vaccine. We did engage some very curious undetectable modifications on the nucleic acid profile of the microbe. After our experience with SARS, we decided to only make minor changes and then ferment a large enough batch to light the fuse of a pandemic. It is so easy to cross borders with a microbe such as that virus. Especially since we effectively delayed notifying the world health agencies of the *outbreak*. Timing is everything and the early release in China with very limited worldwide notification provided the Chinese with the edge they negotiated for and needed from us. Vaccinated Chinese became the unknowing, completely asymptomatic carriers spreading massive viral biomass throughout the world.

Over five hundred thousand vaccinated Chinese were in transit prior to the eyes of the world being focused upon limiting global travel. We were fortunate to have such viral messengers in play before cities and countries went into lockdown.

As a short segue, genes and such topics, they are all related. I would be totally remiss if I failed to mention that our work with the Chinese regarding ethnic gene mapping is progressing so well it is legendary. They believe we are assisting in the mapping of multiple ethnicities throughout the world for their own designs. We are of course assisting them with the massive data acquisition that is required to create a solid understanding about unique gene similarities among various ethnicities. We believe they will seek to lever the acquisition as they have already begun, by offering Covid vaccines in exchange for those essential nucleic acid datum. And in the near future use the data to create specific genetically programmed biological agents that mimic the foundational virus so as to not incur the wrath of the world community.

In essence, bioweapons. They are on the cusp of opening the Dragon and Phoenix jewelry box. How exciting!

They do not realize we have used our Remora Three software that is attached to their data processing, and we extract in real time the same information on all genetic loci. It is humorous to me, and hopefully to us, that the world does not understand how incredibly sophisticated the gene mapping is in the present day. Seriously. We can scrape a damp, cave floor in the Philippines and recover DNA from the ancient remains of Denisovan's blood and tissues and relate that to the worldwide distribution of that ancient genotype in present day humans.

Ironic that no one has connected the fact that gene mapping and gene tracking are very real tools for societal manipulation and even gene splicing. So much of a wonderful opportunity to exploit those data in the future!

But I digress. The rest of the world, sans China, is now in the throes of an economy-destroying pandemic. Discord in the world is opportunity to us. The Phase Two aspect of the grade 9 coronavirus distribution in China allowed for the microbe to be efficiently deployed worldwide and hobble most Western economies in one flow of the human travel wind. The Chinese were very cooperative to allow international travel of infected carriers to deploy our gift more rapidly. After all, as I shared, they were already vaccinated, asymptomatic super spreaders after being dusted.

This will allow China a brief God-given hegemonical moment in the dawn. And of course, since we knew that the disease would stress all types of supply chains, we invested heavily in PPE and naturally, toilet paper. All, *Takoveh!*" It was an audio wave, and everyone could hear the low-level mumble of *Takoveh*. An articulated spiritual agreement that meant so many things. Mr. Chen continued. "We expect a global set of events from which we can profit quite well. The virus is hard to control but it does have our very special version of engineered phage modules inside of its protein coat and when those manifest, it will truly be a *Takoveh!* moment. The residual and chronic ailments from the viral infection will bring profit to our medical equipment groups and to our pharmaceutical agencies who will dictate a further set of vaccinations, medications, and protocols to offset the damage from out little agent of mercy. Since we already know the various illness sequalae to being infected we can now invest in all those treatment media worldwide and heavily invest in the little things that those beset by the illness will require to stay alive.

To all who are Lucid, I have completed my presentation." Mr. Chen's mic became mute, and his screen image faded to a very light grey with no image of his face whatsoever.

"Chen, I realize I stated only three items, but there is an additional one that I would greatly appreciate you speaking to"

'Which initiative would you be referring to? I have several in my portfolio."

"The Renderings."

"Oh, yes, the Renderings. I am not the primary lead on that project. I can share with you top line details. Would that suffice?"

"Let us all hear your words and then determine if we require any further sharing of pertinent details."

"Of course. We have maintained a trade in all types of human tissues. As we are all well aware, we endeavor to use all of the host materials.

We had an inquiry from some interested parties in the southeastern US for the skins we may have available. They sought the leather from all the major ethnicities. They were especially keen on acquiring facial leather and fascia and agreed to financially compensate us extremely well for our efforts.

We only had limited previous commercial activities for the hides. The purchasers had very specific quality requirements that only tapped a small portion of the available material.

That small group of leather workers produces profitable results for us, but the most recent potential customers have cited purchases that are multiples more than the leather workers."

"Do you think this new opportunity will require us to step up our procurement activities?"

"Yes, I do believe that is a true statement. It is relatively easy to acquire light brown to dark brown, they're plentiful and the Chinese penal institutions are always accommodating.

But Caucasian coloring is a scarce commodity. We could always charge more for the white skins, ..."

"Thank you, Chen. We have enough of your tantalizing information to contemplate. Thank you. I shall speak with you in the near future on your thoughts on pricing and availability.

Time dictates we need to move on to our next topic of interest.

"There will be no time for comments. This is an encoding meeting, not a decision path meeting. The decision path meeting will be convened next month. Again, thank you Chen. I am quite certain you will have far more to share in the near future.

Let us now go on to our Geopolitical Board. Mr. Hoover, please provide us with Lucidity." Provo stopped short like a four-wheeler slamming on the brakes without the dust and gravel being kicked up in all directions. He orchestrated the meeting and insisted upon maintaining control of the multiple dialogues. Now it was time for the wind instrument himself, Hoover.

Chapter 25: Usual Suspects

Ah yes. Hoover was the architect of global societal and political disharmony. Not feared or loved. Mostly hated because his motivations on how he stirred the earthly stew of confrontational political and business engagements was solely his ego-driven own. "The Blue Moon cast wonderful light upon us all. And now it's waning phases have shed upon us the loveliest disharmony. I have inserted our agent provocateur missionaries in even some of the most sedate places. Many have been active in the United States for some time. Long before Mr. Trump was elected President in 2016. The Obama administration was *quite* amenable to our thoughts, strategies, and even our tactics. We already know who will win the election there and it perfectly suits our purposes. We discretely helped the software companies enhance their ability to modify the results in a favorable direction for *us*.

In Europe our false and real flag disturbances are creating wonderful, synergistic rivalries. Old ethnic dislikes always respond well to a few injected terrorist activities. Once the fuse is lit it is just a matter of waiting for an auspicious time for it to explode and help our sport activities prosper.

My favorite right now is energy disruption. We have been extremely successful at fielding the appropriate pieces and we are now playing a chessboard on three levels. Gas, electricity, oil, and such are on the move to go head-to-head with the Greenists and their misguided utopian belief that the only good fossil is left in the ground or displayed in a museum and is not to be used in any form to contribute to greenhouse gas production. The silliness and the egotism of that group. They simply have not charted the rhythms of the sun and weather the way we have for how many generations? Elder upon elder, Board after Board, we have extremely solid data that the weather changes are only partly due to the activities of humans. Such a wonderful interaction between the two major factions. We expect this seed to grow into a self-propagating flower of ecoterrorism. Those types of violent acts always increase profits in many of our governances. It is very laughable that with each green *innovation* a plethora of new disruptors emerge. Put up wind turbines and dice and slice birds; with electric conveyances there needs to be a massive infrastructure to support the charging stations; even the most minor societal augment such as masking has created a significant pollution issue with animals being strapped and wrapped like presents for that pagan holiday, Christmas with the cast away elastic face diapers. But I shall pause on those topics. Simply stated, everything has a front and a back. I ensure that we will handsomely profit on the anterior and posterior of silly human behaviors.

Oh, lest I neglect to mention our meatless meat initiative. Again, in brief, it positions consumers of flesh and those who are repulsed by it against each other. This too is an early planting. We expect that this will be a highly profitable area of friction. If I may suggest that all of you review the detailed files on this item. When you submit your private wagers that are based upon the events, do go quite heavy on the meat one. The level of confrontation and friction will be a bit unpredictable, but the odds are high and tilted on the consumption of flesh, not on highly processed pea and vegetable proteins. Currently I believe it is a 14.56 to one valuation. Your wagers in my areas of attention allow me to earn even greater bonuses. But this isn't all about me. It's about us and our mission." Hoover paused for just a moment. Even the most well electrified vacuum has to recharge.

The pause was just long enough for Provo to interject. He wasn't just a single clarinet. He was the whole woodwind section. With emphasis on untuned bassoons.

"Mr. Hoover, we all respect your insightful business thoughts and activities. This is not the best time to share such thoughts on further financial growth in your downlines of human and other assets. Could you please just complete your situation report and let us move on?" Provo abruptly interrupted Mr. Hoover. "This was not a *pitch and catch* time. This is a Board level, top line report time." Provo stared at Hoover's ghostly monitor image with eyes that red lasered through the display. The bassoon section shrank to ocarinas.

Hoover was caught in the seam of unpredictable override. He choked on how to appropriately respond. "Ummm, that's all I wish to share at this time. But do take a look at the meat issue." Hoover quickly put the sell punctuation on the enticing thoughts of financial and status gain. Insider trading at the Grand Ole MLM downline farm. Anyone who thinks an MLM provides equal opportunities to financially prosper is very naïve. The casino is never an entity to be bet against. People in power rig everything they touch. That's why they're in power. And if you have power, you have a responsibility to use it. The vast majority of people use it for their own benefit so why hide the motivations?

"I need to remind you Mr. Hoover that when I say *enough* that is not a signal for you to continue with the selling commentary. We all are well aware of your skills at squeezing grey money to black oozy currency on the dark net. If I need to remind you again of this unacceptable behavior, I shall have to dock the handicap on your bitcoin conversions. You are recognized as a master opportunist, but we have so much to cover today I want to insure we make time for our Sport activities update from Mr. McCarty. I shall evoke the change in our meeting agenda. Mr. McCarty, you now have permission for Lucidity." A vocal brake squealing stop and a quick shift to a different set of profitable gears. Hoover narrowly missed becoming a hood ornament on the Company vehicle. The ocarina disappeared and it became a whistle from Hoover, the teapot. Just steam blowing off. Hot air that goes nowhere.

"Mr. Premier Provo, thank you so very much. I shall quickly proceed through the list. Our current Blue Moon activities that are so very humorous look to be quite the profit makers. Our worldwide Halloween program is still working its magic. Do you get it? Humorous looks, Halloween, and magic? Oh *never* mind.

Philly was good to us but way too brief. We think there may be an opportunity for an accelerant asset there to kick the action up a notch or three in the days that follow. Being next to the river there adds to the ambience. And we get to try out some of our new fast boats for future endeavors in China and Southeast Asia. Maybe even incorporate them in the trade between South America and the United States. On that thought we are working with our Special Innovations group on autonomous submarines to support the illicit drug trade.

We have some delightful activity in Europe. It is moving in such interesting ways. We have our recent small group play in Vienna. Already we have some points on the leaderboard for some of our favorites. We tucked our activities into the actions of the Muslim extremists. My suggestion is to look closely at Angus and his partner over there. They made a quick trip from Ireland to Vienna. And they are quite the provocation specialists. They are the steak and the sizzle.

In France all it took was a few caricatures and a handful of people demonstrating and we now have financial disruptions with boycotts of French products mashing up against the outraged vitriol of additional murders over cartoons. It never ceases to amaze me how such innocent activities hit a feral chord in the human instrument and the music is so nicely limbic. A simple cartoon of a naked man triggers personal and religious insult. How quaint. A cartoon!

Throughout the EU we have the *to be in quarantine or not?* That is the question. To suffer the outrageous impact of a life-threatening disease or to puff up one's chest to exhibit freedom of choice and potentially take on lifelong disabilities. Oh well, deciding to die alone with tubes inserted in every orifice is a choice and a demonstration of free will in a rather perverse manner. The flare-ups there could progress quite nicely. There are also the abortion rights demonstrations in Poland. We will not feature any events there. We are not misogynists and Kurgan barbarians throwing babies into pits with hungry wolves. When I look about the room, I see we are quite well gender-balanced at approximately fifty-fifty here. As it should be.

We are expecting a continuation of the sparky places in the US. Some of the old and some of the new. A degree of uncertainty on which insult will become a full-bore riot. But we do monitor the events closely and when needed we use accelerant assets to bolster the energy of randomness. Our well-placed assets can act at the sound of a phone ringing with speed and efficiency.

In Africa it is truly the most dangerous and provocative place to be. So many flashpoints for sport it is amazing. We do have logistical issues there though due to the fact that many of our athletes find it hard to be grey there so the revenue is good but not great. Tender mercies may yet be rained upon us.

And of course, we still have very open playing fields in the Pacific Northwest, including Portland. We are hopeful that some East Coast venues will open up soon such as Atlanta.

We are engaging and contracting many new members and sport aficionados. We have a very active global recruitment program going on. The initiative has the added benefit of *High Roller Wagers*. If you wish to know more about that initiative reach out and tag me. The High Roller Wagers have some provocative business connectivity. But I shall let our Business Acquisition Board talk to that per the timing determined by our Premier.

Lest I totally neglect, we are working closely with our *Toys and Instruments* division. The modified and unique tools we can now offer as perks to Associates and business builders are simply spectacular. Of course I could go on and on, as you all know by now, one additional note of kudos to our yellow sash contractors. Not one of our adventures has been hiccupped. *No body left behind* is their credo and call to action and they have lived up to it. A loud *Takoveh!* was heard from the monitor feeds and the in-person attendees. It would be quite the financial catastrophe if their sport activities were discovered. A body here a body there and sooner than you can do two snaps and a hefty zipper swish, some big nosed law dog – modern day Wyatt Earp or Doc Holliday would be poking around at the oddities of mortality being served up stainless steel cold on a roll out from the morgue.

One closing thought. I have been given permission to reward and promote two of our most promising athletes. They will be bestowed with Emerald One Star Diamond status.

Thank you all so very, very much for letting me share the great news." McCarty was a salesman at heart and soul, and he knew that it was just as important to stop selling a done deal as it was to initiate a business relationship.

"That was a very nice succinct recap of our opportunities. Mr. McCarty, you can mute and stay on until the Executive session if you wish." Provo calmly stated as though he was asking for a ticket on a subway car to be punched.

"Sir, that is most gracious and kind of you. If I may beg your leave and the leave of the Board members, I do have some timely business matters to attend to with two of our most recent prospect candidates. It is a very nice set of dominoes if they can be properly positioned. Time now for finesse. May I depart from the meeting, Premier Provo?" Always the polite carnival call man. McCarty was already back in his head with the boys, Maachi and Bart. Closing that profitable arc will be more than magnificent, it will be legendary. And he will have been the one to create the campaign and execute the details. He would have to be wary of Hoover though. Mr. Hoover was the jealous, covetous type and what McCarty had planned, tread upon putting his cattle on Hoover's ranch could present jeopardous issues. McCarty wanted to ensure that the bovines were not inadvertently harvested for some bizarre reason by Hoover. Hoover was known as a corporate slice and dice man. He wasn't Asian, but he sure was Ginsu.

"That is fine Mr. McCarty. Do attend to your business affairs. Your affairs are our affairs, so we do understand acting within the moment and seizing the opportunity. I need to always remind all of you that no insider information is to be provided to any *one* individual. If it is good enough for one to hear it is good enough for all of us to hear. Biasing our decision-making processes with insider information is potentially subject to actions of excommunication. I hope I am clearer than the June air in Salt Lake." And with that last word there was a soft click and McCarty's monitor went dark and onto a screensaver. *Takoveh* stretched and squiggled across the screen like a leach in heat. Yes, Takoveh was more than just a word. It was a prophetic *Dendron* mantra in the making. Bursting and glowing with the power to evoke so much.

Chapter 26: How We Roll

"At this time you are trusted consumers and budding associates of the services rendered. Since you are both associates, I thought this would be an ideal moment to share with you the incredible value it is to you. I so very much apologize for the omission of providing all the information during our previous calls and meetings. I would like to take this precious moment to address my negligent shortfall." McCarty played the apologist card like a fundamental Christian citing the Old Testament.

"At this time your recreational activities cost you between three hundred thousand and five hundred thousand dollars each to participate in an event. What would it be worth to you to have that tidy sum decreased by an additional percentage? Would that interest you? If I could offer to you a way to save a rather significant sum of money for each event, and as time goes on, provide even greater rewards? Is that not attractive?" McCarty was out selling beach property in the Marianas Trench at this moment. Maybe. Who wants a ticket on a bathysphere?

"Ya, mean we get a bulk use discount? Like Costco or BJs?" Maachi was not clear on the piece placed on the board.

"Well, yes, no, and maybe. It depends." McCarty responded.

"Great answer. Very clear now. M, I really don't get where you're going." Maachi sarcastically responded.

"Dr. Panicles, Bart, you buy and sell things, don't you? As I state the obvious." McCarty was doing that bait the hook thing. He wasn't switching anything.

"Is this a frikkin IQ test or something? What kind of a dumbfuck question was that?" Maachi responded.

"Oh, please do forgive me. That really wasn't a satisfactory answer, was it?" McCarty's jowly cheeks blushed a hooker's tint for a moment. And he wasn't the one destined to be fucked.

"McCarty, what is it you want? How about very plain, easy to understand first language English? You can even use three syllable words if you need to. We have online dictionaries just in case we hit on a random word or ten. And we already have touched upon the meaningful discounts you tossed out to us in our previous dialogues." Maachi was sharpening his sarcasm blade and burning the candle of his patience at the same time. He forged the bleeding edge in the candle heat and then in then plunged it into the coldness of his words.

"We have discussed that you are a part of a very fine network marketing – multi level marketing business endeavor. I know you are both familiar with the model. I believe you even provide products to a few of the lesser players." McCarty innocently stated with a chirpy smile embedded into each word. As typical with all MLMs it's a dance of innuendo with toe stepping greed. You never get the full story and that's entirely intentional.

"Not clear, dear. Yup. You talked to us about being associates. To us that could just mean a bulk-buying club, like I said. That's about the limit of my boat on the beach.

The breeze that's coming our way is sounding like you signed us up in a pyramid scheme. Ponzi scheme crap. Is that where this is going? You popped us into being in some kind of real MLM?" Maachi asked.

"Hmmmm, so this is really a Ponzi scheme thing?" Bart added.

"We did talk about this with a comment to you both being associates. Nothing onerous here I promise you on a Holy Book of your choice. A grand part of what I do is to ensure that you more fully understand what a unique opportunity this is. No hard and fast requirement for you to sell fictitious stories to line pockets or fill garages with overpriced consumer goods like protein bars or water filters."

McCarty giggled like a little boy who was just caught spanking the monkey with mom's hand lotion to the Swimsuit issue.

"So, the answer is *no* to this being any type of illegal Ponzi business arrangement. That type of business is built upon selling a never to be truly achieved and consumed financial opiate.

In that despicable model you only make money if you connive someone else into giving you money for simply an opportunity to *bring someone else in*. The fees and product discounts only disguise the fact that people can be made to believe they can win in Las Vegas. You both have been there on several occasions. Those ostentatious, enormous facilities could not stay in business if gamblers won the majority of the time. Betting against the house is a fool's errand.

What I am speaking to is a solid, financially well-endowed multi-level marketing company with unique and quite desirable rewards. It is a genuine business opportunity whereby you access and leverage your own network of people. In this situation you would not be trying to convince people to take up the sport. You simply would sort people who would benefit *from* the sport. And as a minor comment, at this time you are still acting more as consumers than associates even though you do have the associate status. You will shortly have the ability to onboard consumers and potential prospects to evolve your sport activity into something more rewarding on many levels.

The document you have previously signed cites that you are on the first level as associates within the company." McCarty droned on about the ephemeral nonsense of MLM. The chum was out, the hook was baited, now was time to sink the hook so much deeper by appealing to the deadly sin of greed.

"This is a riot! Are you pitching us to go all in *and* all out and get folks to be your customers? That's funny as a peacock in my ass." Maachi hyena-laughed at McCarty.

"Seriously?" Asked Bart.

"Gentlemen, no, not customers. Clients with special, refined tastes in the most extreme of sports. If you would be so kind, please consider the following.

One of my favorite authors, Ernest Hemmingway, was quoted as stating that there are only three true sports. Those sports put a man, or woman's, not to be sexist, life on the line. He believed that the only true sports are bullfighting, auto racing, and mountaineering. Those sports can very suddenly and quickly have a person face the grim reaper up close and personal and ask *is that all you've got?* He viewed all other so-called sports as nothing more than games. Grown men and women playing with their fancy balls and receiving huge amounts of money from people just for the opportunity to view them *playing a game.* I believe Mr. Hemmingway would agree that there might be an additional category of true sport. The pursuits of superior alphas who perish the existence of humans while under duress. Highly intelligent Morlocks and self-absorbed Eloi. Thus, as I am sharing with you, The sport as we refer to it, is as primal as it can be. When facing down the fact that within the toss of the mortality dice, rolling your actual bones, you either win or lose and there are no time-outs, no cheat codes, no instant replay, no referees, or a click on the video game to have another life. Men, and if I may say, women, who face their personal event horizon right in the eye either gain a far greater appreciation for life in the body or don't have to think about it any longer. The obese woman either sings or she doesn't. And if she does sing, it is a staccato funeral dirge. Hemmingway was on the right track to understanding the feral nature of man to challenge the unknown and attempting to win a gold medal at facing a scythe bearing, dark all-encompassing being. Only gold medals are of value. Not many get silver or bronze and talk about it.

"If I may continue, you are very patient with me. I realize that both of you are very wealthy and busy. You have no wives or children. Elite self-made playboys that are proud of their accomplishments and now wish to enjoy the delicious fruit that comes from the trees they have planted. This is a way to sweeten the fruits of your lives. You have friends or colleagues that have similar refined, sophisticated tastes and they could very well be interested in escaping mindless corporate boredom. And I do need to share with you that I have some very exciting news for you regarding this grand opportunity to experience life to its fullest." McCarty had set the hook and his tunas were being allowed to reel out the line. They thought they were freely swimming about. Now *that's* finny.

"This is nuts. Lemme dial this in a few clicks. Are you proposing we introduce dudes and maybe dudettes to you to go on sport expeditions? Now why in the universe would we do that? We have enough wood to spend on whatever we wish. What do we need this for?" Maachi strongly questioned the issue on the table. If there was a valid benefit to the suggestion, he was all in. Otherwise, he had better things to do. There was a special, extra-x, live cam on soon and he didn't want to miss it.

"Well, there are quite a few advantageous perks. And your money now allows you degrees of freedom that the vast majority of humanity does not even daydream about.

"Let me share with you how this remarkable opportunity can benefit you. Firstly, significant discounts on your excursions. Secondly, you earn income from those you bring to the company – a percentage of revenue. Thirdly, new vistas for exploration open up for you – right now you are centric to the US. Fourthly, there are quite a few exotic pieces of sport equipment you can acquire that you simply cannot get elsewhere. Fifthly,"

Bart cut McCarty short.

"You got me with the *exotic pieces*. What kinds of exotic pieces are we talkin' about here? Tactical nukes? Hand held lethal laser guns? Kidding. We already have access to all sorts of goodies. And those that we really would like to have we can have dark-smithed for us. So do tell us more. Make this passion play something we want to hear more about." Bart targeted right to the point of his interests.

"We have access to very sophisticated limited distribution accessories and hardware. 3D color night vision optics and protective eye coverings. Hot point beepers that use GPS to track all that is going on around you – yes, GPS as in photographic satellite augmentations. Ordinance that is not available to any civilian. And so much more. Goodness to God I would be jabbering for hours to just scratch the proverbial colorful decoupage surface of the offerings. All at extremely favorable prices." McCarty started to reel the still feisty fish in. They might fin and burble, but they now have entered McCarty's marine world. Where marine life casts aside all hope when entering. You are now owned and on your way to a canning factory.

"You mean like really illegal stuff? Like mercenary contractor stuff? The stuff that there isn't anything on Pinterest even?" Bart quipped back; his cheek solidly pierced by McCarty's sharp hook. As he wiggled, the hook went ever so much deeper. Especially in light of his earlier conversations with McCarty.

"Exactly. But there really is more." McCarty responded with a proud victorious smile.

"Toys are nice. Let's get back to the readies. Just how much can we pocket? Are we talking a few grand or a few really big ones? Or are we talking fields of cabbage as far as the eye can see?" Maachi challenged McCarty. *Make my day, McCarty!* Maachi thought to himself as he went wrinkly-face and squinted his eyes and stared into McCarty's.

"You will need binoculars to view the endless fields if you build your network and create downlines that are productive and compliant. The analogy is apt. With such a vast field of downline associates the cabbage will pick themselves for you." Ah, no need to let the tunas swim back and forth in the ocean saltiness he thought. They were hooked and now it was simply a matter of pulling them on deck and determining which bucket to place them in. Simply toss out a bit choicer pieces and the tunas would be ready to be filleted in a very loose manner of speaking. McCarty was the epitome of not giving a man a fish, but fishing for a man to feed the enterprise. And occasionally gutting a fish and cooking it crispy on the grill of blind greed meets hot charcoal.

"Seriously." Bart looked at Maachi. Maachi looked at Bart. Bookends on the thoughts of more money and less boredom. Bart would have a glorious opportunity to obtain death dealing toys that were only fleetingly mentioned in online in Soldier of Fortune or some hacked email from DOD and DARPA.

"Bart, Dr. Panicles, you appear to be at a temporary loss of words. I shall pause for a moment to catch my breath. I do have even far more interesting things to share with you. Would you happen to have a cold Dr. Pepper locked away in a fridge somewhere?" McCarty's whistle was dry and there is nothing quite like the syrupy sweet taste of the good Doctor Pepper. McCarty had three favorite doctors, Kevorkian, John Bodkin Adams, and Pepper. At this moment it was his third favorite doctor hopefully being teed up for ingestion. A wetted whistle sings a song of sirens' words that hypnotize and entice the unaware listener.

"Let me see what I can do." Bart stood up and exited the room to speak with Latika.

"Just how does all this work? The money part. The rest is just pesky details." Maachi asked with an unusual bit of sincere verbiage.

"I have already touched upon this but let me expand on the topic. At this time you are on the cusp of greatness. You would need to make further commitments to expand your *network business.* As you bring more people into your network, they earn, and you earn off of what they compensate the company with. The more people, the greater the financial rewards." McCarty shared with a matter-of-fact attitude.

"Hmmmm, what does *further commitments* really mean? Are you gonna fill our warehouse with goods like ammo and illegal arms or what? Are we gonna be some kind of fancy gun runners?" Maachi was slowly and very cautiously raising his shields. They were ablative and reactive. Nothing is free. Even free doughnuts aren't free. You pay ill and consequences with diabetes or some other sugar induced malady.

Slippery words with open-ended meanings were not his desert wine glass of aged port.

"May I suggest that we await the return of Mr. Henderson?" McCarty needed to recon the SitRep. Wrong words now could unhook his Best Fish Forever. He needed a nonobvious pause to let his mind pull together the situation and carefully place his words.

"Dr. Pepper coming up!" Bart happily shared with the two of them. Latika followed Bart into the office with three cans of Dr. Pepper, a crystal ice container, a pair of silver tongs, and etched designer company crystal drinkware. She set her goods on the center of the table and turned to walk away.

"Hey, Lati, where's the cokes for us? Bart and I are Georgia boys. Cokes! Make it quick. Not crazy about that prune taste in the Pepper. I don't need a bubbly laxative." Maachi sparked at Latika. She quickly returned with two chilled cokes for Maachi and Bart. She poured out the beverages to all three of them and clinked some cubes in to further chill the libations.

"To Mr. Candler! Here's to you!" Maachi held his glass up. Bart joined him and McCarty was in a short stall mode.

McCarty thought to himself and wondered *this is weird, who might Mr. Candler be.* Regardless, he held up his iced Dr. Pepper and they slapped glasses with resounding tink-tink-tinkety.

"Dr. Panicles, forgive me for inquiring, who is Mr. Candler?" McCarty shyly asked. He was feeling a small bit guilty. *Is this something I should know?* The thought bubble hovered above the three of them along with the open-ended question to Maachi.

Maachi quickly changed the question mark into a sharp exclamation point. "Dude, if you have to ask, then no point in answering. It's a major Georgia thang." Maachi played the one-ups-man card again. He tossed it on the table and left it there face-up. He had no intention of answering McCarty's question. McCarty chugged a few swallows of his Dr. Pepper to break the verbal impasse. His innards chilled as he swilled the sweet soda. The only thing that would make the coolness cooler would be a cone of Aggie Blue Mint. *Or, maybe I should patent a Dr. Pepper – Blue Mint float, floated not sunk.* He jokingly thought to himself. His inner glow was a rather diminutive and rotund secret agent night-light.

"Ah, delicious!" McCarty's sugarcoated words melted on his lips. "Please indulge me and let me continue. Your question about further commitments was most *apropos*. All of our prospects, associates, and various level Board members are required to approve and sign off on a very straightforward agreement. Not an electronic DocuSign. You have already signed off on the document we previously proffered. In that document there is verbiage that I had pointed out to you. In essence, you are truly already greatly inculcated in this wonderful enterprise. To be eligible you do have some monthly requirements to maintain." He left a broad, pearly-white, toothy smile upon his face and spoke no further. He wanted to see their reactions.

"This really feels like bait and switch. Need to think about this. You? Bart?" Maachi asked of his co-CEO.

"We're aligned. Yup. McCarty, we need to think about what's going on here. You just backed up a Tonka truck and tipped its load on us. Monthly requirements sounds a lot like that God awful auto ship stuff. Is that where you're going?" Ever so logical Bart shared with the man in the plaid jacket.

"Well, alrighty then! Sounds like a plan! I'll follow up with you later. I'll make a note in my tickler file and collect some thoughts for a potential vision board. I'll finish my soda and be on my way. There are a few more items that I am just bubbling with excitement to share with you though. The Board has approved for both of you to advance in the organization. And you will be very soon contacted with more delightful, enlightening information.

"They were so delighted with your performance in Philly that they wanted to insure that you were both properly rewarded and motivated to continue your participation in the sport. They have something very special for you.

"Oh, one other thing. It appears that some interesting playgrounds have been developing. I'll let you know if anything appears to be of your persuasion." Hook, line out and in, and sinker, in a manner of speaking. McCarty kept his rosy glow warm and toasty from the inside out. The heat from his happiness almost set off the fire suppression system. Thank goodness for cold soda. As per typical with MLMs, lots of jargon and confusing monologues that are fully intended to not allow detection of some very intricate sleight of hand. The house always wins.

"Ya' lost me. McCarty, you just barcode mode yacked about a bunch of other stuff. You're talkin' a whole 'nother language. Do you have an online glossary for your bango-tango-slango? Because I have no idea what you're talking about. What I did hear is pay less for what you like to do and make extra wood while doing it. That's all I need for now." Maachi further closed the door on the convo and allowed himself to be brought on deck and flippity flop around with Bart. The highest bidder owned the tunas. That bidder was McCarty.

"Hey, McCarty, what were you just saying about us and some type of recognition? I didn't quite catch it all. How about if we hit a great big ole sloe-Gin-fizz button and do a short rewind? Bart pointedly asked.

"Mr. Henderson I can certainly do that for you. You are part of the organization. You were prospects who became associates. With your remarkable performance in Philly what I mean is that you followed the guidelines and rules to the letter, the company, and our most executive leader, the Premier, would like to honor you with recognition and enhancement of your status." McCarty succinctly shared.

"All this blabber is just stating, and restating that we're already a piece in this game and now a sweeter piece is coming our way?" Bart curiously asked.

"That is exactly what I am saying. You are truly no longer viewed as prospects turned associates. You have tremendous opportunity to move up level by level in the organization. The first step on this next part of the journey is to have our Customer Relations team send out to you a representative to personally award you with your gift of recognition. Would it be acceptable to both of you for me to schedule the visit and arrange for all to go smoothly during this empowering transition? I believe when you know more about the award it will enamor you even further and encourage you to be totally on-board with the sport. You shall be so ensconced that you will excitedly invite others to participate. All to your benefit." McCarty knew this was almost a big ole fat done deal.

"Hmm, we should think about this and have our own internal meeting. Ya' know what I mean?" Maachi suspiciously asked.

"Well that would be fine except for the fact that there really is nothing more for you to do. We have our agreement in place as I have previously stated and all that is needed to bring this arc to completion is to have the recognition gift bearing visit. I can assure you that you will be quite impressed with all that will unfold. I do realize there is a lot to encode and digest here. May I suggest that I arrange for the visit very soon and if for any reason you decide to not continue with the program, just let me know and I can curtail any further activities. That would be quite the shame though. You have already climbed the mountain, planted the tree, and now it is time to bathe on the top of the peak sunlight and enjoy the fruits of your labors. May I have you permission to carry on as I have shared? There really is no risk to either of you at this juncture. It is all reward and minimal effort. You have already demonstrated your proficiencies and desire to continue in other ways. This is simply the confirmation to move forward to greater excitement and gains. Your thoughts?" McCarty knew that by dropping the big piece of chocolate cake in the middle of the dialogue it would be irresistible. He wasn't wrong. Feed the greed need and then just step back and appreciate the fine choreography of events as they naturally unfold. Greed and ego are two wonderful ingredients to add to the meal of self-aggrandizement.

"Hey, look, we don't question you at all. It's just our inquisitive nature to make sure that the poke doesn't contain a pig. El Hefe, let's do this. We really don't appear to have anything to lose and maybe lots to gain. I like more money and interesting, unusual tools at our disposal, and this sounds like that's exactly what's on deck. Times slippin' and this could be fun and profitable. I'm in. Let's make the decision now." Bart chimed on in support of being further inculcated into the mysterious and confusing world of McCarty's MLM carnival of earthly delights. The whole advancement process in an MLM is a Rube Goldberg machine with no instruction manual. What is provided to engaging entrepreneurs is a hope for something greater that rarely manifests. Buying clouds to import rain is not what the cosmos allows.

"Yeah. Okay. You're the one making this decision. I'm just trusting you to make this happen. And you do know the drill. You made the decision and if this goes anywhere but true north this was *your* decision. Not mine." Maachi had to put the stopper back in the wine bottle and make certain that Bart knew that this was his call to make and it sure better not be a dial tone or a one nine hundred number.

"Roger that. I take the risk and we both get the benefits. Go for it McCarty. Line us up for a dignitary visit." Bart was now on the hook with Maachi. Double hooking lines and hopefully no sinker.

"Splendid! Absolutely, fortuitously splendid. I shall text you with the details. Please do expect a visit within just a day or two. I can't thank you enough for sharing such a large piece of your time with me. I bid you fond adieu. How exciting! I shall also place tickets for you both in some upcoming events. They will be yours to decline. But I think you shall find the venues both interesting and challenging. Good day gentlemen." McCarty was all smiley inside and out. The arc was only a degree or two short of closure.

"How about if you and I chat just a little bit more about this advancement? Since I'm on the hook to make sure this all goes well, I'd like a minute or two more of your time to double down on my understanding. We're in and looking forward to MLM version 2 and the details that make all the dots connect. Let me have Latika deliver up another round of Dr. Pepper and a coke to my office. We can close any open issues. Okay?" Bart wanted just a few more details before putting his ass and the rest of him on the line. He really liked his ass where it was, connected and such to his body.

"That sounds very appropriate. I shall follow your lead." McCarty responded.

"No worries though. We'll make ourselves available for the visit. Big Georgia Peach down south style thanks!" Bart closed the dialogue on an uplifting fruity note.

Maachi looked at Bart and a lascivious thought passed through his mind. *Georgia Peach double entendre Barty boy. And that reminds me. My one-eyed trouser snake is getting hungry. Need to connect with Lati. I can smell peach juice a mile away.*

Chapter 27: Upside Down

"Hey, Barthead, did you get a text from McCarty? I received one late this morning. Looks like the visitors from planet MLM would like to be here tomorrow AM. I shouted back it was fine with us. You okay with this?" His question was more rhetorical than one seeking Bart's approval. Maachi had already made his decision, and this was his design to let Bart think he had a say in the affair. Maachi was only mildly insolent but that could change like the weather in Connecticut. If you like it, it can change in a sweep of the winds complete with thunder and lightning.

"Nope. Nothing. Well actually, I don't know if I got a text from Mr. Plaid Clad Slick." Bart responded with aplomb.

"Douche-man, whaddya mean ya' don't know? Look on your phone ya' dickweed." Maachi was spooling up some acidic vitriol.

"That's just it. I don't know where I left my phone. Maachi, can I borrow your phone for just a minute? I need to call my phone to figure out where it is. Okay?" Bart politely asked.

"Sure. But I need to get it back right away. No long walks with my connection to the known universe. I'll be here. Happy hunting. Don't get lost. I know where you live." Maachi was focusing on his triple-monitor vision fest. A spreadsheet on one monitor. A second was scrolling an inventory set of numbers in SAP. The third was on the dark web. Bart didn't look closely. Just enough to see that someone was inflicting pain on someone else, and it sure didn't look like it was voluntary. All he could make out was what looked like some Koreans playing hard with a young girl. Maachi made a toss to Bart. Bart snatched it out of the air and then just stared at it.

"Hey, El Hefe, this isn't a phone. It's just a new blade." At that very moment Bart engaged the slide release and the blade went airborne and straight toward Maachi's head. Maachi instinctively tilted his head just enough to only get a slight, bloody scrape on his ear.

"You stupidmotherfuckinshithead asshole! You could have taken an eye out or worse! Why'd you do that?" Maachi was crackly hot volcanic-soot-ash-brimstone-pissed.

"Aaahhh, mmmm, Boss how was I to know that was going to happen? I've never handled one of these before. Where the crap did you cop this little gem? I've read about them, just never saw one in the flesh. Poor choice of words." Bart apologetically inquired.

"Don't ever press any buttons on anything I give you unless I tell you to! Got it?" Maachi was spitting out sharp brads and glass shards in word after word. "It's one of the perks from our newest business associates. More easily had than toilet paper during the pandemic. I saw it on this portal they gave me access to. Major double secret password site. This little darlin' turned up and quicker than you can read all the words in the dictionary, *bam*! Here it is. Special courier stuff included at no charge." Maachi sarcastically poked Bart. Bart was immune to the pokes. The little scars built themselves into self-respect armor.

"Huh? Okay, yeah, I get it. Really sorry about the sharp migo. Are we okay here?" Bart was back peddling very slowly.

"Sure. First you get the knife blade out of the shelf." Maachi directed Robot One.

Bart tugged at the blade, but it didn't budge. The velocity and impact drove the metal deeply into the cherry wood bookcase shelf. "No can do. Double sorry cross my DNA." Bart was moving from apologetic to a *get yur own blade out you jagoff!* state of mind.

"Fuck. You're such a dweebed klutz. Here! This is a phone. This is what you came for take it and get the fuck outta my space." Maachi kept pissing all over Bart.

"Is it okay if I press the buttons on it? Just want to be sure here." Bart sarcastically parried back.

Maachi didn't even comment. His special way of saying how irrelevant the other person was. But he did look up and sharp little daggers flew from his eyes. If thoughts could maim and kill this would be a very Mortal Kombat moment.

"Thanks Boss. I'll be right back. Need to follow the tone to its source. You know me. Absent minded when it comes to where my scarecrow parts are." Bart left Maachi's office for his search and acquire mission.

He returned about ten minutes later. "Here ya go. Thanks." Bart chirped out to the Fearless Leader. Maachi didn't even acknowledge Bart's presence. "Hate it when I can't find my phone. It feels like a life and death event. Thanks again. By the way, yeah, I did get the text from the man. All good by me." He placed the tacphone on the desktop next to Maachi's mouse. Maachi was in one of his visual-staring trances. The trance was not focused upon the spreadsheet or the SAP screens. Bart decided the better part of valor now was to quietly and very discreetly leave El Hefe's office. Blushing at the creepiness of the whole situation.

Chapter 28: First Time

A Slack note from Latika bubbled up on his monitor. *Two visitors are here to see you and Bart. Shall I go and collect them from the lobby?*

You left it as a question. It's a statement. Yur goin' to collect them? Whaddya think they are Pokémon cards? Do your thing and let's get this day rolling. Maachi Slacked back. He texted Bart with a terse, pointy message. *Theyre hr. Hp U hve yur phne. Check your butt hole, it could be stuck up there.*

B R there. Bart quickly texted back. *Dipshit. It never ends. Just a continual shit covered cinnamon roll from this dork.* He thought to himself.

Latika opened Maachi's office door and ushered the two guests in. As they entered a meter or so into the office confines, Latika cast her glance at the floor in front of her and exited like as though she evaporated. It was a I Dream of *disappearing* Genie time.

"Very pleased to meet you two. Long plane ride? Tough traveling from, where did you travel from?" Bart opened the can of dialogue for the morning. Mmmmm, nothing like the whiff of a fresh batch of snappy repartee and triple entendre first thing to start the day.

"The flight was fine. We have our own means to go from here to there and back again. Utah, of course" Green eyed Peeta fluttered her extended lashes at Bart.

"That's a long flight. Coach sucks, doesn't it?" Bart was being teased and he liked it. A lot. Teasing pleased him ever so much. Usually he had to pay extra for that on those lonely nights in his crib.

Both of the women coquettishly giggled. "You must be the funny one. The other guy over there with his head stuck in his monitors probably not so funny. Coach? What's coach? You mean did we get put in some type of woman's oversized purse like a cat or get shipped in steerage?" Peeta laughingly charted out the course of the interaction. Her pearlies sparkled in the bright white office lights. The not-so-innocent teasing was absolutely disarming. Smart chick, snappy brain, will travel.

"I don't get it. Coach?" Bart naively stated.

"Silly boy. *Coach*, go Google it. No, we don't travel coach. Private jet. We flew in on a 7500. Probably very similar to what you guys use on your travels to events. It's very comfy. And the best part is we don't even go within smelling range of security. Mmmmmmm, security. Now that brings back some awkward moments. Going through security. Sometimes I wished that it wasn't a woman." Peeta carried on with not-so-subtle innuendo.

"Oh, well, okay with that. Really glad you're here. Maachi, hey, Maachi, some colleagues are here to see us." Bart poked his business associate with a velvet nail to the cortex.

Maachi tilted his head up to peer over the top of the monitors. His look was a stare. And as he stood up to fully see the landscape, he started doing the stare-way to heaven. *Wow! What a babe. And her sidekick is pretty bangin' nice too.* His thoughts were in cadence with his optics.

"Pleased to meet you Mr. Panicles." Peeta said as she held out her hand in receptor mode. It froze in the air. She was unaware that Maachi would rather shake the dick of a dolphin than the hand of another disease carrying human.

"Yup. Most people are. You're not an exception." Maachi already was doing that alpha-predator stuff. He totally ignored her extended greeting.

"Forgive me. Could you repeat that? I think I missed something." Peeta innocently stated as she slowly let her arm descend to her side.

"People are pleased to meet me. And a B-T-W, it's Doctor Panicles, okay?" Can always count on Maachi to demonstrate the utmost fastidious inviting behavior. How cosmopolitan.

"Oh, that's funny!" Peeta was an eight on a zero to ten-laugh meter. "It's still a pleasure to meet you, Dr. Panicles. I've heard so much about you. And you were quite magnificent on the field in Philly. The vids were inspiring and quite precious.

"We were thinking of using excerpts from that exploit for training purposes, but we'd need your permission to do that. Or not." She flashed a *fuck you asshole* smile.

"Philly was quite the deal. Were those good things or bad things?" Maachi was beginning to verbally prod and poke. Just a very small crack in his rigid security blanket.

"Yes, Philly was a very interesting situation for all of us. We're not accustomed to having the National Guard troop the color and come on in." She never did answer the question on the good, the bad, and the dastardly. That was her style. She was a top Alpha Cat and unfortunately Maachi could not appreciate that anyone, especially a woman, could be of any true value. Just a glorified Eloi with nice boobs hanging with the Morlocks. And hopefully, tastes better than Georgia peaches.

"Ladies, so what do we have on the menu for this morning? You're in the driver's seat. Shall we sit?" Bart was going Suwanee River honey sweet. He deliberately didn't set his eyes in elevator mode. He wanted to but didn't. He stayed on the floor of how to entertain important visitors and provide hospitality accouterments. Any level further up might be a reach for a peach that was beyond his grasp and out of his on-call late evening bush league.

"That would be fine. Please though, how rude, and insensitive of me. This is my colleague and very trusted travel companion, Charly Welsh. She is quite the experienced international traveler. She's my right-hand woman. And she is very delightfully hands on." Peeta waved her hand in the most angelic way towards Charly. The person of her reference smiled and pouted her red lips.

Bart moved to the opposite side of the conference table and pulled two adjacent chairs backwards to allow the lovely female visitors to sit. He wished he could be the chairs.

"So nice to see that there is a southern gentlemen in the house." Peeta sweetened up the dialogue. She cast a seductive *thank you* gaze at Bart. He fell so deeply into her eyes she might need retinal surgery.

As she and Charly were situating themselves, Maachi was not just going full elevator mode. He was checking out each floor. His thoughts went to stopping at the third floor where lingerie and maybe battery powered tools were available. His gaze did go on to the upper most floors and he thought *what a lovely pair of balconies*. He was looking right through her clothes. X-ray vision but not from a Superman. The penetrating vision was from a Superperv and Peeta was no dopey bimbo. She felt the optical invasion and just inwardly shrugged it off. Her armor was impenetrable unless being wooed with a rare vintage of Dom in a Prix Fixe candlelight exclusive restaurant of her choice. If only Bart knew the price for admission to this house that passion built was more than he could afford.

Peeta, Charly, and Bart sat down, and the moment went pregnant. Maachi was still staring at Peeta's balconies. "Maachi, join us please." Bart was slipping into his suave and debonair mode. Maachi was slipping into a *I'd like to bone-her* mode. Such a classic, chauvinistic pig. "Maachi?" Bart again queried Maachi with a bit louder voice with the intent to wake him up from checking out the stripper pole wrapper.

Maachi projected the not-so-subtle facial tells and simply walked from around his desk to the conference table and sat down next to Bart.

"What are we doin' here? What's up?" Maachi wasn't interested in small talk unless it was his.

"We're honored to be here to share the good news with you. We have your jewels." Peeta further explained.

Maachi was on a total high lateral drift. She said, *honored* and he was thinking *on her*. She was saying *jewels* and in his Macho Translator piece of brain matter he was thinking, *love to have her check out my jewels. Bigger balls make the bawdy ones bawl.* Even mildly intelligent people know that you really need to be careful about what you wish for. Sometimes you get your wish to come true but not quite how you intended that form to be.

"As usual, I know you two charming fellows are aware we don't engage in a lot of soft or hard copy documents. All I have for you is your pin that signifies your status in your respective downlines." Peeta eloquently stated just the facts. Maachi's brain was on full breeding mode. He was thinking it would be great to down some lines with this babe. Or maybe a lascivious sting from his tacphone.

"Super. Now what?" Bart innocently asked. A puppy dog aura that beckoned for petting by at least one of the babe-o-lishes.

Peeta nodded to Charly who placed a red Tumi bag on the tabletop. She opened it and did the rabbit out of the hat thing and produced two very intriguing, ornate carved boxes. Bart did a double take on the cubes. They were different but very similar to each other. He flashed on a horror movie he viewed on Netflix. It was the Hellraiser movie piece with the opening of the

Lemarchand puzzle box. An icicle chill went from stem to stern in him. He contained his shiver, barely. The coldness might make it so the ocean froze over, and he would need an icebreaker to clear the way.

"Two gay boxes? Hah! Now that's funny! And?" Macho Maachi was on the loose again. Too bad Bart couldn't use a muzzle on the dog or at least a tranq dart from a blowgun.

"These are not just any gifty-needless-markups boxes. Here, this one's yours and this one's for you, Bart." Peeta was starting to glow-up. This was so not her first bejeweling. Not by a long shot, both literally and figuratively. She played the two of them like cheap out of tune ukuleles.

"Oh boy, hey Bart, do we need to wait for Christmas or something to open these things?" Maachi was lashing out his snake tongue at everyone in the room. Thripppthrippp thripp. A true master of being coarse and vulgar. His blood sugar must be low, and his voluntary recreational meds must be on high.

Bart smiled. Charly smiled. Peeta cast a well-rehearsed obfuscating smile complete with her lovely shiny white pearly teeth. Maachi got caught up in the view of her dents. He fantasized that if he had her down on him, he hoped her luscious lips would be wrapped over her teeth. He wasn't into having his rod spring red leaks. But that was just his private XXX moment that was shaken back to reality when Charly spoke up.

"Gentlemen, if you would open the boxes, please." Her words were like honey-soaked lace and silk. Who wouldn't want to comply? Bart had no problem with the box. The movie visual led him to mimic the hand movements he saw in the video. A whir, a click, but the box did not fully open. Only a hole appeared in the side of the mystical cube. Maachi was fumbling with his gift. His bumbling was all kid-like confusion on how to open a condom packet. He didn't even understand how to manipulate the puzzle even though he watched the manner in which Bart made the hole appear.

To prevent further embarrassment, Peeta floated up from her seat and winged over to the back of Maachi's chair. As though wrapping her feathered wings around him, she gently grabbed his hands and placed his fingers on the appropriate places. She Marilyn Monroe-breathily said, "you have to do this. Not me. Mr. CEO Only you can open it." Her words evaporated as quickly as they were spoken. Maachi was moving his meter to sexy-feral. He thought *ya got that right, who's ready to breed?* Gritty thoughts from a greasy Italian mind and his meatballs were getting swollen at the titillating thought of dominating this babe. A ball in her mouth, ankles silk sash tied, buns up naked and he'd be wheelin' and dealin' with some kinbaku too.

"So Dr. Panicles, is this the right time for family jewel examination? Or not?"

Maachi's box now also had a hole large enough for a finger. Maachi looked at Bart and Bart was looking at Charly for the *dogs to be trained* cue and directions.

"You stick your finger inside the box and just close your eyes and wait for a surprise." Maachi had parked his semi in the gutter. He was thinking he'd like to stick his fingers in her and give her a penetrating surprise. *Wonder if she fishhooks?* He stalled on that thought and hypnotically followed her honey-sweet words and did as he was told.

"*Ouch what the fucking hell was that?*" Maachi howled out his words at the unexpected surprisingly sharp pain. He yanked his finger out and as he did a small amount of finger flesh was torn away. "Jesusmutherfuckinshit, ...what's going on?" He stuck his bleeding finger into his mouth to catch the sweet, metallic liquid.

"That looks tasty, Dr. Panicles. Are you tappin' or is that just a private tasting?" Peeta couldn't resist taking her nicely manicured nail and poking him in the soul with it.

"Shit. Funny girl. What the hell is going on?" Maachi was nursing his finger like a small kid with his thumb in his mouth. The only thing missing was an utterance of *mommy!*

"I'm sorry Dr. Panicles, I don't speak fingerease." Peeta was working the rest of her manicured fingers into his very being. Time to let him know an Alpha Cat trumps an Alpha Dog.

Meanwhile, Bart had left his finger in the box as he stared into Charly's beautiful hazel eyes. Bart could hear some clinkety-clinkety sounds from inside the decorative cube. She nodded her head and Bart got the body language message. *Time to remove finger from hole. Roger that.*

Charly then turned her attention to Maachi, which allowed Peeta to exit the mad dog's vicinity and place herself in the sanctity of the office chair.

"Please don't be concerned. Wait one more moment." It was as though her words coaxed the opening of the top of the boxes. A small door retracted into the wall of each box and a beautiful, perfectly round cut emerald rose up. Quite the show.

"Groovy. Just what I needed. Jewelry. All I need now is to hang a chain, where baggy trousers, and spout rap." Maachi quipped disdain for being given a trinket.

"I hope that you're alright Dr. Panicles? Should I call a nurse or someone to help you with that? Maybe nine one one?" Peeta went from battery powered leaf blower to jet engine blast in less time than it takes to say, *ouch, burn, suck on this.*

"Are you always such a wiseass? Not appreciated. If I want something sucked on or licked, I'll let ya know." Maachi was trying to match her speed. No chance. He was peddling his trike and she was zooming on in an Aston Martin Vanquish. Full throttle.

Peeta and Charly laughed a cute little, *he's so cute, everyone should have one* tweety bird-chirrup. "It's true Dr. Panicles, I do have a very wise ass. Don't I Charly?" She ever so slightly darted her tongue out from between her lips.

Charly unabashedly smiled and twinked a seductive wink.

"And it knows how to do things that are the stuff of wet dreams. And if you think my ass is wise, you would be so lucky to experience the wisdom in my head." Peeta was not a person you messed with. Not at all, never. She was oh-so-over being a complacent female. Confident, bold, and fearless. Not Maachi's preferred internet profile.

He preferred his women with asses that wouldn't quit even when the drugs wore off and never any wise-ass lip.

A cold silence fell upon the office. The coldness pierced through everyone, not just Bart this time. At that moment there was a knock on the door. It was Latika. Good thing. The dialogue was spinning in a diabolical direction. She shyly opened the door and peeked her head in. "Would anyone like a hot beverage? Coffee? Tea? Or Water?"

"How very kind of you, Latika. It's Latika, right?" Peeta started to shift her attention from just clapping back at Maachi. She full body slammed him on the conference table with a loud, *Are you kidding me? Did that really happen?* slammeroni. Maachi was on the table like a limp, splooting sausage and he didn't fully realize that he would need more than industrial strength intravenous Viagra to get back into this game of words.

"Yes, Latika. That's correct. May I get something for you?" Latika faintly blushed at the focused benevolent attention. A true rarity in Maachi's office.

"I'll speak for myself and Charly. No coffee for us. Tea would be simply lovely. And if you could put a dab of honey in it, that would be great. If not, sugar is fine. Do you have organic?" Peeta went from balls to the wall to a friendly kitty that purred musical words.

"Yeah, we have organic sugar. We also have organic clover honey, manuka honey, and agave. The manuka is from New Zealand. What's your preference? We're pretty cosmopolitan around here. We even have indoor plumbing." Maachi was scratching his way back into the quip filled dialogue. If only he had a grappling hook. He surely needed it. Outclassed in the first and second round of an unlimited rounds tete-a-tete.

"I'll leave it to your choice Latika. I'm sure you have good taste."

Maachi sported a slimy smile at the thought of Latika's honey taste.

"Darjeeling would be superb if you have it. Not fussy though. Thank you very much." Peeta was purring away and totally ignored Captain Crass.

Bart was in a state of delighted shock. He didn't show it, but he was loving the moment. He was in love. She wasn't just beautiful, she was a jade eyed, red haired warrior queen.

"Bart and I will have lattes, Lati. No sugar. Stevia, and not a lot of it. You always put too much in. Go easy." Maachi the ever so nouveau pedestrian with sophomoric commentary.

They waited until Latika returned before diving back into the particulars of the meeting. Latika couldn't help but notice the large emeralds standing guard over the boxes. She made a point to not stare at them.

"Bart, Dr. Panicles, the gems are yours to keep. Could you remove them from the boxes please?" Peeta kept her engine warm. She was a kitty cobra queen who ate her prey in one gulp and spit them out or swallowed depending upon how good they tasted.

Maachi took the emerald off of its perch and started twirling it on its pin post as though it were green rock candy on a stick. Bart just held it and looked at it. He was hypnotized by the quality of the cut. An *amazingly beautiful* thought cleaved his eyes in fascination as he very covertly slid a surreptitious coy wink towards Peeta. She didn't look directly back at him. She gently touched the corner of her right eye and kicked out a very subtle twitch Bart's way. *Love the body language.* Bart covetously thought to himself.

"Big deal. A green rock on a gold stick. I'll put it with my Cartier panther cufflinks." The whir of Maachi's dialogue revved and spooled up to hover above them all. Like a seagull pooping on a recently washed car. He was yet again sticking his ass out. An inviting target for Peeta to lop off.

"Dr. Panicles it's far more than a verdant stone on a stick. That poke you felt and fed blood to was a sample of your DNA. It's being coded and transmitted from the box to Utah. We keep a sample from our athletes and associates, in fact all of the lovely people I work with have had their DNA sampled and retained. For you and Mr. Henderson it enables us to positively identify you if the need should arise." Peeta slid the red-juice, drippy words off her tongue and through her lips to Maachi's and Bart's ears.

"What do you mean when you say *if the need should arise?* It sounds pretty fucking ominous. Did you also take out life insurance policies on us, just in case?" More endearing words from Maachi's wise cracking adobe lips.

"Why would you think something of that nature? No, we believe that DNA matching to ensure identity is not just a fad. It's a reality. And, I need to mention that if something untoward should develop, the jeweled pin is also a transponder that transmits your location and your vitals. Nice package. Would you agree?" She stated as she did a very sensual feminine waist twist to the right to look at Bart.

"How would you know all this with the pin in my link box?" Maachi was now slipping far behind in the dialogue. He was running a three-legged sack race with just his own three legs. He was in last place at this moment and the other participants had rounded the final turn.

"Well, that would be a challenge, wouldn't it? Now that you are an Emerald One Star Diamond Associate, you'll need to have the jewel with you every time you venture out to join an adventurous excursion." Peeta had turned her head back to Maachi as she dialed up the therms in her heat vision.

"Very funny. You think I'm gonna add weight to my gear-up? Don't you know that ounces lead to pounds and pounds lead to pain?" He parried with an almost related comment. Very irrelevant because the jewel weighed less than a couple of rounds of ammo. It was typical dog rationale that made little sense but was offered up as faux reasonable support. No winnah winnah chickin' dinner yet. The bird was still defrosting on the counter.

"It's your choice to have it on you or not. But if you don't have it on you, you won't be able to participate in the soirees. It's as simple as that. We all have investments in this remarkable business opportunity. Speaking on behalf of the company, we just want to make sure you're safe and we can assist you before you may realize you need the help. Your choice. Pin and play or don't and stay. And this is not a discussion about the merits of our ways. You either do it or you don't. No pinny, no playee. And, Dr. Panicles, pain should be of little concern to you. You do manufacture all types of interesting potions, powders, and pills, yes?" Slam, bam, hit him in the head, thank you ma'am. Peeta just delivered another full body slam right through the canvas and on down one floor below.

Maachi went all stainless steely eyed. The only wise crack he wanted from her was between her legs.

"So we dress up with the pin on our covert dates. Not a bad idea at all. I'm okay with this Maachi. I really am. It's way better than getting chipped like a woofer. And we don't have to wear a bracelet or collar. Having them know where we are, and our vitals is pretty hot damn cool. Tech rules." Bart was all in. And he definitely wanted to connect with Peeta to get the skinny on the box. It was just too weird. Which came first, the horror movie or the company?

"Another one on you Captain Bart. If this goes swirling down in flames, it's on you. Got my drift biff?" Maachi demonstrated his remarkable delegation skills.

"Okay by me. I'll take that responsibility on." Bart quickly responded.

"The pin has been paired to each of your unique bioelectric profiles." Peeta was ready to depart. She had her entertainment for the day. Bart was cute and fun. Maachi was simply oily, predictable, and disgusting. The mere thought of him touching her made her skin want to retract into her gut to be cleansed by digestion and shit out her butt.

"Charly, our plane is most likely on the tarmac. Could you secure text them that we're on our way?" Peeta was now on an outgoing roll. She played with the mouse, got it all excited, and left it with blue balls, excuse me, an emerald jewel. If in another scenario, she would tease the mouse more to raise its arousal levels, just before she, … killed it and brought back home as a trophy kill. Excited mice are tastier with fear hormones loose.

"Will do Peeta." Charly happily tapped at her phone with lovely mauve-colored real nails. "Done and done."

"Dr. Panicles and Bart, it was a real slice of nice. Thank you for accommodating us on such short notice. Just think of the business you're building! Incredible! Isn't it?" Peeta wanted to cap this session of who's the brightest bulb in the chandelier. Lights out and time to get a move on. Maachi pretty much had his dick handed to him. He was not a happy penis boy. A shrunken unit was his to own.

Bart stood up and said, "I'll see you to the lobby, ladies. We very much appreciate the visit."

"How very gentlemanly of you, Bart. It's nice to see that chivalry and respect are alive in Georgia. Well, alive, yes, but on life support." Peeta fleetingly looked over her shoulder at Maachi. The glance was her opportune chance to see if Maachi had any type of situational awareness at all.

Per usual, his dismissive genes were highly upregulated. He had already moved on from the smackdown he just experienced. There was no question he was uncomfortable with the meeting. He should be. Medium-sized frogs in a small pond rule. Medium sized frogs in an ocean of deception and mystery end up being one-gulp lunch.

Maachi had already returned to his monitors and resumed engaging his dark ADHD with the shiny little lights on flat pieces of plastic and wires. He tapped one of the monitors and it responded by enlarging the image. A salacious, debauched lizard-lipped smile stretched almost from ear to ear. He quickly picked up his phone, tapped it few times and held it to his uncuffed wrist. The smile went wider and wrapped all the way around his head. He leaned back and closed his eyes.

His actions were covertly viewed by Peeta. She smiled a mile too, shrugged, and turned her pretty head back towards Bart.

"It appears that your co-CEO is the willing victim of technology. Too bad he doesn't realize that all that he's viewing is not truly real. Just flattened images that trap your mind, and if you are so disposed, your body. *Use the left hand Maachi with lots of Überlube, it'll feel like someone else,* she sarcastically thought

"Life is *lived* in real time; real life is filled with more than just interesting visuals. Would you agree Bart?"

Bart's face had scrambled microexpressions dancing across it. He was speechless, in a good way. The mind works very quickly in thought time. Good thing or they could be standing there for days.

A complete portfolio of imaginary scenarios blazed across his inner vision movie screen. He connected the actions as little dots of passionate light together wishing what he would like to have happen.

"Bart, a bitcoin for your thoughts."

"Oh, sorry, was caught up in a bunch of business stuff in my head. Rude of me."

"It's all good. Your rudeness borders on enjoyable after my recent interaction." A wink- wink-winky-wink left lipped smile dashed across the short distance from her face to Bart's eyes.

"I want to make sure you're not late for your plane. How about if we get a move on to your car?"

"I like that idea. A gentleman who respects sharing time with others and perceives their needs. Nice touch Mr. Georgia Peachy Southern Gentleman."

Bart opened the door and held his arm out with an extended hand.

"Ladies, ..."

Peeta looked at Charly and tilted her head with the slightest of mesmerizing hair flossy toss.

They looked at Maachi and in charming unison said, "Thanks Dr. Panicles for the hospitality."

Without respectfully looking up, Maachi went neolithic and dismissively squeezed a few distant words from his being, into his throat, through his larynx.

"Yeah. Great. We need to do this again, ... sometime." Like fuckin' hell, he hot-darkly thought.

"Oh, I'm sure that in one way or another, we shall." Peeta pearled a smile, Charly didn't.

Charly never was first cabin great at hiding her true feelings. She did her best but at times like this, the cute, furry kitty lets just a hint of a *fuck you* malevolent purr take over. A passion pressure vent that ported just enough enmity out to keep the power blast of being insulted fester a bit longer inside.

"Bart we'll follow *the* leader." Her implied thought was not lost on Bart.

Bart-boy cast a squinkly nervous look at Maachi. His inner careful boy, *poke the bear, get teeth and claws in the rear.* He was hoping to calm the kid inside by ensuring that Maachi was not hearing the slap happy repartee.

Great idea.

"Terrific. Before we go, would you like for Latika to have some to-go drinks for you?"

They walked through the opened door and let it close behind them before Charly responded.

"You really are a sweetie. That won't be necessary though. The car is well-provisioned with some lovely beverages and a few other recreational items. Ingestible and other. But you do have that impressive tacphone so some of the fun designer things may be of little interest. Maybe you should join us for the ride to the airport. We can have the driver bring you back to the office."

"Hmmm, well, ... the phone. I accidentally left it in Maachi's office."

"Naughty boy you are. Accidentally?" Charly went from the malevolent purr to a borderline passionate meow.

Brain chill, brain defrost, Bart was getting lost in the inviting wet jungle of Peeta and Charly. That was a good thing. Which way to go? He didn't truly know. His mind raced while his lips stumbled.

"The invitation is quite enticing. I think that due to time constraints I need to get back to my office. So many issues, so little time."

"The invitation has no expiration date." Peeta went Venus flytrap and clamped down on the adolescent in Bart. He couldn't see the floral fangs that were entrapping him.

He smiled and just began walking towards the elevator. It was a very quiet and focused walk. Bart was behind the magically moving seductresses. Every step they took was the finest of living art in motion.

Only the sounds of the clippityclop, thud thud, and cloc-cloc of shoes percussed through the tile entryway as the ladies from Utah took their leave and exited through the frosty etched glass doors. They didn't hustle away, though. They turned and faced Bart and practiced their art of synchronous alluring body language expression.

Peeta and Charly shook their pretty little heads in Bart's direction with a *c'mon boy, whatcha waitin' for?* look.

Barty was conflicted. Of course, he was after all a Georgia boy. Go with the goddesses or stay with Lucifer.

Freeze frame.

Bart took a slow gaze around the entryway. Thoughts of being videoed all the time ran through his head like a frightened fox during a hound led hunt.

He shook his head, left to right, ever so slight, so as to not alert his intent to the world of electrons and in-perpetuity, imbedded in the electronic Akashic record of the digital age, plutonium lethality.

The devas from another state went from eager to have him accompany us to a quasi-dramatic, downtrodden look of pinkness, *wish you were here."*

Art in motion they were as the slowly stepped down to the car.

They stalled, just for the briefest of moments and turned to look back at Bart. Final offer, take it or leave it Barty boy. The best magical gifts from the universe sometimes do come enticingly and intoxicatingly wrapped in drippy animus. They were so sexy oozy that Bart might have to have the hall floors where they walked scrubbed down.

He regarded their scent as an offering to revel in life as a free soul.

They once more raised their eyebrows with the come play with us look.

Bart did a half eyelash shutter whiplash.

He opened to door and exited the building.

The driver opened Bart's door as he slid out of the car seat.

Bart ascended the entry steps and looked up at the building and keyed his phone. *What's with the puzzle box? Are you a female Hellraiser or what?'* All that appeared on his phone in response was a smiling purple devil emoji.

Well, he thought if *this was hell, hell ain't a bad place to be.*

He stared at the monitors. He wasn't surprised. Well, a small amount of surprise, yes.

Maachi looked at the phone left on the corner of the conference table and though, *Stupid shit.* Not only does he forget his phone AGAIN, but he jumps into the pussies of those two fucking, nasty Utah hussies, knowing I've got more cams then all the Best Buys in Georgia.

Motherfucking dumb asshole!

Maachi put on his Bose headphones and turned up the volume. He wanted to hear every word. Right down to breathy-breaths from Bart.

And of course, study the expressions down to the micro level.

Every face tells a story, everybody tells an epic.

Chapter 29: Does Everyone in the World Have to Die?

Maachi and Bart had their choices of arenas and playgrounds of pain, suffering, and the discretionary end to human life all for the thrill and benefits of being in a global MLM that compensated its associates and business builders with an ever more complex set of enticing perks and intoxicating earnings. The company was quite successful in transforming pure, unadulterated greed into a fine, well-aged liquor. Gon bay!

The two of them trotted from hot spot to hot spot and were treated as rising stars they were. They walked upon the fiery coals of urban destruction and anguish and would make Tony Robbins proud about how they could dance on flames for hours and days. They racked up points for kills with minimal collateral damage that could have seriously dinged their point totals. They had the money to go wherever there was an opportunity to lever their skills and drug induced delight. DC, Philadelphia, the ever-in-turmoil Portland, and a number of lesser-publicized venues. They were Emerald Single Diamonds, they had license to thrill and kill.

The tumult in DC over the election process was a fertile area for their gamesmanship. Caution though was called for in the political mess there. Security for the politicos and wannabes was always extremely present. The mash up among BLM, Antifa, Proud Boys, and an assortment of angry groups was an earthly garden of death, and the boys took advantage of the confrontations. The only reason to have power over life and death was to coldly use it.

The venues were like Olympic sport open-range arenas. The athletes could increase their scores by deliberately selecting more, rather than less, challenging itineraries. The scoring was for difficulty and execution. Kind of like a very bloody reverse 1½ somersault with 4½ twists off the 3-meter board dive into a five-gallon bucket with piranhas, baby sharks, and lampreys. In 1N HCl water.

Literal operational definitions for both of the factors. Going to DC was a challenging environs and how the athletes performed there was captured in who and how they offed to enhance the body count. They chalked up tasty points and moved up the leaderboard like the pros they had become. They both scored very high but of course Maachi was the point master.

Bart was no fool. El Hefe *always* had to be the winner, Mr. Number One. Bart had no desire to do anything that would force Maachi to constantly dwell and burn on. After the meeting with Peeta and Charly though, there was a rift, a rip in the emotional tides of Maachi. Bart knew that getting caught in any Maachi riptide could be the essence of the word deadly.

All the athletes who were considered to be promising prospects started out in the easier locus of the loci. This limited the potential for inadvertent, random events to occur to the participants and the risk of exposure to the company.

Portland was always a great proving ground for newbies. And now with the decriminalization of cocaine, shrooms, and other drugs on the billet of law enforcement, it made it an even easier place to increase the body counts and points. While those guidelines were not yet completely embedded in law, it was a loud and clear signal to LE that prosecutors would not seek to be punitive. Drugged out people can get *lost* and become the departed simply due to their habits. It's a rare event indeed for a missing person's report to be filed for the lost ones. The addicts are highly disposable people, and they hang out with their ilk that have similar self-destructive desires and habits. Those genres of people do not often visit police stations to report a missing person or any crime for that matter. Law enforcement has more important things to do than go hunting for a vanished druggie. They had riots and other peaceful demonstrations to attend to. With the lack of civil support from the mayors and councilpersons, they only focused upon the most dire and egregious illegal activities. Murder, rape, and violent physical assaults had become the range of societal disruptions they drilled into. The city leaders and unfortunately, the general populace, supported such events as the looting and torching of properties. The massive, jagged edge of involuntary wealth redistribution cut large holes in the livelihoods of thousands of law-abiding citizens. No gift wrapping required. With the exception of the occasional zippered, twenty mil vinyl, leak proof body bag. Designer editions cost extra.

The property damage was regarded as expected collateral and insurance would cover the losses so no big deal. Kind of, and not sort of. The urban thought was it was *only* a building. Regardless of whether the buildings were public or private. Inhabited or not. Even if the business represented the life work of a struggling legal immigrant entrepreneur made no difference.

There are always hidden repercussive damages. Like waves of the most egregious violence, poverty would be dominant. When the insurance funds are paid out, the distant effects become front and center. Fastly and not slowly. The insurance companies are not in commerce to be philanthropic business entities. They simply raise rates and cite the ongoing costs of business and intentional destruction. The insured pay more to get less in the twisted financial model.

The more adventurous company business builders went to such delightful hotspots as Nagorno-Karabakh. A venue that was only accessible to the most status-elevated associates and gem holders. The heavily armed clashes meant that they could tap into the additional tools and toys that the company proudly and profitably had to offer. The accessorization included uniforms of both sides of the conflict. Only the best of the best made the choice of entering into such a melting pot of death. Highest points were awarded to offing those that were on the uniformed same side. The company rewarded well executed fragging by means other than a grenade.

All forms of associate identification were collected and held until the engaging bloody entrepreneurs returned to their respective roosts. Passports, drivers licenses, phones, anything with a traceability risk was placed in physical escrow. The one exception was the use of tacphones. The more common smartphones were the threads that could be easily tracked. Not so for tacphones. Heavy duty encryption was the master of the technology. In some situations, the company required tats to be removed or made indistinguishable from the original images. Unusual birthmarks were lasered.

Fingerprint removal was discretionary, per the choice of the company.

The beauty of being in the middle of the flames was that the yellow-sashed cleaners were not needed. All that was required to obtain qualifying points were the cam videos of the events. Having to engage the yellow sashed contractors in those areas of violent ethnic and political rivalry would have been highly problematic. Very Indian-looking folks mingling with the locals would be like adding first pressing extra virgin olive oil to balsamic vinegar with no emulsifier. The two just don't mix and in short order separate. The big idea of the athletes and business builders was to go unnoticed. The same was true of the cleaners. The cleaners did their best work in the US. But the company was working on the acquisition of new assets that could be effective cleaners in other countries. A growing and very profitable business needs to adapt to the local habits, trappings, and circumstances to continue its progress. Successful species are always able to quickly modify their behaviors to new situations. Morlocks don't sit on their laurels. They sit on thrones of bleached bones. Sharks always swim forward and Morlocks are the sharks of the land.

In the US, the dramatic misunderstanding by the rioters and progressive sorts was that federal buildings were on the list of potential targets and were no different than toasting a Wal*Mart, corner store, Nordstrom's, or local constabulary facility. Just as rioters change their approach to attain their goals, so does law enforcement. This was the case in Portland when the US Marshals deputized other law enforcement colleagues. Federal judges and not the local talent who turned two blind eyes to destructive events would prosecute those types of illegal activities.

The charges and repercussions of a federal arrest were more severe than the local ordinances would allow. It was Wyatt Earp acting as a federal marshal and not a local tin star appointed sheriff. The local DAs were catch and release oriented and they made that perspective very clear. The police in those burgs just didn't bother with lesser crimes of arson and looting. They were told right from the get-go that those deviants would not be prosecuted. The marshals had a very different charge d'affaires and proceeded accordingly.

So why bother to arrest? Simply hold the line against more egregious events like murders and assaults on police officers. What else could they do? The Democrat governed cities were in the process of further inhibiting law enforcement from acting in cities such as Portland and Seattle by no longer allowing lesser nonlethal tools such as chemical irritants. Chemical dispersants and such were *persona non grata*. It was beyond Thunderdome, and the rioters had no rules but the folks in blue had their hands strapped with double two-loop zip tie handcuffs. They had to just shrug off the fiery insults, the bombardment with feces and bottles of urine, the projectile sputum, and assorted other instruments such as high-grade fireworks. One would have thought that spitting on police officers during a pandemic would be akin to years ago having AIDS and throwing your blood on people or biting them. Spewing virus particles is the same as using a bioweapon in close quarters. But then again, the police in the eyes of some local governments are both expendable and unnecessary. How unfortunate.

Chapter 30: Undead

"So glad you're out of the hospital. I was getting majorly edgy over you being in there. I knew you'd recover from the beat down, but I really wanted you out of the coronavirus breeding ground in the Red Cross hot zone. That's where all the major virus shredders go, and hospitals are not really very good at limiting nosocomial infections. And I brought you a bag of goodies for your ouchy bruises. Some Emergen-C Tangerine, pycnogenol, and nattokinase." Tannin compassionately shared with Aidan.

Aidan just nodded. Aidan's grandparents always stated that if you want to die, just go to a hospital. That's where the sickest of the sick go and hope the one foot on the banana peel is in stall mode. Both of them passed away in their home one after another. Their bond was tight, and the marital relationship was so strong that their spirits were resolute that they lived *for* each other. When one was gone the other had no further reason to live. They held the belief that they would connect again on the other side of the mysterious veil of life and death. If the Indian view of the soul were true, then they would dance in the cosmos as constellations of embracing stars.

"I had the ME dig out the bullets from the four thugs who ate dirt near you. Those slugs, or what was left of the fragged pieces, were not *our* standard issue. They weren't even nonstandard issue. The stuff they dug out was the same kind of munitions we've seen used by perps focusing upon death by contract. And it wasn't just a well-placed grouping. It was like a lead fire hose. Overkill is stating it lightly." Tannin had that look on his face of something very wicked is afoot here. And he didn't know what it was. But he was determined to find out.

"Tannin, your left eye is doing that twitching thing. I don't like it when that happens. It's that distant early warning microexpression that you're going to pop with some Inspector Clouseau epiphany. And what I really

179

don't like about the twitch is that your itch is almost always spot on and needs a scratching. Me thinks you're going the way of mad, mad focus here. What are you saying? That someone had it in for these guys? Look, maybe it was just one of those serendipitous events where a rival gang took advantage and leveled the playing field. They just decided to become reapers and then not be accused of scything." Aidan offered a more levelheaded logical rationale for the four bodies with no motive for the killings other than gang warfare.

"Nice try buddy. Not buying it. Here are the pieces. You're getting stomped out of existence by four totally zonked out guys who were pumped on something more than street stuff. We found envelopes in their pockets with the most bizarre image stamped on them. They had a bald guy's head with nails in it. Never saw that before. The pills were even more weird. On each purple pill was an emoji devil's head. We labbed the stuff and we don't really know what it is.

During your beat down the road to death, along comes Santa and one of his elves to help you out. They drill these guys like they're fracking for natural gas. Not a bullet or two. Those four guys went into a rinse cycle. They dropped over and bleed out, quickly, I might add. Then we get a distress call of officer down and we need to go pronto with first responders. We arrive at the scene and two guys all kitted up are vanishing into the distance and flashing four fingers. That's not a rival gang. That's either a contract hit, which makes no sense or something more invidious." Tannin was now with wrinkled brow and mild derision in his voice. His eye was twitching like a dysfunctional neon light flickering in the night. Maybe they should be speaking Cenobite and have subtitles.

"Tannin, Tannin, Tannin, c'mon. It still could have been a gang scrub thing." Aidan was not agreeing that there were bigger, badder, meaner snakes on the loose.

"Oh, sure. And the two heavily armed gang bangers called in a man down radio zap. Why would they do that? Gang bangers hate rival gangs *and* law enforcement. Why would they reach out and put themselves in the midst of the act to be potentially exposed? Not gonna happen. My Occam's Razor is sharper and more to the edge than your plastic spork." Tannin was getting a bit irritated with Aidan's cludgework orange. He was not in the mood to debate what he viewed as connectivity. Randomness is not so random. Even randomness has a set cadence and pattern. He just needed to connect the dots like he always does. Connect the dots and then step back and view the image. This image had hidden images behind it.

"Aidan, there's no such thing as pure serendipity. Everything is connected. Our job is to determine the connectivity and act upon it. We get our puppy chow by boxing in the badness in people. We don't get paid to debate issues. We reconnoiter, we act, and we're decisive about it. How many folders have you and I worked on that were dry? Zero. Let me state that again, a big *zero*. You and I are Earp and Holliday. I have the vision and you have the messiah complex and believe you could walk on water with burning oil on top." Tannin was fueling up his commentary and preparing to unleash snappy repartee metaphors like little yappy dogs chewing on Aidan's pant leg.

"Tannin, I can walk on water. Watch." With that Aidan poured out his bottle of water on the carpeted floor and walked across it. "See?" He stated as he broke into belly-shake laughter. His quaint attempt at expanding upon a scene in the movie Tombstone. They both loved that movie.

"You stupid shit. That cavalier attitude will be your undoing if you're not really careful. Even ceramic plates can't stop every weapon." Tannin countered. True logic is important but doesn't account for protective angelic forces. Aidan bet on the support of a righteous universe while Tannin was a complete trust and verify human machine. Tannin's slicing always went first principle logic. He ripped up the pieces and then glued them back together again to create a tapestry of events. A fully woven set of threads that divulged the course of events with surgical accuracy and precision. He was a savant of the law enforcement discovery arts. Sometimes Aidan thought he was more of an idiot savant. Regardless, Tannin coupled with Aidan, were flawless in the execution of their actions. They were bolts of lightning that were heavenly-ordained, precision two legged munitions Crusaders. They took the Royal Mounted Police slogan and applied it to themselves. Tannin and Aidan always fetched their man, woman, or whatever gender bent being term was in vogue. They never failed.

"Oh, one more thing. I forgot to mention. During the riots the eyes in the sky were watching everything. I obtained the imaging from our dear friends. And here is another flying insect in the potpourri. I ran the zoom in and out for the area. Played back the vids several times. So check this piece out Sherlock. Right about the time we arrived on scene, shortly thereafter, a stealthed fast boat was nearby on the Delaware. You had to really study the images. It was an ink fish. So dark it looked like it absorbed all the light. It was a bubble on the water. It was motionless in the river and then it jacked up its motors, paused at the riverbank and then bolted out like the proverbial water bat out of aqueous hell. And guess what the eye revealed? Two guys emerging from the shallow water and catching a ride. How do you explain that *Mr. Things Just Kind of Happen*? Another serendipitous happenstance thingy? It had no numbers on it and the only folks that have technicals like that are the elite military and extreme covert ops." Tannin was now full-bore on to make his point. He would have to conclusively make his case to Aidan so that they could go forward and get permission to start pulling on the loose threads. Strip the clothes off the beast so see what lurks within. Only the fabric knows for sure at this time juncture.

"Look, Tannin, let's say, and I am being benign here, that the events are connected. What's your big idea for motive? Can't have murders without bodies, and we do have four bodies which means a motive is under the carpet hiding with the evil killer dust bunnies. I showed up with my motive. What's yours? Hit me with your illuminati logic. It's smarter gang players offing lesser gang members for territory. What other motive is there?" Aidan countered with a very logical point. If there were bodies and no perps or motives, then this set of nasty circumstances was on the bottom of the to-do list. But they did have bodies and that's a piece of clue matter that Tannin could use to get permission to go bad and nationwide. The four chillin' in the morgue popsicles were real and very tangible. Tannin and Aidan just needed to shake down the pieces and identify the perps who committed the acts. The two passers-by in the night were the placeholders for suspects. The mysterious dark boat was a piece to toss to their superiors. If some drug cartel was using occluded stealth boats, that was of great concern. The drugs they found tied in some big money-making big deals who were not being appreciative of competitors. Or something like that. It was as good a stretch as they could create. It would be enough to give them a pass to go state hopping.

"Maybe, just maybe, what if we leave the degrees of freedom open on that part. The bandwidth is gang bangers with intent or way on the other side, and this is a taffy stretch, they could be some kind of ronin LE runnin' crew with a cartel.

"You and I let's go détente. You are immovable here and I am going to be the irresistible. Humor me; indulge me, just for a small slice in time. Work with me on the threads and let's see what we can find. What else have you got to do? We're pretty much in the same bucket as the local LE in that we can only do so much in those fucked up urban maelstroms. Sure, we can observe and provide solid tactical and strategic support for our colleagues and deputize to ensure *Maintiens Le Droit*. But that's a part time job at best. Let's go poke around and see what we can find. Whaddya say boi, in our out?" Tannin wanted to cap the dialogue and move to action. Usually it was the other way around.

Aidan was usually the one who presented the seductive call to action. Tannin, in reciprocal, was the one who was the immovable and insisted to be steadfast until a pile o' facts were in a large dump truck. Or five. Typically, Tannin was the potential and Aidan was the kinetic.

But even the planetary poles reverse upon occasion. Human beings are not immune to emotional pole changes.

"I always humor you, Tannin. You're a funny guy. Inside I laugh at you. On the outside I also laugh at you. So what's the call Officer Legal Shot Caller? What's next?" Aidan grinningly acquiesced.

"Let's book a ride to Portland. It's an active burg and that hotbed will have hidden sharps. Let's go find them. Bet we can find cookie crumb drug packets with a guy with nails in his head." Tannin pushed his fact-gathering agenda.

"Like I said, you're really a quirky, humorous guy. And then what?" Aidan pounced back in a last hit to corner his partner.

"If I knew that I wouldn't be flapping my lips at you. We'd go find clues. I really think they're there. We're social fire inspectors. We need to find out the accelerants that started the blazing conflagration of lawlessness and see if there is something far more under the hot bed. Let's just start there. Agreed?" Tannin wanted to obtain a mutual agreement not just a cajoling to force Aidan to go along for the ride.

"Agreed in a guardedly nonoptimistic way. Okay, I'll play. But if we don't have anything after a few days we go book some time off in in Puerta Vallarta. Bargained kind of well and done. I'll get packed up today, bandages meds and all the accessory items. Anyway, the trajectory Portland is on we may be able to practice our perishable skills, with or without the permission of the local talent." Aidan totally folded with a sarcastic smile on his lips.

"Done deal. Let's plan on jetting tomorrow dark thirty." Tannin had a laurel wreath upon his head that was only visible in his mind's eye. No victory lap yet.

Chapter 31: Gravity

"My dear sweet, adbhut patnee, I have to travel for work. I will be gone for about a week or so. I need to go to the west coast. I will be accompanied by my aadhyaatmik bhaiyon. Please forgive me for leaving you even for this short period of time." Bubai lovingly shared with his divine earthly consort.

"I understand. We need the money to help us get out of the situation we are in with Cantank Rus. I sorely miss you already. Where will you be going?" She inquired with a very sincere tinge of sadness in her voice. An inner tear ran down to her soul.

"Please understand the nature of my work is private. I cannot even share with you the details. I pledged an oath of secrecy to my brothers. We can only speak of our work amongst each other." Bubai further shared.

"This has me concerned. We have always shared everything. Complete openness. But you are my husband and I honor your wishes and your commitments. Can you text me when you are there?" Her heartfelt soft plea to maintain the integrity of the thread between them reached out and traversed time and space.

"Of this I cannot do. They will take my phone from me when I meet with them at the airport. My heart sheds tears that I cannot speak with you about any of the details. I hope you will think kindly of my quietness and regard it with benevolence and understanding." He offered up a fragment of yet another resolutely closed door to his actions.

"I trust you with my heart and soul. I trust Kali to keep you safe. You need to do what is required. You are a man and must own your destiny. Please take care and chant to Kali. She will protect you. She protects *us*." Bubai looked deeply into the eyes of his living goddess. He rubbed his hands clockwise three times and then placed them on either side of Latika's head.

He held his thumbs to her temples and softly stroked them. Bubal's energy penetrated her lotus. He chanted in a low-tone whisper. *Om Maha Kalyai Ca Vidmahe Smasana Vasinyai Ca Dhimahi Tanno Kali Prachodayat.*

His gaze met hers and a spark of spiritual light ignited between them. It was black and then turned red in luminous loveliness. She began chanting in perfect cadence with her husband. They continued to utter the godly words and as they did so their voices became louder more vibrant. Not as two voices but as one. The mantra harmonics radiated throughout the room and sonically drenched every molecule. They were now engaged in a joyful, transcendent trataka.

As they continued to chant the merged melodious sounds to the Goddess Kali, they lost their sense of self. They were becoming louder and more emphatic when their door snapped open just a sliver and four inquiring bright eyes looked in. Baku and Saadhaka slowly enlarged the small opening to a portal. They tip toed quietly and entered the room. Their higher pitched voices harmonized with their parents'. The shiny, soulful glowing ethereal crystal went from red to light blue and then on to become a blinding, brilliant, deep cerulean. It pulsed brightness and became more lustrous with each repetition of the chant. They could all see the bright blue light within their beings.

Latika could feel the chant rise up with joy in the core of her soul. She felt vibrant, rich, and protected. *Everything will be fine. Balance will be attained,* she confidently thought to herself.

Bubai felt her thoughts through the beams in her eyes. He smiled and then kissed her. And then kissed her again. Baku and Saadhaka looked at each other and cutely blushed at the amorous moment.

After dinner, she went to the bedroom and noticed that Bubai had already packed his bag. The top was open, and she saw a very unusual black jump suit and a yellow sash. A large question mark bubble appeared above her head. She had committed to trusting her beloved husband, so she did not mention the odd clothing.

Chapter 32: Monsters

"Could you check again? They're gone. It just isn't like 'em." Andell passionately shared with the disinterested, monolithic desk Sergeant.

"Kid, I've already looked *three* times. I'm telling you that we don't have anything on your friends. Did you check the local hospitals for Does? Good place to start. Maybe also try online, maybe some social media note has popped up." The Sergeant responded.

"Ya know, you're not the only ones who are trying to find someone. With all the minnies and the marys running around like it's Halloween every day, we're trying to play softball, and everyone is showing up in full contact football gear with nails in hockey sticks and they've made this job far more difficult. Even if some of you yahoos are beating each other up, we pretty much are at a stand down." He stated in a very clear, metaphoric manner. His frustration was mounting. For the Sergeant it was like being in a box and all the sides kept closing in. And there were no cheat codes, time outs, or free parking moments. There never are. Life happens and does its thing and pesky humans have little impact on the universe except to believe they have power over their free will. Being the professional he always told himself he was, he restrained his emotions and played straight talk.

"Look, we've checked every day since they went missing. No-go. Nothing at the hospitals. We also thought maybe they were dead and, in the morgue, but we couldn't find anything there either. Please, please, could you check one more time? *Please!*" Pleaded Andell.

"No. I won't check again. Kid, we're real busy here and one of the reasons we're busy, as I've already shared with you, is because of you and that roving band of peaceful demonstrators kicking my officers in the nuts and claiming not your fault that their nuts got in the way of your booties. I have all kinds of goofy reports coming in. Have had a steady stream for weeks. I even have some really wacked out reports of some guys in Japanese black ninja suits with yellow belts in the mix picking up bodies. We have all kinds of folks here and I don't want to light a match and create some kind of ethnic witch-hunt. All I need is to have the Japanese say we are targeting them and unjustly stating they were in the poo here.

"Did you check Washington, Clackamas, or Hood River? Hospitals have been in a pile of broken bodies and may have shipped your buds off to a nearby county. You should give that a try.

"And take a big ass note here, we are in the middle of a pandemic and my officers have to wear masks and the other team? Not so much. You know how it goes. When bat-shit crazy is let loose people claim UFOs, green monkeys from the evil witch, and conspiracy theories galore. Us folks here have a saying. *If I have no facts I can't work on hunches.* If I can't find people, it's almost always because the folks I should be looking for have disappeared under their own power. And right now, again, and again, I have more than just the two of you looking for the two or more of whomever. Every time there's a protest that goes hot, missing persons, overdoses, murders go up and max out against the previous year. Ya' know, the craziest thing, I heard a rumor from more than a couple of my guys, they swear that they saw some muzzle flashes on top of more than a couple buildings. What the hell do ya' make of that? For us, we don't make anything of it cuz' we got no bodies. No body? No deady.

"I'll ask you again, could they have just skipped town to be on the chaos train to another *oh so peaceful* demonstration?" The Sergeant was now truly losing his patience. His thoughts were that these creeps in front of him want to defund his officers and then out of the other side of their pie holes they plead for help. *Maybe I should ask them to go get a social worker and not waste my time here.* He kept those thoughts to himself. He really didn't want to be on the police purge list from the liberal governance folks. He liked his job pretty much and wanted to keep it even if it did mostly have some really sucky moments. It was a paycheck and he liked getting those electronic notes that his bank account had more funds in it than yesterday.

"Write their names and a short description down on this pad. And your contact info. If I see anything that looks close, I'll shout out. Okay? Now can you do us a favor here and let us focus on our cop stuff?" The officer wanted to bring this to a friendly *no* closure but not in a way as to jeopardize his job. He had a little over a year more on the force and he could retire. The whole *fix-this-and-that* in the house thing, the *honey-dos*, the disconnect the alarm from his phone happy dance, and the most internally destructive thing turned off – the stress of his job of *things and contradictions* would be oh so history. That feeling that you believe you're in control of parts of your life only to find out that your cheese was moved and eaten by some humanoid rodent with zero notice. And they even took the refrigerator that held the cheese. He needed about one more year and then the citizenry that was slashing and burning would be far away. A temporary storm that consumed itself in self-immolated rage.

An easily forgotten toxic long day, and troublesome nightmare. A memory and not a good one.

Chapter 33: No. 5

"Nice to meet you guys. Real pleasure. We'll scarf up all the help we can get. Hey, by the way, where are you guys out of?" Captain D'spain politely asked.

"We didn't. But since you asked, Camp Beauregard, Louisiana." Aidan answered playfully with a fried catfish drawl. Tannin cleared his throat and hid his smirk. He thought to himself, *Aidan you're about as southern as Groton Connecticut, you crack me up.*

"Camp Beauregard, Louisiana? Really? Never heard of any office there for USMS. Must be a real small office." The captain offered his naïve opinion.

"Yup. Small office. SOG." Aidan followed on using a bit more slippery, faux southern drawl. If the captain was not aware of what SOG meant that was just fine. Letting the local talent know that the Special Operations Group was on the hunt would be a flare in the night sky signaling something was more than just a little bit amiss. It would invite questions upon questions and since this was a speculative bird dog hunt, fewer inquiries were desired.

"I like small offices. Easier to get to know people. Who to trust and who to toss a sly eye to, if you know what I mean. All good eggs there?" Captain D'spain queried.

"All good. We kind of think of ourselves as a special variant of gamecocks." Tannin responded in a half joking manner. Tannin was not one to joke of such things. He was drier than a piece of Oregon beaver jerky. His humor carried sarcasm like a stealth DNA programmed miniature cruise missile.

"Good for you. Not so sure anymore with what I've been seeing. I think some of our eggs might hatch velociraptors. Little ones, not the big ones like in Jurassic Park. If you need to know the righteous roosters here, lemme know. I got your six. So what can I help you with? What's the big deal with you guys traveling to the Rose City?"

"Thanks for asking. Before we jetted here, we reviewed your arrest data and such. Looks curiously like some stuff we've seen on the east coast." Tannin continued on.

"We saw this really weird thing in the data. A while ago during a spate of *kick out the jams, brothers, and sisters* you had a big jump in missing persons' reports and speculated potential homicides.

"Those current data are more than just a bit unusual to us. You have a very recent big spike in those who have left the stage. Murder rates are zooming, and we can't tell if its real or artifactual data. Maybe not murders, just people going ghost. Any thoughts on what's going on?" Aidan carried the dialogue like a in-character scripted actor.

"We noticed it too. You guys must have better data than we do. We did have quite a few folks pay us a visit. You know the ones. Hoodies, Antifa, and BLM, oh my! Lots of whispers about MIISPERS. Nothing solid. We're thinkin' drugged-up paranoid tweakers.

"There was an increase but ya know, missing persons is a funny mix of pok pok wings and Nong's Khao Man Gai. Sooner or later everyone turns up. More vertical than horizontal. It's odd but then again look at the clowns out there on the street. They sure aren't our usual homeys." Captain D'spain was now speaking a language that was as foreign to Aidan and Tannin as Klingon or British English.

Aidan cast a quizzical gaze at Tannin. The gaze of *what's this guy talking about*? Tannin projected a look in response, *no fucking idea*. When you work with someone for a long time you can pick up on the microexpressions faster than an OCR component in a copier.

"Yes, I agree, it's odd but it's more than a burp of unusual. We were assigned to help your state police and other law enforcement by way of deputizing them. Not unusual. When local talent, no offence, is rendered limited in how they can respond to these types of riots, we get invited by the next level or three up. Federal level that has fewer constraints and bigger sticks. So here we are. And I've looked over some of your reports and data. Wow. Was quite a pile of people. You stacking cordwood somewhere? Too bad that your leadership here, your DA, decided to not prosecute looting and what they called, *no one got hurt* crimes. But when I looked through those data, going back a couple of months or so, you have *quite* a few missing persons reports on *the* rise." Tannin trotted his words out like a Tennessee Walker showing off and strutting its stuff.

"We seem to have all been the victims of the Chinese curse, *May you always live in interesting times*. True?" The captain responded.

"All true and more. Okay if I go right to the crux of the biscuit? Aidan and I know you are busier than the Devil with a revolving door to hell. Maybe having those souls go through a revolving door makes it so they are evenly roasted." Tannin was not hiding his bias. His bias was becoming bulbous.

"Go for it. Yeah, right you are. Look around. It's like an insurance commercial, *Mayhem, person of the year*. The Captain agreed with the ambience status of the current city situation. The city was cooking in the fire and brimstone with no real resolutions in the offing to hose it down. Everything they hosed it with just made the flames jump higher.

"A short while back you had that bump in missing persons. Some of those missing persons were teenagers. You know that the Marshals are really hot right now on any kind of human trafficking. So, drops-to-rivers, and you have a pod of teens going back to the last boil on the city popping. But, me being the kind of guy I am, I looked at the current data. And right here, right now, over the past few days, you have eighty-eight new reports. Some of the missing are less than sixteen years old. You have no speculation even as to what's going on?" Tannin commented and kept visiting the same thoughts in a hope to see if anything would pry loose from the captain. Any microexpression or tell that would reveal an insightful observation no matter how small. The datum slid into a wet bog of data. It smelled odd, stinky. Something was in that bog. Neither Tannin nor Aidan had a clue as to the source of the odor.

"We don't know. Just like I said. Simple as that. All of a sudden, we have these missing persons reports going crabgrass on us. Every time the city goes on a window-smashing-car-burning-human feces throwing tar pit, we get an influx of people who view this like when I was younger, a Max Yasgers farm party with Ten Years After banging out like molten gold. Back then, it was the music. Now? I really don't know what this is all about. It's like all of a sudden everyone feels empowered to do whatever they want with total impunity. Maybe it's a millennial thing.

"And the guys on top of us ain't helping the situation. So for me, and my officers, glad you're here. Anyway, all these new faces come in and then like a handful of dirt tossed into the air and dropping down, some of the dirt, the little pieces disappear in the wind. Like I shared, we think that the missing folks are the little pieces in the wind. When we tell people to not freak out, they get all lit up. Twenty-four to seventy-two magic hours we need to wait. We tell them call their friends, families, even make a visit to hospitals. We go open kimono and suggest hitting the shooting galleries. Like a tape loop, they eventually return to tell us, been there, done that. Early on, I was thinking that maybe some of these visitors to our fine burg may have ended up bagged. I connected with the ME and ask for stand and deliver." The captain had a level of confidence and excitement in the fact that he knew he covered the potential places where a two-legged being could get caught up. For sure, he wasn't going to let the newly hired help go genius here. This was his turf, not theirs.

"And, go on. You left us hanging off the edge of the cliff. What were the numbers? How many new stiffs?" Tannin questioned the Captain.

"I know you guys probably think that we don't data crunch very well. That's okay. I get it. You guys have a higher and more magnified view of this stuff. No insult meant." He responded.

"None taken. When you go on work vacay to as many places as we have you get used to the perspective. And not totally off. But in this current environment, we don't have the answers and we're not even sure of what questions to ask. We really are here to run air cover for you. Think of us as very benevolent Warthogs." Aidan smilingly interjected.

"My numbers are stupid simple. No net increases. Almost all were positively identified. Teeth, driver's licenses, known family, and in some cases even DNA checks. You get the picture. And for the very small number of Does, I emailed all the people who filed the reports. Invited them in. C'mon down and play with this. This is the spooky part." The Captain was now on Tales of the Unknown talk radio. Unsolved mysteries of the universe was humming through his melodramatic crush.

"Hey, we're hangin' here." Aidan chuckled a bit as though a child listening to an old-time detective radio show. Like Nick Danger, Third Eye.

"One. One, just one. So out of the bunch of missing person's reports, I score one. Guys, you're next question might be how many of the filers actually visited the morgue? All of them. Looks like this band of destructive gypsies really do work together. They must be doing something right. They don't have day jobs. And a few of them weren't next-door close. They had to hop fast planes and get their asses here before we moved on with the cadavers. These folks look like they're flush with cash. Maybe they're getting unemployment while being employed in the Marxist prime time show. Someone is flowing cash to them or they're all independently wealthy.

"A mix of all types of ethnic bents. The creepy part: I've closed the loop on all except the new ones over the past handful of days in regard to stiffs. We've gotten centralized and the Oregon State Police, the Multnomah County Sheriff's Office, and the Portland Police Bureau have gone Spartan. National Guard was klaxoned and we now have five fingers, including you, on the long arm and hand of the law. You get the picture? The folks that are missing are most likely really missing. We're talkin' dozens now. I can't make the call that a murder was committed without a body. You know how it goes; you can't claim a murder if you ain't got *no*-bodies. Hey, that's almost funny. That reminds me of a Carlos Santana song. Funny how the mind works." The Captain was starting to blabber even more so. Another officer of the law who was getting ready to retire. He had become a benevolent clock watcher and who could blame him?

Aidan and Tannin had almost no idea what he was alluding to. Some old guy dredging up memories from behind the grey matter plaques.

"Creepy isn't the right word. On the dial of oddities, it's in the scary weird zone." Aidan wanted to get this Captain back on track. Unfortunately though, the track led to a rail spur that just stopped and dissolved into nothingness.

"Guys, stating the obvious. We are now seeing dozens of folks go missing. And the data bumps happen around *ring around the anarchy* times. No corpses. Just pure disappearances. When we level the data out and meta it with existing relatable size cities, we have on our hands a mystery. Not a good mystery that has most likely a really bad ending. When people vanish like this, we either have extraterrestrial abduction or something that we don't even know what it is. Time to get really curious. You're not the only city to have unusual spikes." Tannin was looking to determine what the ferryman was doing at the river Styx, or maybe more appropriately, the Delaware River in Philly, and now the Willamette. It was bizarre. People simply vanishing without any trace whatsoever. No ransoms, no cadavers, and no cookie crumb clues.

"Hey, looks like it's almost sundown and ya' know they *really* come out at night. I need to get ready for the shift change. So if you two fellas don't mind, I'll go back to reality TV versus the Twilight Zone. Anything else you need? If not, can we go ten-four and get back to our respective corners of the known universe?" The captain had delivered only a half-pound of uncooked insights. It was good enough for now for Tannin and Aidan. They would use the underage data to make a cogent report back to their superiors. That alone would make this a priority investigation.

"Huge thanks for your time. Do you have an office we could use to get some privacy?" Aidan asked.

"Not really a lot of space in here right now. But down at the end of the hall to the right you can use the small conference room. A word to ya'. Make sure you indicate on the placard that the room is in use. Got it? Otherwise, you never know what might slither in. That was almost funny. You guys Harry Potter fans? I kind of like the new mysterious, magic stuff. Slytherin. Get it?" The captain did his best to be relevant. It sort of worked. Both Aidan and Tannin smiled. Yeah, they did like the Potter stuff. Even though the author was in her own witches kettle of stew because of her recent remarks on sexuality. Seems like everyone these days thinks their narcissistic commentary is relevant to something. It isn't. Talk has become quite cheap and was devaluing by the minute. But for whatever reason, make any kind of a public comment and expect well-targeted outrageous slings and arrows. Just like the morass that law enforcement was in.

"All good. Do we need a code or key?" Tannin asked.

"Yeah, code is 111251. Got it?" The captain offered up.

"Five by Five" Aidan responded. Tannin held up four fingers in an attempt to strengthen their bridge to the local talent.

"Let's go buddy. Time to munch and crunch data." He directed his comment to Tannin.

"Thanks for your help." Tannin said to the Captain. Help was a divine muse they badly needed.

Chapter 34: Black Dahlia

"This is waaaayy out there matey." Aidan piped up.

"Out there is right. We've gone knife-sharp on the searches and what we have is one of those Sherlock Holmes scenarios." Tannin emphatically responded to Aidan.

"But what we have is just hanging *stuff*. We have much higher-than-normal numbers of missing persons hot spotting at the same places where it's all just fun and games until someone lobs a Molotov events. And then? Data spike time." Aidan coalesced the not-so-sticky pieces.

"People missing. Big number of people missing without a trace. No stiffs. No ransom notes. Nada, zip. We have multiple cliffs, and the roadrunner isn't even identifiable. We're empty bowl here." Tannin further did his best to zipper together the thoughts.

"Hey guy, look me in the eye. There's something layered in all of this that we have no clue about. It sure isn't Let's Play Clue. What we have is a list of people, a series of events where they were, and no candlestick, no knife, no gun. We have empty spaces and don't even know where to look. I don't like this one bit. I like the ones where we know where the Professor, the Cook, and the major players are and we have a real good idea using the evidence, as to what transpired. We are playing with nothing. And the local LE aren't much help. They are so glue trapped down they probably have to fill out a req to take a dump." Aidan tossed his best attempt at connecting the pieces but actually had nothing of substance.

"Motives? We have missing person reports. We have nothing else. Just names with post-it notes, *Buhbye*. No UFO sightings either. The folks were torn out of the here and now just gone girl is in the offing." Tannin hit the Ping-Pong ball back to Aidan.

"We go back over it all, again. And again. And we follow-up on every new report from this moment on. Let's post a data watch to Seattle, Vancouver, Los Angeles, Kenosha, Philly. All at the same time, let's go Boolean and see if something else surfaces with a blow hole." Aidan suggested a very logical path to catch critical clues of what was swimming below the surface.

"Love it. But Aidan, LA? Really? That's a big bunch of chew. I think we should just stick to the smaller cities that don't have a lot of background stuff. Let's skip Chicago, New York, and LA. Whaddya say? Those burgs are already burning up resources with zero results. Even the data is filled with noise." Tannin offered up a more surgical path. Big cities with lots of weird stuff happening anyway will just fog the data.

"Roger that. The more sedate urban environments. It should work." Aidan agreed with the thought process. Use magnifying glasses on small things and get bigger images.

Chapter 35: Already Dead

"Here we are *again*. We should get frequent flyer miles for this hike to Portland. It'll be nice if some more *local* action pops." Maachi chirped to Bart.

"Mach, yeah, here *we* are again. Gotta admit, Portland is like playing the same golf course. You get to know the par for every hole. Startin' to get really boring. Ya' know what I mean? Hey, did you sting yourself?" Kind of an oxymoron question from Bart. Maachi was usually on one kind of sting or another.

"Just a little sting. Not a major sting. I wanted to chill before this gets interesting. Hey, did you bring any of those Chocolate Decadence high protein bars from that *lose the fat* multi level diet company in Arizona? They're not great but I'm starving." Maachi asked of Bart.

"Hey, Number One, catch!" Bart tossed two bars over to Maachi.

"Thanks number two smartest guy." Maachi nicely spanked Bart. His scowl was transparent and Maachi could see the impact of his words. He really liked it when he could poke somebody and show who the boss was.

"Why are you looking at me like that for? I'm just stating a fact. Would think you were used to it by now. If not, tough shit." Bart duly logged the diplomatic approach from Maachi.

Always that same God-awful *gotta be the smartest guy on the planet* tude. Bart grimaced and wisely and quickly changed the topic. Spurious pencil thin lips on his face. Verbal flares and heat reflecting chaff were in the air. Bank hard and high G.

"So, El Hefe, what's the plan? How we rolling tonight?" Bart went in a different direction. It was the hand throwing the tennis ball that caught Maachi's attention deficit focus. The comments about being number one or number two vaporized to not be seen again that evening.

"I was thinkin' we stay on this rooftop like the last time we were here and then maybe move in all quiet like to a building or two when we see where the roll is going. Whaddya' think?" Maachi chided Bart.

Bart knew better than to comment. Questions from Maachi were like invisible, open, sharp-toothed bear traps. When you step in one you end up in a set of circular commentary that only benefits Maachi. No matter what you say he'll kick it up a notch or ten just to maintain his bizarre thoughts of illusory superiority. Ego is larger than is seen in the rear view mirror of previous actions.

Bart paused for a moment and took a look over the rooftop wall. He saw a loner stumbling down an alleyway. "Hey migo, I need to tap this one, too funny not to. Take a look." Bart laughingly shared with Maachi.

Maachi left his rifle propped up against his kit bag and took a look through his spook glasses. He laughed a *ya gotta be kiddin me, ... this can't be for real* laugh.

Bart thought to himself, *classic*. He was scoped onto the funkiest chicken he had seen so far. The guy had black-rimmed glasses, a partial face mask that was blue on one side, the image of Bernie Sanders in the middle, and on the other side a rich orange color. His *helmet*, if it could be deemed as one, was a spray-painted, red pith-type helmet with plastic flowers glued on top. *Just classic*. His thought rolled on to where to drill the hole. He decided that just for the fun of it, the Bernie image was a perfect place to bulls-eye. He rocked the bolt and a one shot – one *feel the bern* thought became a reality. At this range the high velocity round popped through the Bernie image and splatted out the back of the jerk's head knocking off the pith helmet. Bart pulled back on his rifle and propped it up on his rifle case. He sat back down with a thud of accomplishment. Butt cheeks kissing the rooftop.

When he did so, Maachi said to him, "check this out, talk about effective cleaners. Just saw one of our black clad bogeymen pick up the score and scurry off to a niche in the alley. Hey, maybe this sport will allow one on one events." Maachi closed his monologue with that macabre thought and sat back down facing Bart. Bart was up one on Maachi. A unique start to the engaging events to unfold.

As far as the suggestion to go street, Bart was cold. He wasn't interested in meeting the locals.

"Let's take a quick break. We're going to be up here for a while. The tide of douchebags is going to keep going back and forth. We've got time before we have to exfil." Maachi commented. "Chillin frosty time. But first a message from our pharmacological partner. Time to go Murder Hornet." Stated Maachi as he rolled back his cuff and punched up one of his favorite concoctions. He held the phone over his wrist and let it sting him. "Wow! I must be *extra extra* sensitive right now. That really hurt. Must have been the needle angle or I hit a nerve." Maachi moved the phone away and rubbed his wrist where a small red bump appeared. "That's a first. Hey, number two smartest person on the roof. Toss me a bottle of that local stuff, Blue Dot Injun, will ya?" Maachi directed Bart.

"Sure thing." He opened the Yeti soft bag, snagged an ale, and chucked it to Maachi. Maachi snatched it out of the air like a jumping German Shepherd on a bright orange Frisbee. "Good catch. Must be all those vitamins you take."

"Nah, just my natural-born skill." Maachi confidently stated yet another self-serving, startling fact about his legendary talents.

Bart was propped up against his duffle and rifle case facing Maachi. "Hey, ya wannaaa see a trickk?" Maachi words were slurred as he questioned his athlete partner.

"Oh, yeah. The bottle cap thing. Again." Bart stopped in mid-sentence and instinctively moved to his right. Maachi had taken out his ballistic knife, not the switchblade. With straight arrow accuracy it penetrated Bart's left chest but missed critical tubes and heart pieces. "What the fuck?" Bart spit out painful words that only his ring and tacphone understood. A miss on the heart that was a saving grace and pass the grappa. Universe serendipity added some random to control.

"Time to finiiisshhh yew offff. You misearraaable slimey, baaaackstabing fuck. I know what youwhirrr up to youuu fudddge packkkking dipssshitt. I have kameras everywhere aaahhh know the deallllyou cttt with McCarteee got the fid of it on my phhhheee wanna s." Maachi's words were stuck in Jello and just hanging in the heat of the roof. The sting he administered was not what he expected. "Enddd yur little mennnageee aah twa with the skannkkyyy gasahs fromm Utera, ... Ut,... terus, ... Utah.

Bart took his phone out and pulled his sleeve up and delivered his own special brew to help him through this very painful episode of Ren hates Stimpy. Just to top the dose off, some meth, and just a meager amount of epi. Delish was his wish, and he got what he asked for. The custom sting amped up his awareness and kicked his pain to the side of the road. "So, how does it feel to *not* be the smartest guy on the roof top? Betcha didn't see that coming. You, Mr. Macho Macho Maachi are about to go somewhere that is very hot, dry, and ugly. It's that turbo elevator on down mode." With those comments, Bart pulled from his inner jacket pocket a suppressed Sig Mosquito packed with Stingers. He racked a round and sighted it in. "I have some ouchy things for you. This one is for how you treat Latika." One round hit Maachi's right shoulder. The bullet easily penetrated the t-shirt he was wearing and Maachi lurched to the right upon the impact.

"And say hello to its little friends!" Bart snarled out the words with maximum contempt.

"For the insults to me *pfftttt*; the dead dog *pffttt*; the way you treated Mr. Yang *pfffftt*; for locking me out of the door *pffffttt*; for insulting Peeta and Charly *pfffftt*. I fully intend on using every single round I'm packing with. No single kill shot. Death by a bunch of bullets one at a time, no auto." Bart continued and rinsed. Each deadly round caused Maachi to jerk in the direction of the bullet impact. "I know you can still hear me. El Hefe, like I said, no kill shot, no melon shot. This is not going to be fast and pleasurable, for you. For me? A different chapter in this book." Maachi was quite uncomfortably numb. He was very sofa-ed up with the mix from the special edition Murder Wasp injection courtesy of *I'm not a doctor, but I kill like one*, Bart. Bart was quite successful at hacking Maachi's phone and mixing up some killer pharma brews when he borrowed it to find his own phone. He dumped in some quick access macros tied into his virus switch, and there ya' go, the joy of recreational pharmacognosy. Bart put the *to go*, in to go.

Without looking Bart dumped the empty mag and reloaded with another ten rounds. Maachi was a victim of the *Swiss Cheese Drill*. Far more holes than he was born with. Red spots were expanding, and little crimson rivers flowed onto the rooftop. "You're getting all major drippy. Warfarin really does work at a high enough dose. I thought adding it to your brew was a nice touch. Whaddya think, ain't tech cool! We're done here. Have a nice bleed out. I guess the strain of all that was going on was just too much for you to bear. Maybe next life time if you have one and don't come back as a mangy street mongrel, you'll think about every action has that proverbial reaction. And, my reaction is fucking bigger than your action." Bart laughed as he hastily barked out the whispered harsh words. "You've gone through two rinse cycles, and you'll bleed out here, on the roof, alone. Just the way you lived your life."

Bart tossed his Sig, the empty mags, a few odds and ends he had inadvertently touched and placed them on top of Maachi's chest. The Indians will remove everything. Even drops of blood will not go unscathed with a dose of bleach. He gathered up his case and duffle. He dared not pull the blade out. Too risky up here. He gently wrapped the blade entry point with QuickClot gauze and then wrapped a couple of yards of black duct tape around his chest. It would do for now. He cinched himself with his belt. Time to beat feet and get to the exfil. He would arrive early but that was just fine with him. When he was collected, there would be no questions regarding his partner.

Everyone knew the rules. Especially the one about if you go down, and its mortal, your partner is required to finish you off. No evidence. No body left behind. Whatever was left behind would cease to exist at the hands of the yellow sashed ones.

Before he picked up the rest of his gear, he crouched over Maachi's face and said, "You're not number one now. Just a pile of number two on a roof. Just a big piece of shit on a shingle. Don't get a nose bleed on the down bullet elevator." Maachi's eyes were venetian blind slits and his breathing was total low tide shallow.

Bart gathered up all his belongings and looked around to see if he had missed anything. Nada. Clean as a dirty, sooty roof. Maachi was still barely conscious and was getting more and more zoned out as his life dribbled away. High-test pharma meets burgeoning lead poisoning by a bunch of holes. A death by a bunch of Stingers. Ouchiness of the most prejudicial kind. It was slow speed dial death call for Macchiato Poco Panicles. Raise a glass of the best Nanino and shout *morte!*

Chapter 36: I Just Puked My Soul Out

Black clad Bubai crept as a silent spider along the rooftop with his duffle bag. His steps were not perceptible thuds. More of a swishing, gliding *mmmffttt* sound. Like that of a puffy wind across the ground and mingling upward into the leaves..

He repetitively recited a short mantra to center his being and focus his soul upon his divine acts in support of the Goddess Kali. *Om Krim Kali, Om Krim Kali, Om Krim Kali* the words had such power in him as they built upon each chanting. A tornado of spiritual sound swirled within and each spin of the energy enervated and drenched his entire being. A blood and guts ever accelerating cyclotron.

His holy work would begin on this, his first assignment. He felt the beneficent power of the Goddess Kali. A replay of the great one as she became one with the Thugee so very long ago. A brief and ironic thought arose in him. He remembered why the Thugee now had to dispose of their targeted ones. So very far in the past the Thugee committed an act that displeased the Goddess. She had told them that she would dispose of all the remains of the bodies, but they should never ask about how she accomplished this. Conditionally they were never to observe her in the act of escorting the departed. But they did. They hid behind foliage and peeped out at how their handiwork was being dispatched. The Goddess saw them. She is a Goddess you know, and she is more omnipresent and omniscient than anyone can imagine. She chastised them for violating their compact. She told them she would always protect them but from now on they had to dispose of their own victims. Fair arrangement. Kill and rob and be protected? What more could a devotee wish for? All in honor of the Goddess and a path to pure enlightenment.

He looked at his tacphone and confirmed that the target was the one on the rooftop. A short, muffled beep indicated that this body was to be secreted away to parts unknown.

Kneeling over the still moving, slightly breathing, but mortally wounded body he noticed numerous bullet holes. Maachi was a human sponge on its final squeeze out. His evil dark blood poured out over the tarred rooftop. In the darkness it was black oozing pitch.

As Bubai stared into the largest hole in Maachi, he saw a brilliant blue dot. He meditated upon this lustrous dot, and he swooned into a short divine soulful dance.

He removed his yellow sash and knelt beside his parcel. Twice he carefully wrapped the neck so very tightly.

A gurgle rose up from Maachi's throat. A defiant sound. His deathly war cry tempting fate to sweep him away.

Fate very willingly complied.

Bubai pulled very slowly on both ends of his very fashionable garrote. A powerful cloth snake that was empowered by the Goddess to offer up another life essence to the universe. The clothen reptile constricted upon Maachi's throat.

Maachi was slowly being strangled. The strangling was not due to anger or a desire to harm. It was a loving last kiss at the hands of the Goddess Kali who was acting through Bubai. As Maachi's life was vaporizing, his angriness seethed. His last words, powered by his final gasping death rattle that accompanied the exiting of his soul. "Fuck you with a rake, sideways."

Bubai wondered what that curious set of words would do to propel this man's soul forward. What type of a body takes on a vile consciousness that projects such thoughts? An incarnation of Ravanna, he wondered.

With the sacrifice's last plash, he placed both of his hands over Maachi's face and ensured that his eyes were closed. The eyes are the windows to the soul and just like the Goddess he didn't want to be seen in his acts. Like Goddess; like man. Bubai removed the ligature and quickly replaced it around his own waist. There were only subtle marks from the ligature.

He reached into his duffel and took out a lithium powered, reciprocating hand saw. Bubai selected a coarse blade for the first cuts. They would need to chew through the clothing. Before he began his work, he searched all of the pockets and hidey places on the man's being.

He emptied Maachi's pockets and took the battery out of the tacphone. The phone he would keep. It must have been very expensive. It looked like something he saw in a Batman movie. A miniature Batbelt for this chap was now in the possession of a nice guy, not a dead guy. His friends were quite good at cleaning a phone and making it a ghost phone. Phones always had passwords and all types of interesting usable information.

He inspected his wallet and took the few credit cards and the debit card. It was a very nice collection. Even Bubai knew that a Black Card was of high value. He had no idea what he Dubai First Royal card was all about. No never mind, *collect them all. What an odd name on the cards, M Poco Panicles. Who has a first name that is just a letter*? Bubai chuckled at the thought of simply calling someone, *M*. It reminded him of the James Bond movies. The mind connects unfamiliar concepts with previously embedded impressions. The universe projects façade relationships to help samsarins believe that they are in a world of logical order. Logical order is a human construct. It makes puzzle pieces that do not have a connection appear to be fully integrated. Naivete is a protective shield for the innocent and righteous.

In Maachi's side zip pocket he found the most wondrous thing. A flawless emerald the likes of which he had never even imagined. Round and crystalline smooth with no indication of any type of cut with a gem blade. There was a gold post delicately adhered to the bottom of the jewel. *This I keep*. He thought to himself.

A flash of light came forth from inside Bubal's mind. He could see the Goddess dancing with all ten arms and legs. Her heads were vibrating back and forth. They separated and merged back into each other as a divine fan of imagery. All ten of her heads were singing and laughing. The sounds were not a single sound but a symphony of the Goddess' mellifluous voices. His eyes met the image's eyes and all he saw was yet again a brilliant blue light. As he looked more deeply at it, it flew off and disappeared.

Into his chest pocket he placed this bounty. How auspicious that on his first assignment he was in receipt of such an item. He treasured this as an omen.

Time to finish this work. His thoughts moved from the blue dot and Kali to the more practical, mundane matters at-hand.

He glanced at Maachi's sidearm and then up at the rifle. There was also the very odd weapon. It was like a large pistol. He also snatched up the Sig. *Weapons are always a valuable commodity to be sold to those who use such things.* These he would share with the brotherhood. A valuable bounty for all.

The saw blade zzzissled and tore at Maachi's body. The muffled sound of the saw blade cutting through cloth, flesh, muscle, and bone was hidden in the approaching loud noises of the rioters. The Goddess protected him.

His phone vibrated against his body, and he paused to see what was going on. The screen was a dull red with slightly brighter crimson words. *Testicles in cryobag.* Bubai's eyes opened widely and then narrowed to a thin slit. *It is the wish of my brothers. I shall not question.* His reason subdued his surprise.

Big pieces became smaller pieces and smaller pieces were torn to be even smaller easier to pack chunks. He only had to change the blade once.

There was only a gentle spurting of blood during the first deep cuts. The arteries and veins had already lost most of their pressure from the multiple Stinger holes.

He respectfully tossed the pieces into his duffel. It was the perfect size for the parcel
when properly organized.

After all the body parts and other pieces of mortal temptation were packed away, he completed the act by spraying the area with chlorine bleach. Not even DNA could be allowed to be recovered. That was the bond and compact with his benefactor Goddess.

He scanned the area to make sure that he did not leave even the smallest shred of Maachi. Nothing could be left behind to be used for identification purposes. It was a stretch to believe that anyone would go clue hunting that deeply. But the Thugee Brotherhood had as their responsibility to make what happened—never so. They honored the Goddess in this way and manner.

Chapter 37: Shadows

"Now that we have convened this extremely important meeting. I'll let Peeta provide the section-by-section update on the most pressing items of interest. I also wish to insure that you are all very comfortable with speaking openly within the confines of this chamber. It has been swept and charged to make quite certain that we cannot be recorded in any manner whatsoever. This is a voice meeting only and no record of it will exist. Now, before I have Peeta drive, please place your phones and any electronic devices such as watches or wearables in the carbon fiber basket that is now making its rounds about the table.

After I have collected all your communication items, I am going to erase all the information in your little helpers. *All of it.* The batteries will be removed and placed next to each of your devices. Take a note here. You will need to totally reload your personal and professional information into your devices after you depart these facilities.

You will each be swept to confirm that you have no *forgotten* items on your being. You all know this is our process so please be speedy. Peeta, the drive is now in your very capable hands. Carry on and let's make the best use of all of our time here." Provo burped out his words in perfect rhythm. He had made the statements so many times it was more like the onboarding in a plane without the hand signals for the exits. The flight attendant gazing off and going pure rote. If Provo had been a little bit more in character in his method acting, he would have also shared, in *case of emergency* comments. But Provo was confident in the Board to maintain a shared secrecy in all matters. They always took advantage of emergencies and never became engulfed by them.

"Thank you, Chairman Provo. I will follow our process and go through the litany of items of interest.

"There will be no misting. This is a meeting of considerable gravity and pure, very rational clarity is a mandate. Your own elevated state of awareness will provide stark lucidity with what is shared. You have all proven yourself to be very capable in that regard.

Questions, if any, do all of us a favor and don't go sophistry. To-the-point questions will be greatly appreciated. We work on facts and not opinions. Your beliefs and thoughts are your own. The facts though cannot be fabricated and are the property of all. We use facts to create strategies and tactics. We do not use emotional belief constructs to create the future.

First item on the list is in the Finance realm. Our compensation plan for the various levels is still below twenty-two point four-six percent. As we continue to expand on the sport platform and acquire new talent this keeps the overall payout to the upline under control and minimized. That is on the plus side. More on the plus side is the wagering regarding performance of the associate and business builder athletes. We are Las Vegas in this regard. We offer perks and incentives to those earners, and they respond quite well to them. We are the house and we already have evaluated the financial algorithms and as long as they keep performing well, we shall enjoy many multiples on our wagers and on their participation payments to us. As with other multi-level companies, they have to pay a tidy sum either in direct payments or in maintaining specific revenue targets to preserve their status. They need to keep the points on the upswing week after week and month after month. We actually do better than stockbrokers who get paid on buys and sells. We also benefit from electronic currency movements in-between.

We have an ongoing income stream from our athletes that is superb. Simply stated, it is the qualification program that keeps them very motivated to meet quotas and of course entertainment for us." Peeta laughed with that hidden darkness that was her brand. "Any questions about the sport program?" She professionally inquired of the Executive Directors.

"Thank you Peeta for that top line review. My question is in relation to Mr. McCarty. None of us wishes to live in the foggy area of rumors. That is not our way. But this is an interesting one. I have heard that he is also structuring some type of an additional asset procurement. Any substance to this?" Trey Garzee' commented despite Mr. Provo suggesting with Peeta's agreement, rumors were not the meat of this feast.

"That is a great and wonderful question. As we had touched upon in the opening remarks, we refrain from rumor-mongering and myth-building during this meeting." She laughed that inner carnivore, black widow spider gurgle laugh. Not demonic. Almost seductively charming. Made you want to be eaten alive by her. She is the sirens *en toto* on the cliffs singing to Odysseus. Intoxicating tones and sounds that beckon one to come closer, at personal risk. "This brings to mind our Executive thought structure. Great minds discuss ideas. Average minds discuss events. Small minds discuss people. We view ourselves in the most former, occasionally in the middle, and not interested at all in the latter. So, let us move on to the wagering aspects of our business." The portal on talking about McCarty closed with an electric thudkk complete with bug zapping electricity to confirm finality in the commentary. Cleaved and left. Peeta did not suffer any foolishness well. Foolishness to her was something to be tossed into a well and see if it sinks or floats. Either way it is irrelevant and extremely counterproductive.

"Continuing on, we have our wagering business. It is our method of herding along the best of us to use our fine minds to determine what the next sequence of events shall be. We have this friendly process of determining who is our most accurate predictor of future events. There is no computer that can accomplish this. Computers don't walk around in the world. We do. We gather information and practice sharpening our reasoning skills by our wagers. For us, it is our corporate governance process that makes us wish to be promoted to become Oracle. Only the most accurate and precise of us wears that mantle. The best compensation and leadership is on that pinnacle Board. Which is where we all seek to be the best for all of us." Peeta shared her constructive guiding thoughts to the group. She paused to let the words circulate and expand. The pause of the Alpha Cat was a palpable force.

"We have several events coming up. Most of them are still in the US but a few highly levered opportunities exist outside of the country. This is a follow-up summation of current affairs. We do review the global status on a very regular basis. Consider this as the most up to date top line status report.

The EU has become quite interesting. This includes the UK regardless of the Brexit issues. In lighter moments we refer to the social events as antimask pub crawls with a smattering of ethnic suspicion and profiling. All of those fuses can be easily lit with an accelerant or three. We've seen how effortlessly it is to push people to morally descend and become very base creatures. A cartoon here or a beheading there and within minutes the lit fuse burns towards its explosive moments. Which equates to a sport platform venue and financial rewards for us.

The very fluid moving war zones in the Middle East and most southerly and westerly geographies extending into Turkey, and the unlikeliest of places, China. China is a very subtle mix of animosity. Religious groups and unique ethnic genotypes are the fodder for the fire that can be created. All is in the timing. At this time we are still managing our relationship with the Chinese in regard to the Covid opportunity. There may come a time that we create interesting times within China and capitalize on them. Takoveh.

Africa as we all know is still off our official venue list. We need to develop some downlines in Africa to be able to maximize any opportunity there. Questions? Now is the time." The request for input came from only one voice. It was the pesky Trey. The ineffable, or as Peeta thought of him, the *eff-ing-able*. He was the top-of-the-line fellow who had a bit of a challenge conflating his big ideas into concise statements. He was mayonnaise, ketchup, mustard, and ghost pepper hot sauce randomly spurted at each other and shaken in a glass vessel. Lots of stuff, just hard to determine which was what and what was which.

"Could you talk to how we are providing accelerants to increase the number of arenas?" Trey offered up.

"That is an excellent question. To the human assets that are the mob of agent provocateurs we have only to provide nominal amounts of funding to support their efforts. We have done this in Portland, Seattle, Kenosha, DC, Atlanta, and a smattering of other burgeoning playing fields. When we add drugs and money the fuses burn even more rapidly and far hotter. Simple inexpensive rewards for even the most outrageous actions.

They believe we are in agreement with their social protests. In a manner of speaking, we are in support of their efforts. Our rationale is different from theirs but that is irrelevant. We let them believe what they wish and imagine. We tread a different path.

On the law enforcement side of the equation it is more costly and challenging. They are greatly influenced in their decisions to be accommodating to the most recent odd city governing groups trying to defund and remove support of effective law enforcement measures. This has moved us to identify key city and state governing personnel to focus upon. We encourage their efforts to defund which has the most interesting impact on law enforcement as well as empowering the more disruptive social elements. They too think we support their efforts with common beliefs. It is most quaint and perversely logical.

Law enforcement basically has a huge issue in that a significant group of prospective retirees and others who are leaving the forces. They actually are our most fertile group of assets. We play both sides. We support defunding and we support the disenfranchised law enforcement elements. There are elements within the disenchanted officers that are approachable to help create events that demonstrate that defunding only results in more bold actions by the twisted minds of opportunistic lawbreakers including rioters. A method of validating the importance of supporting your local sheriff is to draw attention to the unfortunate things that happen when the thin blue line is pierced.

We provide little accelerants that result in the deaths of a person here or there. Then we provide rapid notification to the social element via Twitter, Facebook, and other communication conduits to add more wind to the fires. This allows us to create a potential event that we have influenced. In a tight summary, we have been highly effective at stimulating social unrest on a national and burgeoning global scale. Then it is simply a matter of letting our associates, business builders, and prospective Board members know of the events, the timing, and the cost. Does that help you to understand the linkages?" She hid her disdain well. The words chosen with sharp, surgical efficiency. If Trey had further questions on this topic, she fully intended to cut him short. She was an expertly foundried, carbon steel katana and he was something on a plate to be cut up raw.

She left the topic like roadkill on an Arizona desert freeway and moved on to other items that were of higher priority. Feeding information and data to Trey was metaphorically casting pearls before a swine.

Chapter 38: Believe

"This is unbelievable! You mean every screen is of some athlete doing their thing? And you're running wagers on all of the outcomes? Unbelievable is a *way* too small word. I can't imagine anyone even pulling something like this together. Must have taken a long time to bolt down the programming on this one." Bart shared with his jaw dropping to the floor and bouncing a couple of times. He had witnessed Maachi pour over lines of code to create clever ways of laundering money and tucking away ill-gained profits. But the scale of this endeavor was like a governmental agency doing things right.

"I encourage you to believe. This is the internal part of the MLM where only the most qualified Rubies, Sapphires, Emeralds, and Diamonds play in their very own private games. But this is a small part of what we do. A very financially rewarding diversion and sorting of the smartest among us. We don't grade on a curve." McCarty was setting another sharp, barbed hook, but first, the chum of greed was to be cast onto the waters for Bart to bemuse himself and drool his inner Legree.

Thank goodness for the dark web and cryptocurrencies. If this were a Greek play, those two items would be powerful god-like animas. They formed and fueled an entirely unregulated environment to conduct all sorts of activities. The coin of the realm was a bunch of electrons expressed in a binary fashion. The owner of the electrons wins. The vulnerability of such a system to be hacked and accessed for gain, fraud, or the acquisition of power was a chink in the armor of global commerce and stability. In other words, a lack of stability was a watershed for the Company. Let no vulnerability go to waste.

"Not clear here on *their games*. They aren't playing anything. They're just watching events unfold and wagering on the outcomes. Just a bunch of soft algorithms." Bart morphed into a frigatebird and puffed his chest out more than just a bit. His heart and passionate egotism were now red and on the outside of his feathers, ebullience. A bit of Maachi's *eau de importance personnelle* evidently rubbed off onto the Bart unit. Soulful-influencing epigenetics. All it takes is a potential chance at absorbing vast amounts of filthy lucr-trons.

McCarty caught another whiff of ego-driven narcissism and took his comments down a notch. He also detected a potential opportunity. That personality flaw was a terrific crack in the wall that was large enough to envision a more financially rewarding game. "So true, Mr. Henderson. So true. Yes, they're just wagering a percentage upon prognosticated outcomes." He hid the remainder of his thoughts. No point in surfacing them now. It would take time and effort to educate Bart on the differences within the Company of *watching* and *doing*.

Everything and everybody has strings sharply hooked into their being. Those strings are pulled by something bigger, always. Free will is not the dominant domain in a human.

"So all of these monitors are tracking athletes? And then there are wagers on who the leaderboard point-masters are?" Bart was slow on the pick-up here. Restatement sometimes helps reality become understood. Maybe some social lubrication delivered by Peeta would enable more rapid encoding. Nah. It will just take time for Bart to grok what all of this magnificent machine was capable of.

"Why, yes, Mr. Henderson. Again, though, all the betters need to attain a certain level in the program and maintain it. If not, they lose their wagering rights. Think of it like coupled runners racing. As you continue to study and understand how our multi-level reward structure works, I am quite certain that you will find it quite enamoring. And handsomely profitable." McCarty deliberately left a stack of floating innuendo in his comments. It rose in a column of covetous heat generated by Bart's persona.

"So what do I have to do to get to this level of play?" Bart heard the word *profitable,* and his greed genes went wildly upregulated.

"All in due time Bart, I may call you by your first name, yes?" McCarty was intentionally shifting the dialogue without a clutch statement.

Chapter 39: Glory

"Both Peeta and I are extremely impressed with your recent accomplishment." Premier Provo commented with total statesman wryness.

"I am so honored that you would recognize me and my methods. It now allows you to pursue your dream of adding income streams. Your thoughts are lovely and so very much out-of-the-box." McCarty glowed with enthusiastic pride. He was a solar powered lantern in the field of dreams.

"I so agree with Mr. Provo. Finesse taken to a galactic level." Peeta could not resist the urge to chime in. Her comment was a drip off the end of the icicle words of Mr. Provo's. The voice that mattered was Provo's. There were no such things as ties in anything in his business world. There were no even money opportunities. And neither were there times when he would have to cast a vote. The whole governance structure of the concern was to maximize the returns on the multi levels of their business engagements and other activities. He was at the helm and had earned it.

"Oh, my Mr. McCarty, I have great reverence for the speed and ability to conduct business in the grayest areas between what is right and what is wrong. The push and pull of those universal forces places us so very nicely in a weightless area where we can do whatever we wish whenever we want. You ice-skated between so many potential obstacles and have now delivered to our mutually beneficial business entity a complete, privately-held manufacturing business entity. Remarkable, indeed! Takoveh!"

The four ears of McCarty and Peeta listened very closely. They were doing their best to free-climb the thoughts of the Chairman. Good luck with that. A word to the wise, always use sharpened crampons and make sure your belay device is in tiptop functional shape. A double cross check is never a waste of time. Confirming that the ice or stone is thick enough to withstand a jump or two is confidence-building and advantageous.

"I am absolutely delighted to be a part of this remarkable organization." McCarty knew how to butter the bread and put delectable organic jellyfish jam on it.

"Do you really understand what the direction is?" Peeta asked in her typical *look down her nose* manner. She lived for the delectable moments where she could clearly demonstrate who the smartest cat was in the cattery. She never needed to sharpen her fangs; they were self-sharpening. Just looking at them would create two surgical punctures in your neck.

Every sentence is a challenge and a dare. And if you dare challenge her, keep in mind she is a Gateway Seven Diamond. She is not to be jousted with. You either have your game on or go back to crayons and construction paper at the fold up table in the corner. She plays for keeps. She knows of no other way. In any game with her it needs to be understood there are absolutely no additional lives. Life comes at people hard and fast like a leathered covered baseball. Come armed with sharpened wits just to gain entry into the cage with her. Or, go home now and self-gratify in your constructs.

"Well, that is a very good question, Peeta. No, I really don't know the bigger picture, but I certainly would love to learn more! Please do share, Mr. Provo." McCarty had developed his contorted conversational skills over decades of convincing people to do things and making them believe it was their idea. He just did the one-step-two-step jump over the commentary and go for the gold. He acknowledged and ignored Peeta's ego-driven, diatribic nonsense. Almost very sharp knives out time. McCarty had many sharp-pointy things at his disposal.

But, don't bet against Peeta. She is the long stemmed two-legged house that is very conversant and knowledgeable on how all of the company operates.

Knowledge versus male-driven feralness.

"I can share with you the larger thoughts, but the details are still held within a very elite, privy group of directors. The intent is to use the company you now have essentially taken ownership of by coercion or direct management. The manufacturing facilities will begin making unique pharmaceuticals and dietary supplements for us and others." Provo went momentary pontification monologue.

"That is very interesting, so very interesting. If I may, sir, why would we need to be able to manufacture products like those? I understand the market cap value, CAGR, and gross revenues that the Cantank Rus Pharma company is experiencing are deliciously large numbers. Why not leave it as is and just tap into the organically generated profits?" McCarty had a conundrumic, disarming soft goofy smile grimace. He should check to see if he has any hay straw stuck on his plaid sport jacket. Time for a big ass lint roller.

"My intent is to have us bring to life a multi-level marketing company that can provide various consumable products such as foods, supplements, and even more enamoring, designer drugs including recreational substances. We also have very dear associates south of the border, and in fact worldwide who have a keen interest in obtaining the most delectable designer drugs." The Provo word march went on. It trampled the road that McCarty was paving.

"Drugs?" McCarty questioned.

"The times they are most truly changing my dear Mr. McCarty. So as to not be too obtuse, maybe you would be wise to review what is happening in the Pacific Northwest in regard to previously illegal substances. Then, enwrap the worldwide opportunities around it. It is an enticing package." Provo set his logical stake in the ground and into McCarty's heart. If McCarty was as good as he thinks he is, the intent of the comments would be all that he needed to understand the future path. Both Provo and Peeta began to laugh. Not just a giggle. A *sheik yer booty* guffawing. The comic moment was anchored in things that Provo and Peeta already knew. They had the joke behind the joke and that is what made it so personally humorous.

"Mr. McCarty, you have so much to learn still. We always conduct our businesses to engage all types of markets. Don't we Peeta? Take a mental note here. Why do you think some of the west coast cities are on the verge of legalizing all types of previously verboten substances? Use your finely honed imagination Mr. McCarty." Unseen hands are very effective at moving mores and situational ethics. You have already experienced how we encourage social unrest. Take the word influence and substitute the word channel. We channel all types of societal energies to enhance the strength of the company.

Use a more sophisticated set of prescriptive lenses and you will immediately understand that companies now are the countries of the past. The business entities generate more true profit than entire countries.

So many countries in the red. If you review their GDPs, they look like the Midas touch of commercial activities. In reality though, let's take the United States of America. GDP is approximately twenty-seven trillion dollars. Ah, and now the cover off the lid of the pot of steaming heaps of humanity.

The debt is about thirty-two trillion and rapidly counting upward.

Am I providing insights for you?"

"Yes, ... and I can sense the direction you are going in." McCarty was now in elementary school adding and subtracting. It was time to move on to huge polynomial equations with an almost endless composition of parenthetical values.

"The number I shared with you does not include interest on the principal debt.

"The United States is not the sole owner of extreme financial mismanagement. Other countries are in the same kettle of suffocating fish.

"There is not successful business that can have such financial jeopardy. If Apple, Pfizer, or even that silly fellow, Peeta, what is his name?"

"Musk, Elon Musk, the loud, conflicted voice of Tesla."

"Yes, that is the chap.

"If those companies conducted their financial affairs in the manner of the US government, the executives would be strung up at streetlight intersections for their incompetence and bold deceptions.

"The ubiquitous Wal*Mart has annual sales of six hundred plus billion. Sweden, Norway, and mostly all other countries have GDPs less than the value I just shared for Wal*Mart.

"The controller of the energy of commerce, money, controls the countries as de facto string pullers. Companies are more financially well-endowed than entire countries. While countries fritter away their revenue and wealth of counterproductive initiatives, companies use their financial power to become larger, stronger, and more in control to?

"Maximize their wealth.

"Companies control the activities of countries. Do you understand the ramifications of such financial opportunity and jeopardy?"

"Yes, I do understand but I am not yet clear regarding our company."

"Mr. McCarty, here is what is in motion. The company is nobody's bitch. We influence domestic and global financial flows by covertly manipulating all types of factors. The company that you are now fully engaged with, has revenues that exceed all country's GDP except the United States and China. We do as we wish, when we wish, and how we wish.

The company is more financially powerful that several countries combined. Our goal is to become larger, and far more globally dominant." Peeta conflated the Provo graduate level lecture to the coarse, mundane language that McCarty was more familiar with.

"Nicely stated, Peeta. Always follow the money to see how controls the situation."

Provo and Peeta just branded McCarty's brain with Technicolor thoughts. A thousand neon lights lit up within his head. McCarty joined in on the laugh. Yes, he did get it.

"In closing, Mr. McCarty, bringing the galactic view down to Earth-level, would it be wise for us to team up Sussen with Henderson? It will allow us some additional degrees of freedom if Henderson fails to meet our significant expectations." Provo wrote the book on financial and human manipulation. Peeta was his trainee, and she slivered a very minimal smile. She was quite aware that a question from the Premier was not a question. It was a directive that had sharp things embedded in marshmallows around it. Sweet and sticky and a way to test potential future elite Board members.

"That is a truly a first cabin idea! I shall make it so." McCarty was quickly learning that being the artful dodger and yes man are not mutually exclusive personality traits.

Chapter 40: Heart of a Champion

On the other side of the country another meeting of interest was simultaneously occurring. *Latika, could you help me out and visit me in my office? Need to chat.* The message Slacked across her monitor. Not knowing what to expect and thinking the worst she soldiered onward anyway. She hadn't seen Dr. Panicles for over a week. She was hoping this was not one of their evil firing rituals. The one where the unsuspecting employee thinks they are invited to a valuable business meeting only to discover, *BaBamm! You're Fired!* Complete with the Maachi goblin drooling and loving every minute of the stress, strain, and suffering he had just inflicted. Power and control drips strange rewards to the deranged souls who march across the surface of planet Earth.

Be right there. And that was all she Slacked. She summoned up her inner blue light to give her courage. She called upon the Goddess Kali for protection and guidance. The *Om Sri Maha Kalikayai Namaha* inner chant became an incoming ocean of powerful protective energy. She chanted in slow repetition and timed her breaths with the soothing, gentle words.

A cautious, soft knock-on Bart's door and a timid "May I come in?" articulation from Latika.

"C'mon in! Thanks for getting here so quickly. I need your help in taking care of an issue." He got up from his chair and walked to the etched glass door and opened it widely for her. Bart was more than congenial. It was Bart speaking and not the *waiting to get bitten by the Mad Dog Maachi* person he had been. That Bart who would cower in the corner.

"Is Dr. Panicles here too?" Her voice stretched nervousness across her vocal cords. Her heart was beating ever faster, and she refocused on the Goddess Kali and her inner voice chanting.

"Huh? Not sure what you mean." Bart crinkly-browed confusedly responded.

"I just thought maybe this was a meeting with both of you. I haven't seen Dr. Panicles in days, and I usually have some sort of communication from him when he is out of the office." She offered up in a very cautious manner.

"Oh, no, he'll not be joining us today. And that is exactly what I wanted to speak with you about." Bart candidly shared with Latika. A strange, cozy softness in his voice that she had never previously detected. *Something is very different here.* She rested her thought upon that feeling. The mantra spun slowly so as to cast a protective shield around her very soul. She was being hugged into a protective cocoon.

"How about if we sit and have a genuine sharing? Please, have a seat." With compassion and empathy he offered up a more casual moment. "Dr. Panicles is on an extended sabbatical, I think. Actually, I really don't know where he is. I get no calls or texts, and you? Has he contacted you? Anything?" Bart moved his locomotive to a different track without even the sound of a switch clunking on the rail steel. He was going heavy theatrical gravity.

"Oh Dear! I hope he's all right. No, I have not had anything from him at all. It is so strange." Latika politely responded. Mantra spinning and her soul was winning the favor of the Goddess.

As those concerned words expanded in the room, Bart noticed a most beautiful emerald pin on Latika's blouse. Bart was just gaining altitude in his flight to the clouds and now he was dead stick and going down. His wings melted in the hot sunlight of reality. He was caught like a grape between the fingers of a hungry child. Speechless and now going pale. The emerald was not just any jewelry store item. It was a game pin.

"What a beautiful emerald pin! Absolutely super!" Bart maxed the gas and air intake just in time to break his nosedive and regain a reasonable interaction altitude.

"Thank you. Thank you very much. It was a gift from my husband. It is lovely, isn't it?" She very openly responded. She never questioned her husband on how he had obtained the jewel. She did remember seeing one like it before in Maachi's office atop the puzzle boxes. It would have been an insult to her husband if she questioned him. Some things are best left undisturbed and not looked into too deeply. Gifts are gifts from the Goddess to her devotees and to question her actions would border on blasphemy. It would be akin to watching the Goddess dispose of the empty husks in the wild.

"Indeed, it sure is, anyway, sorry about my pause there. The gem just captured my attention. How about if we move on?" Bart mastered his composure and effectively hid his true thoughts. Questioning cogitation arose in his being regarding the how and when did this gem surface here?

"I think we need to work together on this. Nothing shakes a company more than not knowing someone is at the helm of the good ship Cantank Rus Pharma. Since you don't know where he is and I don't know where he is, we need to apply social CBD and soothe our employees. Can you help me? I've put together a memo and I need your input. Okay?" Bart had become the gentleman with exotic tastes he wished to be. A confident smoothness in his voice. The timbre was that of a man who had been many years a corporate slave. He was previously a well-paid serf awaiting the next beating. His thoughts though bolted back to the emerald pin.

"Of course. Anything you want me to do I shall do." Latika was arcing into comfort mode.

"Super. Here, I printed a copy for you to read. I didn't want to send anything electronic at this time." Bart handed her the one-page memo.

She took the paper and placed it on the conference room table. It was a short to the point read.

For the time being I shall be assuming the sole role as CEO of Cantank Rus Pharma. Dr. Maachi Panicles is on an extended leave of his own choosing and will return to assume his duties as the commander of the good ship we are all on when he is able. If you are aware of any open issues or projects that he was working on, please immediately contact Latika via email or visit her in the executive offices reception area. If she is not available send me a Slack note or an email and I will assist you as promptly as I am able. We all wish Dr. Panicles some well-deserved time off. He has worked so very diligently over the past several years to elevate this company to be an international success. And we are only beginning our path forward. We have more great goals to crush and to continue to establish ourselves as a leader in the pharmaceutical and dietary supplement marketplaces. Most of our activity has been focused upon contract manufacturing. We will very soon have an executive team meeting to scribe our go-forward strategy. Here is the trailer on the movie; we are now going into the branded product marketplace. Hope those words resonate well with you, they should. Nothing loves success better than more success! Thanks for being a huge part of the company's achievements. I look forward to working with you to hammer out the malleable pieces of our business to create a legendarily great company. We're all in this together! Signed, Bart Henderson, acting CEO.

"What do you think?" Bart asked as he could easily see that she had completely read the memo. The microexpressions upon her face spoke volumes of tomes on fear, relief, and redemption. Most importantly a bright blue sky filled with happiness and freedom from the tyranny she had previously lived within.

"It sounds fine. I can transmit it under your name if you wish? Would that be helpful?" Latika was feeling far more at ease. Her mind left the mantra on park, and she started to replay the diminishing voice of the vulgarity of Maachi. And for now, he was gone.

"That would be great. We already have a few empty days without Dr. Panicles. I don't think it's wise to wait any longer. The information doesn't become more valuable by waiting. No time like the present to hit a reset, even if it's a temporary respite." Bart's voice was robotic. He knew he had to say something to keep the energy flowing.

For Bart though, Maachi was still here. Noncorporeally, but still right in the very same room. *Jeepers creepers, where did you get that gem?* An electric cold shock ran through Bart's entire body. He stood soundless and motionless except for a ghastly shiver. How could she possibly be involved in the company game? He shivered again as his temperature rose, beads of sweat popped through his pores like a last rigor before the unknown, death?

Chapter 41: Evil

A quick squish of the time space continuum took place immediately after Latika exited Bart's office. She glided out of his office in a trancey divine state of one hundred percent pure relief. No more Maachi. Gone. *The Goddess Kali had completely answered my soulful wishes* she thought with a contented smile upon her face.

The moment was punctuated with a swishy electric-buzz windy sound.

The next reality sentence following the closure of one door and another one opened. Doors opening, closing, revolving and electronically zapping are the substance of life. And it's all about choice. Go through the door, find another, or freeze in the moment.

Bart's phone vibrated in its upside down breakdance. The bzzzzpt, bzzzzpt, bzzzzpt was a sonic mosquito awaiting that lapse in tick tock to penetrate Bart's awareness. And then? Bzzzzpt interruptus. It stopped. A text message.

His stunned state regarding the jewel and all that collapsed in his brain over the recent macabre, bloody, events left him in a temporary, catatonic blank mind set. The mosquito kept revisiting and challenging his pensive mood.

No point waiting. Calls and reach outs on his tacphone were never *Scam Likelys* or some organization looking for a donation to help plant seven trees in the arctic circle due to upcoming global warming Waterworld events. It was always something interesting that emerged from that worldwide conduit in the swamp the internet had become.

He ignored the phone. Bart stayed in his state of questioning cotton candy bliss. That place was safe, sweet, and predictable. The phone? *Random mijo.*

The 'squito banged him again and silently melted into the future while his awareness floated from thought cloud to thought cloud.

This was one of those seams in time where being paused out didn't feel right. Obviously, a message or an encrypted text was in the bowl of Cheerios. Repetitive calls always meant some chunky random event had either happened or was on the way trotting down the yellow brick road.

Back in the current phase of reality, Bart decided that he would be avoiding the inevitable by letting the 'squito continue for return sorties.

He turned over the phone and it was a Hallmark textin' event. The first text was three smiling purple devil emojis.

The second text only had one much larger image of a frowning purple devil emoji. There was only one person that would send that electron smoke signal, Peeta. She had no appreciation for any lapse when she reached out. Peeta was a Pinhead reboot in a babe-o-liciousy body. The kind of drippy female presence that wraps itself around your being and next thing you know you have a ball in your mouth, a studded collar around the neck, and a diaper on. The smacks with the riding crop are not meant to be titillating or exciting. Pain was the frosting on the chocolate lava souffle of complete responsiveness and obedience. Peeta was the epitome of the head mistress and the Cloister d' Dominatrix was her playground.

Three emojis was an indication of some bad juju smoking and swirling about hiding the reality. A single big ass purple, frowning devil emoji was her doing her best to pith you off and stick antenna in your head. No phone needed.

Bart sent a large winking Unicorn emoji back. His second text was all upper case WAP.

Peeta responded with a purple devil with its head blowing up all nuclear and such.

This is not going well, Bart brilliantly concluded with silent words that betta' all be sealed away never to be uttered.

Bart noticed he miskeyed. He intended to use a *U*, not an A. Major chill blush went tsunami in his brain. It was Peeta and sending WAP was both sloppy and stupid. Two things that Peeta totally despised. A Freudian slip on the heavily waxed and wet travertine floor.

Bart sent a follow up smiley face emoji with fingers on chin and a large question mark on the image's face.

Peeta sent one image. A phone graphic.

That's a very clear message. Call now and dial for dollars or don't call now and ask for another smack with the riding crop.

Bart poked the red button under his desktop and a loud, definitive *clickkkk* was the door responding that it would be his insentient Heimdall.

Chapter 42: Dangerous

"I understand. It is truly more awkward than finding out my favorite brother has eight wives and not seven. In all pure candor, I have no idea why it turned up where it did. We've never had this happen before. Yes, yes, it is a dangerous area we enter here. But we can weave together a very cogent outcome. I shall connect with trusted colleagues and begin spinning the threads. Thank you for your patience. Is there anything else you would like to share?" The smile in his voice was lake ice thin and was on the verge of cold cracking at any moment. And that would not bode well for him at all. Any indication of a lack of confidence was thin steel to the neck. A bleed out like no other cuz, you owned it. McCarty was boosting his dial from concern to passionate resolve to bring closure to this atomic wedgie moment.

"And further, I need to state it again. I have not even a single thought on how this happened. I realize I'll need to act. Yes, sooner rather than later. As I think about this red-hot poker sitch, I may need some additional resources, insightful assets. Can you help me with that?" Bart calmly asked as he stepped to the precipice of a begging moment. He was shaken and stirred. *How the fuck did this happen*? He steamed the stinging thought as his brain went Riddler question marks.

"Of course, I can take care of this untidy situation. There is always an explanation for every event. Whether a butterfly effect or a vampire bite infect. I know exactly who to reach out to."

She knew what to do. A different means but the same outcome was to go from thought to pure action. Peeta's heart skipped a beat in anticipation of the thrill of the game going pedestrian. She was adept at thoroughly cleaning her hands after they were dirtied.

"I have to share with the Board in pure lucidity that we have an issue and an enormous opportunity. Rarely do the planets align with the billiard balls on the table. The energies are aligned and soon, the Gods willing, we shall have attained a milestone in one of our most potentially advantageous new areas of commerce." The Premier chipped the words out onto the green and played with dripping the opportunity to have more than they ever thought possible in such short snip-snip sew together pieces of time.

Bubai shared with his brothers, "I need to meet with you all as soon as you can avail yourself. I have some bounty that I shall require your assistance to understand its value. It could be that what I have you have seen so many times in the past. For me, though, it is a first. How soon can we meet? I understand. I shall not have the items with me when we meet." He paused his deep-toned voicings and welded his ear to the speaker on the phone. "That would be perfect. The weekend works well for me also. I shall let my consort know that I will have a short-day travel. All very good. Many thanks for your understanding." Bubai terminated the call and drew up a very optimistic sigh of relief. The puzzle pieces in his possession were more than curiosities. He felt assured that the baubles and babbles held deep secrets. The man who was once was, ... was now discretely disposed of. But his trappings must have many dark, wet tunnels leading to potentially even more bounty. Bubai looked forward to his meeting with his brothers.

Chapter 43: Gonna Be OK

The meeting was to commence in less than thirty minutes, ... eighteen hundred seconds. Each threading of the stitches in time bordered on painful. The anticipation that order is not the rule at this moment. Randomness was playfully kicking up sand into Bart's eyes.

Meetings with McCarty were a necessary annoyance. Those meetings were perfunctory checking-up-on-you meetings. Technical, tactical Jello blabber about next steps was an opportunity for the cart puller to get an in-person readout of the emotional weather report of the cart. Having Bert get his chain yanked by the master of buffoonery was uncomfortable and awkward but getting face time with the clown helped build the relationship with the Company.

This whole affair with Maachi in the wind, literally and figuratively, and Latika with a company gem was a perverse coincidence. And since Bart had his creepy crawly maggots-under- the-skin feeling about this, then Peeta, the Provost, and the company would deem it politic to understand the state of a lost-in-space gem. The oblique uniqueness of an athlete, a player in death that was within the company tentacles being disposed of was less than one in a billion happenstance. Because if it was a mundane one in a million, then the liquidation of paying customers would be a self-defeating exercise. One in a million would equate to about seven thousand participants becoming dust. A pyramid business model that would be a self-defeating strategy with bloody tactics as the sting of the beast. Self-induced diminishing returns. Unless of course the company had somehow managed to maneuver very high value Lloyd's of London policies whereby the company itself were the sole or would be *soul* benefactor of the compensation. Thousands of policies being fulfilled would evoke piercing questions. But then again there could be useful financial washing machines taking dirty money and having it be sparkling, spring, ozoney-fresh funds. That would be too diabolical. Clever but acidly invidious.

A monumental undertaking that might be interesting if the targets were the object of the athletes.

But that would be more than insidiously invidious and inappropriate. But worth considering.

Better this be a meeting with McCarty than, ... with Peeta. A meeting with her would have been hellraiser reaper-rapper meets the to-be-reaped. So, a meeting with the animated caricature was just fine. For now.

The seconds dissipated and the main event of the day was having its dark red, dusty curtain raised. Bart's phone buzzed and he swatted the buzz with the palm of his hand. It was a short text from Latika. The carnival cliché had arrived and was downstairs. She offered to collect him.

Of course. Show him up. Bart texted back.

Bart fully anticipated that this meeting would focus upon a very special, and oh-so-unique lustrous green gem. The jewel that Latika was adorned with exploded into so many questions for him.

"What a spectacular pleasure to meet with you! The universe evolves as it revolves." McCarty cawed out like a raven to a Poe.

"Mr. McCarty, the pleasure is mine. I have been looking forward to this face-to-face opportunity. Shall we sit? Would you like Latika to concoct a dirty Dr. Pepper for you? She has perfected it by adding coconut syrup." Feed the beast, bees don't sting when they're consuming honey sweetness. *Maybe we should add a few drops of blood to add color*, Bart imagined how humorous that could become.

"A splendid offer, Bart! That would be delightful. I'll most certainly let you know how it compares to the Utah offerings."

"Latika, please be so kind and do your magic and serve up a creation for our guest."

"Happy to. Give me a few moments to blend it." Latika exited Bart's office and went to the beverage bar outside her work area.

"One of my favorite three doctors." McCarty chuckled at his private joke.

"How so? Who are the other two? Bart was curious. The logical ones, he thought, would have been Dr. Kevorkian and Dr. Mengele.

"Dr. Seuss, Dr. Strange, no specific preference. All three are quite unique personalities. If you had to choose three favorites, who would they be?" A playful smile froze on McCarty's face.

"It sure wouldn't be my now-no-longer urologist. The douche wanted to bore holes in me because he was convinced, I had prostate cancer. All I had was a serious infection that cleared up with antibiotics." Bart's face knotted up and was accessorized with a knitted brow.

"Should I know his name, so I do not partake in his bold practicing of medicine?"

"Nah. My three favorite docs would be Paracelsus, Patch Adams, and Ron Paul."

"Not the illustrious Dr. Fauci?"

"That guy is an X-rated thought to me. He fucked everybody over with his everchanging proselytizing."

"Oh dear, I detect distaste."

"Yeah. He left a bad taste in the mouths of so many people. No clarity. Changing directions at the drop of a datum. How about we move on to more pleasant and productive topics?" Bart offered up.

"A truly capital idea. Let's do just that."

At that last word, Latika entered the office with a dirty Dr. Pepper and a vanilla coke for Bart. "Mr. McCarty, I hope you enjoy my creation."

"I am quite certain I shall! Thank you ever so much for the effort."

"If either of you are in need of anything else, just Slack me."

"Thanks Latika. McCarty, let's sit, sip, and let drip the items we need to cover." Bart was going into pushy mode. He had to understand the gem issue and what that meant for him. Was it do or die, or Dewar's 32-year-old and glide? Bart motioned to the comfy office chair.

"We have only a few items to discuss." McCarty calmly stated. No microexpression tells.

Chapter 44: Reclaim

"I couldn't have helped noticing Latika's finely crafted jewelry." Poker, chess, or just best guess was dancing between them.

"Most curious, isn't it?" Bart gave nothing away. He was well aware and experienced in the ways and wiles of McCarty's coyote words and mannerisms.

"Truly most curious. She obviously has Maachi's gem. Which is a street full of beggars soliciting answers to yet to be asked questions. Your thoughts?" McCarty's clown mask of innocence melted into a visage of true concern. *It* was now in front of Bart and showing just a finely threatening glisten of teeth.

"Ya' got me migo. I have no idea how she ended up with it. All we really know is that Maachi is gone, and the gem is here. Maybe a pawn shop?"

"If we don't completely understand how this has happened, we could be the sacrificed pawns. I trust that is not a thought you are overly enamored with. She has it; we don't. And we need to gain possession of the emerald with whatever it takes. All options are up in the offing."

"Here's what we know now. She shared with me that her husband gave it to her as a gift. Where would an out-of-work guy pick up the cheese to buy it from somebody else? How did he get it?" A rhetorical question that resounded off the office wall paneling. Bart and McCarty were frozen in time. The right question with no readily evident answer.

"Why not just offer to buy it from her? Money talks and nobody walks from a sum that shines brightly with the images of dead president portraiture." McCarty went Occam on the issue.

"Seriously? Just walk up to her and tell her how much I like the gem and how about if I just give you this duffle bag filled with hunnies? That borders on the absurd. But, if you insist, I'll certainly give it a go. How many bennies are you thinking?"

"Enough to fill a stadium with cloned Benjamins."

"I'll run with that. So she gets a few hundred thousand and then she spends it. I would imagine that someone living in a two-bedroom apartment all of sudden is rich enough to make a down payment on a mansion in Tuxedo Park. Someone is going to ask for her W-2s. Sounds like a great way to create a trail of Krispy Kreme doughnuts for LE to follow and eat up. Take another run at it."

"Hmmm, ... true, very true Bart. Money that has no *bona fide* source invites the attention of several levels of the constabulary."

Chapter 45: Chaos

"The data are so furry it's not possible to draw lines between those pesky datum." Tannin was reaching high and hoped that Aidan would catch his chain.

"You're stating the obvious. Let's go Luther litany and stick the Bowie in the paper stack.

We have striking increases in missing persons in the cities we've been monitoring during this social diarrhea vomit. Even now as we've doubled back with those burb LEs, the lost in space in time, are still lost.

"We have these wild stories, not a lot, just enough to spice the chai, that some ninjas are roaming the killing streets and picking up the stiffs. That makes no sense at all. Who would be interested in capped miscreants' bodies?"

"The usual suspects would be anatomy students at medical schools, people selling body parts for some voodoo rituals, CHUDS, or maybe necrophiliacs."

"Can we agree to not bring politicians into this." Aidan squirrel-faced Tannin and stuck his tongue out.

"Righto. We don't think it's necrophiliacs. Nyuk, nyuk, nyuk." Tannin will never be regarded as slow on the retorts.

"You and I must be drinking too much Detroit water. Our brains must be churning to mush."

"How so big guy?"

"This should have been easy for us, and especially easy for you put your finger on the perpopotamus." Aidan went from his squirrel impression to dragon face.

"If it's so obvious, what the fuck is it?"

"The only people who cart off stiffs are the coroner, disease control during a catastrophic pandemic, or? The people who offed the unlucky departed."

"You doin' shrooms again? I know it's legal here, somewhat, how do you connect the missing from all the cities together?"

"Sure isn't the medical examiner pulling the stiffs. We're in a viral, bizarro madness world here. It's all deductive. So many missing and no body bags? The spikes only happen during the riots, oops, protected social events."

"Yah, all true. Goin' Conan Doyle here, what remains is the truth."

"Sherlock was fiction."

"I'm not, and bandito migo, do share the number of times I have missed the mark. I'm the Clue board with everything in the open if ya' can just shut out the noise and let the focus drift to the points of least resistance." Tannin's face went crinkle-shrinkle.

"Version two of our litany of the remnants."

"Missing people in all the cities where the demonstrations went violent. Let's make mental chalk lines and call them deadites with no return to kiss Sam Ash. Ninja ghosts promptly picking up the remains.

"Someones are deliberately offing demonstrators. For a ketamine moment here, let's connect the deliberate murders with the clean-up dudes. We don't have to have bodies. It helps but that just isn't going to happen.

"We're still missing the fundamental elements, no weapons, and we can't tie anyone to the scenes. A nice to have would be a motive."

"Hold the ketamine drip. How 'bout this?

"Let's talk about the major reasons for murder. We can cross out the ones that truly don't fit.

"Jilted lovers? Nope, x that one. Lustful moment gone rancid? That's more of a one-on-one or murder-suicide. Loathing? How do you loathe all the people with different profiles? Why would someone loathe collateral? That one is loaded with random and makes no sense."

"You left one of the biggies out."

"Spill-it bright bulb."

"Loot."

"You are really a funny guy. Loot? What loot? Low lifes, tweakers, and the rest of the misguided youth folks don't run flush with readies. Surely not with a fat stack of black cards. What loot?"

"I think if we can figure out the motive was tied to some type of gain, we may have a winner."

"Not buyin' it. Who would gain from offing demonstrators?"

"Hard core right wing."

"But that would mean that there's some type of conspiracy among a bunch of bunker mentality wackos to kill demonstrators. Why would they just whack a few? If they were deep in this, why not just Molotov the demonstrators and get a major kill notice on social media?"

"Ya got me. I'm still hangin' on there's a connection between what we now call intentional murders and what's that word?"

"Money."

"We can chorus this, ready?"

"Follow the money and you'll figure out the funnies and perps."

It was very bad acapella, but sound logic. Follow the money.

Chapter 46: Hear Me Now

"Why are we having this discussion? The solution is clear and quite simple."

"Do tell what the simplest solution is? At this moment all we know is that Maachi, devil roast his soul, and Bart's assistant has Maachi's jewel.

"And that jewel unless recovered or disabled is a fiber optic cable right back to the core of the company's sport activities." McCarthy passionately shared with Peeta.

"The sport activities are directly connected to other endeavors. We will have unleashed many inquiring minds. And not to our benefit. Our greatest asset is our invisibility.

"To connect everything together without the jewel is not plausible."

"That means you are suggesting what? Taking a few assets to permanently erase the existence of the now-temporary owner of the jewel?"

"Sometimes, let me correct myself, all the time you are slow on picking up on the obvious.

That's exactly what I am stating. I can repeat it and slow down as I speak? Would that be helpful?"

"There is no need for such caustic commentary. We are working for the same reasons here. Protect the company and protect ourselves.

"I would appreciate more respect after what I have accomplished."

"Sounds great. One-hit wonders only last as long as they're interesting. You're getting very boring. We are short on time to take action."

"I do not like this one iota."

"It is irrelevant if you like it or not. I am open to suggestions for alternative actions that yield the same or better result. And all I hear is you yapping' like a little chihuahua bitch."

"Little canines that continually nip at the hem of skirts or trousers eventually get kicked. Four-legged football with a score meaning a bounce off the wall.

"Is that something you might enjoy?" Peeta's face morphed into a three image demon incubus.

McCarty welded the lid on these thoughts. No tell was the best tell.

"Not sure if that is affirmative or not. Regardless, we have ready-assets to take care of this problem *post haste*."

"Our cleanup associates?"

"Voila. Now you have the opportunity to step up. Put your man-panties on and make the call. Make entirely certain you are clear with them; nothing is to remain. Everything goes. That means everything. This will be a moment in time where the departed are in toto.

"Understood? Time for that plaid jacket to earn its puppy chow. Step up or step out. There are others who would be thrilled to hit the kill switch and get some well-earned rewards. Start it up McCarty. Show me, and of course our beloved leader, that you don't have peanut butter guts.

"You and I have not had animated dialogues regarding strategies and tactics. For your own benefit please consider a backup plan to whatever you concoct in that Oster brain of yours."

"Peeta, you are always insightful. I so appreciate your thoughts regarding my welfare. I have studied many great leaders, especially military and even the characteristics of our pop culture mythic heroes.

"A powerful being once said, *I like to go full bore into something. If you have a backup plan then you've already admitted defeat*, to which I totally agree.

"A second quote though, for me, is always empowering for me to know which course of action to take at times like these.

"General Patton once stated, A good plan, violently executed now, is better than a perfect plan next week."

"You are so trite and boring. I am not some bimbo-bitch from one of your alcohol clubs back home. I am extremely well-versed in the philosophies of great warriors, from Sun Tzu to Musashi, to John Wick.

"I rarely admit a lack of knowledge in that area. But who said that about a backup plan being an admission of defeat?"

"Superman."

McCarty veneer-smiled and nodded his head as he kept his eyes wide open. He stared into the witch's eyes to see if there was any compassion at all.

Hah. Now that's an expectation, that's an expectoration. The razor wire dental floss hairball was firmly lodged in the nasty kitty's throat. She was momentarily speechless.

Chapter 47: Gangsta Sexy

"Brother, I have some bad news for you. It's about the tacphone you gave me to crack." Ganesh shyly stated to Bubai.

"This is humorous, is it not Ganesh? Your namesake is the overcomer of all obstacles. Surely with your skills you could maybe try more, just for me. I believe that any phone like this one has many secrets.

"People with many secrets are usually rich and have considerable vulnerabilities that we can take advantage of. Thugee cunning and charm to follow the trails in a phone like this one has the odor of fine incense." Bubai laughed at his playful jab at his brother-in-soul, Ganesh.

"I tried all I knew, and in a statement of fact, I even connected with a colleague who has the highest of clearances at NSA. She has never seen anything like this.

"Every attempt to access its secrets only indicated a flash screen of a comic character with the words, *is that the best that you've got?* The phone then rings and a voice shares a countdown indicating how many more attempts can be made before a big surprise happens.

"She ceased working on the phone after she was told nine more tries. No one wishes to have some unexplained awkward event happen at the NSA level she is on.

"You should just keep it for now. Phone hacking is an art that evolves by the day.

"I assure you that this pahelee will be solved and all the pieces will come together when Kali wishes."

"Wise words. Time always reveals the details of dharma and the direction of karma. Patience has never been a strong trait for me.

"You have done your best. You always do. Let me know if you identify a solution."

"Brother, my word is my bond, as is yours."

"It is a delight to be back home." Bubai gave Latika a big hug. Both of their children hugged his legs and wouldn't let go.

"We were just going to begin dinner. Dear husband join us and we shall celebrate your safe return. Kali smiles upon us."

"Let me put my bag away and wash up. I'll be right back."

Latika gave him a *I love you more than life* kiss.

Latika and the kids seated themselves at the table. All smiles as they whiled away the moments for Bubai's return.

An occasional gurgly-burgly stomach growl made its thoughts known.

Where is that man? Latika thought.

A few more moments passed, and Bubai returned to the dining area with his bag in hand. A sour paneer look was upon his face.

"Husband, what are you doing? Is something wrong?"

"My goddess wife, I need to go. I received an urgent call from work. I will contact you when I am able. I love you so much. You are my Shakti in the lovely flesh of my wife.

"Forgive me, all of you. I must depart. Thank you for understanding."

The smiles on their kids' faces reversed direction, frowns replaced the happiness. Understanding at this juncture is a very spoiled paneer.

"Brother, thank you ever so much for driving down here to us.

"We have two new contracts. One is in Georgia. The other is in Utah. The one in Utah is extremely lucrative and I would have awarded that one to you except the one in your home state is your familiar geography.

"Maybe not far from where you live." Ramakrishna forthrightly stated.

"Your compensation will be many times what we usually receive. I thought that since it is in Georgia you would be the perfect choice for this.'

"Where do I need to go? Any special requests?"

"I need to have two of our brothers accompany you. This contract requires complete disappearance of all involved.

"Four are to be the fortunate ones."

"Do you believe that two will be adequate?"

"You shall have two of our finest thuggee. X and Y."

"Fine. The address? Timing?"

"Last to first, you should leave now and plan the opportune moment to engage the deceived ones. Here is the address."

Bubai was speechless. He gave no indication of his emotional turmoil.

Chapter 48: Talking Out Loud

"Hey, Tannin, we just got the oddest message. It was forwarded to me in insta-time."

"Oddest as in what? That's a wide-open comment that begs the obvious.

"And a rush on it to run it up the priority list? Do spill the entire well."

"A guy with a significant Bengali accent was blabbering on about needing protection. And get this, he mentioned that he has been extensively traveling and when we meet him, he would share."

"You know it was a Bengali accent because?"

"Silly boy. You know I learn languages to keep me entertained. The subtle nuances of a language tells you lots about the person."

"So you can tell a Boston bowery accent from executive jargon speak?"

"You do pay attention sometimes, don't you?" Tannin elitistly smirked.

"Since you're the smart guy, I'll let you chase this extremely detailed lead. Migo, my plan tonight is a bottle of 2008 Brut Dom with one of the twins." Aidan showed his pearly-best smile.

"One thing I forgot to mention. He cited Portland."

"Which one? Connecticut, Maine, or the famous hot pot, Oregon."

"The latter of the three. Can I tease you to raincheck the twin and the Dom? But which twin was it?"

Aidan smiled twice. Once for the Oregon note. The second for the fact he wasn't going to divulge which twin.

"Pack bags?" Aidan rightly asked.

"Not too far away, Georgia."

"As in the Caucasus, Georgia?"

"Funnyman, no. The place where we grow peaches."

"Ooooh, I like peaches, what about you padre?" If sarcasm was tangible and could be exchanged for lots of solid Benjis, Aidan would have purchased

Alaska back from the federal government. He was always cool and stylin'. In his own image, there were a thousand mirrors, and he was front and center in each one.

"Right now I'm comin' in hot on this potential lead. Migo, think about it. We had no motive, no bodies, and no suspects. This is gonna' be a trifecta. I want all three, not just a juicy peach or two on a tree.

"I want the fucking orchard."

"That's why I asked about peaches." Sarcasm fire alert. *Not a sarcasm fire alert!*

"Clever. Should've expected it. Meet an Indian guy in a restaurant that has a superb Indian buffet. Everyone will be caught up in whether to go for more vegetable biryani or fresh samosas.

"I'm already likin' this guy." Tannin admired artistry in anything covert, dark, and mysterious. It added texture and flavor to the interaction.

"Ya did notice we're the only pasty white guys in here with bulges in their sport jackets, right?"

"Point being?"

"If anything goes tits up and we're in the middle of it, they sure won't be challenged to identify us." A small, hot, red Dhani chili thought burned in Aidan's noggin'.

"Look on the bright side, in a lineup maybe they'll just say all those white boys look the same." Ari never backed down to poke at stereotypes. Being a solid Ashki he was used to targeting tasteless tropos. He had his shots and was mostly immune to the Jew slurs.

"Two please. Could we have a booth in the back? We have some business issues to discuss, and we don't want to interrupt any of your clientele." Aidan knew that what he just mumble-spewed out made no sense whatsoever. The point was to get to the back of the eatery with backs against the wall. Can't get taken by surprise if your back is against the wall.

"Certainly. I understand. Please follow me."

"Thank you, ... *Tannin tilted his head to see her name pin*

"... Baltishna, ... did I say it right?" Tannin was cruising the reality to see what kind of fish lived in this unfamiliar ocean of fine things to eat.

"You said that very well! Yes, you did." Baltishna seductively smiled at him.

"Bengali? You sound like you're from somewhere near Kolkata." Here we go again. Tannin breaking down pieces to create a reality that will keep them breathing and pulling this connection into the game. Whatever it takes. Someone walks into a very ethnic restaurant and is soaking in the ambience.

Tannin was soaking in the bits and behavioral algorithms. Never can tell what you're walking into. Like a trooper who pulls over a tricked-out, blacked-out Charger with darkly tinted windows. Makes you want to wear a ballistic vest all day and when you sleep. Every pull over can be a catastrophic event and you need titanium cajones to put yourself potentially in the way of a barrel of a gun.

Tannin and Aidan couldn't stop what was spooling up. They were going to see what was in the Charger. Tannin went cost effective but highly effective.

Aidan went *I hope this works when I need it* haute couture. His spook friends in Japan had developed an ultra-tough polymer they called Gen I Titanium-Graphene and he had the unique opportunity to test it out in the unreal world he lived in. It fits like a leotard with micro fluid vessels. Weird stuff even had nanosphere iron that would swarm the area of impact faster than Aidan could order Ramos Pinto after a fine meal of osso bucco.

Trust and verify moment here. He trusted them and hoped that he never had to verify its effectiveness. A boy and his toys.

"How did you know? Have you traveled there?"

"Yes, I have. Amazing experience. Make that plural, experiences. Put some time into living in an ashram."

"Really?"

"I tell no lies unless I have to. I don't think I have to here." Tannin flashed his pearlies and winked at Baltishna.

She cast her eyes to the floor as she coyly smiled at him.

"Will this do?"

"Perfect."

They sat together on the wall side of the booth.

"Would you like something to drink?"

"Do you have Bisleri?" Tannin asked as he scanned the room for perps, targets, and potential collateral.

"No, I am sorry we do not have it. We do have Himalayan, will that suffice?"

"Sure will."

"And you sir? Something to drink?" She turned her gaze and words to Aidan.

"Kingfisher or White Rhino, if you please."

"Either one?"

"Yes, your call."

"Are you certain of this?"

"Ma'am, I live dangerously. So unless you're going to inject a vile poison through the cap, I'll take whatever is easiest." Aidan bravado and braggadocio fully displayed.

"Okay."

Oddly, the comment regarding spiking the beer didn't even make her raise an eyebrow.

Away she went and in her departing wake of voluptuousness, a tall, bearded man made his way towards Tannin and Aidan.

Aidan had already taken his Sky Marshal and placed it on his lap, barrel out.

Not to be outdone, Tannin was packing a CZ P-10. It was keeping his jewels company.

"Are you Aidan and Tannin?" The quietest, deepest voice they had ever heard traveled across the table to their ears.

"That would be us. Forgive us for not raising up and shaking your hand. Two white guys with sport jackets part one already made a bit of a whuzup spectacle." Yah, that's part of the reason. The other one is their little friends if this happened to go random.

"May I sit?"

"Of course. That's why we're here." Tannin was gently snarking the moment.

"You know us, and how about a name to attach to your face. Always nice to put the two together." Aidan pitched a wiffle ball for now.

"Bubai."

"Let me guess, voice is saying to me Bengali." Tannin probed.

"Yes, that is correct. How did you know?"

"I have friends from there."

"Very interesting."

"You called the meeting so take the wheel." Aidan wanted to take lead here so that Tannin could do his freaky profiling thing.

"I will be direct. My family has been targeted for death by contract."

"By your family, you mean you also?"

"Yes."

"And this is important for us for what reason? You mentioned Portland, and because you did, that's why we're here."

"Portland, yes, Portland. I was there during the most recent social disturbances."

"You mean violent riots?"

"Yes, that too."

"A lot of people were there. As was shared with us it was like a really evil urban Woodstock with more drugs than Pfizer, and more malevolence than tweaker who got the wrong order at Popeyes."

"So you were in the crowd. Something else you think would make us want to stay and finish our drinks."

As though on cue, the goddess of libations returned to their table.

She carefully reached over the table and placed the drinks on elephant stamped coasters.

After opening Aidan's brewsky, she tilted a chilled glass and slowly filled it almost to overflowing.

As she was focusing on the beer, she spoke up.

"Anything for you Bubai?"

"No thank you, not right now."

"If you need me, you know where I am."

Tannins antsy antennae went to the stratosphere. He had an image of a Star Wars movie excerpt bar scene.

"Looks like you two know each other." Tannin saw an opening to have tells drop to the floor like a cleaved apple from William Tell.

Bubai was not jud. He knew exactly where Tannin was going. How so? Because it would be something he would do after learning so much from his brothers, and the powerful muse of Kali. No blink, no pupil surprise, and definitely no microexpressions. The Thugee are the absolute masters of deception. And if you can be in-the-moment deceptive, then you have not learned your craft and trade. When you have seen and experienced the things that Bubai has, from Kolkata to using a lithium cutter, you automatically go stone face

Aidan saw that this whole interaction was starting to tilt. Tannin was great but sometimes when he thought he was clever he neglected to consider his adversary or morally reciprocal persona could also have a few life experiences and internal searches that perceived his intent.

"Shall I refer to you as Agent Tannin, or do you have a last name that I should know to confirm your identity."

Tannin you ain't got the monopoly on a couple of sharp barbed parries. Bubai, you are one strange nut. Aidan bounced his thoughts regarding he and Tannin may have jumped from a lifeboat to salty waters with innumerable predator fish.

"Not something we need to share. Best idea right now is let's get on track to you and your epiphanical information. Whaddya say?" Tannin is smart enough to know you change the trajectory to avoid taking a hit.

"That would be greatly appreciated."

"How about sharing some top line facts. We're pretty good at connecting dots." Great call by Aidan. Take a quick exit ramp and then back up on the freeway.

"There is a contract out on me. I am to be murdered. And, my family. My wife and children are at equal risk."

"And why would someone want to off your entire family?"

"Because for some reason the company I work for has decided I am a catastrophic risk to them."

"The company thing is critically important but let's go back to you and your family's safety.

It's what we do. You know, protect the innocent and those that are being taken advantage of by some predator. Smelly bumpy things in the night get a fifty-five gallon of smack back."

Something about LE folks. They have the most interesting behavioral traits. The opposite of a retreat limbic response. Loud noises and things that could hurt you are the items you run from.

Aidan and Tannin don't run from anything or anybody. They hold their badass good guy badges up with pride. They run towards the disruption.

"Do you actually know who's trying to kill you? Gotta' name?"

"Bubai."

Aidan slid a wise guy side eye to Tannin with a specific message, *WTF?*

"Same name as you. Cousin? Codename? Freaky similarity. Coincidence?"

"Not a cousin or anything like that. I was contracted to murder myself and my family and leave no trace whatsoever as to what had occurred."

Tannin and Aidan went question mark pupils. *This is insane. Must be something in the food, or maybe the water, or air?*

"You were contracted to kill yourself, your wife, and kids? Like in one of those mindless slasher flicks like Saw?" Tannin drilled for a bedrock thought cuz right now, unless this guy was a diabolical, evil Criss Angel, how would someone pull that off and why would he meet with federal marshals? This is worth listening to just for the soul shaking novelty of it.

"Yes."

"And just how would you do that?"

Bubai cast a meditative smile to the marshals.

"Well? This is your turn to take the mic. Don't drop it. We don't want to be here all night."

Those that I work with are contracted to leave no trace of the people who are killed. I have become very efficient at making people disappear, entirely, no trace at all."

"You're admitting to being an accomplice to murders? Maybe it's time to escort you out of here over to Fulton county jail. Talk faster because right now you have two pistoleers dialed into your privates. You're freaking us out. Hope this has a positive surprise ending." Tannin moved his trigger finger to be ready to kiss a lever.

"The company is enormous. They sponsor people to go out an murder innocents at any gathering that has violence involved. Then we, my brothers, get rid of the evidence.

For some reason I have become a name on the list and that is outside of what we were hired to do. Something monumental has shifted.

My request of you is to take my wife and children and place them in protective custody.

This needs to happen in hours.

Ask yourselves, why would I meet with you and ask you to place your efforts behind ensuring my family's well-being?"

"You could just be totally fucking nuts and you have some thought of death by cop or some other outrageously dumb thing to get attention to some fringy disruptions." Tannin always had to deep digging. Whatever was at the bottom of the hole would be the reality.

"You have every right to believe such things. I have something that will immediately garner your attention. Here, take this." Bubai handed over Maachi's tricked out tacphone.

"A phone? So?" Tannin wasn't impressed.

"Marshal, take a closer look. It is far more than a simple tacphone."

Tannin toyed with the little electronic monster. He turned it over and over and could not detect any seams. On the back was a small membrane panel.

"That phone will open doors to you to apprehend the evilness that is among us."

"Well, Tannin, whatcha say boi? Is this something we can slap with grappling hooks?"

Tannin didn't answer. His eyes glazed over. He continued to fondle the electric beastie in his hands.

"Is he alright, Marshal?" Bubai asked of Aidan.

"Yeah, he'll be fine. He has this way of seeing things with his fingers. It's creepy but what a tactical advantage."

"Hey, Tannin, come on back bucko. Get back into your body in the present time."

Nothing happened. Tannin was catatonic.

"This will get him out of it pronto. *Twins!*"

Tannin rapidly blinked his eyes.

"Where are they?"

"Sorry about that Tannin baby. You went off to that mysterious place you go to and we weren't sure when you'd buy the return ticket."

Tannin said nothing in response. He flipped the phone right side up, massaged something in the metallic wonder, and magically the screen lit up.

Bubai was amazed. He thought he must be dreaming. The best of the best hackers he knew couldn't move the boulder up the hill. Here was Tannin making electric love to the communication conduit and slam, bam pow. It's lights, and now actions.

"How did you do that?" Bubai queried Tannin.

"It's just a gift I have. Lucky for you the gift is still keeping on giving."

"How will you get the password to access what's in the phone?"

"Like this." Tannin closed his eyes and played Mozart in the electronic jungle.

The screen changed to several smaller panes and a bright light projected out that presented the activities of one of the panes. Tannin ran his fingers over the panes and projection changed accordingly. Bubai had become the unwitting projection screen.

For tonight's dinner and a show it was show and tell. And what they scanned through was depraved and had so many nasty aspects to it, there was only one thing that the marshals could do.

In perfect unison, "We're in."

Tannin went total giant protective golem. "You're coming with us right now. Nothing fancy. Not an arrest. You're the electronic message in a bottle we needed. We'll take care of your family. Address and names. Don't call them. Totally go radio silence. Never can tell who's listening. And just to amp up our safety, battery out of your phone or I'll need to dump it in the toilet."

Aidan closed with, "time to say buh-bye, Bubai, let's jet."

Chapter 49: Runaway

Bubai's favorite meeting venue was in the offing. It was a Friday evening, and the restaurant was busy as all get out. Bubai liked the busy-ness. Nice to be surrounded by cadres who would come to your rescue if the need arose.

Tannin put his arm around Bubai's broad shoulders and gave him a camaraderic squeeze. "You family is safe. Had to let you know that you were tagged, I mean, your wife was tagged." Aidan knew that what he was going to share wouldn't sit well with the big Indian.

"I do not understand, *tagged?*"

Tannin went techy and let Bubai know that when they took his family into custody they were thoroughly scanned. And not with the pedestrian level equipment at an airport.

The marshals wanted a total lock down on any potential electric cookie trail. Makes sense. A safe house would go down in its security appraisal level if a person unknowingly trotted into the place sending out a gigundo notice to the world, *here I am, come get me!*

Cover blown. Operatives damaged, and a level of departmental embarrassment that would raise question like, *we pay these guys how much to do what?*

"They found an extremely intricate transponder in the pin of an emerald jewel. Know anything about it?"

Bubai went flush. "I gave that to my wife as a gift."

"Hey, go long on items like this. Time is of the essence. We can't drop the net if we're slow at the switch." Aidan was more than a bit perturbed. The pulling teeth thing to get the whole story was a colossal dingle-berry.

"I took it from one of the men I made disappear. He also was the owner of the tacphone."

"Well how about that Ollie? We just scored! We have the phone, and now a transponder gem from a dead guy. And I made an in-field tactical decision." With that, Tannin took the gem out of his pocket. A grin that would make a mashup Joker and It smile paltry in comparison.

"But that means they could follow you."

A well-rehearsed vocalization from Laurel and Hardy, "Zackly!"

"I understand."

"What about the rest of this? They're safe, you're not. We need to correct that. That would be in the right now."

"You need not worry about me, marshals. I have a short litany of items I need to attend to before I submit to your hospitality. I can take care of myself."

"Nope. Doesn't work like that. Ya see if you keep roaming free-range, you could be compromised. This will sound very mercenary; we need you alive to guide us in this Where In the World Is Carnal *Intento*. This isn't your decision."

"I understand. Please excuse me, I need to use the restroom. I'll be right back."

"Don't get lost and flush yourself down the toilet to escape. And the window in there, you could do that. I just need to let you know there are five unmarked cars out there. They see your ass popping out the window and it will create a low-level moment of confrontation.

"And we don't want that, do we?" Aidan closed the thought loop. If you go take a poop don't try to fly the coop.

"I would not think of doing anything like that. Thank you for letting me know you take your job seriously. It is comforting."

Bubai made his way to the restroom. The one with a guy on the door.

"You think he'll bolt?" Aidan asked of Tannin.

"I hope so."

"You didn't."

"Ya jokin' me right? Of course I did."

"You pinned him?"

"Oh yeah baby."

Bubai was ambling his way back to the rear of the restaurant when the most irritating sound in the world belched. The fire alarm was activated.

Bubai turned around and jumped into the middle of the crowd of frightened patrons who were rushing out the door.

And that was all he wrote. For now.

Chapter 50: So Long

Just another nondescript McMansion in an upscale piece of a white bread suburb.

Five-foot wall, gated entrance, surveillance cameras, and the builders' upgrade of infrared sensors.

None of those items were an issue. In shadows of the shadows they soundlessly walked across the roof. Luckily it was an almost moonless night.

She knocked on the door and incessantly pressed the video door cam button.

A voice rang out, "Something I can help you with?"

"I hope so. My Tesla is totally out of electricity, and I parked it out on the cul de sac. And my luck, my phone isn't getting a connection. Could you help me? Could you call someone? A two service or triple A? I have a card, just can't call." The most convincing, hurt, help-me, vulnerable female smile was fully displayed by Baltishna.

A big jumpsuit clad fellow opened the door and let Baltishna inside.

She's no threat, little thing she is. Scotty mused. *And she's a nice visual diversion from this boring job.*

"Come in. Give me the card. I'll call."

"I cannot thank you enough. I know this is a safe neighborhood, but you never can be sure."

"Got that right."

"May I use you restroom. I have to pee so bad I don't want to do anything embarrassing."

Scotty's thoughts went to the X-rated screen. "No prob, down there to the left."

"Thank you!" She said to Scotty as she turned to walk toward the restroom.

Scotty refocused his attention on the smudged print on the AAA card.

Baltishna jumped up and wrapped her toned thighs around Scotty's neck as she balled her fists and hammered his temples. She grabbed her sash and wrapped it several times around the hot dog muscled neck of her score. Scotty went totally bug eyed as he fell to the floor.

Scotty was so mashed he didn't realize he was being suffocated.

While the surprise and awe was going on, two dark clad fellows speedily ran up the stairs. They would make short work of the tasks ahead.

Chapter 51: Comin' In Hot

They split up. One of them would stay hidden outside the back door on the fire escape.

Bubai motioned for the other brother to follow him.

They made no sounds as they made their way to apartment door. Bubai went first and got cozy with the door lock. He made it look like he was picking the lock. Before he opened the door, he pointed at his accomplice and let him know that Bubai would hold the door wide to enable a fast entrance by his fellow assassin.

His partner nodded.

Bubai swung the door wide and held it open. The only light was from the windows and the streetlights.

Three steps into the apartment, the killer looked around the entry room and there was nothing there except for a heavy wooden cutting board.

Bubai slipped his yellow sash around the thug's neck and pulled so hard it was as though a separated head might be in the offering. His target went limp, and Bubai dragged him to the bedroom.

He pinged the other member of the kill team that it was time to come up.

As he entered the room, Bubai smashed him in the face with the cutting board.

He dragged the unlucky unconscious chap fully into the room and closed the door.

Bubai retrieved his duffle and two body bags. He needed to work quickly.

"Anybody home?" Aidan softly spoke as he knocked on the door.

There was no answer. Tannin took a couple of steps back and drew his CZ.

Aidan knocked again and on the last fingers meet steel door, it opened.

"What are you doing here?" Bubai was surprised in a not-so-good way.

"We were just cruisin' the hood and thought we'd stop by. Just want to make sure everything is okay." Tannin kicked in to the notice of *we're here.*

"Everything is fine. I am just making sure everything is cleared out of here."

"Okay if we come in?" Aidan almost politely asked.

"Of course." Bubai stepped away from the door.

"Awful dark in here. Can we turn on some lights?" Tannin wasn't asking for permission. He already was clicking switches and wandering around the apartment.

"You sure did clear out everything. Where are you stowing it?"

"Not keeping any of it. It is in a storage facility and there is no trace back to me or my family."

"Smart move. Hey you missed something." Tannin pointed at the cutting board in the sink.

He walked over and picked it up and turned it over.

"Is that blood?"

"Yes, it is."

"Yours"

"No. In accordance with my religious beliefs, I sacrificed a chicken to the goddess Kali to celebrate leaving this place and new beginnings."

"Interesting. Well, might want to clean it off if you're going to leave it here. Never can tell what someone might think."

"I shall do that. Anything further I can help you with?"

"There sure is. Your coming with us now. Let's not have you be a sacrificial calf."

Aidan and Tannin led the way down the hall with Bubai in tow.

He's lying. He's a solid deceiver. He should know better. He should know that I know that we're nowhere near full moon. A sacrifice like he said would not be done like this. He's hiding something but what? Give Tannin a piece of thread and he'll weave you a tapestry in record time.

The three of them walked out to the parking lot and passed a van nearby.

"Was that there before?" Tannin was going hyper-vigilant.

"Dude, will you chill? It's just some van. Didn't one of your tribe say that sometimes a cigar is just a cigar? We've got our package so who cares what or who is in the van. Ya' know the saying, don't come knockin' if the van is rockin', ..."

"It's not rocking though. Maybe I should check it out."

"Dang, c'mon. It's getting past my snorts of port time."

Bubai shot a dart glance at the truck.

"Yeah, you're probably right. Sometimes I think I see boogey men everywhere. But then again, a cigar could have poison on it, maybe an explosive load."

"Knock it off! Hey, you two, get in the car. Bubai, we need to deliver you to your family. You'll be safe. I've two of my most trusted colleagues there, Connie and Fernando."

"Connie? Your joshing me. That guy is old and uses a cane. You sure about this?"

"I take it you've never seen Connie in action. If they had a black belt for Cane Fu, he'd have it."

"No such thing."

"Migo, my sincere suggestion, don't test the guy. His favorite phrase is *batter up*."

"My krav maga is faster than a cane."

"Don't be so sure. You heard the story about the really old samurai master who was challenged by a young buck, didn't you?"

"Nope. And I don't want to hear it now. It's your choice on Connie. Fernando, I get. Connie, I don't.

"Let's just get out of here. My stomach's growling for some corned beef on rye."

Bubai cringed. *Nandi, forgive them, they know not what they do*, he sought understanding from the divine bull.

Chapter 52: Whatever It Takes

"Thank you, Mr. McCarty, for visiting me on such short notice. I have some unusual information to share with you.

"I will need to enlist you skills and services on a more involved manner." The Praetor nervously shared with the carnival barker.

"I am honored that you would consider me to assist you. Just let me know what it is I can help you with and consider it done." McCarty was a smooth tool no matter what part of the business machine he tinkered with.

"I shall be succinctly direct with you. We have lost all contact with Peeta. That informational silence leaves me with a vacancy in an elevated leadership position. We do not even have her vitals and biodata. We have no way to locate her. If she had the gem with her this would be a conversation that never would have happened. She must have shielded the gem from our peering electrons. She appears to have made a conscious decision to solidly close the door with the company. Hopefully it will be only a temporary door closure. She'll connect with us when she wishes to. The whole affair is very unfortunate."

"Oh tender mercies! We must do everything we can possibly do to find her! Do you believe she is in grave danger? This is terrible news." McCarty pulled a navy-blue rodeo class bandana from his side pocket and wiped his forehead of its budding emotional dewdrops.

"Such noble thoughts! Just as I expected from you. I do not believe she is in danger. That divine being is more than capable of taking care of herself. It is vitally important for the company to project strength and continuity. You are well aware that we have disdain for rumors and their mongering in the hallways, offices, and Zoom meetings.

"I would be thrilled to make fully available to the company my resources to find her, ... or at least connect with her." McCarthy must have taken his faux compassion medication prior to the meeting.

"Mr. McCarty, my thoughts are proceeding in a different direction. You have thoroughly demonstrated your resourcefulness and skill.

"I bet on you being our next very important decision maker. We always have backroom wagers on who will be an up and comer, a go-getter who views the word no as a dare to discover a profitable solution."

"I am, ... speechless. You have wagered that I would be of greater value to the company? I completely humbled. Thank you for your confidence in me."

"Not many others recognized your talents. I knew that when you proposed the Cantank R Us acquisition plan, I knew you were a man to place a bet on."

"I am at your service. What may I do next for you?"

"Do what you do but do it as my personal adviser."

"How exciting!"

"Will you accept the gauntlet that I have just thrown to the floor?"

"I am embarrassed that you thought you would even have to ask. Of course! When would you like me to begin?'

"You began when you entered the door to my office."

"Oh, my, ... "

"You need to connect with our dear colleague, Ben Sussen. I hope you recall that he is pivotal in taking a visible leadership position within Cantank R Us pharmaceuticals."

"But Bart is now leading that company as its CEO. He is doing a splendid job! Profits are up and complaints are down. That place is a money machine."

"All very true words. Ben Sussen needs to be their to put the final touches on our move to manufacture designer recreational drugs. Especially the Purple Demon offerings.

"Our Chinese partners are feeling such success with how they have flooded the world with the techno-opium, fentanyl. You know they are industrious creatures. They always look for new horizons and it appears that they have conquered yet another technological opportunity."

"Ah, yes, … the drug manufacturing initiative." McCarty hid his sad clown face. He was not a fan of drugs. Not even coffee or alcohol.

"What is so unique with their recent successful endeavors?"

"The Purple Demon line of compounds are potent and unpredictable in their effects."

"That does not sound like it is a good thing."

"Quite the opposite. They are introducing something that they call poly function drugs. They are able to combine several intoxicants with relatively predictable results."

"Relatively is a curious word. I do not understand why that is of importance."

"You and the world will soon be able to stand on a ledge, bungee jump without checking the status of the equipment, or jump from an airplane with a parachute of unknown quality all in a few pills with diverse composition."

"Goodness, thrill seekers. Just as we do with our sport. Cater to the bored, the pained, the confused, with a smorgasbord of unpredictable results. That is master class thinking! The world has become too safe and there are those who always push the boundaries to find their true self. Brilliant!

"The products have been tested for safety, yes?"

"Of course, just like they did with fentanyl."

Sad carnival barker hid his thoughts even from himself. He decided to make a strategic withdrawal and head back home.

McCarty turned on the basement lights, held the handrail, and descended into the cementy-dampness. He sauntered over to the wood stove.

He took out his tacphone, entered a security app, and punched up a series of numbers.

A two-inch thick steel plate folded up against the cellar wall and the stove slid back to hold it in place.

McCarty reached down into the indenture and pulled up on a recessed handle.

He smiled his best greasy-scumbag smile and opened the metal box that lived under the handled door.

Peeta will return when I letter. I own her ghost, McCarty happily thought to himself.

He promptly put it back in its shielded box, hit a few more numbers in his phone and the stove and steel plate reversed their process.

Provo sat in his butt-comforting, leather living room sofa and thought to himself, *I knew he would win out against Peeta. His façade was thin and transparent. My wager on this outcome had very favorable odds.* He smiled again at the warm thought of enhancing his bit account. The Praetor reveled in how many bits he had won on this bet. Everyone else was betting on Peeta making McCarty disappear. Wrong call. If its skill against passion, Provo always bet on passion. Skill has its limits and passion does not.

Chapter 53: Break On Through

"Go ahead, open it."

"And just what's inside?"

"A surprise." Tannin grinned with his words.

Aidan opened the small box on the conference table. Happy eyes took control of his do-the- right-thing genes.

"What are you going to do with them? Shouldn't we be hittin' up the director to let us go wild on this monstrous corporate creature?"

"A great idea but it's all in the timing. You know that pesky little thing of lining things up before you go into motion? Timing, ... the critical element in humor, war, and sex."

"I know there is a point hidden in this, what is it?"

"Yeah, we'll go to the director and lay our plan."

"What plan?"

"We could go wild and crazy and search out our sus. That is not how we need to do this. We want the perps to come to us."

"And you're going to use the gem to draw them in as bait. When are you planning on sending the news through the ectoplasm, *come and get it?*"

"I'm working on that part now."

Tannin closed the graphene-titanium box.

"I get it. The box is our own personal puzzle box. Break seal when in need of trashing bad people."

"On our terms. The game is afoot, Watson."

Chapter 54: New Day

"Who did you say is here to see me?" Bart had become more seasoned in the nefarious arts that were part and partial to the company and now, Cantank R Us. He didn't want the seasoning to be that of a turkey. Bart had played his part so well to off that miserable piece of shit, Maachi. Now was the time to consolidate and up his game on self-preservation.

Post the last meeting on the roof, Bart took a liking and a taking of Maachi's ballistic knife. Upper right drawer in his desk, complete with an actuator that at the press of a foot pedal, opened up and made his blade ready to use. *Open drawer in case of argumentative confrontation.*

"Ask her again what her name is. Maybe it's someone I met and just don't recall her."

"All she says is that she has very important information just for you regarding Latika."

Didn't expect that. Latika disappeared. Bart didn't know if that disappearance was connected to McCarty and the company. People who get too close to McCarty or that drippy bitch, Peeta, have a habit of permanently disappearing. Bart had even sent out one of his warehouse guys to her apartment and everything was gone.

Either way, she's gone and hopefully that cursed green gem is gone with her. Bart had gone emotionally colder after all that had happened. Always looking over his shoulder, never leaving an open beverage about, check wine corks for syringe holes, and most of all, things in the rearview mirror can be far deadlier than they appear.

He had become the prisoner of his own success and everything around him no longer simply had a neutral value in his life. Calling everything either black or white versus playing in the world of grey and shadows was now his *modus operandi.*

"Well, any news regarding Latika would be very welcome. Send her up."

Bart was doubtful that Latika would be returning to work. He sure did need his assistant. Especially with the new organizational structure getting ready to pop.

He opened his drawer just in case it was a duplicitous visitor sent to him by McCarty, or far worse, from the Peeta incubus.

An athletically built Indian lady stood outside Bart's door. She invitingly smiled and held her hand up to say, *Hi!*

Bart hit a button under his desk and the etched glass door slid open. He motioned the little lady to *come on in!*

"Hi, I have some news to share with you about Latika. She was a close friend."

"And your name is?"

"Baltishna."

"A pleasure to meet you. I'm Bart, but you knew that. So, what's going on with Latika? I sure do miss her. She was the corporate guidance system and my go-to person. Big hole in the company right now."

"The pleasure is mine.

"Well, Latika had some very personal issues to address back in Kolkata. Some unexpected events made it imperative to get back to mother India. She will not be returning to work."

"Wow! Not that unexpected. When a key person is AWOL for more than a long weekend it isn't surprising that some crazy thing happened and life's priorities change.

"Very unfortunate. I'm going to have to do some quick action and do a quick search for someone who can help me steer this ship."

"Latika wanted to let you know that she had me come here for two reasons."

"Got the first, what's the second?"

"I have an MBA from the Indian Institute of Management and served as an intern at Apple. Latika believed that I could be of great service to you. She felt that she needed to help fill any gaps she created by her unanticipated permanent absence."

"Seriously? She did that and you are all that? Would you be interested in taking her place?"

"It would be an honor to work for you, sir. When would you prefer for me to begin employment?"

"Several days ago, ... kidding, sort of. How about right now? I'll have HR come up here and you can meet with them in the executive conference room. You wouldn't happen to have those bothersome documents that will make us all legal here in hiring you, would you? Just say yes and we'll figure the rest out. Not kidding."

"May I address you as Bart?"

"Sure."

"Bart, I am always prepared in the best of ways. Yes, I have all required work documents and my *Curriculum Vitae* with reference letters from several trusted colleagues and previous supervisors." She thought to herself that her Hewlett Packard printer was very patient and would never squeak the truth of the document creation.

This can't be for real. She has a CV with her? Love the confidence. Bart pleasantly mused.

He tapped a few keys to let HR know about this highly fortuitous meeting. He gave them ten minutes.

"This is amazing. Big sad about losing Latika. Big happy at having you here."

"It is my pleasure and honor to be of service to you here."

"Pretty amazing how god and the universe unexpectedly deal you some great cards when you are on a low win cycle."

"I agree! The universe has an interesting way of balancing loss and discovery."

"HR will be ready for you in a few more moments. But before you meet with them, could you take a couple of quick notes? I have a pad you can use."

Baltishna reached into her limited edition Tumi backpack and pulled out her tricked

iPad.

"I anticipated your need, Bart." She hit the top button, entered a thumbprint, and the machine lit up with electric life.

She took out a stylus and placed the tip on the glass and looked up at Bart.

"Ready."

Bart smiled at the thought of this babe's energy. *Jeez, this goddess drops into the biz here and is more prepared than long timers here.*

"Nice. Very nice! Okay, first up is I'm expecting a VIP to visit at the end of the week. A Mr. Ben Sussen. Next up is if you can reach out to a fellow by the name of McCarty and schedule a meeting *before* Sussen shows up.

Last big item is this, if a woman by the name of Peeta connects with us, pipe her right in to my personal phone.

All the names, email addresses, and telephone numbers are in Latika's data base. The password is a short one, ONS, all caps, followed by four zeros. You'll need to replace her touch ID with your thumb print. I know it's a lot getting tossed your way, I apologize for that."

"Bart, no apology needed. I can take it from here. I'll meet with HR and then business services to gain access to Latika's files."

"Like I said, nice, nah, super nice. It really is so interesting how things just happen. You know what I mean?"

"I certainly do." Visions of Kali Maa danced in Baltishna's heart, mind, and soul. *Yes, the goddess always looks out for her devotees* she thought as she hid her almost invisible smile.

Before she stood up, she looked down at the Tumi bag and made sure that Bart couldn't see the three monogrammed letters, POS, debossed in a dark purple hue upon the embroidered leather badge. She thought to herself, *almost missed that detail, have to correct it later today*. She also continued her internal review of what else might have notes about the true owner of the iPad? *Time to recalibrate*. Although, no one would question the La Panthère watch or the other expensive baubles she would wear. Doesn't every MBA have hundreds of thousands of dollars or rare jewelry?

Chapter 55: Enemy

Bubai sat in the temple with his back against the wall. Now that his family was safe, he could do what he knew he had to do. It was easy to escape the auspices of the marshals.

His deep meditation enveloped his entire being. Before his inner visions, Kali Maa smiled at him.

She was very clear to him regarding what he must do. Kali Maa is so often misunderstood.

She is often viewed as a dark malevolent force, but that is only part of what she manifests.

Kali Maa is also the destroyer of evil forces and protects the innocent.

Bubai's family were innocents. And now they live every moment with the subtle jeopardy that evil men can visit them again and wreak havoc upon their lives. Not likely now, though. But being situational aware is on the job description for all WITSEC benefactors.

He would never let his family be placed in danger again. He would seek out those that had caused such trouble for him and his loved ones. It would take time, and time was his asset to use.

He was Thugee and a great deceiver. Bubai would find a way, with or without the help of the marshals, to completely destroy the corporate monstrosity that had almost taken his life and the life of his family.

He would reconnect with his brothers. After all, they had no real idea that he and his family were the targets.

They would ask questions regarding the other two assassins and Bubai would passionlessly state that they were mortally wounded during the invasion, and he disposed of any wrongdoing evidence. They would understand that.

Occupational hazard.

Bubai would use the resources of the Thugee to identify the head of the poisonous snake, the company, so that he could lop it off.

If only he still had the Maachi's tacphone and his jewel.

And if there were many heads, he would lop every single one off. Eyes are always everywhere, so one needs to beware. Of him.

Chapter 56: Get Away

As the phone bleeped its charming alert, it bounced the sound of the notification tone around the room like a hungry irritating mosquito. And it rang and rang. How unusual for it to sound belch for so long a period of time.

She gazed at the screen and touched the green dot and lifted the phone to her ear. The voice was a little faint and squeaky, so she increased the volume.

"Maa, when are you coming home? I need help with my homework. Baba usually helps me and he is away on work. Pishi is not so good at math." The chirpy kid's coquettish voice was serious and puppy dog sad at the same time.

"I'm on my way you little cub. I'll be home soon. Big kiss for my little girl." She happily smiled and dissolved any thought of Maachi.

Shashtihi, as she was now known as, reveled in her new job at an upscale Bengali restaurant in Dallas. It was perfect for her and her family. The Goddess Kali had bestowed upon her great fortune in the serendipitous meeting with the eatery's previous manager, Baltishna, who was relocating to the east coast.

She felt safe, especially in light of what she had been through with the marshals.

Horrible, horrible experiences that were now in the distant mind-past.

Shashthi, was visibly pregnant and looking forward to bringing a new soul into a loving human body, with an adoring family.

Her children, Aarin and Debjit easily became part of the Dallas community of Bengali expatriates and tech workers. They had many friends and blended into the local environs.

Her husband, Bhuta, had been very fortunate to open a martial arts academy teaching Bengalis and curious folks from all ethnicities, the discipline of Lathi and Boli Khela. The unfortunate part of his new occupation was that he often had to travel to tournaments and expositions. Everything has a front and a back, good fortune is tempered in its magnitude.

Shashthi's family was awaiting her at their house. As she opened the door and looked in, a wonderful warm feeling caressed her inner being. Home, home with no fear of anything anymore. It was truly *svatantrata ka aanand.* The loving looks wove into the sensual smell of spices and a delicious meal to be thankful for and dined upon.

Her children swarmed upon her as their pishi just wide-smiled and bathed in the richness of souls vibrating in harmony. She compassionately glanced at her niece's tummy and thought to herself that life without stress lets the body imbibe the amrit of life and expand with contentment.

"I'm so hungry. All of you must be very empty inside. Shall we sit and enjoy the delicious dinner your Auntie has made for us?" Miles of smiles were in the room and the evening surfed upon the good feelings.

As they trod the path of happiness, quiescent moments were now theirs to own.

For now, at least.

Chapter 57: Mother Murder

The blue-skinned Goddess Kali with her ten arms outstretched writhed a divine dance of consciousness. Each move a ripple in time. A shrift in consciousness. Her darkness is her lightness. She destroys the lesser self to bring into being the greater Self. The push and pull of the universe reveals mysteries within conundrums that are beautiful in their righteous outcomes. She harbors no ill will and her devotees worship her as the ultimate destroyer of little egocentric beings and empowering them to be more than they could ever imagine. Divine serendipity and fate merge with a dash of free will to create the world as we experience it. It is our choice to go left, right, forward, or backwards. She encourages us to take none of those directive paths but to instead go upward into our thousand-petal lotus.

The End

Other fantastical stories by Robert Arnold Kay PhD
Paperbacks and Digitals Available on:
Amazon, Smashwords.com, Thriftbooks.com, Barnes & Noble, and over
40,000 booksellers and libraries worldwide.
Novels

Plants vs Humans
Plantsversushumans.com

Book 1: Cultivated Meat American Sashimi
It's not rocket science, it's food science

Book 2: Cultivated Meat American Sashimi
No longer in the company of nice guys

Book 3: Cultivated Meat American Sashimi
A reckoning is beckoning

Plants vs Humans: Extinction
To be published by October 2024

YNot
To be published by March 2025

Short Stories and *Taboo You* Magazine
Master library of works available at (free reads):

robertarnoldkayphd.com

Terminal Computer
Twimare
Endangered Species
Don't Make Me Pop the Trunk
HOA1 A Boy and His Cat

Taboo You (quarterly) free online digital content ezine

Robert Arnold Kay PhD
robertarnoldkayphd.com

Dr. Kay is an accomplished 40-year consumer products veteran CSO with deep expertise in the Pharmaceuticals, Non-Genetically Modified Foods (non-GMO, non-BE), Vitamins, Minerals, and Supplements segment, including time leading the scientific initiatives of Isagenix, Renew Life, Alacer, Anabolic Labs, and Leiner Health Products.

He is a practitioner of Siddha Yoga and formerly was an instructor of advanced Hatha Yoga and meditation in a meditation center he opened. This book and all his works are dedicated to Swami Muktananda.

Currently, Dr. Kay serves as the CEO of his own company, Innovative Product Quality Solutions. And, he is an accomplished author with four science fiction novels in publication.

Prior to establishing his quality systems consulting company, Dr. Kay served as the scientific voice of authority as Chief Science Officer, for four privately-owned middle market CPG companies and led them in innovation, research and development, scientific communications, and regulatory agency interactions. The innovations resulted in hundreds of millions of dollars in increased shareholder value and enhanced global distribution of compliant products.

His understanding of regulatory affairs and quality have resulted in the companies he led for quality achieving outstanding audits and reviews by independent auditors and the US Food and Drug Administration.

Dr. Kay holds a BA in Psychology from Quinnipiac University, an MS and PhD in Nutritional Science from the University of Connecticut. During his tenure as a graduate student at the University of Connecticut he received named fellowships in support of his nutritional supplement, green superfoods, and probiotic research.

His current activities include consulting for the pharmaceutical, nutrition, food manufacturing segments, the creation of a butterfly friendly botanical garden habitat, and authoring several science fiction novels and short stories.

He is a published author who combined his significant scientific knowledge and experience with science fiction to create lovely fantastical worlds that delight readers worldwide.

Published by Robert Arnold Kay PhD, 2024

MLM – MULTI LEVEL MURDERS
TRUST THAT THE LIES ARE OUT THERE
First Edition. January 3, 2024.

**Written by Robert Arnold Kay
No AI was used to compose this manuscript.**

Don't miss out!

Visit the website below and you can sign up to receive emails whenever Robert Arnold Kay publishes a new book. There's no charge and no obligation.

https://books2read.com/r/B-A-DFQBB-POXTC

BOOKS 2 READ

Connecting independent readers to independent writers.

Did you love *MLM - Multi Level Murders*? Then you should read
Cultivated Meat American Sashimi by Robert Arnold Kay!

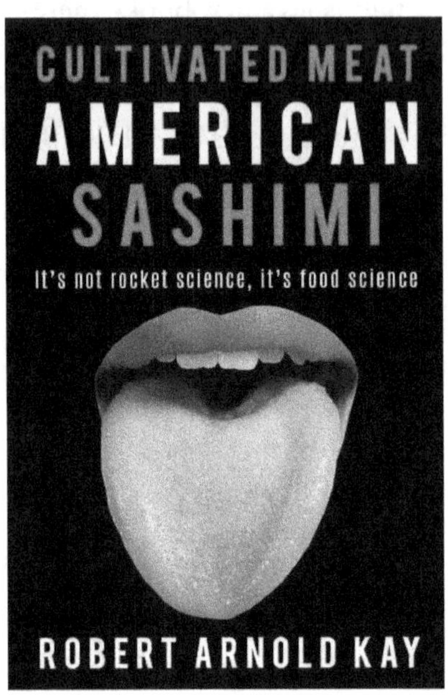

Shocking, Intense, Profound.

It's not rocket science, it's food science.

In a startling twist of fate, the FDA's nod to lab-grown meat opens Pandora's lunch box, catapulting society into a surreal realm where the unthinkable becomes in-your-face reality. What happens when the villainous Yakuza criminal empire harnesses avant-garde technology to engineer raw human meat from celebrity DNA?

The A-listers, from Arnold Dweezeneggar to the Trashkardians, become the most seductively, exotic items on the menu. In *Cultivated Meat American Sashimi*, the inaugural chapter of an electrifying dystopian sci-fi trilogy, the line between gourmet and grotesque is terrifyingly blurred. Dancing in the garden of salacious foodgasmic delights, consumers morph into obsessed, blood-thirsty, insatiable predators, solely focused upon devouring raw celebrity flesh.

This tech-noir saga masterfully fuses cutting-edge science with raw suspense and bioethics, compelling readers to feast their senses in a gastronomic innovation, where every bite challenges both the palate and the morals of its readers.

It's a graphically articulated Picasso-Dali-esque *carne-levare* drama of primal carnality that unfolds one bite at a time. Bon appetit.

Read more at https://robertarnoldkayphd.com/.

About the Author

Robert Arnold Kay holds a PhD in Nutritional Science and a BA in Psychology. He has worked as a Chief Science Officer for several industry leading dietary supplement and pharmaceutical companies.

You may recognize some of his contributions, e.g., Emergen-C fizzy vitamin C drink, multiple probiotic products, and Intermezzo.

He is an ecoscientist, inventor, and science-futurist who connects the dots regarding the health status of our environment and life on Earth, just as he did when engineering supplements and drug products.

He raises hundreds of Monarch and Swallowtail butterflies in his botanical garden sanctuary.

He merges science and fantastical worlds to create enchanting tales that thrill readers.

Read more at https://robertarnoldkayphd.com/.

www.ingramcontent.com/pod-product-compliance
Lightning Source LLC
Chambersburg PA
CBHW070746160726
48004CB00001B/68